DEEP STRIKE

ALSO BY RICK CAMPBELL

The Trident Deception
Empire Rising
Ice Station Nautilus
Blackmail
Treason

DEEP STRIKE

RICK CAMPBELL

ST. MARTIN'S PRESS NEW YORK

First published in the United States by St. Martin's Press, an imprint of St. Martin's Publishing Group

This is a work of fiction. All the characters, organizations, and events portrayed in this novel are either products of the author's imagination or are used fictitiously.

www.stmartins.com

Design by Steven Seighman

Library of Congress Cataloging-in-Publication Data

Names: Campbell, Rick (Navy Commander) author.
Title: Deep strike / Rick Campbell.
Description: First edition. | New York : St. Martin's Press, 2021.
Identifiers: LCCN 2020047435 | ISBN 9781250164773 (hardcover) |
ISBN 9781250274830 (ebook)
Subjects: GSAFD: War stories.
Classification: LCC PS3603.A48223 D44 2021 | DDC 813/.6—dc23
LC record available at https://lccn.loc.gov/2020047435

First Edition: 2021

10 9 8 7 6 5 4 3 2 1

To Brett Campbell

You brought smiles and laughter to places where there were none, and made everyone you came in contact with a better person.

A SIMPLE BOY MADE ALL THE DIFFERENCE

He sits,
He can't walk.
He's quiet,
He can't talk.

Born quadriplegic,
Smiling nonetheless.
Severe cerebral palsy,
Was just another test.

Everything that comes his way,
He seems to enjoy.
He is clearly different,
But he's still just a boy.

His gentle warmth radiates
To everyone around.
His body always struggling,
But never seems run down.

A rewarding sense of self
Flow to those who care.
He provides a new experience
For those who stop and stare.

Only caring souls
Can take on this endeavor.
He is a part of me,
He changed my life forever.

Days and nights go by,
One after another.
But nothing ever changes,
He is still our brother.

—Caitlin Campbell

MAIN CHARACTERS

-COMPLETE CAST OF CHARACTERS IS PROVIDED IN ADDENDUM-

UNITED STATES ADMINISTRATION

Kevin Hardison—chief of staff
Tom Drapac—secretary of defense
Dawn Cabral—secretary of state
Nova Conover—secretary of homeland security

CENTRAL INTELLIGENCE AGENCY

Christine O'Connor—director (DCIA)
Monroe (MK) Bryant—deputy director (DDCIA)
Patrick (PJ) Rolow—deputy director for operations (DDO)
Tracey McFarland—deputy director for analysis (DDA)
Jake Harrison—paramilitary operations officer (Special Operations Group)
Maxim Anosov—paramilitary operations officer (Sochi, Russia)
Pat Kendall—specialized skills officer (National Resources Division)
Khalila Dufour—specialized skills officer (National Clandestine Service)

USS *PITTSBURGH* (LOS ANGELES CLASS FAST ATTACK SUBMARINE)

John Buglione (Commander)—Commanding Officer
Rick Schwartz (Lieutenant Commander)—Executive Officer

K-561 *KAZAN* (YASEN CLASS ATTACK SUBMARINE)

Aleksandr Plecas (Captain First Rank)—Commanding Officer
Erik Fedorov (Captain Third Rank)—First Officer

GADZHIYEVO NAVAL BASE

Anatoly Bogdanov—ordnance supervisor
Vasily Morozov—ordnance supervisor

NORTHERN FLEET JOINT STRATEGIC COMMAND

Mikhail Korenev—command center watchstander
Arkady Timoshenko—command center watchstander

OTHERS

Murray Wilson (Captain)—Commanding Officer, USS *Michigan* (BLUE) / USS *North Carolina*
Lonnie Mixell—former Navy SEAL
Issad Futtaim—Syrian weapons dealer
Ayman al-Zawahiri—leader of al-Qaeda and ISIL factions in Afghanistan and Pakistan

DEEP STRIKE

PROLOGUE

INDIAN SPRINGS, NEVADA

"High value target. That's all you need to know."

It was already ninety degrees at Creech Air Force Base, the morning sun burning down on several dozen trailers neatly arranged in four rows. Captain Mike Berger, seated inside one of the dimly lit, cramped, and chilly trailers, kept his right hand on the joystick and his left on the throttle as his eyes scanned one of the fourteen displays built into the two-person control station. Beside him and sharing a center console was First Lieutenant Dee Ardis, likewise studying her screens.

Berger and Ardis were seated inside an MQ-9 Ground Control Station controlling a Reaper drone, with Berger piloting the aircraft while Ardis operated its sensors. For the last twelve hours, the Reaper had been circling high above Khyber Pakhtunkhwa, a Pakistani province bordering Afghanistan. This section of the province was mainly no-man's-land, a disputed area sparsely populated with villages containing only a dozen or so families each, a region where the Pakistani government had ceded authority to tribal warlords. In the center of Berger's visual display was a single dwelling at the end of a long dirt road, if you could call it that—more like a trail worn into the rugged terrain, snaking through the wilderness.

Most days, it'd be just the two of them in the control van during their six-hour shift, even during combat missions taking out the bad guys. But Berger had been surprised this morning when he arrived to relieve the off-going team, finding an entourage of four high-ranking Air Force officers—his supervisor and his boss, plus a colonel and brigadier general he hadn't seen before—further cramping the small trailer as they monitored the mission. Berger sensed the tension the moment he stepped into the trailer. When he was briefed on the operation, he'd been told, "High value target. That's all you need to know."

Thus far, it had been a boring four hours, with Berger keeping the MQ-9 Reaper at ten thousand feet to keep it out of sight and earshot of anyone inside or approaching the isolated dwelling. It was clear that today's mission was combat-related and not just surveillance, and the Reaper was well equipped for the task, carrying four Hellfire missiles and two Paveway II five-hundred-pound bombs, all laser-guided to their target by equipment in the sensor ball mounted beneath the Reaper's nose.

Although Berger and Ardis flew the drone, operated its sensors, and released its weapons, the mission was coordinated by an attack controller, a special operations type who Berger figured was probably sitting in a windowless concrete bunker somewhere in the Middle East. In the past, different controllers had provided Berger and Ardis with varying degrees of freedom over their attacks. Some were micromanagers, directing the drone approach angle, weapon selection, and impact point.

Other attack controllers were more hands-off, simply saying, "Kill these two targets," letting Berger and Ardis make the optimum selections. Berger still didn't have a feeling for this attack controller, as they'd had few interactions thus far. Things began to pick up, however, when Berger noticed movement on his optical display.

A white bongo—similar to a pickup truck but with a wider body—appeared on the left edge of the display, dust billowing behind it as the vehicle traveled up the dirt road toward the dwelling. From ten thousand feet and a thirty-degree offset, he could tell there were two occupants inside the bongo, but nothing more.

The attack controller's voice emanated from Berger's headphones. "Request visual target confirmation."

Berger acknowledged, then tilted his joystick, sending the Reaper closer to the ground so its camera had a low enough angle to get a good look at the faces of whoever was in the truck.

The drone leveled off at the new altitude as the bongo stopped beside the dwelling. When the two men, both wearing white dishdashas—long white robes traditionally worn by Middle Eastern men—stepped from the vehicle, they were greeted by two other men who emerged from the building. Ardis zoomed in, taking a picture of each man's face.

Berger waited as the facial recognition algorithms worked in the background, watching the percentage under each photograph churn until the reading under one of the pictures stopped at ninety-three percent. The man's name remained blank on Berger's display, but a green *Target Confirmed* appeared beneath the image as the four men entered the dwelling.

"We have confirmed jackpot," the attack controller declared. "You are cleared for weapon release. Paveway in the center of the building."

Berger selected one of the Reaper's two Paveways, then waited as Ardis slewed the laser designator onto the building.

Release solution valid appeared on a display in the center console.

Berger armed the Paveway—*Master arm on.*

Finally, *Ready for release* appeared.

After a final glance at the laser designator, verifying it was locked on to the center of the building, Berger pressed the red button on his joystick, releasing the five-hundred-pound bomb.

As the Paveway descended toward its target, Berger assessed the probability of mission success. A five-hundred-pound bomb would normally kill everyone inside a dwelling that size, but they had no building schematics and no idea of the structure's internal layout or composition.

Berger watched as the Paveway completed its journey, hitting the building dead center. An orange fireball erupted, billowing upward above a trail of black smoke as debris rained down on the surrounding landscape. As Berger examined the display for survivors, two men ran from the building.

"We've got two squirters," Ardis announced.

Berger focused on the squirters, a drone term for someone who runs—squirts—from the scene of an explosion.

"Kill the squirters," the attack controller ordered. "Payload your choice."

Berger selected a Hellfire missile, which could be guided more effectively toward nimble targets on the move. The two men were close together and running in the same direction, so Berger directed Ardis to guide the missile between the two men. After Ardis adjusted the laser designator to the escaping pair, Berger released one of the Reaper's Hellfire missiles.

As the Hellfire began its journey, Berger evaluated the advance warning that would be provided to the two targets. An incoming Hellfire missile would create a sonic boom, with the time delay between boom and impact up to eight seconds depending on the azimuth—the angle the laser designator was aimed toward the target. After years of drone strikes in the Middle East, the bad guys had learned—if you hear a boom, it's time to run.

"Four-second warning," Ardis announced, having done the mental calculation.

Four seconds ought to be short enough between boom and detonation, Berger figured, providing insufficient time once the targets heard the boom for them to realize what it was, change direction, and flee far enough from the impact point to survive.

The Hellfire streaked toward its targets, and just before it arrived, the two men altered their escape route, turning abruptly and splitting up. The Hellfire detonated a few seconds later, filling the center of Berger's visual display with another explosion, albeit much smaller than the Paveway's.

Ardis waited for the dust to clear, then zoomed in on the area, searching for the targets. Both men were lying immobile not far from the Hellfire crater, one man on his back with his eyes frozen open, and the other facedown with red splotches spreading through the sand, outward from his body.

Post-mission analysis would be conducted to assess the results of today's mission, but Berger was confident the men's status on his display would be updated from *Target Confirmed* to *Target Deceased*.

The attack controller's voice came across Berger's headphones again. "You are released for further duties."

Berger tilted the joystick, turning the Reaper toward Kandahar Airfield in southern Afghanistan for refueling and rearming.

ONE YEAR LATER

1

NEW YORK CITY

Standing at the back of the United Nations General Assembly Hall, Mel Cross surveyed the 1,800 men and women in attendance as they listened to the man at the podium. Like many of the attendees, Cross wore an earpiece, although for a decidedly different reason. There was no need to translate the speech being delivered by the American ambassador to the United Nations; Cross was one of the Diplomatic Security Service agents assigned to the ambassador's detail. In the other rear corner of the assembly hall, Agent Jill Mercer also kept a watchful eye as they waited for Ambassador Marshall Hill to finish his speech, which was just now becoming interesting.

"Over the last year," Ambassador Hill said, "there has been an increase in terrorist attacks around the world. The United States has evidence of Iran's involvement, providing funding, arms, and training to organizations intent on harming those who do not align with Tehran's ideology. Additionally, we have proof that Iran has been refining uranium for nuclear weapons. Evidence of Iran's transgressions will be provided to the Security Council, and the United States will be working with member nations to strengthen the sanctions already in place.

"Let me be clear—if Iran's leadership continues its belligerent and aggressive behavior, developing weapons of mass destruction and supporting those who harm others, the United States will work with its allies to address the situation. Various military options are within the realm of potential responses."

There was a murmur throughout the assembly hall after Hill's last statement. Cross paid no attention to the comments. His eyes swept across the audience, searching for that one small detail that seemed out of place. His gaze stopped on Agent Mercer, whose watchful eyes also surveyed the occupants.

His thoughts dwelt for a moment on Jill, an attractive brunette who had been assigned to the ambassador's detail two months ago. She was a recent widow with two young kids—her husband had been an NYPD cop, killed a year ago in the line of duty. Jill had remained aloof since her assignment to the ambassador's detail, failing to provide Cross with an opportunity to determine whether she was ready for, or even interested in, a relationship with him.

Cross forced his eyes to keep moving, admonishing himself for the lapse in his duties. He had dwelt on Jill for far too long. Fortunately, the United Nations General Assembly Hall was as safe a place as any in the city.

Upon completing his speech, Ambassador Hill stepped away from the podium, and Cross moved to intercept him. The ambassador was on a tight schedule, heading to LaGuardia Airport for a flight to spend time with his family in Rhode Island, instead of returning to his penthouse condominium a few blocks away. Jill reached the ambassador shortly after Cross did, and the two agents bracketed the diplomat as they approached the exit.

Cross received a report on his earpiece. He spoke quietly into his sleeve, then informed Ambassador Hill, "Transportation is ready."

The ambassador nodded his understanding. He had already been briefed on the enhanced security measures. Based on the administration's position against Iran and its aggressive response to the recent wave of terrorism, along with Hill's role as a primary messenger, his security detail had been augmented. The ambassador would travel with two DSS agents in the second of three vehicles, with two more agents in the lead SUV and Cross and Jill in the third.

The convoy was waiting as they exited the General Assembly Hall lobby, and Ambassador Hill stepped into the middle of three black Lincoln Navigators while Cross and Jill slipped into the vacant third, whose original driver had moved to the first vehicle. The lead SUV pulled out, with the other two SUVs following close behind. The convoy turned onto Second Avenue, beginning the short trip to LaGuardia Airport.

A few blocks from the United Nations headquarters, Lonnie Mixell waited patiently in the driver's seat of a rented Buick Enclave, parked alongside the curb on East 37th Street, a hundred feet from and offering a clear view of the Second Avenue and East 37th Street intersection. After evaluating several locations over the last week, he had selected this intersection because at this time of day, in the middle of rush hour, the traffic backed up at the red light. The vehicles of interest would be either stopped near the intersection or moving slowly through it.

Normally, after a day at work, Ambassador Hill would have walked to his residence a short distance from the UN headquarters, offering Mixell a slim chance of completing his assignment in the manner desired by his employer: a method that would be captured on video—the aftermath, that is—and played repeatedly on news channels and internet browsers throughout the world. Mixell had eventually connected with one of the ambassador's aides, who for the right price had shared his boss's schedule. It had taken more money than Mixell had planned, but it didn't really matter; he wasn't the one paying the bills.

Inside the Buick, Mixell's eyes were fixed on the video playing on his cell phone, relayed from a small wireless camera placed on a windowsill inside the Millennium Hilton, across the street from the United Nations headquarters. The hotel room, rented under an alias, provided a clear view of everyone exiting the UN General Assembly Hall. Mixell watched the three-car convoy pull away from the building entrance, then turn left onto Second Avenue.

Jill Mercer sat in the passenger seat of the third SUV while Cross drove, scanning the traffic and passersby for anything out of the ordinary. It was a beautiful day, a clear sky with the temperature in the mid-seventies, unusually pleasant for this time of year. The forecast for the next few days was comparable, likely the last patch of decent weather before winter set in.

She planned to take advantage of the warm afternoons, spending time outdoors with her children this weekend. The last year had been difficult for the kids, adjusting to the loss of their father. It had been tough on her as well, and as she approached the one-year anniversary of her husband's death, she wondered if she was ready to move on, or if pursuing another relationship so soon would dishonor his memory.

As her eyes moved left across the traffic, she noticed Cross's thumbs tapping on the steering wheel. It was a nervous habit of his, and she wondered what the issue was. Today's transit was as straightforward as they came and there were no indications of anything amiss. After reflecting for a moment, she realized his nervous glitch appeared only when the two of them were alone in a vehicle. It was clear that Cross was attracted to her, as she frequently caught him gazing in her direction. Thus far, however, he had made no advance.

"So," Cross said, interrupting Jill's thoughts, "do you have plans for the weekend?"

Jill repressed a smile. Cross had finally worked up the courage to ask her out.

"The weather's supposed to be nice," she replied. "Maybe I'll take the kids to Central Park. Other than that, I'll probably just relax."

"Care for company when you visit the park, or perhaps dinner one night?"

Her reaction to Cross's question was unexpected. Her chest tightened and a lump formed in her throat. She'd been wondering if she was ready for another relationship, and she had the answer. She turned away and looked out the side window, hoping Cross hadn't noticed her reaction.

"Not this weekend," she replied. She tried to phrase her response delicately, not shutting the door completely. She was interested, but now wasn't the right time. "I'm not ready yet. I hope you understand."

"Of course," he said quickly. "I can only imagine how difficult things have been for you. Whenever you're ready, let me know." He offered a smile before returning his attention to the traffic, slowing for the red light ahead.

Mixell checked his watch. He had timed the route from the United Nations headquarters several times, and the ambassador's convoy should arrive in the next fifteen to forty-five seconds. He spotted the lead Lincoln Navigator not far from the intersection, stopped for a red light, but the other two vehicles were hidden behind a corner building. It wouldn't be much longer, however. He slid the driver's side window down.

Beneath a blanket on the passenger seat was a Milkor MGL Mark 1L—a six-shot, revolver-type, shoulder-fired grenade launcher—which could fire a variety of 40mm rounds. This MGL was loaded with XM1060 thermobaric rounds, a fuel-air explosive consisting of a fuel container and two explosive charges. The first explosion would burst the container open and disperse the fuel in a cloud, which would mix with atmospheric oxygen as it expanded. The second charge would detonate the cloud, creating a massive blast wave, killing anyone nearby and destroying equipment and even reinforced structures.

The traffic lights along Second Avenue turned green and Mixell waited as the traffic began moving again, the vehicles establishing the desired spacing between them like an accordion stretching out. He'd have only one shot at the target as it passed through the intersection, which, if successful, would bring the three-car convoy to a halt. Accuracy wasn't an issue, as the MGL had an effective range of just over four hundred yards and he was only thirty yards away. The response time of the ambassador's security detail was a concern, however. For his escape plan to work, he couldn't have DSS agents charging up the street toward him.

When the lead Navigator began moving, Mixell pulled the blanket from the passenger seat and lifted the MGL to his shoulder, aiming at his primary target.

It happened almost simultaneously. A thin trail of white smoke appeared as the ambassador's Navigator erupted in an orange fireball, the explosion sending glass fragments and metal shards pelting off Jill's SUV. Cross slammed on the brakes, bringing their Navigator to a screeching halt, as did the driver of the lead vehicle.

Jill turned toward the origin of the attack, spotting a man in an SUV about thirty yards away, shifting the aim of a shoulder-fired weapon toward the lead Navigator.

"Weapon at two o'clock!"

The words left Jill's mouth a second before a projectile slammed into the first Navigator, detonating before either agent could exit.

"Get out!" Cross shouted.

His warning was unnecessary, as Jill had already kicked open her door. She darted from the SUV and circled behind the vehicle, joining Cross as he squeezed off a three-round volley. The bullets missed the perpetrator, shattering his vehicle's front window instead. Jill added another three-round burst while Cross fired again. The assassin ducked down and slipped from the vehicle via the passenger door, then fled up the sidewalk as pedestrians scattered, scrambling for cover.

Cross directed Jill to take the right side of the street while he moved left, and they crossed the remaining lanes of Second Avenue and sprinted up both sides of East 37th Street toward the suspect. Jill headed up the sidewalk on the opposite side of the street while Cross ran up the other side, keeping parked cars between him and the suspect.

Mixell had planned to leave the grenade launcher in the SUV, strolling from the scene with his hands in his pockets, moving toward his escape vehicle parked not far away. Unfortunately, the two agents in the third vehicle had reacted quicker than he had hoped. They had a bead on him and were already charging up the street. Mixell shifted to his backup plan.

He stopped beside a parked car, swinging the grenade launcher back toward the two agents pursuing him, with the man being closer. Before Mixell could target him, both agents fired their weapons. He ducked behind the vehicle and waited for the hail of bullets to end. Then he popped over the hood and fired a round into the car closest to the male agent.

The XM1060 detonated after it pierced the car and the explosion shredded the vehicle, sending glass and metal fragments in every direction. Nearby pedestrians had taken cover, either behind vehicles or in nearby stores, but those near the explosion were hit by shrapnel. The lead DSS agent was one of the casualties, his scorched and lacerated body writhing on the sidewalk.

After a quick assessment of the results, Mixell sprinted up the street, hoping to slip away from the last agent.

Jill Mercer tried to push the image of Cross's smoldering body from her mind as she raced up the sidewalk, shifting her thoughts from wondering whether he would survive to getting a clear shot at the perpetrator. As she moved up the street, she periodically regained her target, glancing between the parked cars she used as cover. She heard the faint sirens of approaching law enforcement; assistance would arrive soon. However, he was traveling up the street faster than she was, opening the distance between them. She couldn't let him slip away.

She picked up her pace, moving as fast as possible while staying in a crouched position, shielded by the parked cars. To make up ground, she stopped checking on the man's progress between each vehicle, sprinting past a dozen cars before pausing to take a look.

Peering over the hood of a Chevy Blazer, she scanned the other side of the street, focused on where the man should have been if he had kept up his pace. Just to the left of where she expected him to be, not quite as far up the road, she spotted the suspect. The man had the grenade launcher on his shoulder, aimed at her.

Jill's gaze shifted to the burning and shredded car near Cross, suddenly realizing her peril. The projectile the man was firing would rip apart the Chevy Blazer she was hiding behind, turning the vehicle into a four-thousand-pound fragmentation grenade.

Bad place to take cover.

The danger coalesced in her mind a moment too late. She saw a thin white exhaust trail streak toward her as the projectile slammed into the Blazer.

Time seemed to slow down after the round detonated. An orange, blossoming cloud expanded from the vehicle as it shattered the windows and shredded the car body, enveloping her in a scorching inferno as shrapnel penetrated deep into her face and torso. The pressure transient from the explosion knocked her from her feet, blasting her backward until she slammed into a building's brick facade, where she crumpled to the ground.

Unbearable pain sliced through her body as she lay there, while blood spread slowly across the concrete. As her world faded to darkness, the last thing she realized was that the agonizing scream piercing her ears was her own.

2
GADZHIYEVO, RUSSIA

Along the curved shoreline of Yagelnaya Bay, as the sun rose above snow-covered hills to the east, Captain First Rank Aleksandr Plecas stepped from his sedan at the end of the pier, instructing his driver to wait. After pulling the flaps of his ushanka fox-fur hat down over his ears, he strode down the pier toward his submarine, his boots crunching through the four-inch-deep layer of snow that had fallen during yesterday's storm.

Winter had arrived early this year and Yagelnaya Bay, along with the entire Murmansk Fjord, would soon ice over. That was of no concern, of course, since Northern Fleet submarines deployed year-round, with an icebreaker clearing a path, if necessary, to and from the Barents Sea. Plecas and his crew would soon make that transit aboard *Kazan*—Russia's newest nuclear-powered guided missile submarine.

The second of the new Yasen class, *Kazan* incorporated cutting-edge sensor and weapon technology. With eight torpedo tubes—double that of American submarines except the three Seawolf class—and eight vertical launch tubes loaded with up to forty land-attack or anti-ship missiles, *Kazan* was a formidable submarine indeed. After operating in the nearby Barents Sea for the last few months, working out the bugs in their new submarine, Plecas and his crew were finally about to take *Kazan* on her first deployment.

Much of Plecas's crew was topside this morning, assisting with the food and spare parts loadouts, transferring the pallets of material from the pier into the submarine through the topside hatches. The weapon loadout was scheduled for next week, which would fill all stows and launchers with torpedoes and missiles.

Plecas crossed the brow onto his submarine, where he was saluted by the topside watch, who announced the Captain's arrival over the shipwide intercom. After climbing down the ladder into the warmth of Compartment One, Plecas was greeted by his First Officer, Captain Third Rank Erik Fedorov, the submarine's second-in-command.

"Good morning, Captain. All preparations are proceeding smoothly, and we are expecting the courier from Northern Fleet within the hour." Plecas nodded his understanding and Fedorov asked, "Will you be staying long today, Captain?"

"Only to sign the necessary paperwork. I'm flying to Moscow this afternoon."

"Spend whatever time you need with your family, Captain. Your ship is in good hands. We will be ready for deployment on schedule."

Plecas appreciated his First Officer's concern, as well as his confidence. Of course his submarine would be ready on schedule, even if he spent more time in Moscow than planned. As Captain, he made the decisions, but Fedorov and the rest of his men did the heavy lifting, and they were a dedicated and capable crew.

Fedorov left to address other matters while Plecas entered his stateroom, a three-by-three-meter room containing only a narrow bed, a built-in desk, and a small table with two chairs. As he tossed his overcoat and hat on the bed, he eyed the two-inch-thick stack of paperwork that had accumulated in his in-box. Sitting at his desk, he rifled through the documents, pulling out only those that had to be approved prior to deployment.

He had just finished reviewing all required paperwork—except one item—when there was a knock on his stateroom door. He answered to find his First Officer and an admiral's aide from Northern Fleet.

"Sorry to interrupt you, Captain," Fedorov said, "but our patrol orders have arrived."

The final item.

The aide entered the tumbler combination and unlocked the courier pouch, then withdrew a classified envelope, which he handed to Plecas.

Plecas signed the transfer document, acknowledging that he now had custody, which the aide stuffed into the courier pouch before leaving. Plecas's First Officer stood by the door expectantly, and Plecas realized Fedorov was hoping the patrol orders would be opened in his presence.

At this point, no one aboard *Kazan* knew the deployment area or duration, although Plecas had an inkling.

There were several unresolved issues related to the deployment, and Plecas decided now was not the right time to reveal the details. "I will brief the officers and crew at the appropriate time," he told Fedorov.

"Yes, Captain," Fedorov replied as Plecas closed the door, the disappointment evident on his First Officer's face.

Plecas sat at his desk and unsealed the envelope, then read the patrol orders.

Everything was as he expected.

He locked the orders in his safe, then checked his watch. His driver was waiting.

3
WASHINGTON, D.C.

Christine O'Connor sat in the backseat of a black Lincoln Navigator, with two Protective Agents in the front, as it merged onto the Theodore Roosevelt Bridge, joining the morning traffic fighting its way into the nation's capital. The radio was tuned to a local station, whose hosts were discussing the previous day's horrific assassination of the American ambassador to the United Nations. Christine tuned out the commentary, as she had heard it all and more.

As director of the Central Intelligence Agency, Christine had access to the agency's vast information network, along with data gathered by the myriad other U.S. intelligence agencies. Late into the previous night, she had studied the evidence. Technically, since the attack was on U.S. soil, the FBI had the lead hunting down the man responsible. However, Christine was convinced the trail of responsibility would lead overseas, which was her agency's forte.

The president had apparently reached the same conclusion, requesting her presence at today's 8 a.m. meeting in the West Wing. Although this was Christine's first meeting with the president as CIA director, she was no stranger to the White House. Prior to becoming the second female director in the history of the CIA, she had spent three years on the president's staff as his national security advisor, occupying a West Wing corner office. Three months ago, the president had nominated her for CIA director.

It was a short trip from CIA headquarters in Langley, and it wasn't long before the Navigator rolled to a stop in front of black steel bars blocking the entrance to the White House. After the gate guards checked Christine's identification and completed a security sweep of her vehicle, the gate slid aside and the Navigator pulled forward, coasting to a halt beneath the West Wing's north portico. Standing at the entrance between two Marines in dress blues was Kevin Hardison, the president's chief of staff—and Christine's White House nemesis.

While Christine served as the president's national security advisor, Hardison had been a thorn in her side. He was the typical Type A, overbearing personality, and she and Hardison frequently found themselves supporting opposite positions on critical issues. She had won more than her fair share of those debates, swaying the president to her side, much to Hardison's chagrin.

As Christine stepped from the SUV, Hardison was the first to speak. "Good morning, Christine. We're meeting in the Situation Room."

Hardison's greeting was surprisingly cordial, considering the animosity that had built up between them over the years.

Christine followed Hardison down the steps into the West Wing basement and into the Situation Room, where there were three empty seats around the rectangular table. She and Hardison took two, leaving one at the head of the table for the president. Of note in attendance were Secretary of Homeland Security Nova Conover, FBI Director John Dehner, Director of National Intelligence John Rodgaard, and Thom Parham, who was Christine's replacement as the president's national security advisor.

After Hardison and Christine took their seats, Hardison buzzed the president's secretary, informing her they were ready for the president, who arrived a moment later. All stood as he entered, returning to their seats after the president settled into his chair.

"What's the status?" he asked.

Hardison replied, "Director Dehner has the lead on the investigation and will brief you on what we know."

After the president nodded his concurrence, Dehner began. "Good morning, Mr. President. I'll start with a recap of what happened yesterday—a summary of the casualties and video of the entire event."

Although most of the country had seen footage of the aftermath, not everyone in the Situation Room had seen the entire event unfold.

"In addition to Ambassador Hill, six Diplomatic Security Service agents were killed. There were no civilian deaths, although eight persons were injured. None of those injuries are life-threatening. Regarding the sequence of events, we've pieced together video from several surveillance cameras in NYPD's Domain Awareness System," referring to the New York Police Department's surveillance network of more than eighteen thousand cameras.

Dehner activated the video clip on his laptop, and the display at the front of the Situation Room energized, showing the traffic intersection at Second Avenue and East 37th Street. Christine watched as the middle Lincoln Navigator in a three-SUV convoy moving through the intersection erupted in a fiery explosion. A few seconds later, after the lead and trailing SUVs screeched to a halt, the lead vehicle was also destroyed.

Christine watched the next two minutes unfold, with the video shifting to other cameras as two DSS agents pursued the perpetrator. Finally, the video ended with the most disturbing image of all and one too graphic for public broadcast—the scorched and bloody remains of the female agent who had been chasing the assassin.

The display went dark as Dehner said, "We lost track of the suspect shortly after he killed the last DSS agent. He either knew where the cameras were located and avoided them, or got lucky. Either way, we don't know what vehicle or transit system he used to depart the area.

"We do know, however, who he is. We got a clear image from one of the surveillance cameras, and facial recognition algorithms matched him to several photos in the FBI database."

Christine recalled one of the briefings she received during her turnover with the previous CIA director. The FBI had a massive library of more than 600 million photos, derived from driver's licenses, passports, and criminal justice records, to name a few.

"He's an American citizen," Dehner said, "a former Navy SEAL who was court-martialed for killing several terrorist prisoners. He was sentenced to fifteen years at Leavenworth, although he was released after eight—a model prisoner, apparently. However, he doesn't seem to have been adequately rehabilitated. Mixell is his name. Leonard Mixell."

"Lonnie Mixell?" Christine asked.

Dehner searched the file and read off the pertinent information. "Alias—goes by Lonnie." He looked at Christine. "You know him?"

Christine nodded, then chose her words carefully. "We went to the same high school. I lost touch with him after we graduated."

There was silence around the table as Dehner scribbled a comment in his file, while Christine made a mental note to discuss the matter back at Langley. She hadn't been aware of this critical information.

Dehner continued, "We now know who the perpetrator is, but don't have any leads yet. Mixell dropped off the grid shortly after he was released from prison. There are no database hits on Leonard or Lonnie Mixell in the last three years. He's clearly using an alias, or perhaps multiple ones."

Hardison asked, "Do we think he was working alone or as a mercenary?"

"We don't know yet, but based on the target, he's almost certainly hired help. We're going with that assumption for now, trying to identify and follow the money trail."

As Christine listened to the exchange between Hardison and Dehner, she noted that the president hadn't yet engaged, aside from his opening question. She found his detached manner odd, especially considering the circumstances: Hill was a close friend of the president. She examined the president more closely and noticed the intensity in his eyes. He wasn't detached. He was fuming.

Finally, the president spoke. "What happened yesterday is unacceptable. Everyone here bears responsibility, to some extent, for failing to discover and prevent the attack. It's only going to get tougher as we lead the effort to combat global terrorism—the United States will have a bigger bull's-eye on its back than before. We need to make an example of whoever was behind yesterday's attack."

The president's eyes canvassed each person at the table.

"I want a full-court press on this. Track down and apprehend the perpetrator and figure out who's pulling the strings. Do I make myself clear?"

"Yes, Mr. President," Christine replied, as did the others around the table. It wasn't like they weren't already trying their best, but the president had a point. They needed to do better.

"Any questions?" the president asked.

There were none.

"Keep me up to date."

The president pushed back from the table. As he stood, he addressed Christine. "Stop by the Oval Office before you leave."

Christine acknowledged and the president departed. After a few minutes discussing matters with the other directors and cabinet members, Christine left the Situation Room and stopped by the president's secretary, inquiring about the president's schedule.

After the secretary verified he was available, Christine entered the Oval Office to find the president seated behind his desk, framed by the tall colonnade windows overlooking the South Lawn and Rose Garden. He stood and greeted her as she entered, motioning toward one of the two couches instead of the three chairs by his desk, where she had sat countless times while discussing issues with him over the last three years. It felt odd being treated as a guest instead of a White House staffer.

The president took his customary place in a chair at one end of the two sofas as Christine took a seat.

"So, how do you like the new job?"

"There's a lot to learn, but I'm getting the swing of things."

"That's good to hear."

The conversation continued, covering nothing of much consequence until the president said, "The main reason I nominated you for CIA director is because you're someone who'll get to the bottom of things. Another reason is that you have no political ambitions I'm aware of, and likely to stay on as director for the long haul. I'd like you to consider staying in the job for as long as I'm president."

"Five more years?" Christine smiled. The president was up for reelection next year.

"Of course," he replied. "Five more years. As long as you manage to stay out of trouble."

The president glanced at her wrists before briefly surveying her face.

She could tell he was searching for the scars left behind during her stint as his national security advisor, when she had found herself in the wrong place at the wrong time on more than one occasion. She was wearing a business suit today and the sleeves covered the marks on her wrists, while makeup adequately hid the faint scars on her cheek and neck.

"Oddly enough," Christine replied, "since I've been director, I've gotten into far less trouble than when I was your NSA."

"I hope things stay boring for you, at least at the personal level."

Now that the pleasantries were over, the conversation shifted to business.

"Regarding Hill's assassination, I have no doubt the trail will lead to a terrorist organization overseas. Pull out all the stops. Find out who's responsible, and do what you can to help the FBI track down Mixell."

Christine replied, "After we identify who's responsible, I assume we're to classify those involved as enemy combatants, dealt with appropriately?"

"Certainly," the president replied.

"And if the CIA gets to Mixell before the FBI? What leeway do we have regarding interrogation?"

The president's eyes searched hers for a moment before he replied, "I leave that to your discretion."

4

LANGLEY, VIRGINIA

Christine O'Connor entered her spacious seventh-floor office after her return trip from the White House, still contemplating the information revealed in the Situation Room. She hadn't let on during the meeting, but she'd been embarrassed, caught flat-footed by the revelation the ambassador's assassin was Lonnie Mixell. The director of the CIA, head of an organization with a vast intelligence collection apparatus, had been unaware of that key fact during her first meeting with her contemporaries and before the president himself.

Upon reaching her desk, she activated the intercom to her secretary. "Are the DD and DDO in?"

"Yes, Miss O'Connor."

"Have them meet me in my office."

When the two men arrived, Christine motioned toward the round conference table, where Monroe Bryant, the agency's deputy director, and Patrick Rolow, the deputy director for operations, took their seats. They must have sensed something in her demeanor, because the two men cast curious glances between them.

Christine joined them at the table, taking a few seconds to determine how best to proceed.

Finally, she said, "I just had an uncomfortable meeting at the White House."

"In what way?" Bryant asked.

"Do you know who assassinated the ambassador?"

"We do now."

"I was blindsided during the White House meeting. I'm the director of the CIA and I didn't even know that the man responsible was someone I went to school with."

Bryant replied, "When it comes to domestic issues, the FBI has access to more data and analysis resources. They're going to discover information faster than we can."

"I don't want to hear excuses," she said firmly. "Just don't let it happen again."

Neither man replied, and as they waited for further direction, Christine evaluated the two men seated before her.

In his late fifties, Monroe Bryant was your quintessential bureaucrat, one Christine found easy to read. In Bryant's mind, Christine and the other CIA directors who rolled through Langley learned just enough to be dangerous, making well-intentioned but often damaging decisions. His self-ordained job was to manage the issues that rose to her attention, ensuring she did no harm.

On the other hand, Patrick Rolow, who went by PJ, was unreadable. The deputy director for operations was a man of average height, weight, and dress, blending into the background of almost any setting. That anonymity was more than a result of his unremarkable appearance. He had spent fifteen years in the field before rising quickly through the management layers in the Directorate of Operations, and in his late forties was one of the youngest DDOs ever.

As both men waited for Christine to continue, she regretted her harsh words—admonishing them for not informing her of Mixell's role before the White House meeting. That the ambassador's assassin was Mixell had hit too close to home.

She hadn't revealed it during the Situation Room meeting, but Mixell was more than just someone she knew. He was the best friend of her former fiancé, Jake Harrison, and for most of high school, the three of them had been inseparable. There had been a fourth wheel during most of that time, as Mixell cycled through various girlfriends, but the three of them had done just about everything together. That Mixell had assassinated the UN ambassador—that he was capable of such evil—was difficult to digest, and she was taking it out on her DD and DDO.

Christine took a deep breath, then addressed both men. "I apologize for being abrupt with you." She went on to explain the details regarding her relationship with Mixell. Additionally, she expounded on Jake Harrison's role in Mixell's downfall.

"Harrison and Mixell were best friends. They joined the Navy together and both became SEALs. They had a falling-out at some point. I don't know what happened, but Harrison was the one who turned Mixell in for killing captured terrorists. He was also the main witness during Mixell's court-martial."

Bryant replied, "We'll track down Harrison. See what he knows."

"I've got a better idea," Christine replied. "He just retired from the Navy, and I'm sure he's looking for a job. Offer him one."

"We'll run the requisite background checks and—"

"He's fine," Christine interrupted sharply.

Her tone wasn't lost on the deputy director, and his jaw muscles worked slightly as he prepared to respond.

Rolow interjected, "I'm sure there won't be an issue. We'll find a good fit for Harrison within the agency, giving him the opportunity to help track Mixell down."

5

MOSCOW, RUSSIA

Captain First Rank Aleksandr Plecas stared out the passenger window as his car passed over the Moskva River, winding through Moscow. Dark clouds drifted slowly over the city, casting a gray pall over the skyline and further darkening Plecas's mood. His driver, a starshina second class, who had met Plecas at Kubinka Air Base outside the city, had tried to engage the senior officer in conversation, but had grown quiet after realizing Plecas wasn't in a talkative mood.

They made a quick stop at Hotel Bogorodskoe to drop off Plecas's luggage, then the car pulled up to the entrance of Blokhin National Medical Research Center. Before stepping from the sedan, Plecas dismissed his driver. He would not need him again until Sunday evening for the return trip to Gadzhiyevo Naval Base.

Plecas entered the lobby and took the elevator to the fifth floor. He stopped at the nurses' desk, asking them to inform Dr. Vasiliev that he had arrived, then continued down the corridor. After passing several rooms of patients, some with visiting family members, he reached his ten-year-old daughter's room. He pushed the door open slowly to find Natasha in bed, her eyes closed, as a clear liquid dripped from an IV bag through a needle inserted into her arm.

Tatiana was seated in a chair beside the bed, holding Natasha's hand. His wife looked up as he entered the room, and the physical and emotional exhaustion were evident in the dark circles under her eyes and her slouched shoulders. There was an empty chair beside her, which he sank into. He said nothing as he examined his daughter more closely. She was even paler and thinner than before; the radiation and chemotherapy had failed.

"How is she doing?"

"She's resting comfortably now. She was up most of the night in pain, but they increased her medication this morning. She's been asleep most of the day. I should wake her—she's been looking forward to seeing you."

Plecas put his hand on Tatiana's arm. "Let her sleep. We can talk when she awakens."

"What is there to talk about?" Tatiana's voice turned cold. "About the treatments that have failed? About how long she has left to live?"

"There is always hope," Plecas replied.

"There is no hope," Tatiana said. She looked away, but not before Plecas noticed tears forming in her eyes.

He placed his arm around his wife and pulled her close. She turned toward him and pressed her face against his shoulder, and he stroked her hair gently. "I made an appointment for this evening with Natasha's doctors. I asked the nurse to let them know I've arrived. Hopefully they will have good news."

The sound of her parents' voices must have awakened Natasha, because she began to stir. Her eyes opened, but it took a moment for the glassy look to fade. She turned to the side and, upon seeing her father, broke into a wide smile.

"Papa!"

Natasha's voice was weak, but her excitement was evident.

Plecas took her small hand in his. Her skin felt cold and damp.

"You made it!" she said.

"Of course, I did. There was no way I could deploy without spending more time with you."

"I'm so glad you came."

"How do you feel?"

"Much better today. I had a good night . . ." She looked at the clock on the wall. ". . . a good day's sleep." She forced a smile. "But you're here now, and that's all that matters!"

Plecas gently squeezed his daughter's hand and she responded in kind, although there wasn't much strength in her fingers.

They talked for the next hour, about nothing in particular or of importance, with the discussion jumping around as Natasha's thoughts flitted from topic to topic. Eventually, she brought up her favorite pastime.

"When you return from deployment, it will still be winter. By then I'll be healthy and we can go ice skating together."

Plecas hadn't discussed Natasha's prognosis with her, and neither had Tatiana to his knowledge. But there was no doubt she understood the outcome if her deteriorating condition wasn't reversed. Through the entire ordeal, she had remained optimistic, holding up better than either parent.

"Yes. All three of us," Plecas replied. "On the pond behind our house."

Natasha smiled. "I can't wait."

Plecas wondered whether his daughter would even be alive when he returned from deployment. The doctors had given her four to six months if an effective treatment wasn't found, and he'd be back in three. But the timeline was difficult to predict with certainty, and her cancer might progress faster than expected.

With *Kazan* preparing for her first deployment, Plecas had considered being relieved of command so he could spend more time with his family. Although his superiors sympathized with his predicament and said a relief could be arranged, they highly preferred he remain aboard for the submarine's first deployment. He was the most experienced submarine captain in the Russian Navy, specifically given command of *Kazan* for its first deployment.

Additionally, command of *Kazan*—Russia's newest nuclear-powered submarine—was a prestigious assignment, and Plecas worried that he might lose the accompanying clout. There were far more children with cancer than beds at Blokhin, and if there were any chance of a cure, he had to ensure Natasha was admitted. That meant remaining in command of *Kazan,* and unfortunately, taking her out for her first deployment.

Natasha grimaced suddenly.

"Are you in pain again?" Tatiana asked.

"A little."

"I'll call the nurse."

"No, not yet. The medicine makes me groggy and papa just got here."

"Let me know if it gets worse," Tatiana said.

They talked for a while longer, her hand in her father's, but her muscles gradually tensed as her discomfort grew, and perspiration began to dot her forehead.

When her breathing turned shallow, Tatiana said, "I'm going to call the nurse now, okay?"

Natasha nodded.

Tatiana pressed the attendant button and a nurse arrived. After evaluating Natasha's condition, the nurse increased the pain medication.

Natasha's muscles relaxed and her breathing slowed.

Plecas leaned forward. "We are going to make you well."

Natasha smiled. "I know that, papa."

Tatiana suddenly stood and left the room without a word. Plecas wondered how much more his wife could handle. Dealing with the death of a child was difficult enough, but it was even more gut-wrenching to watch her life fade away day by day.

He caressed his daughter's hand as her eyes began to glaze over again. Her eyelids slowly closed and she drifted off to sleep. Tatiana eventually returned, slumping into the chair beside him. He held her hand in silence as they waited.

A half-hour later, an intern stepped into the room. "Dr. Vasiliev will meet with you now."

Plecas and his wife entered a conference room filled with a half-dozen men and women—the team assigned to care for their daughter.

Dr. Vasiliev greeted Plecas and his wife warmly, then gestured to two vacant chairs. After they took their seats, Vasiliev introduced the members of his team, with each doctor specializing in a different aspect of Natasha's care.

"Captain Plecas, Tatiana, I know how difficult this last year has been for you, and I want to assure you that we are doing everything possible for your daughter. Unfortunately, Natasha's cancer hasn't responded to any of the treatments. Unless you've come up with the necessary fee to pay for the experimental drug we discussed during your last visit, there is nothing more we can do."

Plecas recalled the details from their last meeting. There was a new drug that had been successful in initial testing. However, it was difficult to manufacture and the limited doses were extremely expensive—

three hundred million rubles. Tatiana's jaw had dropped upon hearing the amount, equivalent to almost five million U.S. dollars.

"There must be something you can do," Plecas said. "Some way to obtain this drug."

"We've already tried all avenues, explaining the unique situation—your daughter being an only child and your prestigious assignment—but the sticking point is the fee. We cannot get it reduced and the government won't cover the cost."

"Who do I need to talk to," Plecas said firmly.

"There is no one," Vasiliev said. "The drug comes directly from the company and they are not receptive to requests for reduced costs. They can manufacture only four doses a month at this point and are not willing to sell it for less than it takes to manufacture. As you can expect, the demand is high and there are enough patients, or their families, who can afford to pay."

Plecas turned to Tatiana, who had tears in her eyes. Three hundred million rubles was more than he'd make in ten lifetimes. Even the combined resources of their extended family would amount to only a tiny fraction. Vasiliev's decision to inform them there was a drug that might save their daughter's life, only to learn they could not afford it, bordered on cruelty.

"I'm sorry," Vasiliev said. "We will do everything possible to keep Natasha comfortable during the final stage of her disease."

Tatiana burst into tears, covering her face with her hands. Plecas caressed her back as he stared at the doctors, his mind going in several directions at once, searching for a solution. Unfortunately, Vasiliev was right. They couldn't afford the drug.

Vasiliev stood. "If there is anything I can do in the meantime, please let me know."

The doctors filed silently toward the door, avoiding eye contact with Plecas and Tatiana, leaving the Russian captain and his wife alone in the conference room. They sat together for a long while before mustering the strength to leave.

They stepped from the medical center lobby into the brisk night air, a light snow falling as they walked to their hotel a few blocks away. Neither

Plecas nor his wife spoke during the short journey, both lost in their own thoughts. Upon reaching the hotel, Tatiana numbly led the way to the seventh floor.

Their room at Hotel Bogorodskoe was small, containing only a single bed, beside which rested the suitcase Plecas had dropped off in the lobby earlier today, and a small window looking out into the city. As the door closed behind them, he took Tatiana in his arms.

She looked up at him. "There must be something we can do. Some way to pay for the drug."

Plecas shook his head. "We don't have the money, and none of our friends or relatives do either."

"The government should help," Tatiana replied. "They should intervene and force the company to provide the drug."

"The government doesn't care about people like us."

She looked up at him. "You have devoted your life to the Rodina and what has she provided in return? The government pays you crumbs and abandons you when you need its help the most."

He couldn't argue against her assessment.

"There must be someone," she said. "Someone you know who can make the company provide the drug."

Plecas was a captain first rank, the equivalent of an American Navy captain, in command of Russia's most technologically advanced submarine. Despite the responsibility, he was still a small fish in the pond, not yet an admiral. Still, he had managed to get Natasha admitted to Blokhin National Medical Research Center.

"I have done what I can. Natasha is being cared for at the premier cancer center in the country, and her doctors are the best in Russia."

Tatiana pulled back from his embrace. "It is not enough! She is going to die!"

"What do you want me to do?"

"Get the authorization for the drug!"

"There is nothing more I can do."

Tatiana's features transformed from anguish into rage. "Then you are a failure as a father! It's your responsibility to protect our daughter. To ensure no harm comes to her." Her eyes turned cold and hard. "You are not a father. You are not even a man!"

Plecas searched for the right words to defuse the situation. Tatiana was distraught and lashing out, and he tried hard to not let her words hurt.

When he didn't respond, Tatiana pounded a fist into his chest. "Save her!"

"There is nothing more I can do," he repeated.

"You lie! You must know someone with the right contacts or with enough money for the drug!"

Plecas shook his head.

Her anger transitioned into fury, and she pounded his chest with her fists as she screamed at him, her face turning flush with emotion. Plecas wrapped his arms around his wife and pulled her tightly against his chest so she could no longer hit him, although she kept trying. After a moment, her struggles subsided and her fury faded to anguish. Tears began to flow and sobs escaped between deep, shuddering breaths. As he held Tatiana close, her face resting on his chest, he felt the warmth of her tears soaking into his uniform.

Tatiana's crying gradually subsided and her body relaxed. He released her and she pulled back slowly; her eyes were vacant and her body listless. She was physically and emotionally spent. He lifted her into his arms and laid her gently on the bed. After removing her shoes, he covered her with an extra blanket from the closet and kissed her forehead. By the time he tucked her in, her eyes were closed. Her breathing slowed and she soon fell asleep.

Plecas sat beside her, staring out the small window as his thoughts drifted into the past—to the day Natasha was born and how proud he'd been; to her sitting on his lap as a toddler playing games; to her running across the pier into his arms upon returning from deployment.

Eventually, his thoughts turned to the future—*Kazan*'s upcoming deployment, and the one potential solution remaining.

He pulled his cell phone from his uniform pocket, looked up the desired number, and called.

The American answered.

"I am willing to discuss your request," Plecas said.

6

LANGLEY, VIRGINIA

In a seventh-floor conference room, Christine O'Connor was joined by Deputy Director Monroe Bryant, Deputy Director for Operations PJ Rolow, and several other deputy directors and staff. The primary topic of this morning's meeting was the status of the hunt for Lonnie Mixell.

Tracey McFarland, the agency's deputy director for analysis, began with the headline item. "We have a lead on Mixell. The FBI has been analyzing video feeds from the major New York City transportation hubs, and facial recognition programs got a match at one of the JFK airport gates. Mixell boarded an Emirates Airlines flight to Dubai three hours after he assassinated the ambassador, traveling under an alias: Mark Alperi."

"Have we located him in Dubai?" Christine asked.

"Not yet. We're running about two days behind Mixell, so he could have already left the city. We'll do what we can, but we don't have many officers on the ground and have limited access to surveillance video in the city. We're moving assets into Dubai and pulsing our contacts there, plus we're monitoring the transportation hubs. Hopefully, something will turn up."

"Speaking of assets," Christine said. "What about Jake Harrison? Have we hired him yet?"

"He turned down the offer," Rolow replied.

"How much was he told? Does he know Mixell is involved?"

"It would have been a standard job offer. No details would have been provided."

"But that's the key issue. He needs to know we're hunting down Mixell."

"We're not authorized to disclose that information. I'll admit it's a catch-22 situation, in that if Harrison was already an agency employee with the proper clearance, we could reveal the information."

"Who's the classifying authority?"

"The FBI."

"What authority do I have as director? Can I supersede the FBI's determination?"

Rolow looked to the deputy director. Bryant answered, "Technically, no. But if you were to direct us to disclose this information, those who could hold you accountable have much bigger fish to fry. Plus, the FBI has leaked far more sensitive information to the public lately, and they probably won't bark up that tree. If you direct us to disclose Mixell's involvement, I'll have HR reengage Harrison."

"I have a better idea," Christine replied. "I haven't made the trip to the Naval Undersea Warfare Center in Washington state for the surveillance program review. Harrison lives nearby. We have a long history and I'm sure I can talk him into assisting."

Bryant shrugged. "You're the director. If you want to spend your time hiring folks, that's your prerogative."

Christine replied in an icy tone. "Thank you for your blessing. Set up the trip and meeting with Harrison as soon as possible."

When the meeting ended, Christine and the other deputy directors and staff departed the conference room, leaving only Bryant and Rolow. The deputy director closed the door, then returned to his seat, eyeing Rolow before commenting.

"She's a royal bitch."

"I like her," Rolow said. "Give her some time. Right now, she's asserting herself, making it clear who's running this place. Of course, that's not entirely true, but don't dispel the illusion. Once Christine settles in, she'll be fine. In fact, she'll be better than fine. She's perfect for the job."

Bryant shot Rolow a curious look.

"Have you reviewed her file?" Rolow asked.

"Just her professional qualifications. Enough to know she's even less qualified to lead the agency than your standard political appointee. She hasn't even served on an intel committee. She's a weapons expert and policy wonk."

"Read the rest of her file. You'll find Appendix C quite interesting."

"Classified personal incidents? She's been a congressional and White House staffer. What could she possibly have done to warrant an Appendix C?"

"She has a remarkable knack for ending up in the wrong place at the wrong time. Fortunately for us, although she might be a royal bitch, she's also a vindictive one."

"How's that?"

"She killed Russia's defense minister and SVR director."

Bryant raised an eyebrow. "I thought Elena Krayev did the deed."

"That was the plan, but we couldn't get Elena in place. The defense minister didn't take the bait and instead invited Christine to spend the weekend with him."

"I'm not surprised," Bryant said. "I'll admit, Christine is pretty easy on the eyes."

Rolow continued, "Elena convinced Christine to complete the task. It was pretty straightforward, but Christine got caught. Semyon Gorev, Russia's SVR director, strung her up and subjected her to a mild case of physical and psychological torture. If you look closely at her left cheek, you'll see the faint scar where Gorev sliced into her face.

"To make a long story short, Christine managed to call an extraction team and could have slipped safely away. Instead, she searched the villa for Gorev and blew his brains out."

Bryant pulled back slightly in his seat as Rolow added, "If I were you, I'd mind your p's and q's around her." Rolow grinned. "The important takeaway is that Christine isn't afraid to do what it takes to accomplish the mission. I think you'll find her more receptive than previous directors to proposals that fall into the gray area."

"She's not going to learn about any of that," Bryant replied. "We feed her, like the previous directors, what she needs to know and nothing more. Keep her desk full of paperwork and engaged enough for her to think she knows what's going on. We leave the tough decisions to you and me, unless we need her buy-in to cover our asses."

Rolow nodded. "Business as usual."

7
KARACHI, PAKISTAN

The bright city lights reflected off the front window of a green Suzuki Mehran as it worked its way through Karachi's congested streets. Inside the small four-door car, based on a three-decade-old design and sporting nearly the same features as the original version, two men rode in the front in silence. Driving the car was Amir Zahed, whose attention at the moment was split between the American beside him and the traffic. Lonnie Mixell sensed the stiffness in the man's posture as he gripped the steering wheel. Zahed didn't yet trust him, and the feeling was mutual. Both men were taking a gamble, one that would cost them their lives if tonight's meeting didn't go well.

Three hours after assassinating America's ambassador to the United Nations, Lonnie Mixell had boarded an Emirates Airlines flight from New York's JFK International Airport to Dubai, followed by a connecting flight to Karachi, where he had waited expectantly for word from Aleksandr Plecas. After the call was received, Mixell made one of his own, arranging tonight's meeting. Zahed had picked Mixell up at his hotel, and aside from a short greeting, the man hadn't spoken, focused instead on navigating the clogged streets. With a population of more than fifteen million and the fifth-largest city proper in the world, Karachi was truly a place where one could get lost in the crowd.

The buildings thinned out as they entered the suburbs, and Mixell sensed they were nearing the end of their journey when the Mehran turned in to a residential area of gated estates. After several more turns, Zahed pulled into a driveway and stopped before a black metal gate. A query emanated from the speaker on the driver's side, which Zahed answered, and the gate slowly opened. As they passed into the estate,

Mixell assessed its defenses. The metal gates transitioned to twenty-foot-tall brick walls that encircled a sprawling three-story residence. In the distance, he spotted three armed men in various locations, each cradling an assault rifle.

Zahed pulled to a stop on a circular driveway outside the home's entrance. Both men stepped from the car as two armed men emerged from the dwelling. Like Zahed, the men wore white dishdashas, although they also carried AK-47s held ready at the waist. The two men greeted Zahed while eyeing Mixell suspiciously, then motioned for Mixell to follow Zahed inside.

Mixell stepped into a brightly lit foyer occupied by two other men, similarly armed, who searched him for weapons. Finding none, they stepped aside and Zahed led Mixell into a living area filled with several couches and chairs arranged around a low table. Zahed settled onto a couch and motioned Mixell into one opposite him. As Mixell sank into the plush cushions, he was surprised that they were the only men in the room.

"I thought we were meeting the leader of your organization."

"He will arrive soon."

Two women entered the room, one carrying a large platter of food while the other carried cups and a pot of tea.

"You must be hungry," Zahed said. "Eat."

Mixell and Zahed had finished eating, the dishes cleared away, when four men entered the room: a man Mixell recognized, escorted by three armed men who made no effort to conceal their Uzi submachine guns. Mixell almost smiled at the irony—Arab terrorists carrying weapons manufactured by Israel Military Industries. These three men were different from the four Mixell had encountered earlier. Conscious of his surroundings and potential threats, Mixell noted that there were now ten armed men nearby. But for the moment, he focused on the man without a weapon, who was missing his right arm and walked with a limp.

The rumors were true. The man had been targeted by an American drone and had barely escaped with his life. Mixell rose from the couch to greet Ayman al-Zawahiri.

Zawahiri had succeeded Osama bin Laden as leader of al-Qaeda. After the rise of ISIL and the presumed death of Zawahiri, America's attention had turned elsewhere and al-Qaeda had slowly regained strength. Additionally, Zawahiri had recently convinced ISIL remnants in Afghanistan and Pakistan to shift allegiance to his leadership, with a goal of unifying all Islamic extremist and jihadist organizations worldwide. Zawahiri yearned for a bold strike that would demonstrate his leadership and his organization's capabilities, convincing other groups to join the al-Qaeda network.

But even though al-Qaeda had regained strength, it still lacked the ability to inflict the type of damage done on 9/11. Not that Zawahiri didn't have resources. He had money, but not the right people or relationships. Mixell was a man who could help. As an American, traveling under an alias and with even a minimal disguise, he could move freely through Europe and the United States and had developed the necessary relationships. But to execute his plans, Mixell needed money. The question was—how deep were Zawahiri's pockets?

Zawahiri studied the American rising to greet him. He was adept at reading men, a trait that had kept him alive through twenty years of Western persecution. It did not take long to realize the man standing before him was a contradiction. He was staring at an infidel in Western attire, a man who could never outwardly be confused as an ally. But the man's eyes told a different story. Within his dark pupils was a simmering hatred, a visceral desire for revenge. The man had suffered a great injustice, it seemed, and had embarked on an unwavering path of vengeance. It was this journey that Zawahiri wanted to explore further.

For his part, Mixell saw a man who wasn't much different from himself. Although they were of different races, religions, and cultures, they were men cut from the same cloth. They shared a common enemy, albeit for different reasons. The differences were irrelevant as far as Mixell was concerned; only the common goal mattered. It was Zawahiri's dedication to this goal—and his ability to fund it—that had drawn him in.

Zawahiri gestured to the couches. "Be seated."

There was no need for Zahed to translate, since Zawahiri had spoken in English, and was fluent in French as well as his native Arabic.

Mixell returned to his couch as Zawahiri sat opposite him beside Zahed, while the three armed men remained in the room, standing behind Mixell. One of the women entered, offering tea to Mixell and the two men facing him, which they accepted.

After taking a sip of tea, Zawahiri said, "Congratulations, my friend," although Mixell was certain the man did not yet consider him a friend. "You executed your task in New York well. I could not have asked for a better outcome."

Mixell nodded his appreciation, then asked, "Do you plan to take credit for the assassination?"

"In due time. If you are successful in your next endeavor, the ambassador's death will pale in comparison. In the meantime, I do not want to focus America's attention on my organization any more than it already is. Let them hunt down only the man responsible for the assassination."

"Fair enough," Mixell replied. "Regarding this next endeavor, have you made a decision? The timeline is tight. You must authorize the first task within the next three days or the opportunity may not present itself again."

"I will decide tonight," Zawahiri replied. "But I have many questions that must be answered first."

And thus, the interrogation began. Question after question regarding Mixell's background, the events that led to his incarceration, what he had done since regaining his freedom, and his motive for assisting al-Qaeda. Throughout it all, it was clear that Zawahiri was trying to resolve the basic issue—could he trust him?

After two hours of questions and answers, Zawahiri turned to Zahed and spoke in Arabic. Mixell couldn't understand their conversation, but sensed the tension in their words. After a few exchanges, Zawahiri spoke to Mixell.

"Step outside for a few minutes."

As Mixell rose from the couch, the terrorist leader offered a small smile, then took another sip of tea.

This was a dangerous time, Mixell thought. The smile could mean anything.

Zawahiri's eyes followed the American as he left the room, accompanied by the armed men. Although Mixell claimed not to understand any of the Arabic dialects, it could be a ruse, and Zawahiri wanted to discuss matters with Zahed in private.

"This American," Zawahiri said. "I do not trust him."

"He did as we requested," Zahed replied, "killing the American ambassador to the United Nations to prove his loyalty and his capability."

"That was but a single act, one that does not confirm his allegiance to the cause. It could easily be a ploy to gain our confidence."

"Do his motivations matter?"

"It does if there is an armed drone overhead tracking his movements, waiting until the appropriate meeting has been arranged."

"I think we've answered that question. You have arrived and there has been no attack."

"The Americans are weak. They do not sacrifice their men. As long as he is with us, we are safe. It is when we go our separate ways that we are at our greatest peril."

Zahed considered Zawahiri's words, then replied, "I agree with you. There is no way to be certain the American can be trusted. But we are not bringing him into our inner circle. He will learn nothing about our leadership or operations. He has offered valuable services, and you risk only money. We must take what Allah provides and be grateful."

After a moment of reflection, Zawahiri nodded his agreement. "Bring him to me."

Mixell entered the room, returning to the couch across from the al-Qaeda leader.

"I will fund both tasks," Zawahiri said. "As for the first, these are the targets."

He glanced at Zahed, who pulled a sheet of paper from his pocket and handed it to the American. Mixell examined the list, which matched his expectations.

"How much do you require for both tasks?" Zawahiri asked.

"What I've proposed is not easy to arrange," Mixell replied. "It will be expensive to purchase the cooperation I require, as well as the equipment. I need sixty million U.S. dollars, up front, with another sixty million upon the successful completion of either task."

Zawahiri stared at Mixell for a moment, his eyes unreadable. Finally, he said, "If you accomplish either task, I will double the sixty million due. Consider the additional funds a down payment for further work."

Mixell nodded his understanding as Zawahiri stood and limped from the room without another word, leaving the three armed men behind.

Zahed made no move to leave, and when Mixell asked what the plan was, Zahed said tersely, "We wait."

A half-hour later, Zahed answered his cell phone. Mixell didn't understand what was said, but when he saw the relief on Zahed's face, he connected the dots. Zawahiri had made it safely to his destination. There had been no drone circling above, waiting to eliminate those who had met with him.

Zahed stood. "We can go now. The required funds will be deposited into an account in the morning."

8

SILVERDALE, WASHINGTON

Angie Harrison looked out the kitchen window as she rinsed off the lunch dishes. The weather was beautiful for this time of year, with clear skies offering a view of the snow-capped Olympic Mountains to the west and Mount Rainier to the east. After placing the last plate in the dishwasher, her eyes settled on her husband, Jake, working in the backyard, clearing the brush along the perimeter that had encroached on their house over the years. Despite the cool air, he had worked up a sweat and paused to wipe the perspiration from his face on his shirt sleeve.

The phone rang with the expected call and Angie let the answering machine pick up. It was Christine O'Connor, letting them know she was fifteen minutes away. After the CIA director hung up, Angie took a deep breath.

She had never met the woman Jake had proposed to twice, and in a few minutes, she would walk through the front door. Although Jake said he no longer loved Christine, Angie was convinced he had just grown tired of waiting. After dating Christine for ten years, he had finally walked away, proposing to Angie a year later. Christine hadn't heard the news and called Jake the following month, telling him she was ready to settle down. Angie didn't know which woman Jake loved more, but she knew he was an honorable man and he had held to his commitment to her. Sometimes, though, she wondered how things would have turned out if Christine had called a month earlier.

Angie turned on the dishwasher, then entered the living room, surveying the area one last time. After ensuring everything was in its place, she stopped by the foyer mirror and examined herself with a critical eye. She normally wore a sweatshirt and jeans around the house, but this morning had picked out a pair of khaki slacks and a form-fitting shirt that accentuated her figure, and had taken the time to put on makeup.

After checking the rest of the house to ensure it was presentable, she stepped onto the back patio. Harrison was still busy with the underbrush, making slow progress. She called across the yard to him.

"Jake! Christine will be here in a few minutes. You need to get cleaned up."

He looked up at her, then shrugged. "I'm fine."

Angie noticed how differently they were reacting to Christine's visit. Her stomach was tied in knots, while Jake acted nonchalant. But she knew him well enough to know he was staying busy to keep his mind off things. To keep his mind off *Christine.*

She started a pot of coffee, then stopped by the foyer mirror one last time. After reaffirming her appearance was acceptable, she spotted movement through the living room window. A black SUV with two men in front and a passenger in the back was pulling up the long driveway. She went to the back of the house and opened the door.

"Christine is here."

Harrison finished clearing the section he was working on, then wiped the grime from his hands onto his jeans and cleaned his face with his T-shirt. He headed toward the house, not looking forward to the pending conversation. He needed a job, but was hoping for something less dangerous than his last, plus he wasn't sure if working for Christine was a good idea.

Fifteen years earlier, after Harrison proposed to Angie, Christine had accepted he was in love with another woman and moved on, getting married a few years later. But after her husband's death three years ago, she ran into Harrison aboard USS *Michigan*. Christine was still a beautiful woman and there was no denying that he was still attracted to her—and it was obvious Christine had similar feelings. During their last private conversation aboard *Michigan,* Christine had asked him how things were with Angie. He had answered honestly, and when he said *Things are good,* he'd seen the disappointment in her eyes.

Harrison stepped through the back door and into the breakfast nook to find Christine, wearing a black business suit and white blouse, sitting across from Angie, who sat stiffly in her chair. Christine rose to greet him, extending her hand. Harrison found the gesture odd. He'd known Christine since they were kids, and he couldn't recall ever shaking her hand. Even when running into her aboard *Michigan* after not seeing each other for years, they had picked up like the childhood friends they once were. If today's meeting had been in a different setting—without Angie—he was convinced Christine would have greeted him with a hug.

He took the proffered hand, noting Christine's firm handshake, then settled into a chair between the two women. As Christine returned to her seat, Harrison noticed Angie scrutinizing the CIA director. Even in a conservative business suit, Christine's beauty was undeniable. It was a good thing, Harrison figured, that Angie had never seen Christine dressed for a night out on the town, wearing an evening dress that hugged her curves. He had seen the effect, entering a bar or restaurant with Christine on his arm. Heads would turn, men and women alike, admiring his date.

Angie rose to pour coffee for all three, and they engaged in small talk for a while until Harrison moved the conversation along. "So, what brings you to the Pacific Northwest? I'm sure you didn't travel all this way just to say 'Hi.'"

"I had some business at the Naval Undersea Warfare Center in Keyport, but I moved the trip up so we could talk."

"About what?"

Christine glanced at Angie before returning her attention to Harrison. "We need to talk privately."

"Whatever you have to say, you can say in front of Angie."

"The details are classified."

"I no longer have a security clearance. Whatever you can tell me, you can tell Angie."

Christine smiled. "You're quite right."

It was obvious Christine was here to talk him into accepting the CIA job, but he had already decided. There was no point in extending the discussion. "If you're going to offer me a job again, the answer's still no."

"There are details you're not aware of that may change your mind."

"Such as?"

"We want you to help track down the man who assassinated the United States' ambassador to the United Nations." She paused, then added, "The assassin is Mixell."

Angie raised her hand to her mouth. "Lonnie?"

Christine turned to Angie, surprised by her response. "I didn't realize you knew Lonnie."

"I dated him before Jake. Lonnie and Jake were best friends—that's how we met. But Lonnie had anger management issues and we eventually split. I started dating Jake a short while later."

"Are you sure it was Lonnie?" Harrison asked.

Christine nodded. "We have him on video. He torched the ambassador and his security detail with thermobaric rounds. The president directed us to put a full-court press on the matter and we want you to help. You have the same training and background as he does and know him well, and might be able to provide valuable insight."

There was silence around the table as Harrison considered the new information. He hadn't realized Mixell had been released from prison early.

"He'll eventually come after you," Christine said.

Harrison didn't respond; the same thought was running through his mind.

Christine continued, "Lonnie's out for revenge against the country he believes betrayed him. If you think he's going to stop there, you're wrong. You turned him in, and you testified against him. He's not going to stop until his revenge is complete."

"When do you need an answer?"

"As soon as possible."

"Let me talk things over with Angie, and I'll let you know in a day or two."

"Thanks," Christine said as she rose from her chair.

They walked Christine to the door and watched her step into the SUV, which drove slowly down the driveway before disappearing around the bend. After the front door closed, he turned to Angie.

She spoke first. "Your mind's already made up, isn't it?"

"I think so."

"You said you were going to get a safer job. One where you didn't have to put your life on the line. Think of me and Madeline, the impact on us if something happened to you. Your first responsibility is to your wife and daughter now, not your country."

"Taking care of my family starts with money. I need a job, and one that pays well. We've got bills to pay and college to save for. Whatever job they have in mind can't be any more dangerous than my previous one. Even more important, I have a responsibility to protect you and Maddy. Christine's right—Lonnie will eventually come after me. You know as well as I do that he's got a mean streak and a get-even attitude. Given what he's done in New York, the sooner he's back behind bars the better."

Angie stared at him for a long moment, and he could see the tears welling in her eyes. He leaned forward and placed his forehead against hers and caressed her cheek with his hand.

"Nothing's going to happen to me. We'll find Lonnie and put him in prison again, and this time, he won't get out. I'll be safe. You and Maddy will be safe. I promise."

"Okay," Angie said, forcing a smile as she wiped her tears away.

Without another word, she headed to the kitchen, Harrison following her, where she moved the coffee cups from the table to the sink. After rinsing them, she placed her hands on the edge of the counter. Her shoulders remained tense as she stared out the window. Something else was bothering her.

Harrison stopped behind her. "What's wrong?"

She turned toward him. "It's Christine. She's even more attractive in person. And you'll be working with her."

"You're beautiful too, and you're the only woman I care about."

"I know I'm attractive, but Christine is . . . elegant. I could never be like her. She's polished and sophisticated, while I'm inner-city trash."

Angie's words reminded Harrison of how sensitive she was about her upbringing, growing up in inner-city Baltimore, reared by a single mom on welfare. Angie had clawed her way out of the morass, earning a college degree while working nights to pay her way through school.

"You're not Bawl'mer trash," Harrison replied, pronouncing Baltimore the way Angie did. He grinned as he placed his hands on her waist. "Christine had her chance and blew it. I ended up with a better woman, and I'm not going to trade you in for her."

"She's got different thoughts. I can tell when a woman is interested in a man, and Christine is definitely interested in you."

"You have nothing to worry about."

"Yeah, right. A beautiful, successful, and powerful woman—someone you dated for ten years and proposed to twice—wants you to work with her on the other side of the country. What's there to worry about?"

Harrison leaned forward and kissed Angie softly on the lips, then locked his eyes on to hers. "There's nothing left between me and Chris."

"I can tell when you're lying, but at least you're saying the right things."

The tension faded from Angie's body, then she rested her forearms atop Harrison's shoulders, locking her fingers behind his neck.

"In case you get any ideas, I'd like to remind you that there's no way Christine is as good as I am." A devilish grin appeared.

Harrison returned the smile. "At what?"

Angie hooked one leg behind the small of Harrison's back, then swung the other leg up lithely, scissoring her legs around his waist.

"A lot of things. I bet one or two come to mind."

Harrison played along. "I'm drawing a blank. Perhaps you could remind me."

Angie tightened her grip around his neck, pressing her body against his as she moved in for a kiss.

9

LANGLEY, VIRGINIA

"Harrison's arrived."

Deputy Director for Operations PJ Rolow delivered the news as he took his seat beside Deputy Director Monroe Bryant at the conference table in Christine's office. "He'll be here shortly, once he's through security."

"What's the plan?" Christine asked.

"Harrison is well trained from a technical standpoint," Rolow replied, "but he'll need to get up to speed on CIA protocols, so someone will hold his hand for a while. When he's working stateside, he'll be teamed with Patricia Kendall from our National Resources Division, which handles issues we don't want to hand off to the FBI or other domestic agencies, or want to pursue in tandem. To chase leads on domestic soil, Harrison will need to interface with the various intelligence and law enforcement agencies, and there's no one with better contacts and relationships than Kendall.

"While overseas, Harrison will be teamed with an appropriate officer. This just in—Mixell was spotted at the airport in Karachi, Pakistan—so that'll be Harrison's first destination once he's through indoc. While in the Middle East or any of the *stan* countries, he'll be teamed with Khalila Dufour."

Rolow had referred to the group of seven countries in Central and South Asia ending in *stan:* Pakistan, Afghanistan, and the five former Soviet republics, such as Kazakhstan and Turkmenistan.

Their conversation was interrupted by the intercom on Christine's desk; her secretary's voice emanated from the speaker. "Director O'Connor, Jake Harrison is here."

"Send him in."

The door opened and Harrison entered, appearing not much different from the last time Christine had seen him, wearing jeans and a polo shirt. After introducing Harrison to the deputy director and DDO, she motioned him into the empty seat at the table. After a bit of small talk, Rolow got down to business.

"You'll be assigned to the special operations group within the special activities center, which I'm sure you're familiar with. For the Mixell issue, you'll be teamed with two officers, one who will help you interface with the domestic agencies, and one who will assist while overseas. You'll meet them shortly; they're on the way up."

Christine's intercom buzzed again, and her secretary informed them that Officer Kendall had arrived. The door opened and an attractive redhead entered. Harrison rose from his chair as the woman stepped into Christine's office.

"There's no need for chivalry," Rolow said, "especially in Pat's presence."

Kendall gave Rolow an icy stare as she approached, then turned to Harrison and thrust her hand out, adding a smile. "I'm Pat Kendall."

Rolow explained the plan to Kendall, who seemed to have already been briefed on her role regarding Harrison. When Rolow mentioned he'd also be teamed with Khalila Dufour, Kendall's demeanor turned cold.

"You can't be serious," she said. "I realize she's your pet, but you should keep her on her leash."

"Zip it, Kendall," Rolow said. "Play nice or you'll be riding a desk for a while."

Pat was about to say something else, but clamped her mouth shut.

The intercom activated again; Khalila Dufour had arrived. A moment later, a woman of Middle Eastern descent entered. Although Kendall was attractive, Christine had to admit that Khalila was stunning. She was six feet tall, only two inches shorter than Harrison, with straight black hair falling across her shoulders, wearing a short skirt emphasizing her long, lean legs.

Pat shot Khalila a wicked look, then fixed her gaze on the DDO as her hands clenched into fists. Khalila, on the other hand, ignored

Pat as she approached, stopping beside her without even a glance in her direction, her eyes surveying Harrison instead. She made no effort to introduce herself, standing with her arms folded across her chest, projecting a *why-am-I-here* attitude.

"Okay, Harrison," Rolow said, "this is how it goes. Pat will accompany you stateside and herd you through indoc. Whenever our leads take you to the Middle East or any of the *stan* countries, you'll go with Khalila. Her contacts in the region and linguistic skills are the best the agency has to offer. Any questions?"

Harrison shook his head. "No, sir."

Rolow motioned for Pat and Khalila to exit Christine's office, then stood and shook Harrison's hand. "Good luck."

Harrison joined the two women as they left the office. After the door closed, Christine turned to Rolow. "There's obviously bad blood between those two. What's the deal?"

Harrison walked down the seventh-floor hallway bracketed by the two women, with neither one speaking until they reached the elevator. While they waited for the doors to open, Pat turned to Harrison.

"Be careful while working with Khalila. Her partners have a habit of ending up dead."

"Only the incompetent ones," Khalila replied. "It's not my fault your boy toy of the month got himself killed."

The elevator doors opened and after they stepped inside, Pat replied, "John wasn't my boy toy. We were in a committed relationship."

"He had a strange way of showing it," Khalila said. "He couldn't keep his hands off me; said I was way better in bed than you."

"I doubt that," Pat replied, "you clitless camel-jacker."

Khalila swiveled toward Pat, her body tensed for action.

Harrison stepped between the two women. "I understand I'll be working with you separately. Which sounds like an excellent plan."

"You don't need to worry about me," Khalila said. "It's Kendall you need to watch out for. I can smell when someone's corrupt, and she's as dirty as they come."

"That's yourself you're smelling," Pat replied.

The elevator doors opened to the fifth floor.

Khalila asked Pat, "How long are you going to have to babysit him?"

"The rest of today and tomorrow," Pat replied coldly.

Khalila turned to Harrison. "We leave for Pakistan tomorrow night." Then she headed down the corridor.

When the elevator doors closed, Pat smacked the symbol for the second floor. "That bitch! She knows how to press my buttons." She fumed for a while as the elevator descended, then turned to Harrison.

"I was serious about watching your back around Khalila. The word is she's very good, but she usually leaves a trail of carnage. Her partners end up dead more often than not. I don't know what the deal is with her, but I've gleaned enough to know that the DDO doesn't completely trust her. He lets her off her leash only on important missions where the risk is worth the gain, and apparently, tracking down Mixell falls into that category."

"I'll keep that in mind," Harrison said, pondering the unusual situation he was in. As a Navy SEAL, he had trusted his team members without question.

As the elevator doors opened, Harrison asked, "What's the plan for today?"

"I'll take you to outfitting, where you'll get issued weapons and tactical gear, and get you a locker to store everything. Then we'll head to the analysis center, where we'll review what they've come up with regarding Mixell. I understand you were good friends with him. Go through his file. Tell us what we've missed."

Harrison nodded.

As they walked down the hallway, a woman carrying a stack of files approached, flashing Harrison a smile as she passed by. The look wasn't missed by Pat. "I bet you get that a lot."

Harrison wasn't sure how to respond; he hadn't yet figured Pat out. She was friendly, at least toward him, yet he sensed a hard-nosed and flip-switch personality; someone you didn't want to get across the breakers with.

He decided to offer a quid pro quo. "I bet you get a lot of looks yourself."

"Thanks," she said. "Nowadays, most guys would have tap-danced around my comment, afraid of being hauled into HR for offering a simple compliment. I just might end up liking you, Jake. If you stay alive long enough, that is."

10

MOSCOW, RUSSIA

Not far from Patriarch's Pond, its surface already frozen for the winter, Lonnie Mixell navigated the busy sidewalk along Spiridonyevsky Lane. Had he not been told what to look for, he might have passed by the entrance—the door to an old house crammed between two modern buildings, marked by a small sign that said *Mari Vanna*. He knocked on the door, which was opened by a man wearing slippers and a jogging suit who took Mixell's coat as he entered.

Mixell scanned the small residence, which had been transformed into a restaurant offering home-cooked Russian cuisine with a complementing ambience: shows playing on an ancient TV, shelves full of photographs, old cameras, and other knickknacks from bygone days, a bicycle leaning against a wall, and a parrot in a cage hanging above potted plants on a windowsill. Adding to the homey atmosphere were a woman in a pink nightgown with curlers in her hair clearing dishes from a table, and a sleepy cat curled in a basket, opening its eyes temporarily to assess the new customer.

The man Mixell was scheduled to meet was already seated at a small table in the back. Mixell slipped into the empty chair across from the Russian captain, who made no attempt to greet him, although there was a flicker of acknowledgment in his eyes. Mixell spoke first.

"I'd like to thank you for your assistance." Since Aleksandr Plecas didn't speak English, Mixell spoke in Russian.

Plecas replied, "Your Russian is quite good. Where did you learn it?"

"My mother is Russian, an immigrant to America. My father knew enough to get by, and we spoke Russian at home."

Mixell's thoughts drifted momentarily to his childhood and the friendships he had developed due to his Russian heritage. Almost ten percent of his hometown population were Russian immigrants, and his mother had become good friends with two other Russian women, getting together often for tea and social activities. As a result, Mixell had become good friends with two other second-generation Russians: Jake Harrison and Christine O'Connor.

Christine, who went by Chris until she left for college, was a tomboy growing up, hanging out with the guys all the way through high school. She was fast and strong, more than capable of holding her own during the rowdy outdoor games, at least until the boys hit puberty, when they gained a significant size and strength advantage. By then, however, their focus was less on roughhouse games and more on girls, and as Chris developed into a young woman, the guys began to look at her in a different light. Mixell had to admit he'd been quite jealous when Chris chose Jake over himself.

Jake Harrison. His former best friend, the man who betrayed him. While sitting in prison, Mixell had made a mental revenge list, and Harrison was near the top. But first, he would pay America back for what it had done to him. He had fought valiantly against his country's enemies, risking his life countless times, but now that America had turned its back on him, his new path in life was clear—he'd help America's enemies instead. Once that score was adequately settled, he would focus on more personal issues, and exact his revenge on Jake.

Mixell smiled briefly and wondered if Plecas noticed. But the man's attention was focused on the ancient TV. Mixell glanced over his shoulder, noting that the programming had shifted to the nightly news: an update on the Russian Navy. Currently being shown were video clips of the disastrous war with the United States a few months ago. Russia's Northern and Pacific Fleets had been devastated, with the video on the TV showing the aftermath: Russian ships floating aimlessly on the surface—blackened hulks or ships engulfed in flames—while the less fortunate ships were already resting on the ocean bottom.

The news program tried to put a positive spin on the outcome, showing black smoke spiraling upward from the four American aircraft carriers during the main engagement. But two of the carriers had remained in action, putting the finishing touches on the pride of the Russian

Fleet: the aircraft carrier *Admiral Kuznetsov* and the nuclear-powered battle cruiser *Pyotr Velikiy*. Both had remained afloat after the battle and had been towed to the nearest shipyard, but it would be two years at least before either warship was returned to service.

Only Russia's submarine fleet had survived relatively intact, with two-thirds of its submarines still operational. Mixell noticed the darkness in Plecas's eyes and wondered if what America had done to the Russian Navy played a part in his decision to help his cause.

A waitress wearing a traditional Russian dress stopped by to take their order. Mixell selected his favorites—borscht and pelmeni dumplings—looking forward to a home-cooked meal he hadn't had in many years, along with kvass, a fermented beverage made from rye bread. While they waited for their order, they talked in hushed tones, so no one could overhear their conversation.

"I'm sorry about your daughter," Mixell said, "and that she hasn't responded to her treatments." It was a lie, of course. Her deteriorating condition was what he had been hoping for, backing Plecas into a corner. "I have the funds you need. Do you have the required information?"

Plecas pulled a letter from his pocket, which he handed to Mixell. "This has everything you need: the name of the drug, the company that makes it, and the contact information for my daughter's primary doctor at Blokhin Medical Center."

Mixell reviewed the information, then replied, "I will arrange for one-half of the treatment before you deploy, and the second half once you complete your assignment. Agreed?"

Plecas nodded, and Mixell retrieved a folded sheet of paper from his pocket, which he handed to the Russian. "Here are the targets. It must be a simultaneous attack, which will increase the odds of overwhelming defense systems the Americans have in place."

The submarine captain studied the targets for a while, determining where he needed to position his submarine.

"How long before you can launch?" Mixell asked.

"I can be within range of all targets fifteen days after *Kazan* deploys."

Mixell pulled his cell phone from a pocket and reviewed the itinerary he'd been sent.

"That's a good day. What kind of a launch window are we talking about? Plus or minus how many hours?"

"My submarine can travel thousands of kilometers and arrive at the launch point within one minute of the specified time. It's a simple math problem—time versus distance—and I will adjust my submarine's speed to compensate for issues along the way. However, if I run into delays near the end of the transit, does an eight-hour window work?"

"That'd be fine."

Beneath the list of the targets, Plecas wrote down a date and time and showed it to Mixell, who memorized it.

"I will launch between this time"—Plecas pointed to the paper—"and eight hours later, Greenwich Mean Time. Understand?"

Mixell nodded. The U.S. military—and apparently Russian submarines—operated on GMT, to which all other time zones were referenced, so that every unit around the world knew when to execute its orders, regardless of the local time.

Plecas folded the paper and slipped it in his pocket as the waitress returned, first with their drinks and then food. As the two men ate in silence, Mixell sensed that Plecas wasn't enamored with the task he had agreed to, but was confident the Russian would follow through.

Meanwhile, Mixell's thoughts turned to the second and more critical element of the plot, which Plecas was unaware of. Mixell repressed a smile as he dug into his pelmeni.

11

MOSCOW, RUSSIA

It was almost midnight at Moscow's Leningradskaya Station as Lonnie Mixell sat at a table in the back of the train's restaurant car, eyeing the other passengers enjoying a late-night snack prior to the train's departure. Instead of a Sapsan high-speed daytime train, Mixell had opted for an overnight journey aboard the historic Krasnaya Strela, commonly referred to as the Red Arrow, Russia's premier train traveling the Moscow–St. Petersburg route during the Soviet era. As the red train pulled away from the brightly lit loading platform, beginning its eight-hour nonstop journey, music was broadcast through the carriage cars—Oleg Gazmanov's "Moscow"—a decades-old tradition on the Red Arrow.

Having landed in Moscow that morning, Mixell planned to depart the country via St. Petersburg. His departure from JFK airport had likely been detected, and the American intelligence agencies were no doubt attempting to follow his trail. He planned to keep moving, staying a step ahead of his enemies, shifting to a new identity periodically and avoiding transportation hubs he had already passed through. The Red Arrow met his need, taking him to St. Petersburg where he would leave the country to arrange the second plot Zawahiri had funded. But for now, he needed to finalize the last element of the first plot.

Mixell made eye contact with one of the men he'd be meeting tonight, sitting at a table not far away, then caught the attention of the second man, at a table at the far end of the restaurant car, who nodded slightly. He texted both men on his cell phone, instructing them to join him in his sleeper cabin in a few minutes. After finishing his cheesecake, Mixell strolled through the restaurant car, passing both men before stepping into the adjacent VIP carriage, where he slipped into his suite.

A moment later, the first man knocked, then entered, followed shortly by the second man.

Sitting at a small table, Mixell invited the two men into seats across from him. The man to the left was Anatoly Bogdanov, while beside him sat Mikhail Korenev. The two men were meeting each other for the first time. Before beginning, Mixell briefly assessed the willingness of his two co-conspirators to execute the plan.

Years earlier, as he stewed in his prison cell at Fort Leavenworth, Mixell had imagined ways to make the United States pay for its betrayal. Something that would make 9/11 pale in comparison. His thoughts frequently focused on nuclear weapons. Between America and Russia, there had been tens of thousands in their arsenals at the height of the Cold War, and tactical nuclear weapons were small and transportable. If he could get his hands on just one . . .

After evaluating the possibilities, Mixell had focused his efforts on obtaining Russian nuclear weapons. However, even if he obtained a tactical nuke, it wasn't the kind of weapon one could remotely detonate with a cell phone. They were protected by the same safeguards as strategic nuclear weapons, requiring arming authorization from appropriate fire control software, and the warheads had complex logic interlocks that prevented inadvertent detonation.

The unlock and launch authorization codes were held by Russia's general staff at their command center in Moscow or backup facilities at Chekhov and Penza. Additionally, the Russians had their version of the U.S. president's portable Presidential Emergency Satchel, commonly referred to as the nuclear football: three suitcase-sized control modules code-named Chegnet—*the monarch's scepter*. One was kept with the Russian president, another with the defense minister, and the third with the chief of the general staff.

Unfortunately, after two years of developing plans and probing for allies who could assist, Mixell had reluctantly concluded the effort was a bridge too far—the Chegnets and Russian strategic command centers were heavily guarded, and obtaining access to a fire control system with the protocols to arm the weapon and the personnel willing to launch it had proven too challenging. Fortuitously, Mixell had learned of an alternative. A software flaw that, with the right assistance, could be exploited.

Obtaining that assistance was still a tall order. There was a significant possibility America would retaliate, and he needed help from those who had no vested interest in their home country. It had taken another year, but he had finally found his men: one bitter, one disillusioned.

Bogdanov was the victim of a nasty divorce that had ruined him financially, and his reputation had been marred by vicious lies spread by his wife during the divorce proceedings. Additionally, Bogdanov was an only child, his parents dead. If America retaliated, he had no family in Russia to worry about. Only his ex-wife, who he'd be happy to see turned into ashes.

Korenev, meanwhile, had been passed over for promotions to senior positions several times, and a grudge against his government supervisors and the administration as a whole had steadily grown. He was now deeply disillusioned, and the opportunity to be recognized for his ability, even if that appreciation came from Mixell, along with enough money to live in luxury in an exotic country for the rest of his life, had been too tempting to decline.

Both men had agreed to their phase of the plot, but accomplishing it was another matter. There were significant obstacles to overcome.

"Have you arranged the assistance you need?" Mixell asked.

Both men nodded. Each executed a different element of the plot, but both required help, as each part was protected by safeguards requiring the concurrence of two persons with the required authorization. Altogether, four persons were required, but Mixell left it up to Bogdanov and Korenev to arrange the necessary assistance.

Mixell pulled a small case from a satchel and handed it to Korenev. "What you need is inside, along with instructions."

Korenev examined the contents, then closed the case.

Mixell then retrieved a suitcase from the closet, placing it on the table before Bogdanov. He opened it, revealing a handheld laser cleaner and a thin disk about two inches in diameter.

After glancing at the contents, Bogdanov asked, "Where is the third item? It's the most critical."

Mixell turned to Korenev, who pulled a thin, handheld computer from his jacket, which he handed to Bogdanov. "This is what you need," he said. "Do you know how to use it?"

"Of course. Does it have the authorization code loaded?"

"Not yet. Once I receive payment, I'll provide the code." Korenev smiled as he turned to Mixell. "Which gets us to the main topic of tonight's meeting."

"I have the money you requested," Mixell said. "Forty million, U.S., for each of you, deposited into separate Swiss accounts." He retrieved two letters from his satchel and handed them to Bogdanov and Korenev. "Here is the account information, along with instructions so each of you can create another account and transfer funds to pay for the assistance you require."

After reading his letter, Korenev said, "This is only half of the money."

"You'll receive the other half after you complete your task."

Korenev leaned forward. "This wasn't the deal."

"It is now," Mixell said. "You're not getting forty million dollars without assurance you've done your part. If you were in my position, you'd do the same."

Korenev gave him a hard stare, then eased back in his seat. "I understand."

Mixell handed a package to each man. "These are the documents for your new identities, both for yourselves and your assistants, so you cannot be tracked down afterward."

Both men examined the fake identification documents.

With Bogdanov and Korenev officially committing to their part, everything had been arranged, leaving one last concern. Persuading Aleksandr Plecas to launch weapons against the United States had been difficult, and Mixell was convinced that if Plecas learned they were armed with nuclear warheads, there was zero chance he would have agreed. It was crucial that Plecas not discover what he was launching.

Mixell posed his question to Bogdanov. "You're sure the submarine captain won't know the warheads are nuclear?"

Bogdanov nodded. "Neither the Russian captain nor his crew will have any idea their missiles have nuclear warheads. If the arming code is already entered into the missiles, they won't query the fire control software, requesting authorization. They will appear the same as missiles with conventional warheads."

Although Mixell had heard it before, Bogdanov's words were reassuring.

With everything arranged, the only challenge remaining was actually executing the plan. "The missile loadout is in three days. We're on a tight timeline."

Korenev replied, "I will obtain the code tomorrow night, but cannot transfer it until the morning."

Bogdanov added, "I'll be ready."

12

SEVEROMORSK, RUSSIA

Shadows were creeping eastward across the snow-covered terrain, the deep red sun descending toward the hills to the west as Mikhail Korenev's car coasted to a halt outside the headquarters of the Northern Fleet Joint Strategic Command. Established in 2014, the joint command controlled Russia's Northern Fleet and all ground and aerospace forces in the Murmansk and Arkhangelsk Oblasts, as well as the offshore islands along its northern coast.

After passing through the building's security checkpoint and nodding to the two armed guards on duty, Korenev rode the elevator to the strategic command center, located several hundred feet underground and encapsulated within a twenty-foot-thick concrete shell. Upon reaching the reinforced entrance door, Korenev swiped his badge and entered his passcode. The door unlocked, providing access to the sprawling but mostly vacant command center.

Although nuclear strike orders would normally be issued from the main command center in Moscow or the alternate sites in Chekhov and Penza, Northern Fleet Joint Strategic Command served as a backup in case the primary and alternate sites were destroyed or otherwise rendered inoperable. Once a year, a heavily scrutinized training exercise was held to ensure Northern Fleet personnel were capable of transmitting nuclear launch orders to strategic units and Fleet ships armed with tactical nuclear weapons. The remaining 364 days of the year, however, were uneventful, and tonight the command center was quiet, with only the watch captain and two other men on duty, manning three of the thirty workstations.

After two hours, with the boredom of the night shift seeping in,

Korenev stood and stretched, taking his snack bag with him to the tea station at the back of the room. As he passed behind the watch captain, Korenev glanced at the third man in the room, Arkady Timoshenko, who nodded his head slightly, signaling his willingness to proceed.

Korenev called down to the watch captain, asking if he wanted a cup of tea. The man replied affirmatively as expected, and Korenev reached into his pocket and retrieved the item the American had given him on the Red Arrow—a small vial of what was presumably eye drops—and he placed three drops of the liquid into the watch captain's tea.

After delivering the drink to the watch captain, Korenev waited as the man sipped his tea, his eyelids growing heavy shortly thereafter. A few minutes later, his eyes closed and his head sagged onto his chest. After convincing himself that the watch captain was asleep, Korenev moved toward the double-door safe containing the nuclear authorization codes, where he was joined by Timoshenko. Korenev knew the combination to the outer door, while Timoshenko could open the inner door.

Before proceeding, Timoshenko asked about his payment. "Have you obtained the funding?"

Upon returning to Severomorsk, Korenev had verified that Mixell had deposited twenty million U.S. dollars into the account. "Everything is arranged," Korenev replied. "Your half of the money will be transferred into this account." He handed Timoshenko a letter.

As Timoshenko reviewed the information, Korenev entered his combination and opened the first door, then Timoshenko opened the second. Korenev pulled the contents from the safe, sorting through the material for the authorization codes for tactical nuclear weapons. Upon finding the packet, he wrote down one of the sixteen-digit codes. Only a single code was required, which could be entered into every warhead, so the launch platform didn't have to individually arm each weapon.

Korenev replaced the contents of the safe, returning them to their previous locations, then shut and locked both doors. A half-hour later, with Korenev and Timoshenko at their workstations reading naval messages on their displays, the watch captain woke from a groggy sleep, then eyed Korenev and Timoshenko to see if either man had noticed his lapse. Both men remained focused on their screens as they heard the watch captain stir, then stand and visit the tea station for another dose of caffeine.

This was a critical part of the plan. Making the watch captain fall asleep instead of killing him was essential, as there could be no indication that the nuclear launch safeguards had been compromised. Until it was too late, that is.

13

GADZHIYEVO, RUSSIA

It was just past midnight as a full moon illuminated a half-dozen nuclear attack and ballistic missile submarines tied up along the piers jutting into Yagelnaya Bay. Not far away, in Gadzhiyevo Naval Base's ordnance bunker complex, Vasily Morozov monitored the security cameras, noticing the arrival of Anatoly Bogdanov at one of the emergency exits, carrying a suitcase. Morozov remotely unlocked the door and Bogdanov slipped into the complex, arriving at the security center a few minutes later.

Neither man spoke as Bogdanov entered the combination and opened one safe, while Morozov opened another, and each man retrieved a key. Bogdanov led the way through the maze of concrete tunnels connecting the ordnance bunkers, arriving at their destination. Unlike bunkers storing conventional weapons, with their doors secured by padlocks, this bunker was protected by two thick metal doors that sealed together with an internal locking mechanism.

Bogdanov stopped short of the entrance doors and opened the suitcase obtained aboard the Red Arrow, retrieving the thin, two-inch-diameter disk provided by the American. He carefully approached the security camera mounted on the wall, ensuring he remained out of view. Reaching up, he placed the disk near the camera lens, facing in the same direction, and pressed a button on its side, taking a video recording. After a few seconds, an indicator on the side of the disk flashed green.

He pressed the button again, sending an electronic signal that scrambled the camera's video, then slipped the disk in front of the camera and pressed it against the lens, where it stuck in place. He pressed the button a third time, activating the disk. The camera would now see a video clip played in a loop instead of a live feed, allowing Bogdanov and Morozov to approach the bunker doors unnoticed.

Bogdanov inserted his key into the security panel on one side of the doors while Morozov did the same on the other side, and both men turned their keys simultaneously. After a heavy clank, the steel doors rumbled slowly apart. Bogdanov retrieved the suitcase and stopped at the entrance, surveying the tactical nuclear weapons inside. In the early 1990s, Russia had removed all tactical nuclear weapons from its ships and land-based units, moving them to secure storage areas. Gadzhiyevo Naval Base was the repository for the Northern Fleet's allocation of nuclear weapons, which included nuclear-warhead-armed Kalibr missiles.

Morozov accompanied Bogdanov as he moved toward the missiles, stopping by the nearest four-tier stowage rack. Opening the suitcase again, he retrieved a tool roll and handed it to Morozov, while he grabbed the laser cleaner. Morozov started removing the bottom missile's guidance and control section nose cone, which was painted in a red and yellow scheme indicating the missile was configured with a nuclear warhead, while Bogdanov focused on the warhead itself. He activated the laser cleaner, stripping the white paint from the desired section, and more important, the warhead's black serial number.

Bogdanov then sprayed the bare metal with white, quick-drying paint, feathering the edges so it blended in, and moved on to the next warhead as the paint dried. After stripping the serial number from all four missiles, he returned to the first, verifying the paint had dried, then pulled a pack of stencils, each precut with a different serial number in the required font and size. He taped the first stencil to the bottom warhead and sprayed the new serial number onto the white surface with black paint. After removing the stencil, he stepped back to assess his work. There was no indication the serial number had been changed, replacing it with one from a conventionally armed missile.

After stenciling the new number onto the fourth missile, Bogdanov moved on to the most challenging aspect of tonight's endeavor. He retrieved the handheld computer Korenev had provided on the Red Arrow and connected it to the guidance and control section of the bottom missile. The computer activated automatically and communicated with the missile, stopping at the critical point. Bogdanov entered the nuclear arming code Korenev had provided earlier in the day, then waited tensely as the computer transferred the code to the missile. A few seconds later, the digital display on the missile flashed *Warhead Armed* in red letters.

Bogdanov armed the other three warheads and looked up as Morozov, who had departed the bunker fifteen minutes earlier, returned with a forklift carrying four conventionally armed Kalibr missiles, whose serial numbers matched the new numbers Bogdanov had stenciled onto the four warheads. Bogdanov repeated the laser cleaning and painting process, stenciling the serial numbers from the nuclear-warhead-armed missiles onto the conventional ones while Morozov swapped the nose cones, then they exchanged the four missiles in the bunker.

Now sitting on the stowage rack were four conventionally armed Kalibr missiles, indistinguishable from their nuclear brethren. The situation would soon be the same in the conventional bunker, with Kalibr missiles armed with nuclear warheads blending in with their conventional counterparts.

Bogdanov checked his watch. They were on a tight timeline—they had until 6 a.m. to complete the swap of twenty Kalibr missiles.

14

MOSCOW, RUSSIA

In the conference room on the fifth floor of Blokhin National Medical Research Center, Aleksandr Plecas held his wife in his arms as she squeezed him tightly. Tears streamed down her cheeks, but unlike a few days ago in their hotel room, they were tears of joy. Dr. Vasiliev had just delivered the news—the expensive experimental drug for their daughter had been approved, and the odds it would cure Natasha's cancer were good.

Vasiliev and the other doctors filed quietly from the room, leaving Plecas alone with his wife. She looked up at him and asked the inevitable question. "How did you arrange this?"

"I have a friend, someone I served with on my first submarine, who is now an executive in the oil and gas industry. It was a long shot, but I tracked him down and explained the situation. He's well-off and agreed to help."

It was a lie, of course. Plecas couldn't admit who had agreed to fund Natasha's treatment, nor what was required in return.

Before Tatiana could ask additional questions about his friend, he added, "I must return to Gadzhiyevo tonight. We deploy in two days and we are scheduled for weapon onload tomorrow."

He reached into his overcoat and retrieved an envelope with Tatiana's name on it. Inside was a heartfelt letter to his wife, along with an explanation of what he had agreed to do in exchange for the money for Natasha's drugs. At the bottom of the letter, he instructed Tatiana to take it to Northern Fleet Command as evidence that he, and not the Russian government, was to blame for the attack, an admission that would hopefully deter the United States from retribution.

"Open this a week before our wedding anniversary."

The timing was odd, but the letter needed to be opened around the time his attack would occur. A week later would likely be too late.

When Tatiana gave him a curious look, Plecas explained, "There are arrangements you need to make, so that everything is perfect on our anniversary."

Tatiana smiled, and after placing the envelope in her purse, she cradled his face in her hands. "You are a good man," she said, and he could tell she regretted her harsh words a few days earlier. "You are a good father and a good husband."

Plecas kissed Tatiana and pulled her close. He held her in his arms, contemplating what he was about to do. If he was fortunate enough to survive and see his wife and daughter again, it would be from behind prison bars.

15
DAMASCUS, SYRIA

The conference room was in stark contrast to the public perception of war-torn Syria. Lonnie Mixell sat in a leather chair at a polished ebony table, facing floor-to-ceiling windows spanning an entire side of the room overlooking the Barada River. Rather than wearing the traditional white dishdasha, the Arab seated across from him, along with his executive assistant beside him, wore slacks and an open-collar dress shirt.

Since the civil war began, travel to the Syrian capital had become difficult. Few airlines offered flights into the country—with most opting instead for nearby Lebanon and Jordan, letting local carriers complete the transit. Fortunately, relations between Russia and Syria remained strong and direct flights from Russia were still offered, and Mixell had landed at Damascus International Airport a few hours ago. It was Russia's support of the Syrian government, and even more important, its supply of military personnel and equipment, that had led Mixell to Damascus.

Sitting across the table from Mixell was Issad Futtaim, the man who could furnish the desired item, and now that Zawahiri's money had been deposited into Mixell's account, the cost would not be an issue.

Mixell pulled a sheet of paper from his jacket pocket and slid it across the table. "This is what I require."

Futtaim reviewed the request for a moment, evidently determining the effort and cost required to obtain the item. Although there was no doubt that Futtaim wondered what it would be used for, he was in a business where those types of questions weren't asked.

He looked up from the paper. "It won't be easy to obtain this. You cannot just *lose* one of these from inventory. Many people will have to be persuaded to alter the books and assist in delivery. The cost will be *very* high. Twelve million, U.S."

"That's retail cost," Mixell replied. "You're not buying it. You're bribing whoever you need to. Above that, everything is pure profit."

"The cost of the bribes is usually commensurate with the cost of the item. Twelve million," Futtaim insisted, adding a tight smile.

Mixell considered the offer. He had budgeted fifteen million, after factoring in the cost of shipping. "That'll be fine. I need the equipment prepared for transport as soon as possible. How long will that take?"

"A few days. Where do you need it delivered?"

"United States. Anywhere along the East Coast is fine."

"Concealed shipping to the United States is difficult to guarantee. Additional bribes will be required to ensure the container is not opened for inspection. Two million, U.S."

Mixell nodded his concurrence. "I'll also need instructions."

"Of course. Instructions will be provided and should be easy to follow," Futtaim said, "as long as you can read Russian or Arabic." He broke into a wide grin.

"That'll be fine," Mixell replied.

The smile faded from Futtaim's face.

16
LANGLEY, VIRGINIA

Inside the darkened facility, Jake Harrison looked up from his computer display, taking a break to examine the large flat-panel displays lining the front wall. Inside the crowded space, several rows of analysts reviewed data on their monitors, the glow from their displays playing off their faces and faintly illuminating Styrofoam cups of cold coffee. They spoke quietly among themselves, occasionally looking up from their computers to examine the large screens.

He'd been at it since yesterday, reviewing Lonnie Mixell's file and the details of his assassination of the United Nations ambassador. After Harrison was issued weapons and a locker to store them, Pat Kendall had parked Harrison at a workstation in the analysis center. More specifically, Harrison was inside a transnational cell—the Office of Terrorism Analysis—which supported the National Counterterrorism Center in McLean, Virginia.

The CIA's file on Mixell was extensive and, Harrison had to admit, quite thorough. It was obvious that the CIA had access to Mixell's military record, along with his security clearance investigations and findings. Nothing out of the ordinary had been noted until Mixell, while still a Navy SEAL, had been accused of killing an unarmed prisoner in Afghanistan. The details were concise and accurate; Harrison had witnessed it firsthand, and after much deliberation, had reported the incident to their commanding officer.

Two items were missing from Mixell's record: one significant and one minor. The significant item was that the prisoner Mixell killed in Afghanistan hadn't been the first. It was the third that Harrison was aware of. The first time, Harrison had pulled his friend aside, asking him what the hell he'd been thinking. Mixell explained he'd been caught up in the heat of the moment—another SEAL had been killed in the engagement. What had been missing from the conversation, Harrison realized later, was that Mixell neither admitted that what he'd done was wrong nor pledged it would never happen again.

Three weeks later, Mixell killed a second prisoner. The man had seen it coming; Mixell reaching for his pistol as he approached, his eyes boring into him. The prisoner placed his hands in front of his face as if they could somehow ward off the impending bullet. Mixell shot through the man's palm, putting a bullet in his head. Afterward, Harrison pulled his best friend into an adjacent room and slammed him against the wall, hoping to knock some sense into him.

Harrison had been prepared for a fight—Mixell was the same size and just as strong, and had a reputation for being a hothead. But as Harrison pressed his friend's back against the wall, Mixell offered no resistance. During the one-way conversation, Mixell displayed no emotion; neither anger nor remorse. His eyes seemed vacant as he listened to Harrison's heated words.

After Harrison explained he would have no choice but to report future incidents, Mixell's response had been short.

I got it, buddy.

Looking back on the exchange, it was clear that Mixell believed no one would turn him in. SEALs were a tight-knit fraternity, men who had each other's back. While that was true, what was also clear to Harrison after the third time was that these weren't unfortunate incidents occurring in the heat of the moment—events Mixell would learn from and avoid in the future. It was a pattern, and he wasn't going to stop. It had been a difficult and agonizing decision, but after talking things over with the other SEALs in their unit, Harrison had turned Mixell in.

A burst of background noise in the analysis facility caught Harrison's attention. He looked up from his computer again. Analysts and supervisors were studying one of the displays; a grainy image of men and women exiting what looked like an airport gate. One man, taller than the rest and Caucasian, stood out from the mostly Middle Eastern passengers. The video froze on a frame with the man in the center. It was Mixell.

Kendall arrived a few minutes later, stopping by Harrison's workstation. "We got a hit," she said. "Mixell's been spotted in Damascus. Even better, the lead is only a day old. If Mixell's doing business in the city, he's likely still there. It looks like you're heading to Syria; Khalila is on her way here."

While they waited, Harrison's thoughts turned to the second item missing from Mixell's file. Before he'd been turned in, Mixell was supposedly engaged to a stripper—his soul mate, he called her, but he'd otherwise been close-lipped about the relationship. Harrison figured that if they could track down Mixell's former fiancée, perhaps she could shed light on his plans, or even where they could find him if he returned to the United States. He passed the information to Kendall as Khalila entered the facility and stopped beside them.

"Engaged to a stripper?" Kendall asked. "Anything else, as in *useful*? Like her name, what club she worked at, or even what city?"

Harrison shook his head. "That's all I got."

Kendall added a note to her smartphone. "I'll have someone connect with Mixell's prison cell mates. He spent eight years behind bars with nothing better to do than pine after his *soul mate,*" she said sarcastically. "I'll bet he poured his heart out to someone."

Khalila folded her arms across her chest and gave Kendall an expectant look. "Are you done with him?"

"He's all yours."

Khalila turned to Harrison. "Get your gear. We're leaving for Damascus."

17
ARLINGTON, VIRGINIA

Jake Harrison leaned back in his leather seat as the Dassault Falcon executive jet lifted off from Ronald Reagan Washington National Airport, banking eastward toward the Atlantic Ocean. Configured to transport a dozen passengers, it carried only Khalila and Harrison today, along with a CIA case officer named Asad Durrani, a naturalized citizen whose family had immigrated to America from Pakistan when Durrani was a child. This was the first time Harrison had met the man, but it was obvious that Khalila had worked with him before.

Durrani pulled three manila envelopes from his briefcase and handed one to Harrison. "This contains your alias identification documents."

Harrison examined the contents: a birth certificate, Social Security card, driver's license, passport, and credit cards issued under his alias.

"Dan Connolly?"

Durrani handed an empty envelope for Harrison to deposit his true identification and credit cards, which Durrani sealed and placed in his briefcase.

The second packet he handed to Harrison was labeled *Background,* which contained a thick printout of his fake personal history: hometown, friends, education, employment history, and residences. The third packet was labeled *Cover,* which contained information on his current employment in Bluestone Security, a CIA-owned company engaged in legitimate business dealings as well as government-funded weapon sales to approved organizations and countries. Harrison was the new assistant director of procurement, en route to Damascus in search of a supply of cheap and untraceable weapons from various foreign manufacturers—whatever suited Bluestone's customer's desires.

Regarding Khalila's cover, she explained that she was a translator contracted to Bluestone Security and other companies in need of a Middle Eastern or South/Central-Asian linguist. There were hundreds of languages spoken throughout the region, with twenty-four different ones in Syria alone.

When she mentioned Syria, Harrison's thoughts shifted to the pending mission.

"What's the plan?"

Khalila answered, "Word on the street in Damascus is that there's been an expensive weapon procurement. My bet is Mixell is involved, and we'll start there. I've set up a meeting with a weapons dealer who frequently sells to Westerners. He's probably not the right guy, since he typically deals with inexpensive firearms, but he may know who made the deal."

As Harrison prepared to study his alias and background material, he wondered how it was going to work—how receptive would a Syrian weapons dealer be to doing business with someone who was clearly Western and likely an American?

"I admit that I don't know much about spying, but I thought we're supposed to blend in, obtaining the information we need clandestinely. I stick out like a sore thumb—I'm a tall Caucasian—and you obviously work for the CIA, traipsing in and out of headquarters in Langley. I assume some of the Middle Eastern organizations you interface with have the ability to figure that out. How does all this work?"

"You being Caucasian is not always a liability," Khalila answered. "In fact, for our current assignment, it's an asset." When Harrison gave her a confused look, she explained. "You have to analyze things from the perspective of the people you're engaging. For example, if you're trying to strike a deal with a Bedouin tribal chief or perhaps an illegal weapons dealer, he's going to avoid meeting with someone who looks like him, a man who could be a rival out to kill him. He'll more readily meet with a stereotypical American—a tall, clean-cut Caucasian. Your appearance generates a measure of trust that otherwise wouldn't exist.

"Regarding my presence at Langley, being contracted to the CIA is part of my cover." Khalila glanced at Durrani before continuing. "If I were a typical woman, how do you think your average Middle Eastern male would treat me? We're talking about societies where women are considered property, where in some countries women aren't even allowed to drive, and where they need a man's permission to get married, travel abroad, apply for a passport, or even to open a bank account. How many high-level business meetings do you think I'd be invited to, and how much sensitive information do you think I'd be able to glean from my interactions?

"On the other hand, working for the CIA as a translator opens doors. I have valuable information—insight into who the CIA sources are, both prisoners and agents, and what information has been divulged. That makes me a valuable asset for numerous Middle Eastern organizations and governments. Of course, the information I'm allowed to provide is carefully selected by the Directorate of Analysis, allowing me to divulge enough information to prove my bona fides, but nothing that would significantly jeopardize American interests."

"So, you work for the CIA, but the organizations you interface with think you're working for them. Isn't that the classic definition of a double agent?"

Khalila shrugged her shoulders. "Call it what you will. But I don't think I cleanly fit any of the CIA officer or agent definitions."

Harrison recalled Pat Kendall's comment in the elevator; that the DDO didn't completely trust Khalila. He now understood why. Khalila was burning the candle at both ends, with the people on one side of the candle being wrong about her true allegiance. Still, this couldn't be the first time the CIA had to work their way through this kind of dilemma. He figured the Directorate of Operations, or perhaps Analysis, had ways of ferreting things out.

"Memorize everything in these packets before you land," Durrani instructed.

Khalila leaned back in her chair, kicked off her shoes, and propped her feet atop the seat in front of her, placing her long legs in clear view, her skirt inching up her thighs. She caught Harrison checking out her legs.

"Focus," she said, pointing to the packets of information. She interlaced her fingers across her waist and closed her eyes. "Let me know if you have any questions."

18
K-561 *KAZAN*

Captain First Rank Aleksandr Plecas stood in *Kazan*'s Forward Bridge cockpit in the sail, monitoring his submarine's outbound transit as it trailed behind the icebreaker *Taymyr*. Large fragments of coastal ice, broken apart by the icebreaker, drifted by as both ships plodded through the Murmansk Fjord. Although the Russian ports along the Kola Peninsula were considered "ice free" year-round due to the warm North Atlantic Current, the coastal areas often iced over during the frigid winter months. But the ice remained thin, easily broken.

A bone-chilling gust of Arctic wind swirled inside the Forward Bridge cockpit, mixing with the warm air rising up the Bridge trunk. The contrasting temperatures reminded Plecas of the conflict swirling inside him. It was good to be underway again. This was what he joined the Navy for—taking submarines to sea. What his crew would do at the end of their journey, however, was not how he envisioned his career would end.

After graduating twenty-eight years ago from Grechko Naval Academy in St. Petersburg, Plecas had been assigned to Russia's newest Project 971 submarine, dubbed by the West as an Akula II. He had alternated between attack and ballistic missile submarines during his career, and was Russia's most experienced commanding officer, having just completed a three-year tour in command of *Gepard,* the most advanced Project 971 nuclear attack submarine, sometimes referred to as an Akula III.

Now in command of *Kazan,* Plecas was taking the submarine on its first deployment. However, what he had in mind was quite different from the planned Mediterranean display-the-flag patrol of Russia's newest military hardware. His thoughts went to his submarine's armament. Yesterday's weapon loadout had gone smoothly and *Kazan* was now fully armed, its vertical launch tubes loaded with twenty Kalibr land-attack cruise missiles and sixteen Oniks anti-ship missiles, plus a full torpedo room. Although firing torpedoes wasn't part of his plan, their employment might be required.

Plecas brought his binoculars to his eyes, scanning the horizon. Aside from *Taymyr,* there were no ships in sight, but that didn't assuage his concern. The real threat to *Kazan* lurked beneath the ocean waves. The United States kept at least one fast attack submarine in the Barents Sea at all times, and *Kazan*'s loadouts would have been observed by American satellites. Plecas figured there was no higher priority than trailing Russia's newest guided missile submarine during its deployment.

The Navigating Officer's voice emanated from the speaker on the Bridge Communications Panel. "Captain, Navigating Officer. Ten kilometers to the dive point."

Plecas's eyes went to *Taymyr* and the thin layer of ice ahead. They would break through in thirty minutes, reaching water deep enough to submerge moments later. He slipped the microphone from the communications panel and acknowledged the report, then turned to his Watch Officer beside him.

"Transfer the watch below deck."

The Watch Officer passed the word over the shipwide announcing system. After a final glance at the surrounding ice- and snow-covered shores along the Murmansk Fjord, Plecas stepped from the Bridge cockpit and climbed down the ladder into the warmth of *Kazan*'s interior.

Thirty minutes later, the submarine's new Watch Officer, stationed in the submarine's Central Command Post in Compartment Two, reported *Kazan* was ready to submerge. All hatch and hull openings were sealed, and communication antennas lowered. Only the Search Periscope—the forward one of two periscopes—was raised, manned by the Junior Watch Officer, circling slowly with his face against the eyepiece.

"Report status," Plecas ordered his Watch Officer.

"We are on course zero-one-zero, ahead standard," Captain Lieutenant Ivan Urnovitz replied. "Hydroacoustic holds one contact, *Taymyr,* the only contact held visually. Electronic Surveillance reports no threat radars. Water depth is one hundred meters. We are ready to dive, Captain."

Plecas ordered, "Submerge to fifty meters, then turn to course zero-seven-zero."

19

USS *PITTSBURGH*

Just off the coast of Russia's Kola Peninsula, USS *Pittsburgh* cruised eastward at periscope depth. Lieutenant Bob Martin, on watch as Officer of the Deck, rotated the port periscope slowly, his right eye pressed against the eyepiece. As the scope optics swung to the south, Martin shifted the periscope to high power for a detailed scan of Kola Bay, the exit point for Russian warships stationed in ports along the shores of the Murmansk Fjord. He paused at the fjord entrance and pressed the doubler, increasing the periscope magnification to maximum.

Still nothing.

This morning's intelligence message reported that Russia's newest guided missile submarine, K-561 *Kazan,* would likely head to sea today. Satellites had monitored *Kazan*'s crew loading supplies and weapons, and the submarine's nuclear reactor had been brought on-line—all solid indicators that *Kazan* was preparing to deploy.

Where *Kazan* was headed was what COMSUBLANT wanted to know, and *Pittsburgh* had been tasked to find out: gain trail on *Kazan* as she emerged from Kola Bay and follow her until she exited the Barents Sea. There were a few options regarding *Kazan*'s destination, with the leading contenders being west toward the GIUK Gap—a naval choke point between Greenland and the United Kingdom, with Iceland in the middle—for an Atlantic Ocean or Mediterranean Sea deployment, or north under the ice for transfer to Russia's Pacific Fleet.

Anywhere was fine with Martin, as long as there was something to trail. There was nothing more boring than walking round and round on the periscope for hours on end, scouring the horizon for contacts. Trailing submarines was far more exciting, and Martin hoped to be the one to snag *Kazan*. He had only one week left. *Pittsburgh* was nearing the end of its Northern Run, and USS *Boise* was already en route from Norfolk to relieve *Pittsburgh* in the Barents Sea.

Martin's thoughts were interrupted by the Sonar Supervisor's report over the Conn speaker. "Conn, Sonar. Hold a new contact on the towed array, designated Sierra three-four, ambiguous bearings two-one-zero and zero-three-zero. Analyzing."

Pittsburgh's towed array was a valuable asset, detecting contacts at longer ranges than the submarine's other acoustic sensors. However, the array was an assembly of hydrophones connected in a straight line, which meant it could not determine which side the sound arrived from, resulting in two potential bearings to the contact—one on each side of the array.

Martin acknowledged Sonar's report and rotated the periscope to a bearing of zero-three-zero, shifting to high power and activating the doubler. There were no contacts. He swung to the south. As he examined Kola Bay, he spotted a small speck on the horizon. He called to the Electronic Surveillance Measures watch. "ESM, Conn. Report all radar contacts to the south."

"Conn, ESM. I hold no contacts to the south."

Martin selected the Captain's stateroom on the 27-MC control box, then with his eye still against the periscope, retrieved the microphone from its holder.

"Captain, Officer of the Deck."

The submarine's Commanding Officer replied. "Captain."

"Captain, Officer of the Deck. Hold a new surface contact exiting Kola Bay with no radar signature."

"Very well," he replied. "I'll be right there."

Commander John Buglione entered the Control Room and stepped onto the Conn—a one-foot-high platform surrounding the two periscopes—and stopped behind Lieutenant Martin.

"Let me take a look."

Martin swung the periscope to a bearing of two-one-zero, then stepped away. Buglione took his place, adjusting the periscope optics to his setting.

The contact had a boxy superstructure, which meant it was either a container ship or one of Russia's nuclear-powered icebreakers. Since it was transiting through coastal ice, it had to be an icebreaker, and it was most likely breaking the ice for *Kazan*.

Unfortunately, Buglione couldn't see behind the icebreaker; the ship was pointed almost directly at *Pittsburgh* and its large, boxy superstructure blocked Buglione's view. They needed to move off the icebreaker's track so they could see behind it. They were on a good course, however, traveling perpendicular to the icebreaker, and Buglione eventually spotted a trailing contact—a thin, black rectangle: the sail of an outbound submarine.

"Sonar, Conn," Buglione called out. "Hold an outbound submarine behind Sierra three-four. Do you hold anything on sonar?"

"Conn, Sonar," the Sonar Supervisor replied. "The only thing we hold is Sierra three-four. It's masking anything behind it."

Buglione studied the outbound submarine's sail. He and all of *Pittsburgh*'s officers had the sail shape of every Russian submarine class memorized, so there was no need to pull up images on the combat control consoles. After sorting through the possibilities, he settled on the best match, which was a Yasen class submarine—*Kazan* was entering the Barents Sea.

As Buglione examined *Kazan,* plumes of water spray jetted into the air from the submarine's bow and stern. It was submerging, venting the air in its Main Ballast Tanks.

Buglione turned to Martin. "Come down to one-five-zero feet and station the Fire Control Tracking Party."

20
USS *PITTSBURGH* • K-561 *KAZAN*

USS *PITTSBURGH*

By the time *Pittsburgh* settled out at 150 feet, Sonar and the Control Room were fully manned. The submarine's Navigator, Lieutenant Bob Cibelli, had relieved Lieutenant Martin as Officer of the Deck, and Martin now occupied a combat control console on the starboard side, one of three workstations configured to determine the contact's solution—its course, speed, and range.

Buglione announced, "This is the Captain. I have the Conn. Lieutenant Cibelli retains the Deck." Buglione would now issue all tactical orders, while Cibelli managed the ship's routine evolutions and monitored the navigation picture, ensuring *Pittsburgh* stayed clear of dangerous shoals.

Buglione stopped behind Martin. "Geo-plot," he ordered.

Martin pulled up the geographic plot on the top display of his dual-screen console. A map of the southern Barents Sea appeared, with *Pittsburgh* in the center of the display and Kola Peninsula to the south. *Pittsburgh* was well positioned at the mouth of Kola Bay, and Sonar should pick up any Russian submarine trying to slip by on either side.

A short while later, Sonar reported a contact. "Conn, Sonar. Gained a fifty Hertz tonal on the towed array, designated Sierra three-five, ambiguous bearings two-zero-zero and one-two-zero. Analyzing."

A discrete frequency with no broadband meant that whatever was generating the noise was designed to be quiet; the contact was most likely the Russian submarine. Sonar quickly sorted things out.

"Conn, Sonar. Sierra three-five is classified as a Russian nuclear-powered submarine, Yasen class."

Buglione announced to the Fire Control Tracking Party, "Attention in Control. Designate Sierra three-five as Master one. Track Master one."

There was no need to maneuver to resolve the bearing ambiguity, since the southern bearing matched the expected bearing of the submerging Russian submarine.

The Fire Control Tracking Party focused on determining Master one's course, speed, and range, using the geographic constraints to deduce valuable information. Buglione's Executive Officer, Lieutenant Commander Rick Schwartz, directed Martin to pull up the geographic plot again. After examining the distance to the shoals surrounding Kola Bay, Schwartz announced into his sound-powered phones, "Maximum range to Master one is six thousand yards."

They also had a pretty good guess for the contact's course and speed. They were within six thousand yards and weren't detecting broadband propulsion noise, so *Kazan* wasn't traveling very fast; no more than ten knots. The submarine's course was bracketed by Rybachy Peninsula to the west and Kildin Island to the east. Given the above constraints, the two fire control technicians and Lieutenant Martin quickly converged on similar solutions.

Lieutenant Commander Schwartz examined the three consoles, then tapped one of the fire control technicians on the shoulder. "Promote to master solution."

Buglione examined the display. Master one was on *Pittsburgh*'s starboard beam, on course zero-seven-zero at ten knots, five thousand yards away.

Buglione would normally fall in behind the Russian submarine, but *Kazan* was still traveling in shallow water, hugging the shoals around Kildin Island in an attempt to slip by any NATO submarines lurking nearby. *Pittsburgh*'s towed array was deployed, and if *Pittsburgh* fell in behind *Kazan,* the towed array would drag on the bottom, damaging it. Buglione couldn't retrieve the array, since it was the only sensor detecting *Kazan*.

Given the requirement to stay in deeper water, Buglione decided to put *Pittsburgh* in the best position possible. "Helm, ahead two-thirds. Right full rudder, steady course one-zero-zero."

Pittsburgh angled toward *Kazan*'s port stern quarter.

K-561 *KAZAN*

Aleksandr Plecas leaned over the navigation table in the Central Command Post, examining his submarine's position on the electronic chart. Kildin Island was sliding by to the south, and thus far they had detected no submerged contacts; only several merchants to the north. But they had not yet deployed their towed array, their most capable hydroacoustic sensor. As *Kazan* began its transit toward the Atlantic Ocean, the primary concern was verifying they weren't being trailed.

Kazan was a quiet submarine, almost undetectable by older Russian subs. If a NATO submarine had detected *Kazan,* it would have done so with its most capable sensor, the towed array. That meant—if *Kazan* was being trailed, the enemy submarine would be positioned off the port stern quarter, farther out to sea where the water was deep enough for its towed array.

Plecas examined the half-dozen bottom-contour lines circling Kildin Island, estimating how close to shore the NATO submarine could come. Assuming its array droop characteristics were similar to Russian arrays and that a trailing submarine was matching *Kazan*'s speed, at ten knots they could not deploy their array in water shallower than 150 meters.

He placed his finger on the 150-meter curve on *Kazan*'s port quarter, then looked up at the Electric Navigation Party Technician, wearing the enlisted rank of michman on his uniform collar. "Calculate a course to intercept a contact starting at this position, heading zero-seven-zero at ten knots."

Michman Erik Korzhev entered the parameters into the navigation chart and a line appeared. "Course three-two-five."

Plecas turned to his Watch Officer. "Captain Lieutenant Urnovitz. Come to course three-two-five and deploy the towed array once water depth is sufficient."

USS *PITTSBURGH*

Pittsburgh's Sonar Supervisor, standing behind the consoles in the Sonar Room, evaluated the changing parameter of their contact, then made his report.

"Possible contact zig, Master one, due to upshift in frequency."

The fire control technicians and Lieutenant Martin examined the time-frequency plot on their displays, watching the frequency of the tonal rise. Lieutenant Commander Schwartz stopped behind the consoles, and after the frequency steadied, he announced, "Confirm target zig. Contact has turned toward own-ship. Set anchor range at five thousand yards."

Buglione stopped beside his Executive Officer, examining the displays. *Kazan* had maneuvered to the north as expected. In the worst-case scenario, *Kazan* and *Pittsburgh* could be on an intercept trajectory. Although submarine collisions were uncommon, they did occur. In these very same waters, USS *Baton Rouge,* a Los Angeles class submarine, had collided with a Russian Sierra class submarine.

Buglione planned to ensure there was no repeat of that incident. He had to maneuver *Pittsburgh,* but needed to know *Kazan*'s course so he didn't make the situation worse.

"I need a solution fast."

Schwartz examined the combat control consoles, his eyes squinting as the three operators slowly converged on a common solution. A minute later, Schwartz informed the Captain, "I have a solution. Master one is on course three-two-five, speed ten."

Damn. The Russian submarine had turned onto an intercept course. They either knew they were being followed or had guessed where *Pittsburgh* was with incredible accuracy. Buglione had to get off *Kazan*'s track.

"Helm, left full rudder, steady course zero-four-five. Ahead standard." They would move out of *Kazan*'s way, let her pass, then fall in behind.

Shortly after *Pittsburgh* turned northeast, a report from Sonar came over the speakers.

"Sonar, Conn. Picking up mechanical transients from Master one."

Buglione waited while Sonar analyzed the sound. Mechanical transients could be almost anything, from innocuous events such as someone dropping a tool onto the deck to torpedo launch preparations.

Sonar followed up. "Conn, Sonar. Sounds like Master one is deploying a towed array."

Buglione listened to the report with concern. Range to *Kazan* had decreased to four thousand yards. The United States had scant data on the new Yasen class submarines and their tactical systems, and he had no idea at what range *Pittsburgh* would be detected.

K-561 *KAZAN*

Plecas checked the red digital clock at the front of the Command Post. They had deployed their towed array ten minutes ago, enough time for Hydroacoustic to check all sectors. Captain Lieutenant Urnovitz must have been watching the clock as well, because he slipped the microphone from its holster.

"Hydroacoustic, Command Post. Report all contacts."

The Hydroacoustic Party Leader replied, "Hydroacoustic holds three contacts. All three contacts are merchants to the north."

Plecas joined his First Officer, Captain Third Rank Erik Fedorov, in front of the hydroacoustic display, searching for patterns within the random specks. Despite Hydroacoustic's report, Plecas was not yet convinced they weren't being trailed. Narrowband detections were not instantaneous like broadband; the algorithms needed time. As the two men examined the display, a narrow vertical bar rose from the bottom of the display. The Hydroacoustic Party Leader's report arrived a moment later.

"Command Post, Hydroacoustic. Hold a new contact on the towed array, a sixty-point-two Hertz tonal, designated Hydroacoustic five, ambiguous bearings zero-one-five and two-six-zero. Sixty-point-two Hertz frequency correlates to American fast attack submarine."

Plecas's fear was confirmed—they were being trailed.

"Man Combat Stations silently."

The two Command Post Messengers sped through the submarine, and three minutes later, *Kazan*'s Central Command Post was fully manned.

Plecas announced, "This is the Captain. I have the Conn and Captain Lieutenant Urnovitz retains the Watch. The target of interest is Hydroacoustic five, classified American fast attack submarine. Track Hydroacoustic five."

Fedorov stopped behind the two fire controlmen, monitoring their progress as they converged on the same solution. The American submarine had crossed in front of them and was now traveling down *Kazan*'s starboard side in the opposite direction. The Americans were trying to circle around and fall in behind *Kazan* again.

Plecas needed to break trail and considered his options. Under normal circumstances, he'd deploy a mobile decoy and engage the electric drive—a quiet propulsion system capable of propelling the submarine at up to ten knots—then turn to a new course, slipping away while the Americans trailed the decoy. However, *Kazan* hadn't been operational for long, and a variant of the mobile decoy, matching the submarine's sound signature, hadn't been developed yet.

Instead, *Kazan* carried stationary countermeasures they could eject—decoys and acoustic jammers designed to interfere with submarine and torpedo sonars—but the odds of success were lower and he didn't want to alert the Americans that he was onto them. There was another plan with better odds; one that was more creative and would eliminate the possibility the American submarine would regain them if *Kazan* slipped away.

"Steersman, right ten degrees rudder, steady course north."

Fedorov approached. "North?" he asked, realizing their navigation plan took them west toward the Atlantic Ocean.

"For now," Plecas answered.

"I do not understand," Fedorov said. "We should attempt to break trail, deploying countermeasures and shifting to the electric drive."

"Patience, First Officer. Now is not the right time. Let us see what the American captain does when we enter the Marginal Ice Zone, and then I will decide."

USS *PITTSBURGH*

Buglione studied the geographic plot, his concern that *Pittsburgh* would be counter-detected by the Russian crew beginning to ease. *Kazan* remained steady on course and speed, proceeding northwest at ten knots, while *Pittsburgh* worked its way around the Russian submarine. In a few minutes, they would be behind her in an optimum trailing position.

When *Pittsburgh* intersected *Kazan*'s trail, Buglione ordered, "Helm, right full rudder, steady course three-two-five. Ahead two-thirds."

Pittsburgh turned right and slowed, steadying up five thousand yards behind the Russian submarine, matching its course and speed. Buglione was pleased with his crew's performance, successfully skirting around *Kazan*.

Lieutenant Commander Schwartz called out, "Possible contact zig, Master one, due to upshift in frequency."

Schwartz stood behind the combat control consoles, his eyes shifting between the displays. "Zig confirmed," Schwartz announced. "Set anchor range at five thousand yards. Master one has turned north and remains at ten knots."

Buglione examined the geographic display again. In a few minutes, *Pittsburgh* would also turn north, staying in *Kazan*'s baffles.

Schwartz turned toward Buglione. "If *Kazan* continues north, she'll enter the Marginal Ice Zone."

Buglione nodded. "Where *Kazan* goes, we go."

21
DAMASCUS, SYRIA

A purple-orange dawn was breaking across the horizon as a Dassault Falcon approached the eastern shore of the Mediterranean Sea, nearing the end of its twelve-hour flight. As daylight crept westward, the jet began its descent toward Damascus International Airport. Jake Harrison looked out his window, examining the historic metropolis. Wide boulevards radiated out from the Old City—an oblong region defined by ancient walls, of which sizable stretches still stood—within which lay most of the city's Hellenistic and Roman architecture. Descending from the Anti-Lebanon Mountains, the Barada River divided into seven branches upon reaching Damascus, irrigating a large and fertile oasis called the al-Ghutah before its waters vanished into the desert.

The jet coasted to a halt not far from a man leaning against a black sedan. Harrison, Khalila, and Durrani descended the steps to the tarmac where they met Nizar Mussan, a CIA officer serving as an executive assistant for Bluestone Security. The introductions were brief, and after placing their luggage in the trunk and joining Mussan in the car, they pulled away from the Dassault Falcon as its twin engines spun down to a stop.

Damascus was only a few miles away, and shortly after entering the city, Mussan stopped by a side street. Durrani pulled a thick envelope of money from his briefcase and handed it to Khalila, then informed her and Harrison that he'd be only a phone call away to provide any assistance they needed. He stepped from the vehicle and disappeared into an alley as Mussan pulled back into traffic.

Mussan stopped a short while later in front of Beit Al Mamlouka, a small boutique hotel on Qemarieh Street, where he unloaded Harrison's and Khalila's luggage and handed a garment bag to Harrison. Upon departing Langley a half-day ago, Harrison had learned that Khalila was already packed, apparently prepared for short-notice departures. On the way to the airport, they had stopped by Harrison's hotel for clothes.

An examination of his wardrobe had elicited a sour look from Khalila, although he wasn't sure what was wrong with his jeans and polo shirts, plus he had a pair of khaki slacks and several dress shirts to choose from. She took a picture of him as he stood facing her, and after learning his height and shoe size, sent the photo and a short message on her cell phone. When Harrison inquired what the photo and information were for, her response was a curt—*You need appropriate clothes.* Apparently the garment bag contained the items Khalila had ordered.

Harrison and Khalila entered the hotel lobby while Mussan waited in the car, since their meeting with the Syrian weapons dealer was in less than an hour. They were greeted at the lobby counter by an elderly Arab who appeared to be meeting Khalila and Harrison for the first time, although Harrison noticed a flicker of recognition in the man's eyes when he addressed Khalila.

While checking in, Harrison learned that Beit Al Mamlouka had only eight rooms, five of them surrounding a courtyard containing a fountain and citrus trees. They were given the keys to a room on the second floor, which contained a terrace overlooking the courtyard.

"Welcome to Damascus, Mr. Connolly and Ms. Dufour," he said. "I hope you enjoy your stay at Beit Al Mamlouka."

It took Harrison a second for his new name to register.

It wasn't until they entered their room and Khalila tossed her luggage onto the single, queen-sized bed that Harrison realized they had been booked into the same room.

"We don't have separate rooms?" he asked.

"We stay together for now. No one will care. If we have to stay overnight, you can sleep in the bed with me, but don't get any ideas."

"Fair enough."

Khalila approached the window and pulled the brocade curtain back slightly, examining the courtyard and adjacent terraces. Apparently satisfied with what she observed, she unpacked her luggage, then shed her business suit and blouse, stripping down to her bra and panties. As Harrison wondered what she was doing, she pulled two knives from her suitcase, each set within a spring-loaded device, and strapped one to each forearm.

"Nonmetallic," she said, noticing his stare. "They won't set off any metal detectors."

Up to this point, it hadn't occurred to Harrison to inquire about Khalila's training. It was obvious she'd been to the Farm—the CIA's training complex in Virginia—receiving at least some level of specialized training. As he wondered how proficient she was in close combat, she donned a pair of slacks instead of a skirt, plus a short-sleeved blouse instead of the long-sleeved one she had removed, then put her black suit jacket on again. After assessing herself in a full-length mirror, she rotated her right wrist outward and flexed her hand sideways, and a knife popped down into her palm.

She turned to Harrison. "Don't bring a weapon. You're a Bluestone executive for now."

Khalila then wrapped a black scarf around her head and neck, adding a matching niqab that left only her eyes exposed. Harrison, meanwhile, unpacked the garment bag Mussan had given him. It contained two suits, several dress shirts, ties, a belt, socks, and a pair of black dress shoes.

"You can ditch the tie for today's meeting," Khalila said. "A suit and open-collared shirt will work fine."

Harrison selected a shirt and suit, which fit amazingly well, and was soon ready to depart.

"During the meeting," Khalila said, "you don't have to do anything except respond to my questions. You're a prop, giving me the cover I need to inquire about Mixell and the large weapon procurement. I'll talk with you occasionally in English, and we'll need to make it seem like you're making decisions and giving me direction, in case anyone at the meeting understands English. Just play it by ear. Any questions?"

"Not at the moment."

Khalila checked her watch, then looked at Harrison. "Time to leave." She slid the envelope of money Durrani had given her into a leather satchel and handed it to Harrison.

Upon reaching Mussan, still waiting by the curb near the hotel,

Khalila provided the address for the meeting. Mussan pulled into traffic, headed for the Old City.

Mussan pulled over and parked not far from the ruins of the Temple of Jupiter, built by the Romans in the first century B.C., near the entrance to al-Hamidiyah Souq, a fifty-foot-wide marketplace over one-third of a mile long. Harrison joined Khalila as they strolled past countless clothes emporiums, craft and jewelry shops, grocery stores, food stalls, and cafés. Contrary to Harrison's earlier concerns, he didn't stand out, since there were a significant number of European shoppers wearing Western apparel. As they moved down the souq, it didn't appear that anyone was paying particular attention to their presence.

After passing one of the larger jewelry shops, Khalila veered to the side, entering a dark alley running perpendicular to the souq. As their footsteps echoed off stone walls, Harrison felt naked without a weapon. Khalila stopped beside an old wooden door and knocked.

"Who is it?" a muffled voice asked.

"Khalila. I'm here to see Hasan."

The door cracked open and a man wearing a white dishdasha studied Khalila and Harrison before opening the door wider. He beckoned them into a small foyer.

"He is waiting," he said, pointing to a dark, narrow hallway.

Khalila led the way and they entered another antechamber, this one occupied by two men armed with PP-19 Bizon submachine guns. A third man, wielding a handheld metal detector, wanded Khalila and Harrison, searching for weapons. Satisfied that neither stranger was armed, he pointed to a nearby doorway.

The two armed men followed Harrison and Khalila into the adjacent room, a well-appointed study with built-in bookcases, an antique desk, and a rectangular table with six chairs set atop a plush Persian carpet. A man, whom Harrison assumed was Hasan, rose from his desk. He made no attempt to greet Khalila as he extended his right hand to Harrison.

Harrison kept his handshake soft instead of firm, as was customary in the Middle East, as Hasan spoke in Arabic, which Khalila interpreted.

"Hasan wants to know if you had a pleasant trip to Syria, and whether you've had an opportunity to enjoy any of the city's pleasures."

Harrison replied and Khalila translated, then Hasan motioned toward two chairs while he sat opposite them. The two armed men took up positions at opposite ends of the table.

The conversation turned to business, with Khalila beginning the dialogue. An unpleasant look quickly formed on Hasan's face and his voice took on an agitated tone. Khalila turned to Harrison.

"He's not happy you're here looking for information instead of weapons."

"What have you told him?"

"That you're aware of a large procurement, most likely by a rival, and you'd like to know what was procured and by whom." Her eyes shifted to the satchel. "Get the cash."

Harrison retrieved the thick envelope and placed it on the table, pushing it toward Hasan.

Hasan pushed it back toward Harrison.

Khalila interjected, talking with Hasan in a conciliatory, persuasive tone. After Hasan shook his head several times, the conversation became heated, with Hasan raising his voice and Khalila's tone becoming sharp. She turned to Harrison.

"He doesn't know what was purchased or who procured it, but he knows who made the deal. That's the sticking point. He doesn't want to disclose the name. There's a code between weapons dealers in Syria—transactions remain private."

"Where do we go from here?" Harrison asked.

"We pry the information from him."

Khalila dropped her right hand below the table. She rotated her forearm and Harrison noticed a ripple of movement down the sleeve of her business suit. He couldn't see her hand, but was certain it now held a knife.

Harrison didn't know what Khalila had planned, but he immediately shifted into tactical mode, assessing the three men in the room. Hasan appeared unarmed, while the two guards each held a machine gun. The one on Harrison's side of the table was two steps away, and he was confident the man could be neutralized. The armed guard on the other side of the table was problematic, since Harrison would need to wrest the weapon from the guard beside him and bring it to bear on the other guard before he reacted. The probability in succeeding in that maneuver, however, was low.

His thoughts turned to Khalila, who had reengaged Hasan in the heated conversation, wondering what her next move was. She couldn't be stupid enough to attack Hasan with two armed men nearby. Plus, what would that achieve?

Khalila spoke to Harrison, her voice turning cold and hard. "Push the envelope back to him."

Unsure whether Hasan or the two guards understood English, Harrison asked a subtle question, attempting to determine her plan. "What if he doesn't accept it?"

"Just give him the money," she said.

Harrison hesitated, and Khalila added, "Trust me."

He pushed the envelope to Hasan.

Hasan spat a retort to Khalila as he reached for the envelope, preparing to shove it back toward Harrison.

Khalila whipped the knife out from under the table, jamming the point into the table between Hasan's middle and ring finger.

The two guards immediately raised their weapons, pointing them at Khalila, while Hasan sat frozen with his face full of rage, the knife still embedded between his fingers with Khalila's hand on its hilt.

Khalila reached up with her other hand, pulling down the veil from her face so she could talk more clearly. She spoke at a measured pace, her tone stern. Hasan's eyes widened and he leaned back in his chair, his eyes fixed on Khalila. The man's anger faded, then he gestured with his other hand, directing the guards to lower their weapons. Khalila extracted the knife from the table and pushed the envelope closer to Hasan. This time, he took it, then perused its contents.

He looked up and began speaking, with Khalila nodding and occasionally asking questions. After a while, Hasan fell silent, his eyes resting on Khalila as she translated for Harrison.

"He says someone made a large purchase from the major weapons dealer in the country, a man named Issad Futtaim. Hasan claims he doesn't know what was procured, but the cost was extremely high based on the size of the bribes. However, he does know that what was procured was Russian made."

"Is there anything else we need to ask him?"

Khalila shook her head. "We're done here."

"Thank Hasan for his assistance."

Khalila relayed his words as Harrison stood and extended his hand.

Hasan exchanged greetings, although he wore an air of defeat, and the man who initially greeted Harrison and Khalila escorted them back to the front door.

As they stepped into the center of the souq, heading toward the exit, Harrison asked, "Where do we go from here?"

"I should be able to arrange a meeting with Futtaim. I know his executive assistant, although we're not on the best of terms. We'll see how it goes."

"Not on the best of terms?"

"There are a few things we don't see eye to eye on."

Upon exiting the souq, they spotted Mussan, parked nearby. After they slipped into the car, Khalila called their case officer, Durrani, relaying what they had learned.

"I need more money," she told him as Mussan pulled into traffic. "As much as you can get authorized, but try for two million. Take it all the way to the deputy director if you have to. The arms dealer we'll be meeting with next will be difficult to bribe. Also, with the amount of money we're talking about, I'll need the funds placed in an account so I can do an electronic transfer."

After her call with Durrani ended, Khalila made another one. Harrison listened to Khalila's half of the conversation, but didn't understand much since she spoke in Arabic, although he noticed that Khalila spoke in concise sentences, her tone terse.

Khalila hung up, then turned to Harrison. "We meet with Futtaim tomorrow afternoon."

She leaned back into her seat, lost in her thoughts for a while, then said, "Our meeting with Hasan did not go well."

"We got the information we needed," Harrison replied. "I'd say it was a job well done, aside from almost getting us killed."

Khalila frowned. "I need to be more discreet."

Harrison agreed. Her tack with Hasan was bold and it worked, but jamming the knife between his fingers could have been disastrous if she'd hit flesh instead.

"What did you say to Hasan after you put the knife in the table?"

"I pointed out his place in the food chain."

Harrison contemplated Khalila's response, plus Hasan's sudden shift in his demeanor when Khalila pulled her niqab down. Reflecting on the encounter, he realized he had misinterpreted Khalila's actions. She hadn't lowered her niqab so she could speak clearly—she had done so to reveal who she was. It seemed that Khalila wasn't just an ordinary woman, as she had claimed on the flight to Damascus. She had some sort of status in the Arab world.

"And where do you reside on that food chain?" Harrison asked.

Khalila gave him a blank stare. She realized she had slipped up, revealing information about herself that she preferred to keep hidden.

Harrison decided to ask a simpler question, harboring only a glimmer of hope she would answer it. "You revealed to Hasan that you are . . . ?"

When Khalila didn't answer, Harrison modified his query, hoping to chip away at the mystery. "I assume Khalila is an alias. What's your real first name?"

Khalila turned away, staring out the car window as they traveled along the congested streets.

22
JDEIDAT YABOUS, SYRIA

The sun was climbing into a clear blue sky as Lonnie Mixell drove northwest on Highway 30M, tapping a thumb on the steering wheel as he traveled along the dusty, desolate road. He was in a good mood; everything was proceeding according to plan, and he would soon be on a flight departing from Beirut-Rafic Hariri International Airport to begin the next phase of his plot.

He was approaching the Masnaa Syria-Lebanon border crossing when his cell phone rang. After verifying the call was the one he was expecting, he answered.

"Everything is arranged," Issad Futtaim said. "Your item has been procured and is being prepared for shipment. The shipping manifest and instructions for pickup at the destination will be emailed to your account." Mixell had a few questions, which Futtaim answered, then the Arab ended the conversation with, "It has been a pleasure doing business with you. Please keep me in mind for future procurements."

The call concluded as Mixell approached the first of two border checkpoints, this one at Jdeidat Yabous, Syria, which marked the beginning of a five-mile trek through neutral territory between the two countries.

Mixell's cell phone vibrated. It was a unique text-tone vibration, set to one person. Mixell picked up the phone and read the text.

The CIA is gaining ground on you. Your friend Harrison now works for them and is in Damascus. He's meeting with Futtaim this afternoon.

Mixell replied, *What time?*

3 p.m. I recommend you tie up loose ends before then.

Mixell slammed a hand against his steering wheel. Harrison was going to muck things up. After contemplating his options, Mixell slowed and turned around, heading back to Damascus. He placed a call.

When the man answered, Mixell said, "I need assistance."

After explaining his needs and verifying they could be met, the two men struck a deal, which included a dozen armed men. They wouldn't be as well trained as Harrison, but there would be a lot of them.

Additionally, Mixell wasn't about to let the outcome rest in someone else's hands. He asked the man to hold as he pulled up a map on his cell phone, then zoomed in to Futtaim's building. After assessing the nearby terrain, a plan formed.

"I need some equipment this afternoon," Mixell said, then detailed his requirements.

"That won't be a problem," the man replied.

23

DAMASCUS, SYRIA

Seated beside an open window in his hotel room on the eighth floor, Mixell examined the weapon on the table before him: a Steyr SSG 69 rifle with a ten-round box magazine, propped up by an integrated folding bipod. He placed an eye against the attached Kahles ZF 95 Riflescope, peering through the center crack of the room's drawn curtains, studying the two men in Issad Futtaim's office across the street, visible through one of the windows.

Although the Steyr SSG was a highly accurate weapon, Mixell had picked up the rifle only an hour ago and hadn't had time to acquire a zero. The dealer had assured him the rifle was sighted in, but that didn't mean a thing; zeros were different for each shooter. Still, for today's distance, the Steyr was more than up to the task. However, in case he failed to obtain a clear shot or somehow missed, a dozen armed men were only a block away, awaiting his signal.

Satisfied his weapon and mercenaries were ready, Mixell shifted his attention to the laptop computer beside him, connected wirelessly to a satellite, and entered his password. Although the software routine he was about to execute had been prepared weeks ago, he was implementing it earlier than planned; the CIA had tracked him to Futtaim much quicker than he had expected. He entered the security code, then halted the routine one keyboard click away from executing.

Mixell peered through the window, studying the street below as he waited for Harrison's arrival.

It was quiet in the backseat of the sedan as it navigated the busy streets. A few blocks from Futtaim's building, Harrison paused from making a mental map of the route Mussan was taking, to examine Khalila beside him. She was dressed similar to the day before, except she wore no niqab this time, just a hijab wrapped around her hair and neck, leaving her face exposed. She had explained that there was no need for concealment; Akram Aboud, Futtaim's executive assistant, as well as Futtaim himself, knew who she was.

Khalila seemed tense, and Harrison couldn't shake the uneasy feeling she was holding something back. Before leaving the hotel, she had tested both knives concealed in her jacket sleeves several times, verifying they were easily and reliably retrieved. She recommended he carry a firearm, but that he leave it in the car, since he would be disarmed upon entering the building.

Their driver, Nizar Mussan, also seemed nervous, although it could've been Harrison's imagination. While looking in the rearview mirror, Mussan's eyes shifted occasionally to examine his two passengers, with keen interest displayed when their case manager, Asad Durrani, called with an update. Earlier in the day, the two-million-dollar bribe had been approved, and Khalila reviewed the account information on her phone.

As they approached their destination, Mussan slowed and pulled over to the curb, stopping a short distance from the entrance to Futtaim's building.

Harrison was easy to spot, standing a head taller than most, as he and a woman stepped from a sedan. Mixell tucked the butt of the rifle against his right shoulder and peered through the scope, centering the crosshairs on Harrison's head as he strolled up the sidewalk toward the building entrance. Mixell released the air from his lungs and was about to squeeze the trigger when a bus pulled in front of Harrison, grinding to a halt in the congested street.

Mixell cursed as he looked up, then pulled the curtains back slightly, trying to regain Harrison when he stepped out from behind the vehicle.

But the bus moved forward, staying between Mixell and Harrison as traffic snaked along, clearing the entrance to Futtaim's building as Harrison disappeared into the lobby.

There had been no guarantee Mixell would be able to take Harrison out on the crowded sidewalk, so he had selected a hotel room across from the building, one offering a clear view of a good portion of Futtaim's office.

After entering the lobby, Harrison and Khalila passed through a metal detector where they were screened by one of four uniformed guards. As Khalila recommended, Harrison had left his firearm in the car, and Khalila's knives went undetected as they cleared security.

They rode the elevator to the eighth floor and entered a reception area adjacent to Futtaim's office, where they were greeted by a man wearing a gray suit and open-collared white shirt, leaning against a desk. Harrison scanned the surroundings, realizing the office's normal protocols had been altered. On the receptionist's desk were a few photos of a woman and her family, none of which contained the man beside the desk. The receptionist had been sent home early.

The man eyed Khalila before introducing himself to Harrison in English.

"I am Akram Aboud, Mr. Futtaim's executive assistant."

Harrison assessed Aboud as they shook hands, noticing a slight bulge under the left side of his suit jacket—a pistol in a shoulder holster—as Aboud inquired about the purpose of the meeting.

Harrison hadn't understood what Khalila said to Aboud in the car yesterday when she arranged the meeting, so he deferred to Khalila, who answered, "We'll discuss the details once we meet with Futtaim."

Aboud whipped his head toward Khalila and his voice dropped a notch. "I'm talking to Mr. Connolly, not you." Khalila shot him a cold look as he returned his attention to Harrison. "Assuming that's your real name, of course." Aboud offered a tight smile.

Harrison smiled back. "As Khalila mentioned, we'll discuss the details when we meet with Futtaim."

Aboud stared at Harrison, who found the Arab's neutral expression unreadable. Then Aboud broke into a wide grin and spread his hands apart.

"Of course. We will meet with Issad. He is awaiting your arrival."

Mixell dropped his eye to the scope again as Aboud entered Futtaim's office, followed by Harrison and the Arab woman. They had entered quickly, with Harrison stopping behind the brick facade between two windows, leaving Mixell with a clear view only of the woman and Aboud, plus Futtaim, who rose from his desk. Considering the circumstances—all three targets in the same location—Mixell reassessed his priorities.

Although nothing would make him happier than putting a bullet in Harrison's head, Mixell's primary objectives were Futtaim and his executive assistant, who knew what he had procured. Tying up loose ends meant eliminating the risk that either man would divulge his secret or that the information could be harvested from Futtaim's computer files. Once Mixell pulled the trigger and the first man went down, the others would have time to react.

As Futtaim approached his two guests, Mixell analyzed the possible permutations in the order of attack.

"Khalila!" Futtaim said as he strode across his office, smiling. "It is a pleasure to finally meet you. Akram has told me much about you."

"All lies, I'm sure," Khalila said as she glanced at Aboud, who offered a cold stare.

A few pleasantries were exchanged as Futtaim shook Harrison's hand, then Futtaim asked, "How can I help you?" He looked first at Harrison, then at Khalila.

Khalila answered, "We understand a customer recently made an expensive weapon purchase. We're also interested in a purchase. We'd like to know who made the procurement and what he bought."

Futtaim hesitated before replying. "That is a delicate subject," he said. "It is house policy to not reveal our customers."

"We're prepared to pay handsomely for this one-time transgression. Two million U.S. dollars."

"It is as I expected," Aboud interrupted. "There is no reason to continue this meeting."

He then shifted to Arabic, addressing Futtaim. Khalila interjected frequently, her voice rising and her gestures becoming animated as she argued with Aboud. For Futtaim's part, he seemed to be on the receiving end of Aboud's and Khalila's arguments as each attempted to sway him to their side.

"You are a disgrace!" Aboud said to Khalila in English. He turned to Harrison. "Has she told you who she is? That she's—"

There was a blur of movement from Khalila as a knife flew from her hand, piercing Aboud's neck.

He fell to his knees, then extracted the knife, but it only made matters worse. Blood pulsed from the wound with every heartbeat. He clamped his hands around his throat, attempting to stem the flow, but blood oozed between his fingers. Futtaim watched in shock as the color drained from Aboud's face, before he tilted forward and landed on the floor.

"He talks too much," Khalila said as she approached Aboud and retrieved her knife, wiping the blood from the blade on Aboud's suit.

She turned to Futtaim, the knife still in one hand. "The information," she said. "In return, we'll pay you two million. You get the weapon sale, we get the information, you're two million richer, and no one will know."

Futtaim pondered Khalila's proposal, then retreated toward a laptop on his desk. As he settled into his chair, Harrison noticed the man's thumb pressing a red button on the intercom panel on his desk. It took Harrison a split second to conclude Futtaim had signaled the security guards in the lobby.

Before either Harrison or Khalila could react, a red cloud jetted from the side of Futtaim's head, and he slumped onto his desk as blood poured from a hole in his temple.

Seconds earlier, Mixell had decided he could wait no longer, even though he still didn't have a shot on Harrison. Futtaim looked like he was about to reveal his purchase. He had lined up the crosshairs and squeezed the trigger gently, putting a round through Futtaim's head.

Harrison was still out of view, but the woman remained in sight. He shifted the crosshairs toward her, squeezing off another round as Harrison bolted into view, slamming into the woman and knocking her to the floor.

Harrison and the woman were still on the floor or staying low, leaving no targets in view. Mixell moved away from the window to avoid counterfire, then dialed the stored number on his cell phone.

"Proceed," he ordered.

He hung up, then turned his attention to the laptop on the table and pressed *Enter* on the keyboard. He waited a few seconds to ensure the program began executing, then slipped the computer into his backpack and left the room.

Harrison had known instantly the shot had come through the window, his assessment confirmed by shattered glass falling to the floor. Khalila, on the other hand, had turned toward the sound of the breaking glass. Harrison dove for her, knocking her to the ground as a second shot pierced Futtaim's office, narrowly missing her before embedding in the far wall.

Harrison scrambled across the floor toward Aboud and searched the dead Arab, finding a Glock 17 in a shoulder holster. He checked the magazine—fully loaded with seventeen rounds.

Two uniformed guards surged into the room and quickly came to the incorrect conclusion: Futtaim—slumped over his desk with a hole in his head; Aboud—sprawled on the floor in a pool of blood; and Harrison—holding Aboud's Glock.

Both guards swiveled toward Harrison, bringing their pistols to bear, but Harrison was faster. He put two bullets into each man's chest, followed by a third round to each guard's head, dropping them to the floor.

Harrison positioned himself against the wall and peered through the broken window, pulling back after a quick glance. There was an open window across the street but no sign of the shooter. However, on the street below, a dozen armed men swarmed toward the building's entrance. They were dressed in ordinary clothes and not uniforms, and Harrison concluded they weren't friendlies.

He relayed the information to Khalila, who had taken cover behind the side of Futtaim's desk, and she called Durrani for backup. Harrison had no idea what kind of paramilitary forces the CIA had in Damascus or how long before they'd arrive, but was certain it would be too late. The armed men were already entering the building.

Still using Futtaim's desk as cover, Khalila reached up and pulled his computer onto her lap. She dragged Futtaim's corpse from his chair onto the floor, then placed his index finger on the laptop's fingerprint scanner.

"We don't have time for this!" Harrison shouted.

"We're not leaving without the information!"

"Then we're going to leave dead!"

This spy crap was complicating things. The tactical situation was clear in Harrison's mind. They were about to be engaged by a dozen men and had to exit Futtaim's office before the escape routes were sealed. They wouldn't be able to fight their way out.

Khalila ignored him, and after gaining access to Futtaim's computer, launched an internet browser to access a CIA website. She didn't have a flash drive with her, so she tried to upload the contents of Futtaim's computer to a CIA database. But when she accessed the hard drive to tag the desired folders, she watched in shock as the folders rapidly vanished. Someone was erasing the files.

"No, no, no!"

She disconnected the computer from the internet, hoping to sever the connection with whatever program was deleting the files, but the folders kept disappearing. She tried to shut down the laptop, but it disregarded the command. A virus must have been inserted into Futtaim's computer, and there didn't seem to be a way to stop it. She examined the back of the laptop, hoping to remove its battery pack, but it was an integrated unit. She flipped the laptop around as the last of the files were erased.

Khalila shoved the computer aside and searched Futtaim's desk drawers, keeping her head below the top of the desk.

"Khalila! We have to leave!"

"Just a minute!"

It was probably already too late. The approaching men would have the elevators and stairways sealed off, and the only way out would be up, assuming he and Khalila could access the stairways before they were trapped in Futtaim's office. However, that escape route led to a dead end, out in the open atop the roof, easy targets for nearby snipers on taller buildings.

After finding nothing noteworthy, Khalila slammed the last drawer shut. Meanwhile, Harrison focused on the more critical issue. They were trapped.

Through a side door in Futtaim's office, he spotted a conference room with glass panels forming one side of the room, overlooking the Barada River. Harrison grabbed one of the dead guard's pistols and tossed it to Khalila, who took a position beside the office entrance as he entered the conference room. He looked out the glass panels, estimating the distance to the river. There was a side street below, which they'd have to clear to land in the water. The question was—could they do it?

The sound of Khalila firing several rounds made the decision easy. They were penned in. He shoved the conference table aside, creating a clear path to the window, then shouted to Khalila.

"Into the conference room! We're going to jump into the river!"

Harrison backed up against the far wall as Khalila squeezed off a few more rounds, then he put several bullets through one of the glass panels, shattering it. He looked through the doorway into Futtaim's office as Khalila ran toward him.

He figured he would have to coax her into making the treacherous jump, but she didn't ease up as she entered the conference room, headed for the opening. She hit the edge at a full sprint and leaped into the air, disappearing as she fell.

At least she follows directions well, Harrison thought.

He followed Khalila, sprinting across the room before leaping from the building.

As he fell, he watched Khalila plunge into the water below, joining her a few seconds later. He remained underwater, swimming back toward the stone embankment as bullets zinged into the murkiness around him, then angled toward a dark opening. He surfaced as he entered a narrow culvert, which provided a drainage path for rainwater from the streets above. He signaled to Khalila, who had surfaced against the embankment not far away, and she joined him in the recess.

"You okay?" he asked, checking her for wounds.

"Never better," she replied, adding a smile.

As she wiped the water from her face and twisted her hair into a knot behind her head, Harrison realized this was the first time he'd seen Khalila smile.

The smile faded quickly, however. They had failed. It was obvious Mixell had made the procurement, but they had no idea what he'd bought or what the implications were.

Khalila had lost her pistol during the plunge into the Barada, but Harrison retained his. As he debated their options—remain hidden, work their way farther up the culvert, or emerge onto the embankment and vacate the area—there was a screech of tires on the road above, followed by an exchange of gunfire. It appeared the assistance Khalila called for had arrived.

24
USS *PITTSBURGH*

Commander Buglione leaned against the navigation table in Control, monitoring Master one's course with concern. *Kazan* had entered the Marginal Ice Zone, a hazardous area for submarine operations. At the fringe of the polar ice cap, wave action and ocean swells broke off edges of the ice floes, creating a zone of broken ice extending outward over a hundred miles.

It wasn't the ice floating on the surface that concerned Buglione. It was the random icebergs scattered throughout the Marginal Ice Zone. More than three thousand icebergs were produced each year in the Barents Sea, breaking off glaciers on Svalbard, Franz Josef Land, and Novaja Zemlja, accompanied by the calving of glaciers on the east coast of Greenland. While most of the icebergs were small, the larger ones descended several hundred feet and occasionally deep enough to ground on the bottom of the shallow Barents Sea.

Buglione called to his Weapons Officer, Lieutenant Ed Reese. "Officer of the Deck, set the Arctic Routine."

Reese repeated back the order and issued commands to his watch section. By setting the Arctic Routine, Buglione had ordered additional sonar consoles manned and the Deck and Conn split, with Buglione and his Executive Officer alternating as the Conning Officer.

After a briefing from Reese, Buglione relieved him of the Conn, announcing to watchstanders in Control, "The Captain has the Conn, Lieutenant Reese retains the Deck."

The Quartermaster acknowledged and continued preparations for entering the Marginal Ice Zone, energizing the submarine's topsounder and Fathometer. The topsounder sent sonar pings up from three hydrophones on *Pittsburgh*'s hull to provide a warning if an ice keel descended toward them. To help avoid the occasional small iceberg, *Pittsburgh* would run deep, closer to the bottom than usual, using the Fathometer to ensure they didn't run aground.

One of the Sonar watchstanders shifted consoles, preparing to energize *Pittsburgh*'s High Frequency Array, the forward-looking under-ice sonar mounted in the front of *Pittsburgh*'s sail, used to detect ice formations ahead. The sonar technician entered the requisite commands, bringing the console on-line, then cast furtive glances at the ship's Captain.

Buglione knew what he was thinking. *Pittsburgh*'s topsounder and Fathometer weren't detectable, emitting narrow high-frequency beams that bounced back to *Pittsburgh* after reflecting off the ocean's surface or bottom. But that wasn't the case with the High Frequency Active sonar, which sent pulses out in front of the submarine—pulses that would likely be detected by the Russian submarine's crew. Having set the Arctic Routine, Buglione had to make the decision he'd been putting off since *Kazan* turned north—whether to energize the under-ice sonar and risk detection.

He announced his decision. "Attention in Control. We will not use our under-ice sonar. We'll let the Russians pick a path through the Marginal Ice Zone and follow directly behind."

Buglione turned to the Helm. "Come left to course three-five-five."

They had been trailing the Russian submarine with an offset to starboard, but needed to trail directly behind while in the Marginal Ice Zone.

After *Pittsburgh* eased into position behind *Kazan,* Buglione turned back to the north.

Moments later, the Quartermaster looked up from the electronic chart and announced, "Entering the Marginal Ice Zone."

25
MARGINAL ICE ZONE

K-561 *KAZAN*

Inside the Marginal Ice Zone, *Kazan* maintained her steady trek north at ten knots while Plecas monitored the ice-detection sonar, topsounder, and bottomsounder. Thus far, the topsounder had detected only sporadic chunks of sea ice floating above them, while the bottomsounder reported the smooth, shallow bottom of the Barents Sea, which averaged only 230 meters in depth.

Plecas, however, was more interested in what the American submarine was doing. He glanced at the navigation table, which displayed the tracks followed by both submarines over the last day. The American crew had detected each of *Kazan*'s baffle clearance maneuvers and calculated its new courses and speeds exactly. They were well trained, which was not an unexpected revelation.

What *was* revealing was that the American submarine was matching *Kazan*'s movements exactly, mimicking them. That, combined with no high-frequency pings from the American submarine, indicated they were not using their under-ice sonar; they were relying on *Kazan* to show them the way.

Perfect.

As Plecas prepared to implement his plan, his thoughts shifted to his submarine's ice-detection sonar. Objects in front of them would appear as a colored blotch, with different colors representing the intensity of the sonar return, with red indicating a large, deep, or dense formation. Unfortunately, ice-detection sonars weren't very good at determining the depth of the object, which is what ultimately mattered. The color of the ice was the key. As *Kazan* closed on the object, shallow ice keels would recede upward and exit the top of the ice-detection beam. As it receded, the color would change from bright red to darker, cooler colors until it faded to black.

The ice-detection sonar used the submarine's depth and a simple geometry algorithm to determine if the obstacle was a threat. If the ice didn't change from red to another color within a certain distance—the Minimum Allowable Fade Range—it was deep enough to present a threat, and Plecas would have to turn or go deeper. The display was currently black; there were no ice formations ahead.

As *Kazan* continued north, small icebergs were sporadically detected, none deep enough to cause concern, until a bright red blotch appeared on the display, twenty degrees to starboard.

The ice-detection sonar operator announced, "Hold ice keel, bearing zero-two-zero, range twelve hundred meters."

Plecas ordered, "Steersman, right standard rudder, steady course zero-two-zero."

As the Steersman complied, Fedorov approached. "Captain, you've turned directly toward the iceberg."

"I understand, First Officer." Plecas said nothing more until *Kazan* steadied on her new course. He then ordered, "Steersman, ahead full."

The Steersman rang up the new speed order, and *Kazan* surged toward the iceberg.

USS *PITTSBURGH*

"Possible contact zig, Master one, due to upshift in frequency."

Lieutenant Bob Martin, on watch as the Junior Officer of the Deck and head of the Section Tracking Party, made the report to Commander Buglione. While they were trailing another submarine, Buglione had augmented the normal watch stations with the Section Tracking Party, comprising an additional fire control technician to monitor the plots, a Contact Manager, and a Junior Officer of the Deck.

Martin moved behind the Plots Operator and examined the contact's tonal on the display. After studying the frequency change and noting a right bearing drift, Martin announced, "Confirm target zig.

Master one has turned to starboard. Set anchor range at five thousand yards."

Shortly after *Kazan* steadied on her new course, the Plots Operator reported, "Possible contact zig, Master one, due to downshift in frequency. Contact is either turning away or increasing speed."

The Section Tracking Party repeated their analysis, concluding *Kazan* had increased speed to twenty knots.

Buglione examined the new solution on the nearest combat control screen. A twenty-degree course change was understandable—perhaps they had detected an ice formation ahead. But why increase speed to twenty knots? Had they detected *Pittsburgh,* and were opening range in an attempt to lose them?

Pittsburgh needed to match *Kazan*'s speed, or they would lose contact.

"Helm, ahead full. Make turns for twenty knots."

K-561 *KAZAN*

One thousand meters to iceberg.

Plecas remained focused on the ice-detection sonar display as the operator called out the distance to the iceberg.

"Captain, what are you doing?" Fedorov asked. "We will smash into the iceberg in ninety seconds if we do not maneuver."

Plecas turned to his First Officer, answering Fedorov's question with a question of his own. "How have the American crew's tactics changed since we entered the Marginal Ice Zone?"

Fedorov answered, "Instead of following us with an offset to starboard, they are now directly behind us."

"Why?"

"Because they are not operating their under-ice sonar, so they don't give their presence away. They are using us to chart a safe path through the Marginal Ice Zone."

"Exactly," Plecas replied.

"I do not understand your plan," Fedorov said. "I realize the American submarine will follow us toward the iceberg, but they will turn away at the same point we turn away, avoiding the iceberg as well. What will we have accomplished?"

Eight hundred meters to iceberg.

"We have also increased speed," Plecas said. "Why?"

Fedorov pondered Plecas's question, unable to determine the answer. Regardless of *Kazan*'s course and speed, when they turned away, the Americans would detect the maneuver and also turn away at the same spot.

"I do not know," Fedorov answered.

"You will understand once we slow."

"When will that be?" Fedorov glanced nervously at the sonar display.

Six hundred meters to iceberg.

Plecas answered. "When we first detected the American submarine, you wanted to shift to the electric drive, reducing our sound signature so they could not follow us. I said then was not the right time. Remember?"

Fedorov nodded and Plecas continued, "Now is the right time." He turned to Captain Lieutenant Urnovitz. "Shift to electric drive."

Urnovitz relayed the order to the Engine Room as Plecas checked the clock. The seconds counted down as *Kazan* sped toward the iceberg.

Four hundred meters to impact.

Fedorov glanced again at the rapidly closing red blotch on the ice-detection sonar. "Captain—"

A report came across the Command Post speakers, interrupting *Kazan*'s First Officer. "Command Post, Engine Room. Propulsion has been shifted to the electric drive. All main engine machinery has been secured."

Plecas responded, "Steersman, hard left rudder! Steady course two-nine-zero!"

USS *PITTSBURGH*

"Conn, Sonar. Loss of Master one."

"Sonar, Conn. Aye." Buglione examined the Sonar display on the Conn. He expected to see the tonal fade, indicating *Kazan* had pulled too far away to be detected. Instead, Master one's tonal had abruptly disappeared.

Lieutenant Reese, the Officer of the Deck, also noted the sudden disappearance. "They must have secured whatever was producing the tonal."

This was bad news. *Kazan* had been their beacon, charting a safe course through the Marginal Ice Zone. Buglione had two choices: activate *Pittsburgh*'s under-ice sonar, giving away their presence, or close the gap on *Kazan* to regain contact. After a moment of indecision, he chose the latter.

He picked up the microphone and selected the 7-MC. "Maneuvering, Conn. Make normal full turns."

The Throttleman in the Engine Room opened the ahead throttles and *Pittsburgh* surged forward.

Buglione studied the narrowband display, looking for the reappearance of Master one's fifty Hertz tonal. After closing the gap at ahead full for several minutes, there was still no sign of Master one, and *Pittsburgh* was approaching the point where *Kazan* disappeared from the display. *Pittsburgh* was barreling forward, and there was no guarantee the path ahead was safe.

Buglione decided to slow as he evaluated his options. "Helm, ahead two-thirds."

As *Pittsburgh* slowed, Petty Officer Alex Rambikur, seated at his console inside the Sonar shack, was listening to the audio output from the spherical array sonar.

"Sonar Sup, I'm hearing an unusual noise. Like someone dropped an Alka-Seltzer tablet into the water."

The Sonar Supervisor replied, "Let me listen."

Rambikur transferred the headphones to Chief Bob Bush, who pressed them against his ears. Unlike Rambikur, who had never been on a Northern Run, Bush had made several, and immediately recognized the fizzing sound created when an iceberg melts, releasing tiny, pressurized air bubbles trapped in the ice.

Bush grabbed the microphone. "Conn, Sonar. We're picking up a bergy-seltzer on broadband. It's close. I've never heard one this loud before."

"Helm, all stop," Buglione ordered.

He turned to the under-ice sonar operator. "Energize the High Frequency Array."

The monitor flickered to life. A huge patch of red appeared on the display, directly ahead at a range of five hundred yards, barely four ship-lengths away.

"Helm, back emergency!" Buglione shouted. "Hard right rudder!"

26
MARGINAL ICE ZONE

K-561 *KAZAN*

Plecas studied the fire control display, watching the American submarine approach the iceberg. It had been a difficult decision—whether to set this trap for their adversary. If the American submarine rammed into the iceberg, it would be severely damaged, and if its pressure hull ruptured, it would sink to the bottom of the Barents Sea. However, Plecas had been trailed by Americans before and knew how difficult it was to shake them. In the end, it had come down to a simple edict.

Kazan could not be trailed.

Plecas examined the sonar display, searching for clues to their adversary's fate. If the American submarine crashed into the iceberg, they would hear it. He picked up the microphone.

"Hydroacoustic, Captain. Put broadband audio on speaker."

The Command Post speakers activated, emitting static noise from surface waves and biologics. The static was interrupted by a loud burst of noise; the distinct sound of high-speed screw cavitation. The American captain had ordered back emergency.

Hydroacoustic's report emanated from the Command Post speakers, temporarily overriding the broadband audio. "Cavitation from Hydroacoustic five. Downshift in frequency. Contact is decreasing speed and turning away."

The Americans had discovered the trap and were trying to maneuver around the iceberg. But had they realized their peril in time?

USS *PITTSBURGH*

Commander Buglione felt tremors in the deck as *Pittsburgh*'s rudder dug into the water and the submarine's screw churned the water in reverse. He glanced at the under-ice sonar display. They were closing rapidly on the red blotch.

Three hundred yards.

Pittsburgh was so close to the iceberg that it filled the entire display. They weren't turning fast enough to avoid it, and they weren't going to stop in time—they were just now dropping under twenty knots. As Buglione prepared for the inevitable collision, a thought occurred to him. They couldn't swerve around the iceberg, but could they go under it?

Buglione checked the charted water depth: 750 feet.

"Dive, make your depth seven hundred feet! Use thirty down!"

As *Pittsburgh* tilted downward, Buglione had no idea if they would get deep enough in time, or if there was enough clearance between the iceberg and the ocean bottom.

Two hundred yards.

Buglione ordered the Chief of the Watch, "Sound the Collision Alarm!"

The high-pitched wail sounded throughout the ship.

Buglione shouted, "All hands brace for impact!"

K-561 *KAZAN*

The cavitation from broadband audio continued, indicating the American captain was still slowing and turning. Then the cavitation was pierced by several loud pops.

Hydroacoustic reported the unusual sound. "Receiving hull pops from Hydroacoustic five."

As submarines went deeper, their hulls compressed slightly due to the higher ocean pressure. The decks inside the submarine weren't welded to the hull—they rested atop deck clips, which let the hull compress without crumpling the decks. However, the heavy decks didn't ride smoothly on the clips, adjusting in increments, with each adjustment creating a loud pop.

The American submarine was going deep, trying to pass beneath the iceberg.

USS *PITTSBURGH*

Pittsburgh tilted thirty degrees down and heeled to port, the distance to the iceberg melting away. As it approached zero, Buglione braced for the collision.

The seconds ticked away and there was no jarring impact. Instead, *Pittsburgh*'s angle leveled off and the Diving Officer reported, "On ordered depth, seven hundred feet."

Buglione checked the HFA display. The red blotch had disappeared. They had passed beneath the iceberg and the water ahead was clear.

The Helm reported, "My rudder is hard right, answering back emergency. Request orders to the Helm."

The request jarred Buglione into action. He checked the ship's speed; *Pittsburgh* was slowing, approaching zero knots.

"Helm, ahead two-thirds, steady as she goes. Dive, make your depth four hundred feet."

As *Pittsburgh* went shallow, Buglione surveyed the Control Room watchstanders, noting the shaken look on their faces. *Pittsburgh* had narrowly escaped disaster.

27
MARGINAL ICE ZONE

USS *PITTSBURGH*

Commander Buglione breathed a sigh of relief. They'd been lucky. The Russian captain had led them toward the iceberg, then shifted to a quieter machinery lineup so *Pittsburgh* wouldn't notice its turn away. He had also increased speed, forcing *Pittsburgh* to do the same to keep up, so the unique iceberg fizzing was masked by the flow of turbulent water past the submarine's acoustic sensors. The Russian captain had set a deadly trap, and it could have ended with *Pittsburgh* on the bottom of the Barents Sea.

That bastard!

The Russian captain had known all along that he was being trailed and had waited for an opportunity to exploit that knowledge. The submarine and its crew were obviously quite capable and its captain very experienced. The latter didn't surprise Buglione; the Russian Navy would not have placed a novice in command of *Kazan*.

As *Pittsburgh* settled out at four hundred feet, Buglione focused on finding *Kazan*. It had disappeared from the sonar screens.

"Sonar, Conn. Report all contacts."

"Conn, Sonar. Hold no contacts."

That wasn't surprising. *Pittsburgh* was on the opposite side of the iceberg from *Kazan,* which had obviously turned away shortly after they lost contact. But which direction had it gone?

Buglione maneuvered *Pittsburgh* around the iceberg then queried Sonar again.

Still no contacts.

He had no idea where the Russian submarine had gone, and the probability of regaining *Kazan* with passive sensors was low. However, there was no need to remain covert. *Kazan*'s crew knew an American submarine had been trailing them. Using active sonar wouldn't tell the Russians anything they didn't already know.

Buglione ran the calculations in his head. They had lost *Kazan* fifteen minutes ago, and assuming she was evading at ten knots from a starting range of five thousand yards, *Kazan* would be about ten thousand yards away.

"Sonar, Conn," Buglione called out, "Transmit MFA Omni, ten-thousand-yard range scale."

Sonar acknowledged the order to transmit Mid-Frequency Active, Omni-directional, setting the system to analyze returns in a band centered at ten thousand yards. *Pittsburgh*'s active sonar system would send pulses in a circular arc, sweeping the ocean around them.

It took only a few seconds for Sonar to complete the lineup, and the Sonar Supervisor reported, "Conn, Sonar. Ready to transmit MFA Omni, ten-thousand-yard range scale."

Buglione ordered, "Transmit."

K-561 *KAZAN*

"Command Post, Hydroacoustic. Receiving active sonar on a bearing of zero-nine-zero, designated Hydroacoustic six."

Plecas picked up the microphone beside the navigation table. "Hydroacoustic, Captain. Is the active pulse repeating?"

"Captain, Hydroacoustic. Yes."

"Send Hydroacoustic six to fire control."

Hydroacoustic acknowledged, and Plecas moved behind the fire control consoles as Senior Michman Topolski determined a solution.

"Use a range of ten thousand yards," Plecas directed.

Topolski dialed in the ordered range, then matched bearing rate. "Hydroacoustic six is on course one-eight-zero, ten knots."

Plecas checked the geographic display on the adjacent console. The American submarine was traveling south while *Kazan* headed west, steadily opening range. They were already on an excellent course, with

Kazan's stern pointing directly at the American submarine—an aspect unlikely to generate a return ping strong enough to be detected by the American sonar at the current range.

Whether *Kazan* was detected would be evident by the American submarine's reaction. Plecas monitored the contact solution. The American submarine kept pinging, holding steady on its southerly course, with no change in speed. It had not detected *Kazan*.

Once Plecas was convinced *Kazan* was beyond the range of the American submarine's acoustic sensors, he returned propulsion to its normal lineup.

"Watch Officer. Shift propulsion to the main engines and increase speed to ahead full."

USS *PITTSBURGH*

They had been pinging for thirty minutes when Buglione secured the active sonar. The Russian submarine was too far away to generate a sufficient sonar return. His only chance now was to close the distance and hope to regain *Kazan* on *Pittsburgh*'s sensors. But it was a big ocean and *Kazan* could have gone almost anywhere, and the odds of regaining trail on the Russian submarine were low. Fortunately, *Pittsburgh* wasn't the only asset available.

"XO." Buglione summoned his Executive Officer, who joined him at the navigation table. "Draft a message to CTF-69, advising them we picked up *Kazan* entering Kola Bay and lost track of her at our current location. Request follow-on tasking."

Lieutenant Commander Schwartz acknowledged and entered the Radio Room to draft a message to their operational commander. The message was drafted and Buglione reviewed it, releasing it for transmission.

"Officer of the Deck, prepare to proceed to periscope depth. We have one outgoing."

Two hours later, after transmitting the message and descending to 150 feet, *Pittsburgh* returned to periscope depth to download the latest round of messages, which included a new operational order for *Pittsburgh,* plus related directives. COMSUBPAC had been alerted to the possibility *Kazan* was undergoing an interfleet transfer, to ensure assets were available to detect and trail the Russian submarine if it appeared in the Pacific Ocean. Of higher concern was the possibility *Kazan* was headed into the Atlantic Ocean, en route to either a Mediterranean Sea deployment or a patrol off the East Coast of the United States.

Undersea Surveillance Command, which monitored the SOSUS arrays on the ocean bottom as well as the data collected by SURTASS ships with their deployable towed arrays, had been notified, and all paths through the GIUK Gap would be closely monitored. Additionally, two submarines would be stationed near the GIUK Gap exits to resume trail once *Kazan* was regained by SOSUS arrays.

USS *Boise,* currently in transit across the Atlantic Ocean to relieve *Pittsburgh* on its Northern Run, would take station between Iceland and the UK to cover the southern routes through the GIUK Gap, while *Pittsburgh* was being repositioned between Greenland and Iceland to cover the northern routes. Of course, that meant *Pittsburgh* needed to reach the GIUK Gap before *Kazan*. Considering *Pittsburgh*'s maximum speed and that *Kazan* would likely be traveling at no higher than ahead full, that would not be a problem.

"Helm, ahead flank," Buglione ordered. "Left full rudder, steady course three-zero-zero."

Assuming *Kazan* was headed west, Buglione intended to take *Pittsburgh* on an arc around the Russian submarine, hopefully transiting far enough away from *Kazan* that the Russian crew wouldn't detect *Pittsburgh* repositioning ahead of it.

Buglione was confident *Kazan* would not escape into the Atlantic Ocean. At least, not without an American submarine trailing it.

28
MCLEAN, VIRGINIA

Jake Harrison followed Khalila Dufour into the National Counterterrorism Center, taking in the scene: the main floor was filled with sixty analysts at their desks, working diligently while supervisors observed from glass-enclosed offices on the second floor. The NCTC, located in the Liberty Crossing Building and staffed by fourteen government agencies, including the FBI and CIA, served as the logistical hub for the collation and dissemination of terrorist-related information within the U.S. intelligence community.

Upon their return to the United States, Khalila and Harrison had headed to the NCTC to connect with Pat Kendall, who was already working on leads from their trip to Damascus.

"Welcome back," Kendall said as she stood, her eyes staying intentionally fixed on Harrison, ignoring Khalila's presence. "Glad to see you're still in one piece." Her gaze shifted to Khalila, who offered a fake smile.

"I reviewed your trip report," Kendall said, "but noticed that only Khalila signed it. It's missing your digital signature, Jake. Normally the junior officer drafts the report and all involved sign it, but I'm guessing Khalila wrote this herself."

Khalila replied, "Harrison isn't familiar with the required format and content, so I thought it was easier to write this one myself."

"Sure," Kendall said as she handed Harrison a printout. "Take a look and let me know if anything important is missing."

Harrison reviewed the report, which Khalila had indeed written during their return flight across the Atlantic. She had mentioned nothing about the protocol of the junior officer writing it, nor had she offered him the opportunity to review it.

The report, which covered the meetings with both arms dealers, was accurate aside from the death of Issad Futtaim's assistant, whom Khalila had slain without cause. The report instead said Aboud drew his weapon after Futtaim was assassinated, prompting Khalila's attack.

After assessing the omission, Harrison decided to address the matter with Khalila later. "Nothing important is missing," he said, handing the report back to Kendall, who stuffed it into a manila folder.

"It's a pity you weren't able to extract the contents of Futtaim's computer," she said. "However, it looks like we got it all anyway." When Harrison inquired, Kendall explained. "A lot of businesses—arms dealers included, apparently—don't keep printed files anymore. It's all electronic, which means they have at least one backup and sometimes two or three, so a hard drive failure on their computer or main server doesn't wipe everything out. Futtaim was no different.

"He likely had a local backup in his office that you might have found if you'd had more time, but it turns out Futtaim had a wireless backup in the cloud. A backup that our friends in the Directorate of Analysis were able to locate and download."

Kendall brought up a directory of files on her computer. "Unfortunately, it looks like the key file we're interested in is partially encrypted." She opened one of the files, which appeared to be a ledger of transactions. The date of each transaction wasn't hidden, but the item procured, the amount, the purchaser, the shipping destination, and additional comments were garbled.

"Not to worry," Kendall said. "It won't take long for the folks in Analysis to crack it, once they identify the encryption scheme."

29
USS *PITTSBURGH*

"Helm, ahead two-thirds."

Commander Buglione looked up as *Pittsburgh*'s Officer of the Deck, Lieutenant Ed Reese, ordered the submarine to slow from ahead flank. Buglione glanced at the navigation display, noting that *Pittsburgh* was about to enter its new operating area west of the GIUK Gap. *Pittsburgh* had been repositioned to cover the northern routes through the Gap, while USS *Boise* had recently arrived on station, covering the southern routes.

As *Pittsburgh* prepared for *Kazan*'s arrival, Buglione wondered whether his old submarine was up to the task. In the Barents Sea, it was obvious that *Pittsburgh* had been counter-detected by *Kazan*'s crew, and that America's Los Angeles class submarines no longer held an acoustic advantage against Russia's newest submarines; at least not against *Kazan*.

As a teenager, Buglione had read Tom Clancy's *The Hunt for Red October,* which featured the Los Angeles class submarine USS *Dallas*. Back then, the Los Angeles class boats, often referred to as 688s, were the most technologically advanced submarines in the world and the pride of the Submarine Force. Nowadays, 688s were referred to as *the old boats,* creaking by until they were replaced by the state-of-the art Virginia class submarines, which were already entering their fourth flight of design improvements.

Inside the submarine, *Pittsburgh* had somewhat kept up with the times, sporting the latest versions of tactical systems. But *the old boats*' weaknesses were external to the hull. *Pittsburgh* and the other remaining 688s still had their legacy sonar hydrophones. It was relatively easy and cheap to replace internal systems with updated microprocessors, displays, and algorithms. Replacing the entire spherical array with the newest technology or incorporating hull flank arrays, like the Virginia class submarines, was cost-prohibitive. Still, Buglione was convinced his crew was better trained than *Kazan*'s, and that would make the difference.

After the Quartermaster reported they had entered their operating area, Lieutenant Reese called out, "Sonar, Conn. Report all contacts."

Two minutes later, Sonar reported no submerged contacts; only a few merchants more than ten miles away.

Buglione turned to Lieutenant Reese. "Make preparations to proceed to periscope depth."

Now that *Pittsburgh* had arrived in its new operating area, it was time to see if *Kazan* had been detected by SOSUS arrays. If not, *Pittsburgh* would remain at periscope depth until they were provided queuing information—which passage *Kazan* was proceeding through.

After four hours at periscope depth, *Pittsburgh* received the message Buglione had been hoping for. *Kazan* had been detected by SOSUS arrays entering the northernmost channel in the GIUK Gap. Buglione stopped beside the Quartermaster at the navigation table, estimating the course to a new station five thousand yards from the channel exit. He was joined by Lieutenant Reese, who likewise estimated *Pittsburgh*'s new course.

"Zero-six-zero?" Reese suggested.

Buglione nodded. "Course zero-six-zero, ahead standard."

30

USS *PITTSBURGH* • K-561 *KAZAN*

USS *PITTSBURGH*

It was quiet in the Control Room as *Pittsburgh* loitered in its new operating area, awaiting *Kazan*'s arrival. Commander Buglione sat patiently in the Captain's chair on the Conn, his eyes occasionally shifting to the geographic plot on the nearest combat control console.

Buglione was confident *Pittsburgh* was well positioned to detect *Kazan* as it completed its transit through the GIUK Gap, but there was no guarantee they would detect the Russian submarine. After all, during their last trail, *Kazan* had vanished from the sonar screens, just before *Pittsburgh* almost smashed into the iceberg.

It was obvious that *Kazan* had shifted its equipment lineup, eliminating the tonals they had been tracking. During *Pittsburgh*'s high-speed transit to the west side of the Gap, Buglione had directed Sonar to analyze the data when *Kazan*'s tonals had disappeared. During the detailed analysis, Sonar had identified a weak tonal that had remained after the lineup shift, one they hadn't been tracking due to the presence of stronger frequencies emitted by the Russian submarine. If *Kazan* shifted its lineup again, Sonar would shift its trackers in response.

Buglione's thoughts were interrupted by Sonar's report. "Conn, Sonar. Gained a fifty Hertz tonal on the towed array, designated Sierra seven-four, ambiguous bearings of zero-eight-zero and two-eight-zero. Analyzing."

Lieutenant Bob Martin, on watch as Officer of the Deck again, acknowledged Sonar's report, then approached Buglione. "Captain, I intend to maneuver to resolve bearing ambiguity."

"Very well," Buglione acknowledged, although he was certain the new contact was to the east. A bearing of zero-eight-zero was close to where they expected *Kazan* to pass through the Gap.

"Helm, right full rudder, steady course north," Martin ordered.

As *Pittsburgh* swung toward its new course, Sonar provided an update.

"Conn, Sonar. Sierra seven-four is classified submerged. Hold additional tonals correlating to Russian Yasen class."

Buglione addressed Lieutenant Martin. "Station the Fire Control Tracking Party."

The order went out and personnel streamed into the Control Room, manning the dormant consoles.

Once the Fire Control Tracking Party was fully manned, Buglione announced, "Sierra seven-four has been classified Yasen class submarine and is our target of interest. Designate Sierra seven-four as Master one. Track Master one."

The towed array's bearing ambiguity was quickly resolved, and Buglione's crew determined that Master one was to the east, headed southwest at fifteen knots.

Buglione, who was now stationed as *Pittsburgh*'s Conning Officer, evaluated the geographic plot. *Kazan* was traveling past *Pittsburgh,* apparently oblivious to the presence of the American submarine. Buglione ordered *Pittsburgh* to swing around and fall in behind the Russian submarine.

"Helm, right full rudder, steady course two-zero-zero."

Pittsburgh angled in behind *Kazan,* arriving at the desired trailing position a few thousand yards behind, and offset to starboard so their towed array had a clear view of the Russian submarine. It was time to match *Kazan*'s speed and course, following her until relieved by another NATO submarine.

"Helm, ahead standard," Buglione ordered. "Right ten degrees rudder, steady course two-four-zero."

Even though things had gone smoothly thus far, Buglione decided to leave the Fire Control Tracking Party stationed for a few hours in case *Pittsburgh* had been counter-detected and the Russian submarine captain attempted to break trail.

As *Pittsburgh* steadied at fifteen knots, matching *Kazan*'s course and speed, Buglione settled into his chair on the Conn, preparing for a potentially long and hopefully uneventful trail.

K-561 *KAZAN*

"Hydroacoustic, Command Post. Report all contacts."

In *Kazan*'s Central Command Post, Captain First Rank Aleksandr Plecas stopped in front of the hydroacoustic display, searching for patterns within the random specks.

In the Barents Sea, it appeared they had shaken the American submarine from its trail. But as *Kazan* completed its run through the GIUK Gap, it was vulnerable. If there was a possibility they would be detected and trailed by another NATO submarine, they'd pick up *Kazan* here.

Plecas was joined by his Watch Officer, Captain Lieutenant Ivan Urnovitz, at the hydroacoustic display, along with the submarine's First Officer, Captain Third Rank Erik Fedorov. As the three men examined the monitor, a narrow vertical bar rose from the bottom of the display. The Hydroacoustic Party Leader's report arrived a moment later.

"Command Post, Hydroacoustic. Hold a new contact on the towed array, a sixty-point-two Hertz tonal, designated Hydroacoustic two-one, ambiguous bearings two-six-zero and two-two-zero. Sixty-point-two Hertz frequency correlates to an American submarine."

The two watchstanders at their fire control consoles adjusted the contact's parameters—course, speed, and range—and slowly converged on identical solutions. The American submarine had fallen in behind *Kazan,* trailing them in their starboard quarter five thousand yards away.

They needed to break trail again, and Plecas evaluated his options. Shifting to the electric drive in the Barents Sea had been successful, but if this was the same American submarine, they might not be able to slip away. The American crew would respond faster than before, closing range quickly to gain other tonals. However, there was only one way to find out if the evasion would be successful.

"Attention, all stations," Plecas announced. "An American submarine has gained trail on us again. We will attempt to evade covertly, giving the Americans no indication they have been counter-detected. If that fails, we will execute an overt evasion using acoustic countermeasures."

Plecas ordered his Watch Officer, "Shift to electric drive and turn ninety degrees to port."

Captain Lieutenant Urnovitz issued the first order. "Steersman, shift to electric drive."

The Steersman complied, sending the order to the Engine Room, and he soon announced, "Propulsion has been shifted to the electric drive. Making ten knots."

Urnovitz responded, "Steersman, left full rudder, steady course one-five-zero."

USS *PITTSBURGH*

"Conn, Sonar. Loss of primary tonal, Master one. Shifting tracker alpha to secondary tonal."

Buglione stood and examined the sonar display on the Conn. The dominant fifty Hertz and associated frequencies had disappeared, but a weak three-hundred Hertz tonal remained.

A few seconds later, one of the fire control technicians monitoring *Kazan*'s parameters spoke into his headset. "Possible contact zig, Master one, due to upshift in frequency."

Buglione waited as the Fire Control Tracking Party evaluated whether *Kazan* had actually zigged, and if so, to what new course and speed.

After evaluating the three combat control console displays, Lieutenant Commander Schwartz, stationed as the Fire Control Coordinator, announced, "Confirmed target zig, Master one. Target has turned to port. Set anchor range, five thousand yards."

Kazan was trying to evade.

Buglione studied the displays as the watchstanders spent the next few minutes discerning *Kazan*'s new course and speed, which could be numerous combinations to port.

Schwartz hovered behind the combat control consoles, talking with

Sonar occasionally, then tapped one of the fire control technicians on the shoulder. "Promote to master."

Buglione examined the Russian submarine's new solution. *Kazan* had slowed to ten knots and turned ninety degrees to port. *Pittsburgh* had been counter-detected again, and the Russian captain was trying to slip away. To maintain *Pittsburgh* in a covert trail, Buglione needed to convince the Russian crew that their evasion was successful.

"Attention in Control," Buglione announced. "It appears we've been counter-detected and Master one is attempting to break trail. We're going to try and fool the Russian crew into believing they've been successful. We'll remain steady on course and speed, passing behind Master one, then open range to the maximum possible before matching Master one's new course and speed. Hopefully, by then we'll have faded from *Kazan*'s sensors and they won't realize we're still in trail. Carry on."

The watchstanders in Control returned to their duties, although there wasn't much to do at the moment. *Pittsburgh* remained steady on course and speed while it passed behind the Russian submarine and began opening range.

Buglione watched the narrowband display as the tonal strength slowly faded, then the Sonar Supervisor's voice came across the 27-MC.

"Conn, Sonar. We've lost the automated tracker on Master one. Buzzing bearings manually to combat control."

Pittsburgh had dropped back as far as possible, and Buglione needed to hold at this distance, matching *Kazan*'s course and speed.

"Helm, ahead two-thirds. Left full rudder, steady course one-five-zero."

Pittsburgh slowed as it turned south, steadying in *Kazan*'s aft starboard quarter again, trailing from six thousand yards. That was the best he could do. Hopefully, *Pittsburgh* had disappeared from *Kazan*'s sensors by now, and the Russian crew had no idea they were still being trailed.

K-561 *KAZAN*

As the American submarine remained steady on course and speed, passing behind *Kazan* and then opening range, Plecas held hope that *Kazan* had faded from the American submarine's sonar screens and was now slipping away. Range had increased to six thousand yards when the Americans reacted.

"Command Post, Hydroacoustic. Possible target maneuver, Hydroacoustic two-one."

Plecas waited while *Kazan*'s watch section determined the American submarine's new course and speed. What Plecas didn't know yet was whether the American crew had lost *Kazan* and were turning in a random direction in an attempt to regain contact, or had maintained trail and were falling in behind *Kazan* again.

A few minutes later, Captain Lieutenant Urnovitz, examining the two fire control console displays, tapped one of the men on his shoulder. "Set as primary solution."

The American submarine had matched *Kazan*'s course and speed, but was now following from a greater range. Their covert evasion had failed.

Plecas decided to execute an overt evasion utilizing decoys and jammers. Regarding propulsion—that was a trade-off. The electric drive was quieter but capable of only ten knots, while the normal steam-turbine propulsion was noisier but could propel *Kazan* at over thirty knots. Plecas decided for a combined approach.

"Attention, all stations. It appears the American submarine has maintained trail, so we will now attempt an overt evasion. After deploying an acoustic jammer, we will shift back to main propulsion and increase speed, hopefully opening range sufficiently before the American submarine penetrates the jammer barrier. Any questions?"

There were no responses, and Plecas issued the first set of orders. "Prepare to shift propulsion to the main engines and eject one jammer."

Urnovitz soon reported that his watch section was ready.

"Launch jammer," Plecas ordered.

After ejecting the countermeasure, which emitted a continuous blast of noise designed to blind passive sonars, Plecas directed, "Shift propulsion to the main engines and increase speed to ahead flank."

USS *PITTSBURGH*

"Conn, Sonar. Detect broadband jammer on the bearing to Master one. Loss of Master one."

Buglione evaluated the sonar display on the Conn.

Damn.

It was apparent the Russian crew still held *Pittsburgh* and were now conducting an overt evasion. That meant *Kazan* would increase speed once the jammer was deployed, hoping that by the time *Pittsburgh* broke through the noise field, *Kazan* would be beyond sensor range. Buglione couldn't let that happen.

"Helm, ahead flank."

As *Pittsburgh* surged forward, Buglione waited tensely until they passed the jammer, gaining a clear view of the water ahead.

"Sonar, Conn. Report all contacts."

"Conn, Sonar. Hold no contacts."

Kazan's evasion had been successful thus far. But *Pittsburgh* could still regain the Russian submarine. At this point, there was no advantage in trying to maintain stealth. *Kazan* obviously knew they were being trailed again, and using active sonar wouldn't give anything away.

"Sonar, Conn," Buglione called out. "Transmit MFA Directional, forward sectors, five-thousand-yard range scale."

Sonar acknowledged the order to transmit Mid-Frequency Active, looking in the two forward quarters, then completed the lineup and reported they were ready.

Buglione ordered, "Sonar, Conn. Transmit," then shifted the sonar display on the Conn to active sonar.

A small blip appeared.

"Conn, Sonar. Hold a new contact on active sonar, designated Sierra seven-five, bearing two-zero-three, range seven thousand yards."

A few pings later, they were able to evaluate the contact's speed—in excess of twenty-five knots—and Schwartz announced, "Sierra seven-five is a regain of Master one."

"Helm, left ten degrees rudder," Buglione ordered, "steady course two-zero-three."

Pittsburgh swung onto its new course. The question now was, could *Kazan* outrun *Pittsburgh*?

The 688-class submarine was old, but designed during the Cold War when the ability to keep up with their adversaries was paramount and the cost of submarines less of an issue. Buglione was a betting man, and his money was on *Pittsburgh*.

Sonar kept pinging as they chased the Russian submarine, and Buglione watched the range intently. After a few more pings, he smiled. They were slowly gaining on *Kazan*.

They kept closing: six thousand yards, then five thousand yards.

Kazan launched another jammer and a decoy, followed by a radical course change. But *Pittsburgh* held *Kazan* on active sonar and ignored the decoy, then blazed past the jammer, turning to match *Kazan*'s new course.

Four thousand yards.

They still hadn't detected *Kazan* on the towed array again due to the propulsion noise *Pittsburgh* generated at ahead flank. However, the spherical array in the bow had a clear view and once they were close enough, Sonar made the expected report.

"Conn, Sonar. Gained fifty Hertz tonal on the spherical array, designated Sierra seven-six, bearing two-six-zero. Correlates to Master one."

Schwartz compared the new tonal to those from Master one, then confirmed Sonar's conclusion. "Reclassify Sierra seven-six as Master one."

Kazan was three thousand yards away now.

Buglione ordered, "Secure active sonar."

Shortly thereafter, *Kazan* tried to break trail again, launching another set of acoustic countermeasures and altering course. The Russian submarine's new course was quickly determined and *Pittsburgh* followed.

As *Pittsburgh* kept gaining on *Kazan,* Buglione evaluated the optimum trail range. As far as normal tactics went, the jig was up. The Russian crew was aware they were being followed, so there was no reason for *Pittsburgh* to try to maintain stealth by trailing at maximum range. Following far behind improved the odds *Kazan* would successfully evade in the future. It was better to follow *Kazan* at the minimum safety range.

Buglione kept *Pittsburgh* at ahead flank until they closed to two thousand yards.

Kazan suddenly slowed.

Buglione didn't have time for the Fire Control Tracking Party to determine a new solution. *Pittsburgh* was traveling at ahead flank and needed to slow. But to what speed? He evaluated the frequency shift on the display, estimating *Kazan*'s new speed. It looked like the Russian submarine had slowed to ten knots.

"Helm, ahead two-thirds."

A moment later, Schwartz confirmed Buglione's mental calculation. "Confirm target zig. Master one has slowed to ten knots. No change in course."

Buglione waited for the Russian captain's next move. One minute turned into five, then ten. But *Kazan* remained steady on course and speed with *Pittsburgh* trailing close behind. Buglione relaxed. It looked like the Russian captain had accepted defeat—*Pittsburgh* had broken *Kazan* like a cowboy breaking a horse.

At least for the time being. There was no doubt the Russian captain would attempt to evade again when the time and environmental conditions were ideal. Maybe late on the mid-watch when there was a strong thermal layer the Russian submarine could hide behind, gaining a few more precious minutes to open range before *Pittsburgh*'s crew figured things out.

If Buglione had anything to say about it, that wasn't going to happen. For the duration of the Russian submarine's deployment, *Pittsburgh* would be on *Kazan* like white on rice.

K-561 *KAZAN*

Aleksandr Plecas folded his arms across his chest, admitting defeat. The American submarine was capable and its crew well trained, and he had learned during his career that Americans were persistent, if nothing else.

However, it was imperative that *Kazan* not be trailed during its journey. If a hostile submarine was nearby when *Kazan* commenced launching its missiles, it would likely attack. That was something Plecas could not allow. Although his fate was sealed—he would spend the rest of his life in prison upon his return to Russia—he had a responsibility to his crew, to not place them in harm's way any more than necessary. That meant—*Kazan* could not be trailed.

Plecas left the Central Command Post and entered his stateroom. He closed and locked his door, then opened his safe, retrieving the yellow envelope delivered to his submarine a few days ago, containing *Kazan*'s classified patrol order. He opened and removed the order, replacing it with a counterfeit version he pulled from his leather satchel.

He returned to the Central Command Post with the order and stopped beside the navigation table. He called to his First Officer. When Fedorov joined him, Plecas pulled the fake patrol order from the envelope and handed it to his second-in-command. Fedorov's eyes grew wide when he read the salient portion of the directive.

Fedorov looked up. "You share this with me just now?"

"Those were my orders," Plecas replied. "I was directed to keep our mission a secret even from my crew until we deployed. As you can see, this is a very sensitive directive."

Fedorov nodded numbly. "What is the rationale for the attack?"

"I will explain to the entire crew." Plecas pulled a microphone from its holder, switching it to the shipwide communication circuit. "This is the Captain," he announced.

"I want to commend all of you for your excellent job preparing *Kazan* for her maiden deployment. Your hard work and dedicated preparation did not go unnoticed by Northern Fleet Command, and I am proud to inform you that *Kazan* has been selected for a special mission.

"I know all of you have seen the videos. Images of the Russian Northern and Pacific Fleets destroyed by the American Navy—our surface ships on fire or oil slicks where they sank beneath the waves. You no doubt felt as I did; the shame of our failure, the anguish for our dead comrades, the anger and desire for revenge.

"We have been selected to inflict that revenge. We are not beginning a Mediterranean deployment. Instead, we will travel toward the United States, where we will launch our Kalibr missiles against twenty American targets. We will send a message, demonstrating that the Russian Navy is still a formidable foe, one that should be feared. A Navy that has a vast reach, capable of wreaking destruction deep into the interior of the United States.

"To ensure this mission is a success, we must conduct our missile launch without an American submarine or surface warship nearby that could attack and halt the launch, much less sink *Kazan*. That means we cannot be followed.

"We have tried to break the American submarine's trail and have failed. We must now take a more aggressive measure. Northern Fleet Command has given me the authority to sink any vessel that threatens our mission."

Plecas paused to let the implications sink in. They were going to engage the American submarine. His eyes moved slowly across the men at their workstations, looking for indications that any were hesitant to carry out the orders that would soon come.

There was no sign that any of the men had reservations. They stared back without emotion on their faces, awaiting direction.

Plecas gave the order.

"Man Combat Stations silently."

31

K-561 *KAZAN* • USS *PITTSBURGH*

K-561 *KAZAN*

The two Command Post Messengers sped through the submarine, spreading the word to man Combat Stations. Three minutes later, *Kazan* was fully manned.

"All compartments report ready for combat, Captain."

Plecas acknowledged his Watch Officer, then announced, "This is the Captain, I have the Conn and Captain Lieutenant Urnovitz retains the Watch. The target of interest is Hydroacoustic two-one, classified as American fast attack submarine. Track Hydroacoustic two-one."

Fedorov, stationed as the Tracking Party Leader, stopped behind each man to check on the performance of his duties. As Fedorov made his rounds, Plecas surveyed the Command Post watchstanders. His men were tense, but their communications remained disciplined, his crew speaking in subdued tones using the succinct orders and reports they had been trained to use.

Plecas announced, "Attention in the Command Post." When all eyes were on him, he continued. "The American submarine is following closely and will have little time to evade, so we will fire a single torpedo. Since we are being trailed in our starboard quarter, we will shoot from a port tube so the hull will partially mask the torpedo tube door opening. Any questions?"

There were none, and Plecas ordered, "Prepare to Fire, Hydroacoustic two-one, single weapon from tube Six, tube Eight as backup."

His crew executed the order swiftly, and in less than a minute, Fedorov tapped one of the fire controlmen on the shoulder. "Send solution to Weapon Control."

It had been easy to determine an accurate solution; the American submarine was trailing *Kazan,* matching its course and speed.

Fedorov announced, "I have a firing solution."

Kazan's Watch Officer followed, reporting they were ready for counterfire from the American submarine. "Torpedo countermeasures are armed."

The Weapons Officer reported, "Ready to Fire, tubes Six and Eight, with the exception of opening muzzle doors and satisfying torpedo circular interlock."

Kazan's crew was ready to fire except for opening the torpedo tube muzzle doors and satisfying a crucial torpedo safety interlock: anti-circular run logic.

Self-guided torpedoes were artificially intelligent weapons with a sonar array in their nose and sophisticated algorithms able to disregard decoys and maneuver the torpedo around jammers. But the one thing they couldn't do is differentiate between a friendly and enemy submarine. Torpedoes occasionally had steering failures, resulting in the torpedo turning around after launch, ending up facing the firing submarine.

There was also the possibility the enemy submarine would evade by turning toward the firing submarine, and the torpedo, if locked on, would follow, potentially shifting its targeting onto the firing submarine instead. For those reasons, if a torpedo ended up traveling back toward the firing submarine, the torpedo's anti-circular interlock would shut it down.

The trailing American submarine was within the anti-circular-run constraints, and Plecas needed to maneuver *Kazan* before firing. He decided to turn slowly, pretending to simply change course rather than attempt another evasion, so as to not unduly alert the American crew.

"Steersman, right ten degrees rudder, steady course three-three-zero."

Kazan swung slowly to starboard.

Partway into the turn, the Weapons Officer announced, "Circular interlock cleared."

Plecas ordered, "Open muzzle doors, tubes Six and Eight."

USS *PITTSBURGH*

Moments earlier, Sonar had noticed the Russian submarine's maneuver.

"Possible contact zig, Master one, due to upshift in frequency."

Lieutenant Commander Schwartz listened to Sonar's report over the sound-powered phones, then examined the nearest time-frequency plot. *Kazan*'s tonals were increasing.

He checked the contact's bearing drift—the bearings were drifting to the right of those projected by combat control, indicating a maneuver to starboard.

Schwartz announced, "Confirm target zig. Contact has turned to starboard. Set anchor range at two thousand yards."

Buglione stopped beside his Executive Officer, examining the displays. *Kazan* had turned to starboard, but the Russian submarine could still be on an opening course or it could have turned farther, back toward *Pittsburgh*. He needed to maneuver to maintain trail and avoid collision, but needed to know *Kazan*'s new course.

"I need a solution fast, XO."

Schwartz studied the combat control consoles as Sonar announced, "Ten-knot upshift in frequency. No indication of speed change."

That was the information they needed. *Kazan* had turned ninety degrees, showing *Pittsburgh* a beam aspect. Lieutenant Martin and the two fire control technicians converged on a common solution.

Schwartz reported, "Master One has turned to course three-three-zero, speed ten."

Now that there was no chance of collision, Buglione relaxed. *Pittsburgh* would remain steady on course until it was behind *Kazan* again, then turn ninety degrees to starboard, returning to the desired trailing position.

In the Sonar Room, the broadband operator, wearing headphones to monitor the sounds picked up by the spherical array sonar, pressed his hands against his headphones, concentrating on the unusual sound.

"Sonar Sup, broadband," he reported. "Picking up mechanical transients from Master one. I can't tell what it is, though."

The Sonar Supervisor, Chief Bob Bush, donned the headphones. The sound had faded, so he rewound the recording to a moment before. The transient was muffled and difficult to identify.

Bush reported, "Fire Control Coordinator, Sonar Sup. Picking up mechanical transients from Master one. Source unknown."

K-561 *KAZAN*

"Torpedo muzzle doors, tubes Six and Eight, are open," the Weapons Officer reported. "Ready to Fire, tube Six, tube Eight as backup."

Plecas stopped beside his First Officer, evaluating the solution to Hydroacoustic two-one. The American crew was following protocol, driving astern of *Kazan* to maintain trail.

He retreated to the aft section of the Command Post, where he had a clear view of all stations, and examined the displays one final time.

Satisfied that all parameters were optimal, he ordered, "Fire tube Six."

USS *PITTSBURGH*

"Torpedo launch transient, bearing two-nine-three!"

Buglione listened to Sonar's report over the Control Room speakers in disbelief. Sonar must have interpreted the transient incorrectly. There was no way the Russian submarine had fired at them. That was an act of war, and could certainly start one.

Another report from Sonar blared from the speakers.

"Torpedo in the water! Bearing two-nine-three!"

A red bearing line appeared on the combat control displays, signaling the detection of an incoming torpedo.

"Man Battle Stations!" Buglione shouted.

"Helm, ahead flank! Left full rudder, steady course two-zero-zero! Launch countermeasures!"

Pittsburgh's propeller churned the water as it strained to accelerate the submarine to maximum speed. As the Chief of the Watch ordered the crew to Battle Stations over the shipwide announcing circuit, an acoustic decoy was ejected to maintain the incoming torpedo focused on where *Pittsburgh* had been, instead of where it was going.

"Quick Reaction Firing," Buglione ordered, "Master one, tube One! Flood down and open all torpedo tube outer doors, tube One first!"

He had skipped their normal torpedo firing process, choosing a more urgent version that forced his Executive Officer to send his best solution to the torpedo immediately, whether or not he considered it good enough for the torpedo to lock on to the target. However, they had a decent track on *Kazan* and it should be good enough, although the Russian captain would also be maneuvering his submarine.

Schwartz shifted his gaze between the three consoles, then tapped one of the fire control technicians on the shoulder. "Promote to master."

"Solution ready!" Schwartz reported.

"Ship ready!" the Officer of the Deck announced, reporting the submarine was ready to launch additional decoys and jammers.

Buglione's eyes shifted to his Weapons Officer, Lieutenant Reese, manning the Weapon Control Console and in communication with the Torpedo Room. He could not report Weapon Ready until Torpedo Tube One was flooded down, equalized with sea pressure, and the muzzle door opened. That took time.

Time *Pittsburgh* didn't have.

They had been following *Kazan* closely, at only two thousand yards. A fifty-knot torpedo fired from two thousand yards would close the distance to *Pittsburgh* in barely a minute. Normally, that would be enough time to counterfire. However, *Pittsburgh* wasn't combat ready. Aside from the Fire Control Tracking Party, *Pittsburgh* was in a normal watch rotation, with only a single torpedoman on watch. He'd have his hands full preparing the torpedo tubes for firing.

Sonar's next report was one Buglione had been dreading.

"Torpedo is range-gating! One thousand yards!"

The Russian torpedo was homing, increasing the rate of its sonar pings to more accurately determine the range to its target, so a refined intercept course could be calculated. The important question was whether the torpedo was about to intercept *Pittsburgh* or its decoy.

Buglione studied the torpedo bearings. They remained the same—the torpedo was locked on to *Pittsburgh*.

"Launch jammer!" Buglione ordered.

The Officer of the Deck ejected a broadband noise jammer into the water, attempting to overwhelm the torpedo's sonar processing.

"Fifteen seconds to impact!" Sonar reported.

"Helm, hard left rudder, steady course one-one-zero!"

Buglione turned *Pittsburgh* ninety degrees again, the large rudder putting a knuckle into the water as it swung sideways, twisting the submarine to port. Hopefully, the jammer and the swirling water in the knuckle, which distorted sonar returns, would sufficiently confuse the torpedo.

But the torpedo was too close. It sped past the jammer and got enough of a return through the water knuckle to detect *Pittsburgh*'s turn to port. It twisted nimbly onto the new course of its target, which loomed directly ahead. It closed the remaining distance in a few seconds.

Buglione watched the torpedo bearings remain constant as *Pittsburgh* steadied on its new course. They hadn't shaken the torpedo.

Wrapping one arm around the starboard periscope, Buglione braced himself for the explosion, but even his firm grip wasn't enough to keep him from being knocked to the deck as the torpedo exploded, ripping through *Pittsburgh*'s pressure hull.

A loud, wrenching metallic sound tore through the ship, and the stern tilted downward—the Engine Room was flooding.

With a flooded Engine Room, there was no hope. *Pittsburgh* was going down.

"Launch a SEPIRB buoy!" Buglione ordered.

The order was relayed to the Signal Ejector Watch, who inserted a SEPIRB—Submarine Emergency Position Indicating Radio Beacon—buoy into the signal ejector, launching it. Upon surfacing, the SEPIRB buoy would transmit a submarine distress message, reporting *Pittsburgh*'s position.

K-561 *KAZAN*

In *Kazan*'s Central Command Post, the torpedo explosion rumbled through the submarine's hull. Plecas put broadband sonar on the Command Post speakers, and a moment later, a deep rumbling sound indicated the American submarine had plowed into the ocean floor.

Cheers erupted in the Command Post, but Plecas didn't share the enthusiasm. He had sent a submarine crew to the bottom.

He stopped by the navigation table, examining water depth. Having just transited through the GIUK Gap, they were still in water just over two hundred meters deep, which meant any intact compartment in the American submarine wouldn't implode. The men in those compartments would survive, at least until their air turned toxic. Hopefully, the crew would be rescued before then.

Plecas turned his attention from the American submarine to his own. Following their torpedo launch, he had ordered *Kazan* to maximum speed and a new course in case the Americans counterfired. As expected, firing from such a close range had left them with insufficient time to respond.

"Steersman, ahead standard. Left ten degrees rudder, steady course one-eight-zero."

Kazan turned south as it slowed, quietly traversing away from the explosion reverberating through the ocean depths.

As *Kazan* began its trek toward the United States, Plecas reviewed the critical elements of his plan in his mind. Now that they had attacked an American submarine, Russia's Northern Fleet would no doubt wonder if *Kazan* was somehow involved and inquire. In the ensuing radio communications, his crew could not learn that their order to launch a missile strike against the United States was fake. Plecas had thought ahead, developing a contingency plan for this scenario.

"Attention in the Command Post," he announced. "Now that we have attacked an American submarine, the American Navy will be hunting us. We must take every measure to ensure we are not detected until we are in position to launch.

"One of those measures is complete radio silence. American surface warships and submarine hunter aircraft have radars that can detect a periscope or communications antenna once raised, and the Americans have satellites that can pinpoint radio transmissions at sea. We will make no transmissions, nor will we proceed to periscope depth to copy the broadcast. Any questions?"

There were none, and the watchstanders returned to their duties.

Plecas left his crew at Combat Stations, just in case there was another American submarine in the area.

32
WASHINGTON, D.C.

"The president wants us in the Situation Room."

Captain Glen McGlothin, the president's senior military aide, looked up as Chief of Staff Kevin Hardison stopped in his office doorway, delivering the news.

"What's up?" McGlothin asked.

"SecDef Drapac and OPNAV N97 are on the way from the Pentagon to brief the president."

McGlothin wondered what could be so important to warrant a visit by the secretary of defense and the Navy's Director of Undersea Warfare. Before he could ask, Hardison added, "Admiral Blaszczyk and Dawn Cabral are on the way too."

Something big was brewing. The Chief of Naval Operations was joining them, and the secretary of state's presence meant the issue had international implications.

"What's the topic?"

"They think USS *Pittsburgh* has been attacked by a Russian submarine."

McGlothin and Hardison were the first to arrive in the Situation Room, joined shortly by National Security Advisor Thom Parham, Secretary of State Dawn Cabral, and Press Secretary Lars Sikes. The president arrived moments later, followed by SecDef Tom Drapac and two admirals: Chief of Naval Operations Tom Blaszczyk, and the Director of Undersea Warfare, Rear Admiral Pat Urello. The president took his seat at the head of the table, joined by the eight other men and women in the Situation Room.

"For those who haven't been pre-briefed," Drapac began, "we believe one of our submarines has been attacked and possibly sunk. Admiral Urello is here to brief us."

Admiral Urello passed around a stack of briefs.

"USS *Pittsburgh,* a Los Angeles class fast attack, was on station in the Barents Sea, tasked with tracking Russian submarines." He flipped to the first page of the brief, which showed a map of the Barents Sea and Russia's Kola Peninsula. "Russia's newest Yasen class submarine, *Kazan,* departed Gadzhiyevo Naval Base earlier this week for her first deployment, and *Pittsburgh* began trailing her when she entered the Barents Sea.

"*Kazan* broke trail, and *Pittsburgh* and another U.S. submarine were repositioned along the transit lanes through the GIUK Gap in case *Kazan* entered the Atlantic, on her way to either a Mediterranean or U.S. East Coast deployment. *Kazan* was indeed detected transiting through the GIUK Gap by our SOSUS arrays, and *Pittsburgh* was vectored to regain trail. Shortly after we expected *Pittsburgh* to encounter *Kazan, Pittsburgh* ejected a SEPIRB buoy."

"SEPIRB buoy?" the president asked.

"A SEPIRB is a Submarine Emergency Position Indicating Radio Beacon, used to report the location of a submarine in distress. After reaching the surface, the SEPIRB buoy transmits a satellite distress message, reporting its position using a built-in GPS transponder."

"Do we know what happened to *Pittsburgh*?"

"We think so," Urello answered. "Shortly before the SEPIRB activated, our SOSUS arrays detected an underwater explosion, which we triangulated to *Pittsburgh*'s operating area. Analysis of the transient is consistent with the detonation of a heavyweight torpedo. Additionally, the explosion characteristics match those of several Russian variants, and not one of our Mark forty-eight torpedoes.

"We've sent several messages to *Pittsburgh,* directing her to report in, but we've heard nothing so far." Urello fell silent, letting those around the table digest the information and its implications.

"Are we certain *Pittsburgh* was sunk by *Kazan*?" the president asked.

"No, sir," Urello replied. "That's why we've issued a SUBMISS instead of a SUBSUNK. There are three submarine rescue alert levels," he explained. "A SUBLOOK message gets issued when a submarine fails to report in on time. Once there's reason to believe a submarine has sunk or is in distress, a SUBMISS goes out and we begin mobilizing rescue resources. Once we've confirmed a submarine has sunk, we issue a SUBSUNK. It's possible *Pittsburgh* is okay and unable to report in for some reason, but it's more likely she's been sunk. In submarine combat, the outcome is almost always a binary result. The torpedo either misses, or you get hit and sink."

"Assuming *Pittsburgh* was sunk, how long can the crew survive?"

"They have enough emergency supplies to keep the air viable for seven days. If they have electrical power, however, they can run their atmosphere control equipment and purify water, so they'd be okay until they run out of food, which would probably be a couple of weeks, since they're at the end of their Northern Run and food supplies would be running low. For now, we're assuming they have no power and time is critical."

Urello flipped to the next page of his brief, which showed a map of the GIUK Gap, with *Pittsburgh*'s operating area outlined in red.

"This is where we think *Pittsburgh* sank. Luckily, water depth is shallower than *Pittsburgh*'s crush depth, so crew members in intact compartments should be alive. Which gets me to our rescue plans."

Urello flipped the page.

He began with the resources most people were familiar with. "We used to have two Deep Submergence Rescue Vehicles, or DSRVs—*Avalon* and *Mystic*—which attached to a mother submarine for transit to the rescue location. However, the last DSRV was retired in 2008. Their replacement is the Submarine Rescue Diving and Recompression System, located at the Undersea Rescue Command in San Diego."

Urello went on to describe the submarine rescue system, which comprised three main components: an eighteen-person-capacity rescue module capable of descending two thousand feet, the rescue module launch and recovery system bolted to the deck of a support ship, and two hyperbaric chambers, each capable of decompressing thirty-four persons at a time.

"The equipment will be transported to Iceland and loaded onto a surface support ship, which should be on station where we believe *Pittsburgh* sank within . . ."—Urello checked his watch—". . . ninety-one hours."

"What do we tell the public?" Press Secretary Sikes asked. He looked to the president, who referred the question to Urello.

"For now," Urello answered, "I recommend we say nothing. It's not uncommon to issue a SUBLOOK, and on rare occasion we issue a SUBMISS and begin mobilizing rescue assets, sometimes just for a training exercise. Until we're confident *Pittsburgh* sank, I recommend we not mention anything unless we're queried."

"I agree," the president said. "Draft something for my review," he instructed Sikes, "in case the story breaks."

Turning his attention back to Rear Admiral Urello, the president asked, "Have we discussed this with any Russian officials?"

"No, sir. But they know we're looking for *Pittsburgh*. Russia is a member of ISMERLO, the International Submarine Escape and Rescue Liaison Office, which is a consortium of every country that operates submarines. They know we're mobilizing to rescue one of our submarines near the GIUK Gap. The critical question, assuming we're correct in our assumption that *Kazan* sank *Pittsburgh,* is whether the attack was authorized, or even directed by the Kremlin or the Russian naval command."

The president pondered Urello's question before responding. "I find it unlikely that whatever happened was authorized by President Kalinin, considering our assistance returning him to power a few months ago. It wouldn't surprise me, however, if an order was issued by a Russian admiral, considering how we devastated their Navy during their recent aggression. Payback, perhaps?"

It was a rhetorical question, which no one at the table could answer.

The president checked the clocks on the Situation Room wall, noting the time in Moscow: 4 p.m.

"Let's find out what Kalinin knows." He pressed the intercom button on the nearby phone, putting him through to the audiovisual technician.

"Place a call to President Kalinin."

33

MOSCOW, RUSSIA

With the afternoon sun streaming through tall Palladian windows behind him, president Yuri Kalinin addressed the man seated on the other side of his desk: Defense Minister Anton Nechayev, who had arrived a moment earlier per Kalinin's order.

"I just received a call from the American president," Kalinin said. "It appears that one of their submarines may have sunk near the GIUK Gap."

"We are aware," Nechayev replied. "The Americans issued a SUBMISS message, initiating submarine rescue operations. We have offered assistance and are standing by."

Kalinin replied, "The Americans believe their submarine was attacked by one of ours. There was supposedly an explosion in their submarine's operating area, with the acoustic characteristics of a Russian torpedo detonation." Kalinin paused, offering a disapproving scowl. "I expect to be kept abreast of critical issues. I should not have to learn from the American president that one of our submarines may have been involved in an altercation."

"That is just like the Americans," Nechayev replied with disdain, "blaming everything on Russia. We have only one submarine in the area, *Kazan,* on her way to a Mediterranean deployment. Her crew would not have engaged an American submarine without orders."

Nechayev paused to evaluate the way forward, quickly putting together a plan. "We will review the acoustic recordings near the GIUK Gap to confirm or deny the American allegation of a Russian torpedo explosion, and we will contact *Kazan*. But I can assure you, the

American submarine was not attacked by *Kazan* or any other Russian submarine."

Upon departing President Kalinin's office, Nechayev descended to the Kremlin basement and entered the intelligence center.

The senior officer on watch, Captain Second Rank Eduard Simonov, looked up from his console. "Good morning, Defense Minister. How can I help you?"

"Can you show me *Kazan*'s track?"

"Certainly," Simonov replied.

After entering several commands into his computer, the large display at the front of the intelligence center shifted to a map of the northern Atlantic Ocean, showing the location of all Russian naval forces. Just west of the GIUK Gap, a blinking blue circle displayed the projected position of the missing American submarine, reported by ISMERLO.

Simonov entered a few more commands, and two red features appeared: *Kazan*'s operating area in the Barents Sea, and a red track departing the operating area, which ran north of Iceland through the GIUK Gap, directly through the blinking blue circle, then south toward the Strait of Gibraltar before entering the Mediterranean Sea.

Nechayev turned to Simonov. "Order *Kazan* to report the status of their transit and any unusual incidents thus far."

34

MOSCOW, RUSSIA

President Yuri Kalinin entered the Kremlin conference room, joining his advisors seated around the table. To the president's right were Defense Minister Anton Nechayev and Foreign Minister Andrei Lavrov, while to his left sat Fleet Admiral Georgiy Ozerov and Nikolai Barsukov, director of Russia's Federal Security Service, one of the two main successors to the KGB and responsible for in-country counterintelligence, counterterrorism, and both military and civilian surveillance.

It had been twenty-four hours since *Kazan* was ordered to report in, and after sifting through the data, Nechayev had requested the meeting—and Director Barsukov's presence—to brief Kalinin on his conclusions.

Nechayev began the brief, opening the folder before him. "We have reviewed the American claim that one of their submarines was torpedoed by one of ours, and here's what we know. First, *Kazan* left several days ago on its maiden deployment to the Mediterranean, and its track took it through the area where the Americans claim their submarine was sunk."

Kalinin interrupted. "I assume *Kazan* was submerged during its transit, so how do we know its track?"

Nechayev turned to Fleet Admiral Ozerov, who explained. "On the surface, submarines are allowed to take whatever route they want to get from point A to point B. Once submerged, however, they follow a preplanned transit route, which prevents more than one of our submarines from traveling in the same waterspace."

Kalinin nodded his understanding and Nechayev continued. "We have also evaluated the American claim that a Russian torpedo detonated in their submarine's operating area. Our analysts agree. There was an explosion at the time and place the Americans claim, and its strength correlates to the explosive load of our heavyweight torpedoes.

"Also, we have directed *Kazan* to report in, but so far there has been no response."

Kalinin considered the information, then asked, "How do we know it wasn't *Kazan* that was torpedoed and the claim that one of their submarines has been sunk isn't an elaborate ruse by the Americans?"

"That's unlikely," Nechayev replied. "The torpedo explosion was characteristic of a Russian torpedo, not of an American one. American heavyweight torpedo warheads are loaded with an explosive compound called PBXN-105, which is slightly more powerful and produces a different bubble transient. Our analysts are confident that the torpedo that exploded was one of ours."

Still not convinced, Kalinin floated another explanation. "Perhaps there was a collision and *Kazan* was sunk or damaged, which explains why she hasn't responded, and one of her torpedoes detonated during the collision."

Nechayev shook his head. "The explosion was characteristic of an in-water detonation, not one inside a Torpedo Room. The torpedo was launched."

"There must be a rational explanation for what happened," Kalinin said. "Perhaps *Kazan* thought it was being attacked and fired in self-defense?"

Fleet Admiral Ozerov replied this time. "Then why hasn't she reported in?"

Kalinin fell silent and Nechayev waited as the president slowly accepted the most likely scenario.

Kazan had gone rogue.

Finally, Kalinin asked, "What are your recommendations?"

Nechayev replied, "First, we continue ordering *Kazan* to report in. Second, we examine every detail of *Kazan*'s deployment preparations to identify any anomalies. Third, and this is why I requested Director Barsukov's presence, we should investigate every member of *Kazan*'s crew, beginning with its commanding officer."

Kalinin nodded his concurrence. "Move quickly. We must determine why *Kazan*'s crew would attack an American submarine, and anything else they may have planned."

35
MOSCOW, RUSSIA

After spending the day with Natasha at Blokhin National Medical Research Center, Tatiana Plecas was preparing for bed when there was a knock on her hotel room door. Peering through the peephole, she spotted two men in the hallway, each wearing a suit beneath a heavy black overcoat.

"Who is it?" she asked without opening the door.

The closest man held a badge up to the peephole. "FSB," was the muffled response. "We need to talk, Mrs. Plecas."

Tatiana considered, just for a moment, not opening the door. The FSB, the successor to the KGB for domestic issues, was feared among the populace. Although some limits had been placed on the FSB's powers, the service had been controlled by KGB veterans and their disciples since its inception and had often been used as a weapon against *dissidents,* with the definition changing as the Kremlin saw fit. However, she decided that refusing to open the door would not turn out well.

She let the two men into the room. The first man, Nicholai Meknikov, introduced himself and his partner, Pyotr Sobakin, as Sobakin's eyes perused the hotel room furnishings.

"We have a few questions," Meknikov said. There was a small table and chair against the wall. "Please, have a seat."

Tatiana eased nervously into the chair as directed, facing Meknikov, who sat on the corner of the nearby bed. He pulled a smartphone from his suit jacket pocket and scrolled through notes as Sobakin wandered around the room, examining Tatiana's belongings. She thought about objecting, but said nothing.

Meknikov looked up from his notes. "I'm sorry to hear about your daughter's cancer, Tatiana. But I understand her new treatment holds promise."

"She's responding well," Tatiana replied, wondering why the FSB would be interested in Natasha.

"I understand the new drug is expensive. Do you happen to know the price?"

Tatiana recalled the meeting with Dr. Vasiliev at the hospital, and how distraught she'd been after learning how expensive the treatment was.

"Three hundred million rubles," she replied, concluding Meknikov already knew the answer: he took no notes.

"How did you obtain the money?"

"My husband has a friend, someone he served with on his first submarine. He's an executive in the oil and gas industry."

This time, Meknikov entered a comment into his smartphone. "What is your friend's name?"

"My husband didn't say."

There was a slight pause before Meknikov asked his next question, using a slightly accusatorial tone. "Your husband managed to obtain three hundred million rubles from a friend, and you didn't ask who he is?"

"It was very rushed. Aleksandr left only a few minutes later to return to Gadzhiyevo to take his submarine on its first deployment. He is the commanding officer of *Kazan,*" she added proudly.

"That is a very prestigious assignment." Meknikov smiled warmly, then asked his next question. "What else did your husband say about this friend?"

Tatiana searched her memory, but recalled no other details. "I've told you all I know."

Meknikov wrote another note, then looked up. "About your husband's deployment. I assume he has deployed many times during your marriage, yes?"

Tatiana nodded.

"Did you notice anything unusual this time? Did he behave any differently, meet with anyone new, or do anything out of the ordinary?"

It was a difficult question to answer, since her husband had been dealing with Natasha's illness. He had traveled to many hospitals searching for the best care, and had pleaded Natasha's case to anyone who might have the means to help.

"He spoke to many doctors, friends we had lost touch with, and all of our relatives, some of whom he had never met. But anything new was related to our daughter's illness, either arranging for her admittance to Blokhin Medical Center or obtaining the money for her treatment."

"Of course," Meknikov replied, adding another note. "We will contact you again at eight in the morning. By then, please make a list of everyone your husband spoke to concerning your daughter's treatment."

Meknikov glanced at Sobakin, who stood nearby, apparently finished poking around.

"Was there anything else unusual?" Meknikov asked. "Anything that caught your attention or seemed odd?"

Nothing occurred to her at first, but then she remembered her anniversary card. A card she had been directed to open early.

Tatiana shrugged. "He gave me an anniversary card I'm supposed to open one week early. When I asked why, he said there were preparations I need to make."

"Is the card here?"

Tatiana retrieved the card from her purse. She was about to hand it to Meknikov, then asked, "May I read it first?"

Meknikov nodded.

She opened the envelope, but instead of a card, inside was a handwritten letter.

As she read the letter, her hands began trembling, then tears formed in her eyes. When she finished, she handed the letter to Meknikov, then buried her face in her hands.

36

WASHINGTON, D.C.

Christine O'Connor entered the Situation Room in the West Wing basement, taking a seat at the conference table. On her way to CIA headquarters this morning, she had been diverted to the White House at the president's direction for an unscheduled meeting. Already seated around the table were SecDef Tom Drapac, SecState Dawn Cabral, National Security Advisor Thom Parham, and Captain Glen McGlothin, the president's senior military aide.

Chief of Staff Kevin Hardison, followed by the president, joined them in the Situation Room. After the president took his seat, he looked to SecDef Drapac.

"Go ahead, Tom."

"Good morning, Mr. President. The reason for this morning's meeting stems from USS *Pittsburgh*'s sinking and our assessment she was sunk by a Russian submarine. I spoke two hours ago with Defense Minister Nechayev, and he informed me that President Kalinin was planning on discussing the issue with you as well."

"We spoke an hour ago," the president replied. "Bring everyone up to speed."

Drapac glanced at the others around the table. "First, we've located *Pittsburgh* on the ocean floor, just northwest of Iceland, and there are survivors. We've detected mechanical transients at periodic intervals, which correlate to someone banging tools on the submarine's hull. Rescue assets have landed in Iceland and are being loaded onto a support ship, and we expect to send a rescue module down to *Pittsburgh* within the next eight hours.

"Regarding Russia's position on what happened, they've evaluated our assessment that *Pittsburgh* was sunk by a Russian submarine, and while they don't concur, they also don't disagree. They've conceded it's possible."

"Why do they think it's possible?" Captain McGlothin asked.

"That question gets me to the main reason for this morning's briefing. Defense Minister Nechayev informed me that they believe the commanding officer of their newest guided missile submarine, *Kazan*—the submarine *Pittsburgh* was trailing—has gone rogue. His daughter suffers from a rare cancer and the only viable treatment is an experimental drug that costs five million dollars. Someone paid the first half of the bill, and the Russians believe the second half will be paid after *Kazan* conducts some sort of operation.

"We think *Pittsburgh* regained *Kazan*'s trail after her transit through the GIUK Gap, and that *Kazan*'s commanding officer decided to attack. It appears he doesn't want a U.S. warship trailing him."

"Do we know what he's planning or when it will happen?" Christine asked.

"We don't know what he's planning, but we have an idea of when it will occur. *Kazan*'s commanding officer wrote a letter to his wife that she was supposed to deliver to Russia's Northern Fleet command in eight days, explaining that the actions about to be taken by *Kazan*'s crew are his responsibility alone—no one on the crew is aware that the deployment orders they're following are fake. He also wanted his letter to serve as proof that the Russian government wasn't involved so there would be no retaliation against Russia.

"That provides a few clues. First, whatever he's planning will occur in about eight days, and second—*Kazan* will be attacking an entity with the ability to retaliate against Russia. Unfortunately, that's a long list. An attack on any NATO country or even a non-ally could provoke a response. Additionally, *Kazan* could be headed almost anywhere—to the Mediterranean per her deployment orders or somewhere in the Atlantic."

"What kind of weapons does *Kazan* carry?" the president asked.

"*Kazan* is a cruise missile submarine carrying torpedoes and cruise missiles, with the current loadout being a mix of land-attack and anti-ship missiles. With the ordnance aboard, the list of potential targets is vast. We need more information.

"While we assist Russia in peeling this onion, my recommendation is to place our Atlantic Fleet on alert, focused on protecting our high-value warships—our carriers—from a potential torpedo or missile attack, and put a full-court press on finding *Kazan*."

"You mentioned that we'd be assisting Russia on this issue," Christine said. "Have specific arrangements been made?"

The president answered this time. "The Russians are working most of the leads—interviewing the crew's families and friends, plus reviewing the submarine's deployment preparations. So far, nothing noteworthy has been identified regarding any of *Kazan*'s crew aside from its commanding officer, who up to this point had a stellar, unblemished career and had been handpicked to take *Kazan* on its first deployment.

"Regarding who is ultimately responsible—who paid for the drug treatment—President Kalinin has agreed to accept our assistance due to the possibility *Kazan* might target the United States or a NATO ally, plus *Kazan*'s likely attack on *Pittsburgh*.

"That's where you come in, Christine. If we can identify who paid for the daughter's treatment, we might be able to discern the target. When it comes to corruption or terrorism, there's an adage—follow the money. Five million dollars had to leave a trail. Find it."

37

NORFOLK, VIRGINIA

In the U.S. Navy compound off Terminal Road, Vice Admiral Bill Andrea—Commander, Submarine Forces (COMSUBFOR)—was reviewing the latest proposals on his desk when there was a knock on his door. Andrea acknowledged and Captain Rick Current, his chief of staff, entered, holding a folder with a Top Secret coversheet.

"This just in from Fleet Forces Command," Current announced as he entered, handing the folder to Andrea.

Andrea read the message, noting the two items classified Top Secret: the assessment that USS *Pittsburgh* was sunk by *Kazan,* and that the Russian submarine's crew was likely following counterfeit orders drafted by its commanding officer. The directive section of the message was fairly straightforward and was summed up in Andrea's mind in two words.

Find *Kazan*.

COMSUBFOR had been assigned the lead, responsible for coordinating all Atlantic Fleet Anti-Submarine Warfare assets: submarine, surface ship, and air.

Andrea looked up at his chief of staff. "We need to put someone in charge of this effort. What are our options?"

Current ran down the list of senior Atlantic Fleet submarine officers, then recommended someone not on it. "All of these men are capable, but I recommend we assign Captain Murray Wilson. He's attached to a PAC Fleet submarine, but it's currently in the shipyard for repairs, so he's available. If you recall, he led a similar effort to locate *Kentucky* when she received the unauthorized launch order."

"That's an excellent idea," Andrea replied, recalling Wilson's effort.

Wilson was the most senior captain in the Submarine Force, having commanded the fast attack submarine USS *Buffalo,* and was now in command of the guided missile submarine USS *Michigan,* BLUE crew. In between the two command tours, he'd been the senior Submarine Command Course instructor, spending three years training every officer assigned to serve as a submarine commanding or executive officer. A few years ago, when COMSUBPAC had been tagged with coordinating a Fleet-wide effort to locate USS *Kentucky,* Wilson had led the successful effort.

"Coordinate with PAC to get Wilson over here as soon as possible."

38

BREMERTON, WASHINGTON

A light rain was falling as Captain Murray Wilson descended the concrete steps into the drydock at Puget Sound Naval Shipyard, a green foul-weather jacket protecting him from the Pacific Northwest's inclement weather. Waiting at the bottom of the drydock was Bill Sullivan, the shipyard supervisor assigned to the submarine's repair effort. *Michigan* had arrived at the shipyard three months ago, after a torpedo had blown a hole in its Missile Compartment.

While in the Black Sea, *Michigan* had been engaged by three Russian submarines and sank two, but a Russian torpedo had returned the favor, sending *Michigan* to the bottom. Fortunately, *Michigan* sank in shallow water and none of the intact compartments had imploded. Additionally, the service and emergency air banks had been fully charged, and Wilson's crew had pressurized the flooded compartment, blowing enough water back out of the hole for *Michigan* to rise from the bottom and engage the remaining Russian submarine.

The shipyard had just completed welding a hull patch, replacing the damaged section, which had been cut out, and few things made submariners queasier than having to take a submarine with a patched-up pressure hull down to Test Depth for the first time.

Sullivan escorted Wilson along the drydock, stopping amidships for a clear view of the hull patch. The coverings protecting the repair site from the elements had been kept in place, as had the scaffolding, providing the radiographers access to the welds. The hull patch hadn't been painted yet—it was just plain metal—and would remain so until the welds had been certified.

"How's the rest of the boat coming along?" Wilson asked.

Wilson spoke in submarine vernacular out of habit, referring to his submarine as a boat. He had learned early in his career that an easy way to insult Surface Warfare officers was to refer to their ships as boats. He'd heard the response often—*It's not a boat, it's a ship. The only boat we have is the Captain's gig.* However, submariners used the term affectionately. Although their submarine was technically a Navy ship, to them it was just *the boat*.

The inside of the boat—the Missile Compartment specifically—was still in pieces. In the Black Sea, they had blown most of the water from the compartment, and the electrical cables and essential components, which were designed to withstand full submergence pressure, had worked in the critical hours while engaging the last Russian submarine. However, there had still been six feet of water in the bilges, well above the lower level deck plates, and by the time *Michigan* pulled into the shipyard for repair, electrical shorts had begun plaguing the submarine. The corrosive effect of the seawater had begun taking its toll.

After evaluating the damage, the Navy decided to replace all of the wetted electrical cabling and equipment utilizing spare components, much of which had been in deep stow for twenty-five years, manufactured as the Ohio class construction program wound down in the 1990s. After three months in the shipyard, the rip-out was complete and they had begun installing and testing the replacement components, which would take a few more months.

Wilson spotted the submarine's duty officer hustling down the drydock steps with a classified message, which he handed to Wilson after catching up to the two men. Wilson was surprised at the message—he was being temporarily assigned to COMSUBFOR, directed to report no later than 8 a.m. tomorrow.

"Where are you going?"

Claire leaned against the doorframe, surprised to find her husband home from work early.

Wilson looked up from packing his suitcase. "Norfolk. I've been temporarily assigned to COMSUBFOR."

"What for?"

"My orders don't say. Temporary duty is all I know right now, although I suspect something is brewing. A SUBMISS message went out for *Pittsburgh* and rescue assets scrambled from San Diego a few days ago."

Claire folded her arms across her chest, examining her husband through smoky-gray eyes, her face framed with short blond hair that curled inward just above her shoulders. Even though she didn't say anything, after almost forty years of marriage, Wilson knew what she was thinking. They were supposed to leave in a few days to spend a week with their son, Tom, and the grandkids.

Wilson was older than most Navy captains because he was a *mustang:* a prior-enlisted reactor control technician rising to chief before receiving his commission.

After commanding USS *Buffalo* and training the Submarine Force's new commanding and executive officers, Wilson had made a difficult decision. He'd been selected for rear admiral, lower half. But riding a desk into the twilight of his career hadn't been appealing. After much discussion with his wife, he had turned down the star in favor of a final command at sea. Another sea tour meant more time away from his wife, but by then the kids were grown and on their own and Claire was well acclimated to Navy life. Nonetheless, he had asked for her blessing, and she had readily given it.

There were only a few available commands. Most of the Navy's submarines were skippered by commanders, with only four guided missile submarines being assigned to officers who had completed a successful command of a fast attack or ballistic missile submarine. The Commanding Officer of USS *Michigan* (BLUE crew) was due for relief and Wilson made the call. A few weeks later, he reported aboard, planning to enjoy a few years in command of one of the Navy's most formidable ships.

For the next few days, or however long his assignment to COMSUBFOR lasted, he'd leave his crew and submarine in the capable hands of his Executive Officer and his grandchildren in his wife's loving care.

Wilson finished packing and approached Claire, leaning in for a kiss. "Give my love to Tom and the kids."

39

GADZHIYEVO, RUSSIA

Andrei Voronin stood in the security center of Gadzhiyevo Naval Base's ordnance complex, eyeing the camera displays across the front wall. The complex was a frenzy of activity today, as every handler and supervisor had been called in for an urgent inventory of all ordnance in the complex. Did his supervisors have any idea of how many bombs, missiles, mines, and bullets were in these bunkers?

Compounding Voronin's irritation was that two of his most senior ordnance supervisors had stopped showing up to work a few days ago—not even providing a simple notice they were quitting—leaving him shorthanded directing the inventory.

Although the inventory was progressing slowly, it was going well. The weapon inventories completed thus far had totaled to the recorded quantities.

Two men in business suits entered the command post, and after questioning the nearest worker, headed toward Voronin. Upon reaching him, they flashed their identification: Federal Security Service.

"How are the inventories proceeding?" the older man asked.

Voronin relayed the results and answered additional questions posed by the agent. When the man asked if he had noticed any unusual behavior from any of the ordnance handlers or supervisors, Voronin saw an opportunity to make Bogdanov's and Morozov's lives difficult—an appointment with the FSB was one of the least pleasurable activities to have on one's itinerary.

He explained how the two men had abruptly stopped showing up for work a few days ago, and finished with, "Why don't you visit Bogdanov and Morozov, and invite them back to work. I could use their assistance."

One of the agents took down their names while the other inquired further, showing an unusual amount of interest in two men who had recently quit their jobs.

40
MCLEAN, VIRGINIA

Jake Harrison sat beside Pat Kendall on the main floor of the National Counterterrorism Center, surrounded by five dozen other men and women focused on their computer displays. The lead on Mixell had gone cold since the trip to Syria, and Harrison had spent the last few days assisting Kendall as she reviewed the thousands of files downloaded from Issad Futtaim's backup cloud server. Khalila, meanwhile, had been mostly absent. She had stopped by the NCTC on occasion for updates, during which Kendall took every opportunity to throw verbal barbs at her, which were mostly ignored.

Regarding Futtaim's files, more than a dozen analysts at Langley were scrutinizing the documents, while Kendall focused on whatever caught her eye, doling some out for Harrison's review. He was doing what he could to assist, but data mining wasn't his strong suit; he preferred to be out in the field.

The time spent with Kendall had been useful, though, picking up on the tricks of the trade, such as how to access information the general public assumed was confidential. That topic had become relevant when the NCTC's primary focus shifted yesterday from Mixell to Aleksandr Plecas, commanding officer of the Russian submarine *Kazan,* which had presumably attacked USS *Pittsburgh.* Plecas's daughter was ill and being treated with an extremely expensive experimental drug.

NCTC was coordinating with Russia to determine who paid for the drug, with both countries sharing information gathered along the way. The treatment provided to the girl was manufactured by Protek, a Russian pharmaceutical company, and the FSB had obtained the payment information: $2.5M from a numbered Swiss bank account with no account holder name.

"That looks like a dead end," Harrison had muttered upon learning the payment had been made from an unnamed Swiss account.

"Not true," Kendall replied. "Switzerland's Banking Act of 1934 prohibited Swiss banks from releasing information about private clients, or even to acknowledge the existence of private accounts. However, the law was amended and Swiss banks now cooperate with tax and criminal investigations. Thankfully, a lot of folks who want to keep their finances hidden aren't aware of the change."

NCTC's main display on the front wall flashed with an update: Protek had been paid via a transaction from Credit Suisse, which had just released the critical information. The payment was made from an account established less than two weeks ago by a man named Irepla Kram, who had made three more disbursements in addition to Protek: two payments of twenty million each, and a third payment of fourteen million dollars, all to other, nameless Swiss accounts.

The NCTC staff commenced a worldwide search for Irepla Kram. Nothing came up, although the Kram surname, of Jewish origin, was most popular in Germany, Poland, and the Czech Republic.

Kendall, meanwhile, was staring at the transactions, which listed the amount and the account the money was transferred to, and seemed to be focused on the last one.

The main display updated with additional information. Credit Suisse had released the account information for the other three transactions, in addition to the $2.5 million Protek payment. Two were transfers to unnamed personal accounts, while the third had sent money to a company named Arabian Securities, which was a Syrian investment company.

The display on the right updated next, showing information provided by Russia's FSB. They had been investigating two Russian government workers, Anatoly Bogdanov and Vasily Morozov, who had quit their jobs as ordnance supervisors at Gadzhiyevo Naval Base the day after *Kazan* deployed. Their location was unknown, with no database hits on their names since the day of the financial transactions.

The photographs and names of the two Russian men were moved adjacent to the two Swiss personal accounts and outlined in yellow. Kendall explained that the yellow outline meant the relationship between the two accounts and the Russian men was suspected but not confirmed.

As the NCTC analysts searched for more information regarding the three additional transactions, Harrison focused on the main account.

Irepla Kram.

There was something about the name that caught his attention, particularly the unusual first name.

Irepla.

After staring at it for a while, it dawned on him. He turned to Kendall.

"The account name. It's a semordnilap."

"A what?" Kendall asked.

Harrison's least favorite topic in school was English, but palindromes and semordnilaps had stuck in his mind since ninth grade English.

"A semordnilap is like a palindrome. A palindrome is a word or phrase that's the same whether it's spelled forwards or backwards, like *racecar* or *kayak,* while a semordnilap is a word that means something different when spelled backwards."

Harrison pointed to the name on the screen. "What do you get when you spell Irepla Kram backwards?"

Kendall focused on the display, her eyes widening when she made the mental translation.

Mark Alperi.

One of Lonnie Mixell's aliases.

But then a confused look spread across her face, no doubt created by the same question in Harrison's mind. What did Mixell have to do with a Russian captain and his submarine, and what were the other three payments for?

"That's why the last account number looked familiar!" Kendall exclaimed.

She turned to her computer and pulled up one of Futtaim's files, listing his financial accounts and investments. Among them was an account number beginning with the initials CS.

"CS must mean Credit Suisse," she said, "and the account number matches the fourth transaction, to the Syrian investment company, which must be a pass-through account for Futtaim."

Mixell had paid Futtaim *and* Protek, plus the two Russian government workers.

Kendall called one of the floor supervisors over to explain their discovery, while Harrison pondered the connection. What did Mixell, *Kazan,* two ordnance supervisors, a Syrian arms dealer, and the assassination of the United Nations ambassador have in common?

One of the supervisors from the second floor descended, stopping in front of the main display, a laser pointer in her hand. Jessica Del Rio was her name, from the Office of the Director of National Intelligence, which was the lead organization running the NCTC.

"Attention on the floor," she announced.

When she had everyone's attention, a dendrite chart appeared on the center display, with the information for each Credit Suisse account posted beside a photograph, along with the man's name and known aliases. The top level of the chart listed the primary account beside Mixell's picture. Beneath Mixell, the beneficiaries of the four transactions were listed: Plecas, Futtaim, Bogdanov, and Morozov, with Futtaim's picture outlined in red, which Kendall explained indicated Futtaim was deceased.

"It looks like Mixell is connected to *Kazan,*" Del Rio said, "and we need to figure out why and what the other three payments were for. We're already looking for Mixell, but focus on these other two men as well." She pointed her laser at Bogdanov and Morozov. "They're likely traveling under aliases and could be anywhere on the planet by now. Determine their aliases and distribute their pictures to all facial recognition capable networks, highest priority.

"One last item. The money deposited into Mixell's account came from outside Credit Suisse. Follow the trail backward and identify the financial institution involved, then have a conversation with those folks."

41

NORFOLK, VIRGINIA

It was 8 a.m. on a cold and drizzly day, eighteen hours after he'd been handed new orders in the drydock in Bremerton, when Captain Murray Wilson stepped into the headquarters of Commander, Submarine Forces. He was greeted immediately by Captain Rick Current, Admiral Andrea's chief of staff, who escorted him to the admiral's conference room, where the senior COMSUBFOR staff were already assembling for the morning meeting.

Current introduced the N-heads—Navy captains responsible for specific areas, such as N1 (manpower) and N3 (operations)—and they were joined by Admiral Bill Andrea, who took his seat at the head of the table.

Captain Dwayne Thomas, the COMSUBFOR operations officer, led the brief, explaining the situation: the Navy's conclusion that USS *Pittsburgh* had been sunk by *Kazan,* the background on the Russian submariner's daughter and the $2.5M payment for her treatment, plus the letter to his wife indicating he was planning something that would occur in about a week.

When the brief concluded, Admiral Andrea took over, directing his comments to Wilson. "As you can see, we need to locate *Kazan* and potentially neutralize her before her crew executes whatever they've got planned. You did an excellent job tracking down *Kentucky* a few years ago, and we're looking at a similar effort here. My staff is at your disposal, as are all Atlantic Fleet ASW assets. We'll have to work through COMSURFLANT and COMAIRLANT, as well as the numbered Fleets, but they'll be expecting orders from us. Do you have any questions?"

Wilson had quite a few, but figured most would be answered after analyzing *Kazan*'s projected position and the Anti-Submarine Warfare (ASW) assets available. The meeting concluded, and Wilson followed Thomas into the operations center, where they examined a large display on the front wall showing the location of all Atlantic Fleet submarines.

Wilson asked Thomas, "Can you pull up all Atlantic Fleet ASW assets?"

"Certainly," he replied, then relayed the request to the operations center watch officer.

The display updated, adding surface warships and maritime patrol aircraft—submarine hunter versions of Boeing's 737 jetliner—armed with lightweight torpedoes.

Wilson focused first on the assets that were already at sea. There were five Atlantic Fleet submarines on deployment, although one was in the Persian Gulf with the *Truman* Carrier Strike Group, both on loan to Pacific Fleet. Four more submarines were underway in the local operating areas, giving Wilson eight submarines that could be immediately repositioned. Another eighteen were in port, most of which could get underway within twenty-four hours; deployment orders had been sent yesterday afternoon to all submarines not in deep maintenance.

The Surface Fleet was in a similar position, with only a portion of its ships at sea. In addition to the *Truman* CSG in the Persian Gulf, the aircraft carrier *Abraham Lincoln,* fresh out of the shipyard after repairing the damage received during America's war with China, was in the middle of a COMPTUEX—a pre-deployment training exercise with its escort ships—just off the East Coast.

The good news was that there were six squadrons of P-8A maritime patrol aircraft available for immediate employment.

Next, Wilson located the SURTASS ships, best described as mobile versions of the fixed SOSUS arrays mounted on the ocean floor, trailing towed arrays over a mile long. But there were only two ships in the Atlantic Ocean.

Wilson then directed the operations center watch officer to populate the display with NATO ASW assets. Unfortunately, Canada had no submarines underway and the British subs at sea were near Great Britain, well behind *Kazan* and on the wrong side of her most likely direction of travel, assuming she was headed toward the Mediterranean or the U.S. East Coast. There were a few NATO submarines in the Mediterranean Sea, mostly in the eastern sector near Syria, which would come in handy if *Kazan* was headed their way.

Given the forces immediately available, Wilson analyzed the scenario, reluctantly coming to a disappointing conclusion, which he explained to Thomas.

"The last datum we have for *Kazan*'s location is three days old. Even if we assume a speed no greater than ten knots, we're dealing with a transit radius of over seven hundred miles. Any containment we establish at this point will be too porous; the arc is simply too long. We can't get enough P-8As, submarines, and surface ships in place fast enough."

Wilson added, "We'll put together the best perimeter possible, but at this point, detecting *Kazan* is going to take some luck. In the meantime, let's mobilize everything available. Send orders to surge all Atlantic Fleet ASW assets to sea. As soon as you can pull it together, I need a list of all deployable units, when they'll get underway, and what port they're deploying from."

Wilson studied the operations center display as he planned ahead.

"Find out if we can get the *Truman* strike group back from PAC. If so, route her into the Med via the Suez Canal to deal with *Kazan* if that's where she's headed. If not, we'll pull the strike group into the Atlantic to assist.

"Also ask PAC Fleet for as many P-8 squadrons as possible. Based on the Russian captain's letter to his wife, we're looking at a scenario where we'll need the extra squadrons for only a week or two, so pry as many away from PAC as possible.

"Let's get going. We need assets, and we need them at sea."

42

SOCHI, RUSSIA

Sochi, located on the eastern shore of the Black Sea, is a palm-tree-speckled sliver of land in the southwestern corner of the Russian Federation. Part of the Caucasian Riviera, Sochi is one of the few places in Russia with a subtropical climate, with the scenic Caucasus Mountains rising to the east and pebble-sand beaches to the west surrounding a vibrant city with a bustling nightlife. With more villas, palm trees, and yachts than any other location in Russia, Sochi is Russia's largest and most popular resort city.

Anatoly Bogdanov strolled down the sidewalk with his hands in his pockets, enjoying the warm weather, a wonderful change from the frigid temperatures in his former home of Gadzhiyevo. He had spent his entire life in a town inside the Arctic Circle, and looked forward to living where he could venture outside wearing slacks and an open-collared shirt for most of the year. With ten million U.S. dollars in the bank and another ten million due after *Kazan*'s missile launch—over one billion rubles—Bogdanov also looked forward to a life of luxury.

His co-conspirator in the effort, Mikhail Korenev, who had provided the nuclear warhead arming code, hadn't revealed where he planned to move, but Bogdanov had gleaned enough to determine it was somewhere in South America. Although spending the rest of his life in a tropical foreign country had its appeal, the language barrier was a challenge he'd rather not deal with. Plus, he figured he'd blend in more easily in Sochi than in a foreign country. Anyone looking for him in South America would just have to ask, "Are there any rich Russians living nearby?" In Sochi, rich Russians were half of the population.

Bogdanov was traveling under a second alias the American had provided, with the funding deposited into an account using the first alias, so there was no direct connection between him and the account, in case the owner was discovered by authorities. He was also keeping a low profile, paying only in cash and venturing from his hotel only when required: to a nearby restaurant, or to accompany a real estate agent who was showing him the available properties worthy of a man with Bogdanov's resources.

He was running low on money tonight, so he stopped by an ATM to withdraw a few thousand rubles. Armed with enough cash for the next few days, and looking forward to a superb dinner, Bogdanov checked in with the maître d' of a nearby five-star restaurant.

43

MCLEAN, VIRGINIA

Jake Harrison took a sip of lukewarm coffee, taking a break from assisting Kendall with Issad Futtaim's files. The work was tedious, searching for clues to what Mixell had purchased from the Syrian arms dealer and where it had been shipped. Harrison had provided one helpful hint—you didn't put fourteen million dollars' worth of weapons in a backpack. Whatever Mixell purchased was either large, or a lot of them, and there had to be some sort of shipping involved. If they could figure out the shipping, they could track down what Mixell bought, which would hopefully lead them to Mixell.

The dendrite chart of Mixell's money trail had been moved to a side display and updated with additional information as it was discovered, and the main display suddenly updated with a man's picture, which created a buzz in the NCTC. The picture matched the photograph of Anatoly Bogdanov, one of the two Russian government workers who had abruptly quit their jobs, and whom Mixell had presumably paid twenty million dollars.

Bogdanov had withdrawn money from an ATM in Sochi, Russia, three hours ago, apparently unaware that most ATMs took a picture of each person making a withdrawal. Facial recognition programs had identified him as Bogdanov, although the account was in a different name.

Jessica Del Rio descended from the second floor again, stopping before the main display.

"We've identified one of the two Russian government workers Mixell paid. Let's get this guy before the Russians do. I want whatever this guy knows firsthand, not just what Russia decides to share. It's not that we don't trust the Russians, it's just that . . . we don't trust the Russians."

Del Rio's comment elicited a few chuckles from the analysts on the floor before she continued. "I want all agency officers and agents who speak Russian in Sochi by sunrise. I want someone on every corner of the city. If this guy steps onto the street for so much as a cup of coffee, I want him."

Harrison turned to find Khalila, who had entered the NCTC during the brief. He wondered if Khalila's visit for an update happened at an opportune time, or if she'd somehow obtained advance notice they had located Bogdanov.

She pulled him aside, away from Kendall. "You speak Russian, correct?"

"Yes. Why do you ask?"

"You heard Del Rio. She wants every officer and agent who speaks Russian in Sochi by tomorrow morning. That includes you." Then she smiled. "And me."

That wasn't the arrangement Harrison had understood from his conversation with the DDO. Khalila would accompany him whenever he needed her linguistic skills, not the other way around. However, he was new to the agency and still had a lot to learn; he didn't even know how to make the necessary travel arrangements.

"Okay. I'll let the DDO know we're heading to Sochi."

"It's best if we not mention anything to the DDO until we land in Sochi. He doesn't let me out in the field very often. But it's what I do best." She placed her hand on his arm. "When it comes to the DDO, it's easier to ask for forgiveness than for permission."

Harrison had to admit that having Khalila accompany him would be convenient. Besides, if he said no, he'd probably be assigned another officer, since he still didn't know his way around. He was getting a feel for Khalila, and liked most of what he saw. The most important factor was—she was pretty good in the field.

"Okay," Harrison said. "We go together."

"I'll make the travel arrangements," Khalila offered. "Meet me at Reagan National in an hour."

Khalila departed and Harrison returned to his workstation beside Kendall.

"Let me guess," she said. "Khalila wants to accompany you to Sochi, even though she's not authorized for that area."

Harrison nodded.

"I don't get it," she said. "Khalila breaks the rules and gets away with it every damn time. If I pulled half the crap she did, the DDO would have my ass."

"Maybe he expects more of you," Harrison offered.

"Yeah, right. If I don't keep my nose clean, I'll end up back on the street where I started."

Kendall turned back to her computer display. "It's your life," she said. "Good luck with it."

44

SOCHI, RUSSIA

Darkness was falling as the Dassault Falcon 8X descended toward Sochi International Airport, nearing the end of a twelve-hour flight. Harrison was seated beside Khalila, and unlike their trip to Damascus a week ago, carrying only Harrison, Khalila, and Durrani, all seats were filled. The fourteen intelligence agencies staffing the NCTC had followed Del Rio's direction, assigning all available Russian-speaking personnel to the effort to track down Anatoly Bogdanov in Sochi, with additional personnel on their way.

Harrison spent much of the trip picking Khalila's brain about CIA matters: protocol, procedures, and relationships, during which Khalila explained the difference between agents and officers. Although the FBI and other agencies employed agents, CIA employees were officers, and agents were the foreign folks they recruited to supply information. She went on to explain the distinction between reports officers and desk officers, and the different types.

Their case manager, Asad Durrani, for example, was a reports officer whose official title was collection management officer. Durrani had met them at the airport in Virginia, providing their Sochi point-of-contact details.

The Falcon 8X landed and pulled to a halt near a private hangar, where they were met by three separate cars. Harrison and the other passengers descended the staircase to the tarmac and broke into three groups. Although the fourteen agencies staffing the NCTC worked together, they had separate chains of command and infrastructure.

A man leaning against a black sedan matched the description Durrani had provided, and Harrison and Khalila approached him. He introduced himself as Maxim Anosov, lead CIA paramilitary officer in Sochi. After Harrison and Khalila tossed their luggage into the trunk and climbed into the back of the sedan, they began the short drive to the CIA safe house in the city.

Along the way, Anosov explained the plan to locate Bogdanov. The city had been divided into sectors assigned to the fourteen agencies, which was then subdivided based on the number of personnel available. Although Jessica Del Rio had wanted someone on every corner, she apparently didn't have an appreciation for Sochi's size: a city of more than three hundred thousand people, sprawled across thirteen hundred square miles. Even with a thousand agents and case officers descending on the city, each would be assigned an area of greater than a square mile.

"We've also got officers canvassing the hotels, restaurants, and grocery stores. The guy's gotta eat and sleep."

"I've got another idea," Harrison said. "Rather than park us on a corner and hope Bogdanov wanders by, I'd like to try and track him down."

Anosov's eyes met Harrison's in the rearview mirror. "What's your plan?"

"I figure Bogdanov picked Sochi for a reason. He's got a big chunk of cash in his account, and he's not going to spend it buying coffee every morning. He'll be looking for a nice place. I'd like to start with the high-end real estate agents and see if anyone new has expressed interest within the last week."

"I like it," Anosov said. "I'll have the city zone assignments redrawn, freeing you and Khalila to run amok." He grinned, then spoke in Russian. "How's your Russian?"

Harrison replied in kind, "My mom says it's pretty good."

"I have to agree," Anosov replied, returning to English. "No accent at all. Plus, you look Russian enough. If you need to blend in for some reason, you can pull it off." His eyes shifted to Khalila. "No hope for you posing as Russian, but there are plenty of Muslim women in Sochi."

"I'm not Muslim," Khalila replied with an edge to her voice.

Anosov's eyes moved back to Harrison. "Is she always this touchy?" he asked in Russian.

"Usually," Harrison replied.

They entered the outskirts of Sochi, approaching the coast. Site of the 2014 Winter Olympics, Sochi had been the beneficiary of fifty billion dollars of infrastructure investment. The crumbling Soviet-era apartment blocks so ubiquitous in other Russian cities were few and far between, replaced with luxurious seaside hotels connected to an ever-expanding ski resort in the mountains by a new superhighway, over which cab drivers zoomed at over one hundred kilometers per hour. Along the shoreline, several cruise ships were anchored in the emerald-blue water, while sleek white yachts rocked gently at their moorings.

Anosov pulled into the underground garage of the CIA safe house, a four-story building in the older part of Sochi that had been renovated into a condominium. Anosov led them into one of the suites, a four-bedroom flat that seemed to serve as the safe house headquarters; the expansive living room was missing the typical furnishings, filled instead with a dozen men and women working at computer workstations.

Harrison spoke Russian but couldn't read Cyrillic, so Anosov had one of the officers help him research real estate agents, making a list of those specializing in properties selling for more than one hundred million rubles. There were a half-dozen agencies, all clustered within a five-block radius in the Tsentralny City District, a triangular region in the center of the city bordering the Black Sea. All six realtors were *by appointment only,* so Harrison made the calls. Several had no appointments available today until Harrison mentioned how much he was willing to spend: three hundred million rubles.

The six appointments were arranged, and a driver dropped Harrison and Khalila off near the southernmost realtor on the list. Harrison wore a blue sport coat and khaki slacks, both to project the image of a wealthy client and to hide his pistol in its shoulder harness. Khalila wore a business suit again, a pistol likewise beneath her jacket, plus the two spring-loaded knives she had carried in Damascus, one attached to each forearm.

The first two appointments were a bust, but their luck changed on the third. The realtor recognized the photo Harrison showed him, although the man went by a different name—Danil Andreyev. Harrison wrote down the alias and asked for the man's phone number, hoping to determine Bogdanov's approximate location during a cell phone call, but the realtor had even better news.

"When I show him properties, I pick him up outside the lobby of the Rodina Grand Hotel."

Khalila pulled up a map on her cell phone; the hotel was only three blocks away.

Harrison called Anosov as they left the realtor's office, relaying the news, and it wasn't long before he and Khalila entered the lobby of the Rodina Grand Hotel.

They were greeted at the counter by a well-manicured woman in her fifties, who asked how she could help.

"We're meeting a friend tonight, Danil Andreyev. Please let him know we're here."

The woman looked him up on the computer, and as she reached for the phone, Harrison pressed her hand down on the receiver. "Better yet, if you could let us know what room he's in, we can visit for a while before heading out to dinner."

"I'm sorry," she replied. "I can't provide guest information."

Since neither he nor Khalila had any official Russian agency identification they could use to encourage cooperation from the woman, he acquiesced.

As she picked up the phone, the woman asked, "Whom shall I say is waiting?"

"Petr Sokolov," Harrison replied, providing the realtor's name. "Let him know that a new property has come available that will suit his desires exactly. It won't stay on the market long, but if we stop by tonight, he'll have the first opportunity to view and place a contract on it."

The woman made the call, but there was no answer.

She tried again. Still no answer.

45

SOCHI, RUSSIA

Anatoly Bogdanov, seated alone at a table for two, leaned back in his chair, wiping his mouth with a cloth napkin. Rather than eating at one of the hotel's restaurants, he had ventured out for dinner tonight, selecting the most expensive restaurant in the city. The meal was exquisite and well worth the price: terrine of quail breast with shiitake mushrooms to start, followed by veal medallions in raspberry truffle sauce, then sea scallops with pureed artichoke hearts. He had skipped dessert, since he was carrying several extra pounds and had decided to shed the weight. As a new—and wealthy—bachelor in Sochi, he was certain there would be a few attractive women vying for his attention, and getting into shape wouldn't hurt.

After leaving the restaurant, he returned to his hotel, not far away. Upon entering the lobby, his attention was immediately drawn to two persons at the counter: a tall Arab woman and a well-built Caucasian man. What caught his eye was that both of them locked their gaze on to him almost simultaneously.

He turned around and stepped back onto the sidewalk, increasing his pace. He glanced over his shoulder to spot the man and woman exit the hotel, then head in his direction.

His pulse began racing. Somehow, he had been tracked down, and he wondered whether he was being followed by Russian authorities or mercenaries hired by the American to eliminate loose ends. Either way, he had to give them the slip, followed by a trip to someplace far away. South America sounded like an excellent idea after all.

Bogdanov glanced over his shoulder again. The man and woman were catching up.

As he passed a dark opening along the street, he bolted into the alley. He had no idea where it led, but there wasn't time to formulate a plan; he'd have to make things up as he went.

The man and woman were sprinting down the alley behind him, and by the sound of their footsteps, were gaining on him.

Ahead, a brick wall loomed. He had charged into a dead end.

The wall was only three meters tall, though, so he gave it a go. He jumped and got a grip on the top with both hands, then struggled to pull himself over as the man and woman closed the distance. With one final heave, he got his hips over the top and he spilled onto the ground on the other side. After pushing himself to his feet, he sprinted down the alley. His lungs were burning and his legs felt like rubber, but the adrenaline coursing through his body kept him going.

Behind him, the man had been in the lead, but the woman was over the wall first, leaping over the top like a freakin' cat. The man followed, catching up to the woman, while both gained on him. It was obvious he was going to lose this footrace.

Up ahead was a building being renovated, illuminated by a string of construction bulbs dangling from the exterior. He broke through the yellow barrier tape into the unfinished ground floor, disappearing into the darkness shortly after entering. He stopped behind a column to catch his breath, peering around it as the man and woman entered the building. Each was silhouetted by the alley lights; both had a pistol drawn and one went left while the other moved right.

As Bogdanov's eyes adjusted to the darkness, he examined the rest of the ground floor. It looked like he was in the lobby of an old hotel. He searched for exits, but found only one—the entrance he had come through. He debated whether to hide in the building or keep moving, then decided on the latter. Much of the building interior had been torn out, leaving nowhere he could successfully hide if the man or woman passed nearby. His only hope was to leave through the entrance unnoticed.

The lobby between him and the alley was fairly well lit from the construction lights, and he had to choose between a quick dash into the alley or a slow, stealthy journey across the floor. Neither the man nor woman were visible; they must have moved deeper into the building.

He took a deep breath, trying to calm his nerves, then took a few tentative steps toward the alley, doing his best to move silently. He was halfway across the open space when a man's voice reached out to him.

"Stop where you are," the man said in Russian.

He stopped and turned toward the voice, spotting the man with a pistol pointed at him. He heard movement behind him and turned as the woman raised her pistol toward him as well.

Bogdanov raised his hands. "Don't shoot!"

Harrison was about to approach the man when an uneasy feeling swept over him; alarms were going off in the back of his mind. He scanned the surroundings for anything amiss, his eyes settling on Khalila, who was staring at him. It was then that he noticed Khalila's aim was off by a few degrees. Her pistol wasn't pointed at Bogdanov, it was aimed at him.

He pieced everything together in a split second. He had learned too much. During the meeting with the first Syrian arms dealer, Khalila had revealed she wasn't an ordinary woman—she had some sort of status in the Arab world. He recalled Kendall's words the day they met at Langley—*Be careful while working with Khalila. Her partners have a habit of ending up dead.*

Khalila's arm was extended, her pistol aimed at him, but she hadn't pulled the trigger. As he wondered why, he saw the indecision in her eyes.

Harrison considered adjusting his aim and neutralizing Khalila with a bullet in her firing shoulder, which should provide enough time to subdue her. But if he swung his pistol toward her, she'd be forced to decide and would likely pull the trigger. Harrison concluded the better option was to talk his way out.

"I don't care who you are or what you've done, Khalila; only whether you're well trained and that you've got my back. I'm certain of the first. What about the second?"

Khalila didn't answer, and he could tell she was struggling with her decision.

"If you shoot," Harrison said, "you had better take me out with the first bullet."

Bogdanov interjected. "It looks like you two have some things to work out. I don't want to complicate things, so I'll be on my way."

Harrison replied in Russian with his eyes still on Khalila, "Take one step and I'll put a bullet in both knees."

Bogdanov raised his palms in a placating gesture. "I'm happy right here."

Harrison addressed Khalila again. "Make up your mind."

Khalila's aim remained steady, but a sheen of perspiration had formed on her face.

Maxim Anosov and two other men surged into the building, pistols drawn. When they saw that Khalila and Harrison had the situation in hand, with Bogdanov pinned between them, they holstered their weapons.

Khalila did the same, slipping her pistol into the shoulder holster inside her business suit, then retreated deeper into the building, disappearing into the darkness.

"Well done, Harrison," Anosov said. "One of my men spotted your pursuit and we got here as soon as possible. We'll take it from here."

The other two men approached Bogdanov, each grabbing an arm. They escorted him toward the exit as a van pulled up outside the hotel. A side door slid open, shutting again once Bogdanov and the two men were inside.

Anosov looked around, presumably for Khalila, who was nowhere to be found.

"Join us at the safe house," he said, then he jumped into the passenger seat of the van, which turned around and headed toward the main street.

Harrison searched the surroundings for Khalila, spotting her in the shadows, seated on a worn bench pushed up against the wall, bent over with her face in her hands. He started toward her, his pistol still drawn. As he approached, Khalila gave no indication she noticed. He stopped in front of her and she still didn't acknowledge his presence. After evaluating how best to proceed, he holstered his weapon and sat beside her.

Khalila still had her face in her hands, and Harrison noticed her slow, steady breathing.

"Look at me, Khalila."

She sat up, placing her back against the wall. It was hard to tell in the darkness, but there didn't appear to be any emotion on her face; just the glint of her eyes, focused on him.

Harrison had already decided he wasn't going to work with Khalila again. But he needed to ensure he made it back to the U.S. alive, and without being forced to kill her along the way.

"I don't have a beef with you, Khalila. There's a saying, 'What happens on travel, stays on travel.' I intend to follow that rule while working with you. Anything I learn about you is no one else's business. Your secrets are safe with me. In return, I need to be able to trust you; know that you've got my back."

There was no visible reaction from Khalila, who said nothing as she stared at him.

"Deal?" Harrison asked, extending his hand to shake on it.

After a long moment, Khalila nodded, then stood and walked away, leaving Harrison with an outstretched hand.

He closed it into a fist.

46

SOCHI, RUSSIA

One of the safe house condominium flats had been converted into a small detention center: several single-person cells, plus two interrogation rooms, each with an observation booth along one wall, separated by a one-way mirror. Bogdanov was seated by himself in one of the interrogation rooms while Harrison and a few others had filed into the observation booth, awaiting the arrival of a CIA interrogator. They were sending the best, Anosov had said, who would arrive shortly.

Khalila entered the observation booth and sat beside Harrison as if nothing untoward had happened three hours ago. After their discussion in the gutted building, when they had made *the deal,* she had walked off into the darkness. Harrison had called for a ride back to the safe house, and as he made his way to the main boulevard paralleling the Black Sea shoreline, Khalila had appeared by his side. Neither spoke during the short ride to the safe house.

As he sat beside her, several emotions swirled inside; mostly anger and curiosity. What secrets was she keeping, and what kind of experiences produced someone who could kill her partner simply for having gleaned a tidbit about her? He suddenly realized that when Khalila convinced him to bring her to Sochi, it had been a setup. She'd been planning to kill him all along. In Damascus, after the jump into the Barada River, Khalila had lost her pistol. If she had retained it, he doubted he would have made it out of the culvert alive. When the trip to Sochi presented another opportunity, she had taken it.

The door to the observation booth opened and Anosov entered, accompanied by a large, barrel-chested man well over six feet tall and north of 250 pounds. Anosov made the introduction—CIA interrogator John

Kaufmann—who asked everyone in the booth if they had any information about Bogdanov that might prove useful. Harrison and Khalila, plus the two men who had hauled Bogdanov into the van, were the only ones who had interacted with him, but their contact had been brief and none seemed to have anything to offer.

Kaufmann entered the interrogation room and sat across from Bogdanov at the small wooden table. He placed a leather satchel beside him, from which he pulled a manila folder. He flipped through its contents in silence, ignoring Bogdanov. The Russian was unrestrained, but he wasn't near as large as Kaufmann, plus it was obvious the larger man was carrying a weapon: there was a slight bulge near his left shoulder beneath his sport coat.

When he finished reviewing the file, Kaufmann pulled a pack of cigarettes and a lighter from his satchel. He offered a cigarette to Bogdanov, who shook his head.

"I'll get straight to the point," Kaufmann said. "What were you paid 1.2 billion rubles for?"

"I don't know what you're talking about."

"There's a 1.2 billion ruble deposit to an account in your name that says otherwise."

"That's a lie. I don't have that kind of money."

Kaufmann pulled a sheet from his folder and slid it toward Bogdanov, then pointed to the first transaction. "A man named Lonnie Mixell—you probably know him as Mark Alperi—deposited 1.2 billion rubles to an account owned by Matvey Petrov." Kaufmann pointed to the second transaction. "Petrov then withdrew ten million rubles, which was deposited on the same day into an account owned by Danil Andreyev, which is the name you're currently using."

"Of course it's the name I'm currently using. It *is* my name."

"We'll go with that for now," Kaufmann said. "So who is Matvey Petrov?"

"He's an old friend of mine."

"Why did he transfer ten million rubles to your account?"

"You'll have to ask him."

"That's the thing," Kaufmann replied. "I kinda am. Your real name is Anatoly Bogdanov, a former ordnance supervisor at Gadzhiyevo Naval

Base, who is using two aliases to prevent being tracked down while you spend 1.2 billion rubles into your twilight years."

Bogdanov didn't immediately respond, but Harrison noticed the Russian swallowing hard.

"If you don't want to make things more difficult for yourself, you can start by telling me what the payment from Mixell was for."

"I have no idea what you're talking about. I don't know anyone named Mixell or Bogdanov, nor why Mixell paid Petrov."

"You are in *serious* trouble," Kaufmann said. "If you don't want to spend the rest of your life behind bars, I suggest you be more forthcoming about who you are and what you were paid to do."

"I'm done talking," Bogdanov replied. "Either charge me with a crime and provide a lawyer, or release me."

Kaufmann kept up the pressure, providing more evidence that the man across from him was indeed Anatoly Bogdanov, who had been paid 1.2 billion rubles by Lonnie Mixell. Bogdanov refused to acknowledge the obvious, steadfastly sticking to the story that he was Danil Andreyev.

After staring at Bogdanov for a while, Kaufmann pushed up from the table and left the interrogation room, then stepped into the observation booth. He spoke quietly with Anosov for a moment, who then left.

Kaufmann announced, "Time for plan B. Everyone into the interrogation room."

There were several wooden chairs along the sides of the room, and Harrison and Khalila sat on one side, while the two men who had stuffed Bogdanov into the van took seats across the room. Kaufmann removed his sport coat, revealing his pistol in a shoulder harness, which immediately caught Bogdanov's attention.

Kaufmann resumed the interrogation, bringing Harrison and Khalila into the conversation, asking Bogdanov why he had tried to evade them. Bogdanov concocted a story of how he thought they were going to mug him, and had tried to run away. Kaufmann tried several tactics, which produced the same result. Bogdanov remained resolute. He was Danil Andreyev, and had been his entire life.

Finally, Kaufmann reached across the table and placed a meaty hand behind Bogdanov's head, then smashed his face into the table. Bogdanov sprung back up with a glazed look as blood oozed from his nose. His eyes cleared, then hardened.

"I'm not saying another word."

Bogdanov seemed rather smug considering the circumstances, blood running down his face, his fingers interlaced as his hands rested on the table before him.

Khalila suddenly stood and approached Bogdanov. She flexed her left wrist, releasing one of her knives into her hand. She reached over Bogdanov's shoulder, driving the knife through his left forearm, pinning it to the table.

Bogdanov shrieked in pain as she stepped beside him, releasing the second knife into her other hand. She placed it against Bogdanov's neck.

"You had better start talking, or I'm going to fillet you like a fish."

Bogdanov looked up at her with a terrified, but otherwise blank look on his face, and Khalila apparently remembered that Bogdanov spoke only Russian. She looked toward Kaufmann and Harrison.

"Would someone translate for me!"

Kaufmann shot Khalila an irritated look. "Do you *mind*!" he said in English. "*I'm* doing the interrogation here!"

Harrison stood and grabbed Khalila by the arm, then pulled her into the passageway between the two interrogation rooms where they could talk in private.

"You can't do this kind of thing."

"I don't need your permission, Jake." She yanked her arm away. "I should've known you'd get in the way again."

Harrison keyed on the usual wording. "Again?"

"I read Mixell's file," she said. "I know what he did, and that you helped put him behind bars."

"So you think it's okay to execute unarmed prisoners?"

"Yes," she replied without hesitation, "if they deserve it."

"Who gets to decide? Are you going to be the judge, jury, and executioner?"

"If necessary."

A short silence ensued before Harrison asked, "It's okay to execute partners too?"

This time, she hesitated before answering. "It's complicated."

"It's not complicated at all."

"Let it go," Khalila hissed. She moved toward the interrogation room, but Harrison grabbed her arm again.

"When your partner almost puts a bullet in your head, you don't just *let it go.*"

Khalila turned back to him. "Did you ever stop to think about how we got here? Why we're tracking down someone who assassinated the UN ambassador and six agents, and paid sixty million dollars for something that could end up killing thousands?"

She poked her finger into Harrison's chest. "It's *your* fault. *You* put Mixell behind bars. *You* set him onto this path. If you had *let it go,* we wouldn't be here today."

Harrison was momentarily at a loss for words. Khalila was right. Turning Mixell in had started a chain of events leading to today. Still, he had done the right thing, and he wasn't going to let Khalila twist it around, especially in light of what she'd almost done a few hours ago.

"Does the DDO know you've killed some of your partners? If not, I'm sure he'd like to know." It was only a supposition that Khalila had been responsible for some of the deaths, but he figured it was a good guess.

Khalila stepped closer to Harrison, stopping a few inches from his face. "Don't you *dare* threaten me."

"I'm just asking a question," he said, keenly aware Khalila still had a knife in one hand.

"We made a deal a few hours ago," she replied. "You don't reveal anything you've learned about me, and I don't kill you. If you break your end of the bargain, I'll break mine."

"I'd like to point out that there's no reciprocal agreement," Harrison said. "That *I* won't kill *you.*"

"I already know you won't kill me. I've met your type before. You're an idealist, constrained by an inflexible definition of right and wrong, convinced that you're better than the rest of us. The truth is, you don't have the *guts* to do what's necessary."

Khalila's words cut into him, and he fought the urge to slam her into the wall. "That's a bold statement from someone who's never been in combat. You have no idea about what I've done; what I'm capable of doing."

"You don't know what I'm capable of either."

"I've got a pretty good idea."

Khalila had put on a good act in Damascus and Virginia, but her true colors had emerged in Sochi. She was a sociopath.

Khalila leaned closer and whispered in his ear. "Then stay out of my way."

"That won't be a problem. I don't plan to work with you again."

"That would be best," she said as she pulled back, offering a disingenuous smile.

She turned toward the interrogation room again, but this time Kaufmann was standing in her way, his arms folded across his chest. He said nothing, but the unpleasant expression on his face, combined with his imposing physical presence, said enough.

Khalila took the hint and slid past him, returning to her seat.

One of the men in the interrogation room had removed Khalila's knife from Bogdanov's forearm and wrapped a towel around the wound, stopping the bleeding. He wiped the blood from the knife, then tossed it to Khalila, who caught it midair.

Maxim Anosov entered the room.

"Good news," he said. "We found Bogdanov's partner, Morozov, and he's singing like a canary. We've got everything we need now."

He glanced at Bogdanov, then turned to Kaufmann. "Kill him."

Kaufmann pulled the pistol from his shoulder harness, aiming it toward Bogdanov.

"Wait, wait, wait!" Bogdanov shouted, placing his hands in front of him. "Morozov doesn't know everything. Only I know all the details!"

With his pistol pointed at Bogdanov, Kaufmann said, "Then you better start talking."

The words spilled from Bogdanov like a waterfall, and Kaufmann took notes along the way. After a while, he pulled a sheet of paper from his satchel—a copy of the Swiss account dendrite that had been displayed at the NCTC—and placed it before Bogdanov.

"Let's make sure we've got everything correct." He pointed to the top level of the dendrite, showing a picture of Mixell, along with his name and two known aliases: Mark Alperi and Irepla Kram. "Do you know this man?"

"Yes," Bogdanov replied. "An American named Mark Alperi."

"His real name is Mixell," Kaufmann said. Then he pointed to the next level, showing Mixell's four payments, along with a picture of each beneficiary: Plecas, Bogdanov, Morozov, and Futtaim.

"Mixell made four payments: $2.5 million U.S. to Protek for the drug treatment for Captain Plecas's daughter, $20 million each for you and Morozov, and $14 million to Futtaim."

As Bogdanov examined the dendrite, a confused expression spread across his face. "I do not know this Futtaim, but Morozov is not correct. I paid Morozov using the money from Mixell."

Kaufmann scribbled on the chart, drawing an arrow to move Morozov beneath Bogdanov. "How much did you pay him?"

"Ten million, U.S."

"Then who was this twenty-million-dollar payment to?" Kaufmann pointed to Morozov's original spot.

"That'd be Mikhail Korenev."

"And who is he?"

Bogdanov explained that Korenev worked at Russia's Northern Fleet Joint Strategic Command in Severomorsk.

"What was he paid for?"

"He provided me with the arming code."

"The arming code for what?"

"The nuclear warheads."

Kaufmann stopped taking notes mid-stroke. He looked up slowly. "He did what?"

"He provided the arming code so I could arm the twenty Kalibr missiles scheduled for *Kazan*'s loadout. Morozov and I swapped conventional and nuclear missiles one night, then I armed the nuclear variants and exchanged the serial numbers and nose cones so the swap wouldn't be detected."

After a long pause, Kaufmann asked, "What are the targets?"

"I don't know. Mixell didn't share that with us. Only Plecas knows."

Kaufmann turned to Anosov, who was already stepping from the interrogation room, pulling his cell phone from its holster.

It was silent in the room as Bogdanov cleaned the blood from his face with the towel wrapped around his arm.

Anosov returned to the room, directing Kaufmann to wrap things up.

"Once we find Morozov or Korenev," Kaufmann said to Bogdanov, "we'll confirm the details. You've been very helpful."

"What? You haven't found Morozov?" It suddenly dawned on Bogdanov that Morozov's capture had been a charade. "You lied!"

Kaufmann smiled, then turned to Anosov. "Well done."

47

GADZHIYEVO, RUSSIA

Andrei Voronin stood at the entrance to the nuclear weapons bunker, surveying its contents. Moments earlier, he'd been ordered to conduct another inventory, immediately, of the nuclear warhead variant of the Kalibr missile, and this time by serial number. The previous inventory of all ordnance at Gadzhiyevo Naval Base had been conducted by weapon type and quantity, and had revealed no discrepancies. All Kalibr missiles, both conventional and nuclear variants, had been accounted for, so he wondered what a serial number audit would prove.

Supposedly, twenty of the nuclear variant were unaccounted for, but there was no chance that was true. However, he had his orders and watched as two men went down the rows of Kalibr missiles, clipboard in hand, taking independent inventories, checking off each serial number.

When they were finished, Voronin approached both men, who handed him their clipboards. Both inventories matched; every nuclear-warhead-armed missile was accounted for.

As he stood between two rows of Kalibr missiles, he noticed a slight difference between the missiles on his left, versus those on his right. The white paint on the warhead section of one set of missiles was shinier than the others. It was probably just a different production lot, he figured. But just to be sure, he decided to count each version. He went down one side, adding up the quantity of shinier missiles, stopping suddenly when it totaled twenty.

He turned to the two ordnance handlers. "Remove the nose cone from this missile," he said, pointing to the nearest shiny version.

The necessary tools were brought out and the nose cone removed.

Voronin stared in stunned silence at the guidance and control section of a Kalibr missile armed with a conventional warhead.

With rising trepidation, he ordered the nose cones removed from every Kalibr missile in the stowage facility, both conventional and nuclear variants. Perhaps the twenty nuclear-warhead-armed Kalibr missiles had somehow ended up in the conventional storage bunker, but he already knew the answer.

He ordered the nearest worker to bring him the ordnance loadout manifest. It was soon in his hand and he went down the list, his finger stopping below an entry.

Twenty Kalibr missiles had been loaded aboard *Kazan*.

48

ARLINGTON, VIRGINIA

Night was settling over the nation's capital, a light rain falling from a blanket of dark gray clouds as a black Lincoln Navigator sped south on the George Washington Parkway. In the backseat of the vehicle, Christine O'Connor's eyes were fixed on the passing scenery, but her thoughts were focused on the upcoming meeting. She had received the president's call less than an hour ago, directing her to conduct a brief at the Pentagon tonight.

Earlier in the day, the staggering information had filtered in: Bogdanov's confession in Sochi, followed by verification of his claims after a weapon inventory in Gadzhiyevo. The classified brief in Christine's lap pulled together everything they knew: Mixell, *Kazan,* nuclear warheads, and Futtaim. There were still many unanswered questions, but enough information to warrant action.

The Lincoln Navigator peeled off from the parkway toward the Pentagon's River Entrance, the portico's bright lights in the distance wavering through the rain, illuminating the steps descending from the Pentagon terrace toward the Potomac River. Her vehicle stopped at the base of the steps as Cadillac One, bracketed by two more Navigators, ground to a halt behind her.

She stepped from her SUV as the president emerged from Cadillac One, joined by Chief of Staff Kevin Hardison, National Security Advisor Thom Parham, and the president's senior military aide, Captain Glen McGlothin. Christine joined the entourage, flanked by Secret Service agents, as another vehicle arrived and Vice President Bob Tompkins and his Secret Service detail hustled to catch up.

There was no conversation along the way as they descended to the

National Military Command Center, relocated to the Pentagon's basement during the last phase of the building's fifteen-year renovation. Upon reaching the entrance, Captain McGlothin swiped his badge and entered the cipher code, then held the door open for the president.

Christine accompanied the group into NMCC's Current Action Center, with several tiers of workstations descending to a fifteen-by-thirty-foot electronic display on the far wall, then into a conference room along the top tier. Already seated and rising when the president entered were the Joint Chiefs of Staff: the heads of the Army, Navy, Air Force, Marine Corps, and National Guard, plus the vice chairman and chairman, General Gil Bohannon. On the other side of the table sat several members of the president's cabinet: Secretary of Defense Tom Drapac, Secretary of State Dawn Cabral, and Secretary of Homeland Security Nova Conover. Christine took a vacant seat at the end of the table, across from the president.

The president looked to Christine. "Go ahead."

Christine passed around copies of the brief, then began.

"There are a lot of unanswered questions, but the high-level takeaway is—we believe the Russian submarine *Kazan* is carrying twenty Kalibr missiles armed with nuclear warheads, and that the submarine's commanding officer has been paid to launch them."

There were murmurs around the table, as some of those present hadn't yet been briefed on the latest details.

Christine flipped to the first page of the brief. "Here's what we know."

She walked everyone through the issue and what they had learned thus far: who Lonnie Mixell was, that he had funded the cancer treatment for Plecas's daughter, paid Bogdanov and Korenev to swap and arm twenty Kalibr nuclear warheads, and that the missiles had been loaded aboard *Kazan*. Based on the letter from Plecas to his wife, *Kazan* would launch its missiles in approximately three days.

There was a somber silence in the conference room as the occupants digested the information.

"What are the targets?" Chief of Staff General Bohannon asked.

"We don't know," Christine replied. "*Kazan* could target anywhere in Europe or most of Africa from the Mediterranean or Atlantic. However, based on the projected timing of the launch, it's likely the targets are along the East Coast of the United States. Using the datum of *Kazan*'s interaction with USS *Pittsburgh* near the GIUK Gap and a transit speed of ten knots, *Kazan* will be within launch range of major cities near the Eastern Seaboard in three days."

The president interjected. "The Navy is already working on tracking down *Kazan* before she launches. What are our options to reduce the number of lives lost if she does?" He directed his question at Secretary of Homeland Security Nova Conover.

"The short answer is—defend or evacuate." Conover then asked Christine, "What's the range of these Kalibr missiles?"

"About fifteen hundred miles."

Conover processed the information, then turned back to the president. "Evacuation isn't an option. If *Kazan* launches from near the coast, her missiles could reach all the way into Texas and Colorado. There's no way to evacuate over half of the country in three days; the roads can't handle it. An evacuation of that magnitude would take weeks."

"That leaves us with *defend*," the president replied. To General Bohannon, he said, "Put together a plan to defend all major cities in the eastern half of the country."

"We'll put something together, sir, but without knowing the targets, our missile defense will be spread too thin. Cruise missiles are difficult to shoot down, and Kalibr is one of the best. For a successful defense, we need to concentrate our assets near the targets."

"Then we need to prevent the launch," the president replied. "Where do we stand on locating *Kazan*?"

Admiral Tom Blaszczyk, Chief of Naval Operations, answered. "*Kazan*'s location is unknown, with her last reported position being northwest of Iceland six days ago. We're sortieing all Atlantic Fleet ASW assets to sea and borrowing what we can from Pacific Fleet, but we're in a similar situation as homeland security—the area *Kazan* could be in is too vast for our resources. Our current containment is too porous. We need queuing data so we can concentrate our forces."

Silence enveloped the conference room as the men and women around the table waited for the president's next words.

Finally, he said, "The way ahead is difficult, but clear." He fixed his eyes on Christine. "First, find Mixell. We need to know what the targets are."

To Secretary of Defense Tom Drapac, he said, "Locate and sink *Kazan*."

49
NORFOLK, VIRGINIA

Captain Murray Wilson stood before the operations center display on the front wall, examining the location of Atlantic Fleet ASW forces, organized into a wide arc across the Atlantic Ocean. Thus far, there had been no detection of the Russian submarine, but that wasn't surprising. The ASW barrier was stretched too thin.

However, Wilson's new directive—prevent *Kazan* from attacking the East Coast of the United States, sinking her if necessary—offered hope of a better outcome. Wilson could disregard *Kazan*'s potential journey into the Mediterranean Sea and focus all ASW resources on detecting the submarine's approach to the East Coast.

Wilson had spent the last hour analyzing the situation, beginning with the capability of *Kazan*'s missiles. According to the Russian Navy, *Kazan* had been loaded with the land-attack version of the Kalibr missile, designated by NATO as the SS-N-30A, with a range of 1,500 miles and armed with nuclear warheads. Kalibr was a formidable missile, traveling at up to Mach 0.8 at ten yards aboveground while automatically following the terrain height, and able to make 147 in-flight maneuvers during its approach.

The key question was—did *Kazan*'s crew intend to attack one city, or twenty separate ones? The answer was critical, because attacking twenty cities meant *Kazan* would have to come closer to shore, so that all twenty cities were within launch range at the same time. If Plecas intended to attack only one city, he could stay farther out to sea along a wider launch arc, stretching Wilson's ASW forces thinner. Wilson decided the Russian submarine captain planned to attack twenty separate cities; it seemed pointless to plow twenty nuclear weapons into one place.

With that in mind, Wilson entered one of the submarine crew tactical trainers, directing the supervisor to load a Tomahawk missile attack scenario. When the supervisor asked which target set, Wilson's response elicited a raised eyebrow.

"The twenty cities along the East Coast with the highest populations. Be sure to include Washington, D.C. Set missile range to one thousand, five hundred miles."

The target set was loaded and Wilson waited while the Tomahawk software calculated the launch basket—the area where all twenty targets were within range. A hatched area appeared on the display, with its outer edge about a thousand miles off the Eastern Seaboard.

Armed with the necessary information, a new plan emerged in Wilson's mind—a revised ASW barrier closer to the East Coast, which was helpful. It was a shorter arc, extending from Newfoundland in Canada down to Puerto Rico. Wilson analyzed the situation further, assessing whether to establish a single-layer ASW barrier, or a layered defense incorporating the P-8A submarine hunter aircraft, submarines, and surface ship assets.

Although the Newfoundland to Puerto Rico barrier was less challenging than one extending across the Atlantic, it was still a wide arc, spreading Wilson's ASW forces too thin for a layered defense. A single line it was, integrating all ASW assets.

If *Kazan* slipped through it, however, there would be no way to prevent the launch.

After fermenting on the issue, Wilson changed his mind. Not having a backup plan was antithetical to Submarine Force training. If something *could* go wrong, it *would* go wrong. He decided to place the cruisers, the Navy's most capable anti-air missile platforms, close to the coast, to shoot down the cruise missiles if *Kazan* made it through the ASW barrier and launched.

Wilson returned to the operations center and issued new orders, repositioning all assets.

50

SOCHI, RUSSIA • WASHINGTON, D.C.

Jake Harrison boarded the twin-engine Falcon at Sochi International Airport for the return trip to Reagan National. Now that Anatoly Bogdanov had been apprehended, flights had begun returning agency personnel to the U.S., and today's flight was full. Upon boarding the aircraft, Khalila sat beside him as if nothing unusual had happened in Sochi.

As the aircraft took off, she pulled the trip report from her satchel and handed it to him for review. As in Damascus, the report omitted critical details. Obviously, nothing was included about almost killing him, nor did it mention impaling Bogdanov's arm with her knife. Harrison signed and handed it back to Khalila, who filed it away before reclining her seat.

She pretended to sleep for most of the flight, presumably so they wouldn't have to engage in conversation, but Harrison could tell she was still awake. His suspicion was confirmed while he was on the phone with his wife, who had just arrived in Baltimore for her annual visit with her mom. After informing her he was on the way back to the country, the topic had turned to arranging some time alone together, as there wasn't much privacy in her mom's one-bedroom apartment. Harrison had mentioned getting a hotel somewhere when Khalila spoke.

"The Hotel Washington in D.C. It's an agency perk. Call Durrani. He can arrange a room for however many nights you need."

Harrison wasn't sure whether to thank Khalila or tell her to never talk to him again. He decided not to respond, then contacted Durrani, who made the arrangement. He called Angie back; she'd be waiting for him in the hotel lobby tonight.

Khalila said nothing more for the rest of the flight, and upon landing at Reagan National, grabbed her luggage and departed without a word.

The century-old Hotel Washington, located on 15th Street NW between Pennsylvania Avenue and F Street, was only a block away from the White House. Harrison pulled up to the entrance to the eleven-story hotel, which was listed on the National Register of Historic Places and had appeared in several movies, with its rooftop terrace featured in *The Godfather: Part II* and *No Way Out.*

Harrison tossed his keys to the valet and pulled his duffle bag from the backseat, then entered the historic hotel. Although the luxurious lobby was well appointed, his eyes were instantly drawn to Angie, seated across the lobby. Her face brightened when she saw him, and she smiled as she rose from the chair and walked toward him. She was wearing a raspberry-colored featherweight sweater that clung to her curves, low-slung jeans, and knee-high suede leather boots.

Angie's smile turned mischievous as her pace increased, and Harrison quickly deduced what she was planning to do. He dropped his duffle bag on the floor and shifted one foot farther back, bracing himself. Angie sprinted the remaining distance toward Harrison and leaped into his arms, straddling his waist with her legs as she locked her lips on to his. When she pulled back, Harrison glanced at the lobby occupants—distinguished guests wearing suits and elegant dresses—some of whom were staring at the couple, but Angie seemed not to notice or care, her eyes locked on to his, an infectious grin on her face.

"You're excited to see me, I take it," Harrison said, charmed as always by her youthful exuberance.

Angie whispered into his ear. "If you think I'm excited now, just wait until we're alone."

51

DULLES, VIRGINIA

It was just before 8 a.m. when the last passengers aboard Air France Flight 21 trudged into Terminal B at Dulles International Airport, toting an assortment of carry-on bags, backpacks, and sleeping infants. For the most part, the travelers felt as tired as they appeared after the overnight nine-hour flight, except for a man near the back of the line, who pretended to rub the sleep from his eyes.

Although he shuffled along with the rest of the passengers, Lonnie Mixell felt quite refreshed, which was remarkable since his journey had been much longer: a three-flight trip from Baku, Azerbaijan, to Bucharest, Romania, then on to Paris for the final leg to the United States—all preceded by a winding drive through Syria, Turkey, and Armenia.

The extra precautions had been necessary. After Harrison caught up to him in Syria, Mixell realized the facial recognition programs had access to far more cameras, and could process the images faster, than he had expected. As a result, he'd begun his journey back to the United States far from Syria, and with a notably altered appearance.

He stopped in a bathroom, and after relieving himself and washing his hands, looked into the mirror. His hair had been dyed black and was now streaked with gray, and his eyes were blue due to a pair of clear-vision contacts. His cheekbone structure had been altered by implants wedged high in his mouth on both sides, and his jawline was more pronounced due to additional implants outside his lower teeth—along the sides and in the front.

Despite the altered appearance, the face in the mirror was still quite handsome, he had to admit. Of more importance, however, the image matched the picture on his passport, issued in the name of David Morrell, an executive of DavRoc Industries, looking to open a distribution center near Washington, D.C. In keeping with his new and wealthy identity, Mixell wore a three-piece blue suit and complementing silk tie, along with polished black wing-tipped dress shoes.

He had previously made an appointment for this morning and had made a call upon landing at Dulles, and waiting at the curb by baggage claim in a red Lexus GS sedan was Sandy Perry, the sole owner of a realty company specializing in commercial properties. She emerged from the car to greet Mixell, who noticed the woman was an attractive brunette in her forties, smartly attired in a white blouse and gray skirt that went midway down her thighs. He also noticed that she wore no wedding ring.

She offered a firm handshake as she greeted him. "Welcome to Virginia, Mr. Morrell."

Mixell smiled warmly. "Please, call me Dave."

After he placed his carry-on luggage in the trunk, he slipped into the passenger seat beside her.

"I've got a good list of properties," she said as they pulled away from the curb. "I'm sure one of them will be exactly what you're looking for."

Sandy was already aware of David Morrell's professional details, and the conversation eventually turned to more personal topics. Mixell learned that Sandy was single, a recent divorcée.

Sandy Perry had been in the real estate business for over twenty years; a well-known and highly respected woman in her community. Her recent divorce had been an embarrassing and frustrating ordeal, and the mere thought of her ex-husband made her hands clench the steering wheel.

She forced herself to relax and focus instead on the client in her passenger seat, whom she had sized up the moment she laid eyes on him at the airport. She glanced at him frequently as she drove, her eyes lingering for longer than they should have, given she was speeding toward Washington at well above the speed limit.

David Morrell was a strikingly handsome man. His black hair was streaked with gray, which she found attractive, and his eyes were the most amazing color of blue she had ever seen. He was tall and well built, filling out his suit quite nicely.

As they traveled down the Dulles Access Road, her mind began to wander. She was an attractive woman, and over the last few months, she had taken advantage of her new single status. Her eyes went to Morrell's left hand, which bore no wedding ring.

"How long will you be in town?" she asked.

"Only a few days."

"Oh," she said, trying to hide the disappointment from her voice. "Will you be back to visit the property often?"

"It depends on how things go."

Mixell noticed Sandy's frequent glances. He got those kinds of looks often, and while he occasionally mixed business with pleasure, business came first today.

He had requested a property in Alexandria, Virginia. Other than that, there were few requirements: a warehouse with at least three thousand square feet of space on the ground floor, and an industrial-sized garage door at least ten feet wide by fifteen feet tall.

Sandy showed him several properties, and one of the warehouses would have worked, except the large industrial doors opened to the west instead of the east. That was a detail Mixell had decided not to share with the realtor to prevent unnecessary questions.

She showed him several more properties, this time pulling up alongside a vacant warehouse at the end of Oronoco Street. As far as the location went, it was perfect. Situated on the bank of the Potomac River and bordered on one side by Oronoco Bay and the other by Founders Park, he doubted he would find a more secluded location, considering his requirements.

Sandy unlocked the heavy steel door and pushed it open for Mixell. The bare warehouse was exactly what he was looking for. The interior was large enough for the planned equipment, there were only a few grimy windows along one wall through which dim light filtered in, and there was a large industrial door on the far wall, opening to the east.

She turned on the lights and pressed the nearby controller; the door slid slowly up, revealing a dilapidated wharf along the riverbank. Mixell stepped from the warehouse to examine the dock, which was in need of repair but serviceable.

Even better.

He took a mental note, making a small change in his future plans.

When he returned to the warehouse, Sandy sensed he was interested and tried to seal the deal. "It's been vacant for a few years, but there's been recent interest. With the new Amazon headquarters development a few miles away, the warehouse won't be on the market much longer."

Mixell decided to string her along. "It's got possibilities."

"It's in a respectable and safe area," she offered, "not far from where I live. While you're getting settled in, I could stop by on occasion."

Her offer caught Mixell's attention, his eyes locking on to hers.

"Only if you want, of course . . ." Her voice trailed off as her cheeks blushed.

She moved to the other side of the garage opening and pressed the controller, shutting the door. As it descended, Mixell turned back toward the Potomac, pretending to contemplate the matter.

When the door closed, he turned to tell Sandy he'd rent the property, but she was facing away from him, leaning over to remove a shoe, presumably to extract a pebble that had worked its way in. She had timed it perfectly, he thought. His eyes moved over her firm ass, then down her lean legs to her four-inch platform heels.

She replaced her shoe and stood, turning to face him. Mixell pulled his eyes up to hers too slowly and she caught his wandering gaze. A small smile played across her lips.

"Do you like it?" she asked, her voice taking on a sultry quality. "Or would you like to see more?"

Mixell's eyes held hers for a moment before replying. "It's quite nice; more than adequate to satisfy my needs."

"So . . . you'll be taking it, then?" Her body tensed in anticipation. "Right now?"

"Absolutely," he said as he moved toward her, shrugging the suit jacket from his shoulders.

52
K-561 *KAZAN*

Aleksandr Plecas stepped into Compartment Two, the first stop on his evening tour, visiting his crew and checking on the status of his submarine. First up was the Central Command Post. It was quiet on watch, as it had been since their encounter with the American submarine eight days ago. He stopped by the navigation table, evaluating *Kazan*'s progress toward the launch point.

It had been a long journey, much longer than if he had been tasked with attacking only targets along the East Coast of the United States. Instead, the target set covered almost the entirety of the country. From the right location, *Kazan*'s 2,500-kilometer-range cruise missiles could attack targets not only on the East Coast, but all the way north to Canada in the center of the United States, and a significant portion of the West Coast. That launch location was in the Gulf of Mexico, just south of the Texas shoreline.

Instead of heading toward America's East Coast at ten knots using *Kazan*'s stealthy electric drive, Plecas had proceeded on the submarine's main propulsion at twenty knots, staying in the middle of the Atlantic Ocean, headed south. Although *Kazan*'s main propulsion was louder than the electric drive, the higher speed meant *Kazan* would be well past any containment the Americans tried to establish around his encounter with the American submarine near Iceland, if they assumed *Kazan* was proceeding at its stealthier, electric-drive speed.

Launching from the Gulf of Mexico had additional advantages. If the Americans discovered Plecas's plan to attack the United States, their ASW forces would most likely be arrayed in a defensive screen designed to prevent *Kazan* from approaching launch range of the East Coast. By launching from the Gulf, Plecas had been able to remain far out in the Atlantic, skirting around any protective East Coast screen.

Kazan had passed east of Puerto Rico two days ago and was now curling westward below Cuba, approaching the Cayman Islands. Plecas was one day ahead of schedule; when providing the American with *Kazan*'s launch date and time, he had factored in an extra twenty-four hours in case there were any unforeseen delays. If there were none, *Kazan* would slow down toward the end of its transit to arrive on time.

Seated at the navigation table was Michman Erik Korzhev, the Electric Navigation Party Technician. Korzhev was busy verifying the operation of the submarine's two inertial navigators. It had been a lengthy transit without any trips to periscope depth to obtain satellite position fixes. Satisfactory operation of their inertial navigators was critical.

Korzhev looked up. "Both navigators are stable and tracking together, Captain."

Plecas acknowledged Korzhev's report, then stopped by Hydroacoustic. In the middle of the Atlantic Ocean, there had been few contacts, but now that they were preparing to enter the Gulf of Mexico, with Central America closing in on one side and Cuba on the other, contact density was increasing. However, as long as *Kazan* didn't proceed to periscope depth or encounter an American warship, the additional contacts were of little concern.

Plecas ducked his head as he stepped through the watertight doorway into Compartment One, closing the heavy metal door carefully to prevent a transient from being transmitted into the surrounding water. Although there were no American submarines trailing *Kazan* or nearby—that he was aware of—shutting the door carefully was a habit, ingrained into every sailor in the Submarine Fleet. Plecas had entered *Kazan*'s Torpedo Room, occupying the top two levels of the compartment, its ten tubes arranged in two vertical rows, one on each side of the submarine.

Although *Kazan* was the second Yasen class submarine, it was notably superior to *Severodvinsk,* the lead ship of the class. *Kazan*'s keel was laid sixteen years after *Severodvinsk*'s due to construction delays, and as a result, *Kazan* boasted significant advances in tactical warfare systems, along with a shortened hull to reduce cost. Although initial plans called for two more vertical launch tubes and two fewer torpedo tubes, *Kazan* had retained the eight-tube vertical launch module and ten-torpedo-tube design of its predecessor.

Seated near the forward bulkhead below the torpedo launch console was Starshina First Class Oleg Noskov, a junior torpedoman on watch, who rose to his feet as the submarine's Commanding Officer entered the compartment.

Noskov was only eighteen years old. It never ceased to amaze Plecas how the Russian military's most advanced weapon platforms—its nuclear-powered submarines—were operated by such young men. Even with Plecas's advanced age factored in, with this being his second command tour, the average age of his crew was only twenty-four. His officers weren't much older: Erik Fedorov, *Kazan*'s First Officer and second-in-command, who was notably older than the officers beneath him, was only thirty-five.

Plecas spent a few minutes talking with Noskov, learning that he was from Yudanovka, not far from Plecas's hometown of Panino, just east of Voronezh. Upon hearing where the young man was from, Plecas's thoughts went to his family. Tatiana was also from Panino; they had started dating while in secondary school and had married shortly after Plecas graduated from Grechko Naval Academy in St. Petersburg.

Tatiana was one of nine children and Plecas one of six, and both had looked forward to having a large family. That hadn't been in the cards, however. Tatiana had difficulty getting pregnant, and after twenty years of trying everything, including in vitro fertilization, they had finally accepted their fate.

A year later, Tatiana became pregnant with Natasha. *Their miracle baby,* Tatiana still called her, and the joy she had brought to their lives had been immeasurable. Natasha's illness had been a devastating blow, threatening to take away their only child. Plecas was convinced that Tatiana, like himself, would do anything to save her. He knew Tatiana would forgive him for what he was about to do. The Russian government, however, would not.

Plecas was jarred from his thoughts by a subtle change in the deck's vibration. The submarine's main engines were straining a bit more than normal.

He bid farewell to Noskov, then proceeded aft to investigate.

53
SERENDIPITY

Sixty miles south of the Cayman Islands, Marc Manis leaned forward in the Captain's chair aboard *Serendipity,* an eighty-foot stern trawler, adjusting the vessel's course to keep station with its sister ship, *Karma,* four hundred yards to starboard. Both trawlers were headed northwest, cutting through sea-state-two wavelets barely one foot tall, traveling beneath a cloudless night sky with the temperature in the low eighties, accompanied by a light westerly breeze.

It all added up to a beautiful night for fishing. *Serendipity* and *Karma* were pair-trawling for tuna, towing a large net between them: eight hundred feet wide by five hundred feet deep, pelagic trawling through the midwater column where the tuna were. They had been out to sea for a week and the haul thus far had been excellent, both in quantity and size, with the tuna stored in a refrigerated compartment below deck. Each fishing expedition, Manis wagered an under/over bet with his crew regarding the size of the largest fish they'd catch, with Manis always taking the *over* bet. Thus far, however, the largest tuna had been a few pounds shy of winning.

Serendipity's 450 horsepower engine suddenly eased up, catching Manis's attention. He leaned out the bridge side window, noting that the port warp—one of two tow cables attached to this side of the net—had gone slack.

Damn it!

Manis set *Serendipity* on autopilot and hustled aft, joining the trawler's first mate, Kirk Murphy, who was staring at the tow cables—both had gone slack. It looked like the net had broken free of both warps. *Karma* would have to reel the net back in, with both trawlers returning to port for a replacement net.

Manis was about to head to the bridge to contact *Karma* when the tow cables dragged across the transom to the starboard side of the trawler, tension returning to the warps. *Serendipity*'s stern started swinging around, twisting the trawler one-eighty until it was traveling backward. To starboard, *Karma* was also swinging around, being pulled stern-first through the water.

Aboard *Serendipity*, the Gilson winches the warps were attached to began smoking as they strained against the tow cables pulling the eighty-foot trawler backward at an increasing speed.

Serendipity was a rugged, seaworthy trawler, but it wasn't designed to travel backward at high speed, and water surged over the transom, flooding the deck and streaming into the compartments below.

Kirk Murphy probably had no idea about what was going on, but Manis knew immediately what had happened. He had caught this type of fish before.

"Release the warps!"

They needed to cut the tow lines, and fast.

Seven years ago, Manis had been aboard a trawler that had snagged a nuclear-powered submarine and the trawler had gone under. Although the captain had been able to get off a Mayday distress call and the Coast Guard had rescued the crew, it was an experience he would never forget.

Manis called down to Dan Metzger, *Serendipity*'s chief engineer, to start the bilge pumps, but Metzger was already on it and the bilge pumps rumbled to life. Unfortunately, the pumps couldn't handle the amount of water rushing over the stern. Their only hope was to release the warps before *Serendipity* flooded or got pulled under if the submarine went deeper.

He returned his attention to the Gilson winches, as John Lojko, the lead foreman, disengaged one while Murphy tackled the other. The two winches began free-spinning, releasing the warps.

Serendipity slowed as the tow cables paid out, until both warps whipped free. The trawler drifted to a halt before moving forward again, its bow swinging around; Manis had left the engines running and the ship was still on autopilot, returning *Serendipity* to base course and speed.

Manis took a deep breath as his pulse began to slow.

That had been a close call, one that could have ended in disaster.

Manis praised Murphy and Lojko for their excellent response during the emergency, then relayed the same to Metzger once the bilge pumps went quiet. As Manis returned to the bridge, he realized that despite the trawler's name, this hadn't been their lucky night.

Then another thought occurred to him. He had definitely won the under/over bet on the largest fish they'd catch.

54

K-561 *KAZAN*

Aleksandr Plecas stood in the Central Command Post, arms folded across his chest, waiting for the watch section to complete preparations to proceed to periscope depth. It had been three hours since *Kazan* became snared in a trawler's net, and Plecas had been waiting until conditions were right—no contacts nearby that could spot the Russian submarine on the surface. It was still dark outside—1 a.m. local—and *Kazan* wouldn't energize its navigation lights, so the odds of the black submarine being spotted in the dark water were low. Plecas was being cautious, nonetheless.

Kazan's Watch Officer, Captain Lieutenant Urnovitz, ordered, "Hydroacoustic, Command Post. Report all contacts within ten thousand meters."

"Command Post, Hydroacoustic. Hold no contacts."

Urnovitz turned to Plecas. "Captain, request permission to proceed to periscope depth."

Plecas approved the request, with a modification to the normal procedure. "Hover to periscope depth."

The change in procedure was required because the trawler net had become wrapped around *Kazan*'s screw, which not only interfered with efficient propulsion, but resulted in numerous loud tonals and broadband noise being transmitted into the surrounding water. *Kazan* was at all stop, and could not proceed on its mission without cutting the net free.

Fortunately, Russian submarines, like American ones, had crew members trained as divers, who came in handy during emergency situations such as this. Two divers were waiting by the hatch in Compartment One, standing by to egress from the submarine once it surfaced and Plecas verified there was no risk of taking water down the hatch.

"Raising forward periscope," Urnovitz announced.

The scope rose slowly from its well, and Urnovitz placed his eye against the facepiece, then ordered the ascent.

"Compensation Officer, hover to fifteen meters."

The Compensation Officer started the hovering pumps, pushing water from the variable ballast tanks, making the submarine lighter. Once the desired amount of water was pumped out, *Kazan* rose steadily toward the surface.

"Fifty meters," the Compensation Officer reported.

At thirty meters, the Compensation Officer flooded water back in, matching the amount pumped out, plus a few thousand pounds to halt *Kazan*'s ascent. The submarine's upward momentum slowed, with *Kazan* settling out at fifteen meters as ordered, and the Compensation Officer pumped the extra few thousand pounds back out, restoring *Kazan* to neutral buoyancy.

"Periscope clear," Urnovitz announced, reporting the periscope had broken the surface of the water.

Urnovitz did a quick safety sweep followed by a detailed search, then confirmed Hydroacoustic's report.

"Hold no contacts."

"Surface without air," Plecas ordered.

Urnovitz relayed the order to the Compensation Officer, who started the ballast tank blower, which pushed air into the ballast tanks, instead of using valuable air stored in the high-pressure air banks. Although running the blower was noisy, it was far quieter than running the compressors required to replace the high-pressure air.

Kazan rose higher as the water was pushed from its ballast tanks, and the blower was secured once air began escaping from the flood grates on the submarine's keel, indicating the ballast tanks were now empty.

Plecas relieved Urnovitz on the periscope, surveying the sea-state condition. It was a calm night with almost no waves, and the topside hatches could be opened without fear of water flooding into the submarine.

As he returned the periscope to Urnovitz, Plecas ordered, "Send divers topside."

It was a tedious task, but the trawler net was cut free from *Kazan*'s screw in just over two hours. With the divers retrieved and the hatch shut, *Kazan* was ready to submerge and continue on its way.

Despite the delay, Plecas had nineteen hours of slack remaining in the schedule. *Kazan* could still slow and reach the launch point at the prescribed time. Plecas decided to slow now, however, and not reserve all of the slack for later. Proceeding at twenty knots, a high speed that reduced the effectiveness of the hydroacoustic arrays, had not turned out well, resulting in *Kazan*'s ensnarement.

"Watch Officer, submerge and proceed at ahead standard."

55

NORFOLK, VIRGINIA

Captain Beverly King entered the operations center at COMSUBFOR headquarters, noting the unusually high density of personnel. Leading the augmented staff was Captain Murray Wilson, who was currently reviewing the Atlantic Fleet's East Coast ASW barrier stretching from Newfoundland to Puerto Rico. There had been no detections of the Russian submarine that King was aware of, although she wasn't entirely in the loop. As the Submarine Force's senior public affairs officer, she dealt with myriad mundane, and sometimes peculiar, issues.

She had stopped by the operations center to evaluate a report received this morning from a trawler captain convinced he had snagged a submarine, demanding compensation for the net he'd been forced to cut loose. Although it was somewhat embarrassing, it did occur on occasion. The thousands of nets dragged by commercial fisherman were silent and undetectable by a submarine's sonar system, and the only way to avoid a net was to avoid the trawlers.

However, a trawler's engine sounded similar to the multitude of other merchants and pleasure craft, and while it was common practice to keep surface contacts a minimum distance away to avoid nets they might be dragging, it wasn't always possible in high-contact-density situations.

A glance at the operations center display told King what she already suspected; the trawler captain's claim was false. There were no submarines south of Cuba. She queried Captain Wilson, just to be sure.

"Murray," King said as she extended her hand. "Beverly King, public affairs officer. It's a pleasure to meet you."

After Wilson returned the greeting, King explained the reason for her visit, then requested confirmation of her assessment.

Wilson didn't need to check the display. "You're correct. We have no submarines in the western Atlantic."

"Thanks," King replied. She was about to depart when she hesitated, then pursued the matter further. "The thing is, the trawler captain knows what he's talking about. He was on a trawler seven years ago when *Helena* snagged its net. He said the situation was exactly the same." King paused to let Wilson evaluate the new information, then added, "Of course, he could be making it up, hoping to make a few bucks by filing a false claim."

Wilson pondered the matter, then examined the large monitor on the front wall displaying the ASW barrier in the Atlantic Ocean. *Kazan* was overdue. If the Russian submarine had traveled at ten knots on her electric drive, she would've hit the barrier two days ago. Either she was traveling slower for some reason, or had already slipped through. But if the latter, she was now within launch range, and what was the Russian captain waiting for? Was he approaching closer to the coast, so he could hit targets farther inland?

Or maybe . . .

Wilson's eyes moved down to the Cayman Islands.

He turned to the operations center watch officer. "Plot a course from the GIUK Gap—from *Pittsburgh*'s position starting at the time she ejected the SEPIRB buoy—around Puerto Rico to the Cayman Islands. Use a transit speed of twenty knots and calculate the arrival time just south of the Caymans."

The watch officer entered the requested parameters and a red line appeared on the display, representing the requested track.

To King, Wilson asked, "When did the submarine snag supposedly occur?"

"Last night, around 10 p.m. local—3 a.m. GMT."

Wilson examined the display. If *Kazan* had followed the track on the display at twenty knots, it would have passed by the Cayman Islands last night at 4 a.m. Greenwich Mean Time.

Son of a bitch.

While establishing the ASW barrier, Wilson had assumed *Kazan* would attack the densely populated East Coast cities, including the nation's capital, launching as soon as possible. Instead, the Russian submarine captain had done an end around.

It was a brilliant plan if the goal was to strike the broadest area possible rather than a quick strike along the East Coast. From the Gulf of Mexico, *Kazan*'s Kalibr missiles covered eighty percent of the United States; an arc sweeping from Los Angeles in the west to the Canadian border in the north, to Boston in the east. Wilson assumed the Russian submarine captain was planning for maximum effect, and would likely approach close to shore, increasing the available target set.

Still, before he repositioned ASW assets to the Gulf of Mexico, pulling them from the East Coast barrier, he wanted to be more confident of his conclusion. If *Kazan* had been snagged in a trawler's net, it would most certainly have wrapped around the submarine's screw. The Russian submarine would have surfaced to cut the net free.

Wilson asked King, "Do you have the lat/long of the trawler incident?"

King looked up the information in the incident report.

Wilson turned to the operations officer, relaying the coordinates. "Pull up satellite imagery of the western Atlantic, zoomed in to those coordinates. I want infrared scans at ten-minute intervals starting at 3 a.m. GMT this morning."

A map of the Cayman Islands and surrounding water appeared on the display at the front of the operations center; a mass of black with intermittent bright spots scattered throughout. If *Kazan* had been running at twenty knots, its nuclear reactor would have been operating at high power and the submarine's Reactor Compartment would be very hot. If *Kazan* surfaced to cut the net, the event should have been detectable.

The satellite imagery advanced in ten-minute intervals, and three hours after the reported incident, a bright white blip appeared at the coordinates reported by the trawler, disappearing two hours later.

There was no doubt in Wilson's mind—the trawler had snagged *Kazan*.

To the watch officer, Wilson ordered, "Plot an area of uncertainty, starting at the lat/long reported by the trawler, expanding outward at twenty knots. Give me four-hour contour rings."

After the rings appeared, Wilson calculated how long it would take to reposition the P-8A squadrons currently in the Atlantic Ocean, then issued orders for a new ASW barrier in the Gulf of Mexico, through which *Kazan* must pass if it moved closer to the U.S. southern shore.

Although the new barrier was much smaller than the East Coast version, it was still a wide arc—over six hundred miles long—spanning from Mérida, Mexico, to the base of the Florida Keys, and Wilson had only the P-8As to work with. The submarines and surface ships off the East Coast would take too long to reposition.

However . . . a thought occurred to him. It was a risky plan, but there was one more asset available, which might prove handy.

Wilson called the COMSUBFOR chief of staff, requesting an urgent meeting regarding *Kazan*'s status.

Inside the admiral's conference room, Wilson explained the situation. *Kazan* had almost certainly skirted the East Coast ASW barrier and was heading into the Gulf of Mexico to launch its Kalibr missiles at a larger target set. The P-8A squadrons were being repositioned, but submarine and surface ship assets were too far away. Except one.

USS *North Carolina* was getting underway today, her first journey to sea since she was sunk two years ago during America's devastating war with China. Fortunately, *North Carolina* sank in the shallow Taiwan Strait in only two hundred feet of water and had been raised from the bottom. With the Navy's normal repair yards swamped, repairing five aircraft carriers and over two dozen submarines damaged or sunk during the conflict, *North Carolina* had been sent to Ingalls Shipbuilding in Pascagoula, Mississippi, for repair.

Wilson made the request. "I'd like permission to employ *North Carolina* against *Kazan*."

Captain Mark Graham, the COMSUBLANT training officer, objected, as Wilson expected.

"This is *North Carolina*'s first time underway since she was repaired. Her replacement tactical systems and hull patch haven't been tested at sea, she's got a new commanding officer, and her crew isn't certified for deployment. One-third of her crew has never even been to sea."

Wilson pointed out, "The crew completed their shore-based tactical training and passed. They're ready to go to sea."

Graham replied, "Getting underway and engaging in combat are two different things. It normally takes a six-month at-sea workup to certify a submarine for deployment. I have a high regard for our submarines and our crews in general, but if we send *North Carolina* against the premier attack submarine in the Russian Navy, the odds of success are low."

"Then we need to improve the odds," Wilson said. "Transfer me aboard."

There was no immediate response as Admiral Andrea and his staff evaluated Wilson's unexpected request.

Wilson added, "That's what COMSUBPAC did during the *Kentucky* incident. I was transferred aboard *Collins* because it was the only submarine within range. It's a similar situation here. Let me take command of *North Carolina*."

Admiral Andrea considered the request. Wilson was well into his second submarine command tour, and with the two tours bracketing his assignment as senior submarine command course instructor, he was the Submarine Force's most experienced captain.

Andrea surveyed his staff around the table; none had additional objections.

Finally, Andrea spoke. "I'm not a fan of the proposal. It places *North Carolina* and her crew at excessive risk. However, I have to weigh the pros and cons, and employing *North Carolina* improves the odds of locating and sinking *Kazan*. Ultimately, that's what matters."

He turned to his operations officer. "Arrange a personnel transfer. Get Wilson aboard *North Carolina* as soon as possible, placing him in command."

Admiral Andrea stood and shook Wilson's hand. "Good luck, Murray."

56

LANGLEY, VIRGINIA

In the seventh-floor conference room in CIA headquarters, Jake Harrison sat between Khalila Dufour and Pat Kendall, opposite Deputy Director Monroe Bryant and Deputy Director for Operations PJ Rolow. Their case manager, Asad Durrani, also joined them, while CIA director Christine O'Connor was seated at the head of the table.

It was a short-notice meeting, with Kendall taking the call in the NCTC from Durrani less than an hour ago. There had been a break in Mixell's case and the DDA was running down another lead. To pull everything they knew about Mixell together, the DDO had directed they meet at Langley.

The previous day, when Harrison returned to the NCTC, Kendall had asked how things had gone in Sochi. It was a loaded question, which Harrison had to answer carefully. Until Sochi, he thought Kendall's opinion of Khalila was off base, colored by her suspicion that she had killed her boyfriend. He hadn't put much credence in her warnings, but now he had to admit that she'd been right.

However, he had made a deal with Khalila and couldn't reveal anything he had learned about her, or anything she had done that hadn't made it into the official CIA reports.

To prevent Kendall from prying into the matter, Harrison had replied, "It went well. Khalila helped track down Bogdanov."

Kendall seemed satisfied with the answer, or perhaps it had been a polite inquiry and she didn't really care, because she returned to her computer screen, studying the document on her display. The call from Durrani had come shortly thereafter, requesting their presence at Langley.

Khalila seemed at ease during today's meeting, as if nothing unusual had happened in Sochi, while Harrison had to focus on his responses and body language, trying not to raise suspicion that there was an issue between them. At one point, Christine cast a curious look his way, then shifted her gaze to Khalila, and he wondered if he had given anything away. Christine had known him his entire life, from the time they'd begun playing together as toddlers through the ten years they dated in high school and beyond. Although he'd been married to Angie for fifteen years, he wasn't willing to wager as to which woman knew him better.

He tried to stay focused on the case, and after the DDO reviewed what Khalila and Harrison had learned thus far, next up was the minor break Durrani had mentioned over the phone. Rolow took the lead.

"We tracked down Mixell's cell mates at Leavenworth, and he talked to one of them about his fiancée. They never married, but Mixell referred to her as his *soul mate,* and she was indeed a stripper, as Harrison mentioned while reviewing Mixell's file. The bad news is that Mixell was tight-lipped about the woman and never mentioned her name. The good news is that we know where she worked. Mixell recommended the strip club to his cell mate if he ever found himself in Baltimore—the Player's Club."

Tracey McFarland, the deputy director for analysis, entered the conference room with a folder, taking a seat at the table.

"What do you have?" Christine asked.

"I've got two more leads," McFarland replied. She opened the folder and handed copies of the first sheet to everyone. It was a picture of a man Harrison found familiar, but he couldn't identify who he was.

McFarland said, "We picked up this image of a man entering the country through Dulles Airport yesterday morning. We didn't get a match until the image went through regression analysis, but we've got a ninety-one percent confidence it's Mixell."

"He's back in the country," the DDO said. "To do what?"

"Hold that thought," McFarland said as she passed several more sheets around the table. "We've broken part of the code on one of Issad Futtaim's files. It's the critical document—the one that lists the weapon procurements. We've linked one of the purchases to Mixell's Swiss account, and although we don't know what he purchased, we know where it was shipped—the Port of Baltimore."

"Where is it getting shipped from there?" Rolow asked.

"Just the port. There are no additional shipping instructions. My bet is—Mixell is here to pick it up."

"Has it arrived?"

"We don't know. We've run the shipment manifest number, but it doesn't come up in the port's database, nor on any ship unloading in the port. It must be off the books.

"One more thing," McFarland said. "It must be a fairly large item. Futtaim shipped it in a CONEX box."

"That should make it easier to find."

"Not really," McFarland replied. "The port unloads over two thousand CONEX boxes a day."

Rolow turned to Harrison and Kendall. "Table the stripper lead for now. Run down Futtaim's shipment at the port. If it's there, find it."

Kendall pulled out her cell phone as they left the conference room. "I'll call Baltimore PD." She looked up the number in her contacts, then placed the call.

"Jason, this is Pat Kendall. I need your help."

She explained the issue with Mixell's weapon shipment to the Port of Baltimore and asked for an immediate quarantine until she and Harrison arrived.

"Thanks, Jason," she said before hanging up. She turned to Harrison. "They'll have someone at all exits within the hour."

Kendall's call to Baltimore jogged Harrison's mind. He was supposed to meet Angie and her mom for dinner in Baltimore tonight, and he had no idea how long he'd be tied up running down this afternoon's lead.

He called Angie. "I can't make it tonight. Something's come up."

Angie said it was okay, but he sensed the disappointment in her voice. He was going to explain why he canceled, but decided against it; the case details were classified and he wasn't allowed to share them with anyone without the proper clearance, even his wife. At least not with Kendall walking beside him. However, it wasn't hard for Angie to figure out the underlying reason.

"You've got something on Mixell, don't you?"

"Yeah. We're running down a lead. I'll be in Baltimore, though, and if things wrap up early enough for dinner, I'll give you a call."

57
BALTIMORE, MARYLAND

Lonnie Mixell sat in the passenger seat of an eighteen-wheeler cab as the semi-truck coasted to a stop at the entrance to the Port of Baltimore's Seagirt Terminal. In the driver's seat was Allen Terrill, Sr., a trucker nearing retirement. Mixell had needed someone familiar with picking up containers at the port, plus a flatbed trailer to load the shipment onto, and Terrill had met the requirements and been hired.

Terrill was the chatty type, talking incessantly from the time he picked Mixell up at the Alexandria warehouse, and Mixell had learned a great deal about independent trucking and their destination. The Port of Baltimore was one of the largest ports in the world, spread across 1,200 acres divided into seven terminals. Altogether, the port boasted the ability to simultaneously load or offload 173 ships, offered more than five million square feet of warehouse space, and had an outside storage capacity equivalent to over fifty thousand railroad cars. If there was a shoreline version of the warehouse in *Raiders of the Lost Ark,* the Port of Baltimore was it.

The semi-truck pulled forward in line, eventually reaching the gatehouse, where Mixell handed the shipping document to Terrill, who passed it to the gate guard seated at the window. The man entered the shipment number into his computer, then frowned. He entered it again, then handed the document back to Terrill.

"You're at the wrong port, buddy. That shipment's not here, nor scheduled for offload."

Mixell leaned toward the driver's window. "You're Charlie Rooney, right?"

"Who's asking?"

"I was told this was your shift. We're here to pick up a shipment in the *secure* section."

"Why didn't you say so at the beginning?"

He left the window, reappearing a moment later with a clipboard.

"Shipping document," he said, as he glanced uneasily at the driver in the truck behind them.

Terrill handed him the document again, then Rooney slid his finger down a handwritten list on his clipboard, eventually finding a match.

Rooney filled out a piece of paper, then handed it to Terrill along with the shipping document. "Here's your pass. Pickup at E and Seven."

As they pulled away from the gate, Terrill explained the terminal's roads didn't have names—just numbers and letters—and Rooney had directed them to find the foreman in that sector of the terminal, who'd be at the corner of E and Seven.

Terrill knew the port layout well and quickly navigated to the requisite corner, passing row upon row of containers stacked four high and seven deep. Towering above the identical metal boxes were rail-mounted cranes in constant motion, depositing one container after another onto a seemingly endless procession of flatbed trucks.

Terrill stopped at the corner of E and Seven and handed the pass to the sector foreman, who, after reviewing the paperwork, spoke into a handheld radio, directing one of the cranes to pick up container A851051.

"Crane delta-twelve," the man said, pointing to a crane that had begun moving toward a nearby stack of containers.

Terrill pulled forward and parked near the crane as it sorted through the stack, digging down until the correct container was located. While they waited, Terrill explained that most truckers hauling containers had no idea what was inside. The containers were locked and sealed, opened only by customs during random inspections. The truckers only ensured the number on the container matched the shipping document and the door seal hadn't been broken, then delivered the container to wherever the instructions said.

Mixell's cell phone buzzed, using a unique text-tone vibration set to one person. He pulled out his phone and read the text.

Harrison is on his way to the port.

Mixell replied, *How much time do I have?*

Don't know.

Mixell turned to Terrill. "My appointment tonight got moved up. We need to get moving."

"Got it," Terrill replied. "This won't take long."

The crane swung the specified container onto Terrill's flatbed trailer, then the trucker verified the CONEX number matched the shipping document and the door seal was intact. He then locked the container onto the flatbed by rotating four metal twist locks—one at each corner of the trailer. A port worker then signed the pass Terrill had been given at the entrance, and they were on the move again, headed back to the gatehouse.

Terrill stopped near the gate, waiting as a dozen trucks ahead of them worked their way through the exit. Mixell checked his watch; it'd been ten minutes since he received the text, and it was taking what seemed to be an interminable amount of time for each truck to depart the port. As the line inched forward, Mixell eyed the road beyond the gatehouse while checking his watch periodically. His concern that they wouldn't pass through the gate in time steadily increased, and he fingered his pistol, hidden in a shoulder harness beneath his jacket.

As they moved slowly toward the gate, Mixell had to admit Futtaim had selected an excellent port to ship to. The Seagirt Terminal sat right off Interstate 95 and only a few minutes from six other interstates fanning out from the coast in every direction. That foresight had proven handy today, in case Harrison or anyone else tried to track Mixell's truck down before it disappeared into the Alexandria warehouse.

They finally reached the gate, where a customs agent inspected the truck, verifying the container number matched Terrill's shipping document and that the door seal hadn't been broken. Meanwhile, the gate guard inspected Terrill's pass, which had been signed by the sector foreman, verifying Terrill had proceeded to the authorized sector.

Terrill pulled through the gate, headed toward I-95. As they approached the entrance ramp to the southbound lanes, Mixell spotted a police cruiser speeding in the other direction, toward the Seagirt Terminal entrance. They had made it out just in time.

58

BALTIMORE, MARYLAND

Jake Harrison's car approached the entrance to the Seagirt Terminal, swerving to a stop beside a Baltimore Police Department cruiser with the trademark blue streak down the sides. The vehicle had been parked by the gatehouse, blocking the terminal exit, creating a long line of trucks waiting to leave the port. The two police officers were leaning against the sedan, while the driver of the lead truck stuck inside the port was leaning out his window, yelling obscenities at the officers; he had a schedule to meet.

Harrison and Kendall approached the two officers; one was in his early twenties, while the other, with a moderate potbelly, was their age. It was obvious Kendall had worked with the older man before, since they knew each other's names.

"Good to see you again, Officer Kendall," the man said, adding a grin.

"Stuff it, Max," she replied. Her eyes looked him over. "Puttin' on some weight there, aren't ya? I bet the Mrs. ain't too happy. Then again, she probably wouldn't be happy if she knew half the crap you pulled when you were younger."

The man's smile disappeared from his face, then he cleared his throat.

"What's the deal here? We were directed to block the port exits and that someone from your agency would explain things when you got here."

Kendall provided the details, then asked Max to accompany them into the gatehouse.

There were three employees inside, only one of whom was busy: a guy manning the entrance window. The other two employees—a woman at the exit window and another man—sat idly in chairs. The man rose to greet the three officers, identifying himself as the on-duty customs agent.

After Kendall flashed her identification and explained the issue to the man, she handed him the sheet provided by the DDA, which listed Mixell's shipment number.

"It's a CONEX box," she said.

The customs agent entered the number into the computer, but got no result.

"It hasn't been shipped here, nor is it on any manifest scheduled for offload. I can check all East Coast ports if you'd like."

Kendall nodded and the man changed the search parameters, then ran the shipment number again. "Nothing. Either this shipment number is bad or it's off the books."

"What if it's off the books?"

"Then you're outta luck."

Kendall stepped closer to him. "If it's off the books, who do we talk to?"

"You? Fat chance of that happening. Even if you figured out who the right guy was and had the cash, his lips would be tighter than a clam's ass at high tide."

"There must be a way."

"Look, lady. If there was a way for folks like us to run this type of stuff to ground, we'd be doing it. These guys are pretty crafty, with key people in critical positions, and they ain't gonna talk. I'm afraid that if this shipment is off the books, you're not going to find it by poking around here. Of course, you could inspect every container at the port, which would take you about . . . ninety-five years."

With her hands on her hips, Kendall studied the man, then turned to Harrison. "Any ideas?"

"Assume Mixell's got the CONEX box by now. He's not going to pull up to a hotel with it, which means he'll be renting someplace where he can hide it or it'll blend in."

"Mixell could be headed anywhere in the country with it."

"True, but we've got to start somewhere. He flew into Dulles, and D.C. has the highest concentration of likely targets in the country, so I'd focus on the District and its suburbs."

Kendall considered his proposal, then nodded. "Let's get back to the NCTC and get the team looking at real estate properties."

As they returned to Harrison's car, she said, "Aren't you supposed to have dinner with your wife tonight?"

"Yeah. And . . . ?"

"Why don't I get a ride back to McLean? You can spend some time with your wife and take her to dinner, then check out the Baltimore stripper lead when the club opens tonight. Besides, I'm sure you'll enjoy running down that lead a lot more than I would."

"Sounds like a plan."

"Try to stay out of trouble." She offered a grin, then turned to Max.

"Can you give me a ride to McLean? I'll call Jason and let him know he can release the units blocking the port, so it looks like you're available."

"Not a problem," Max replied.

59

ALEXANDRIA, VIRGINIA

The return trip from the Port of Baltimore to Alexandria was uneventful, and the nonstop conversation, led by Allen Terrill, helped the time pass quickly. Upon arriving at Mixell's warehouse, Terrill pulled the truck into the building through the rear garage door.

Mixell lacked the equipment to lift the container from the flatbed, so he had arranged to rent the semi-truck for a week. After dropping down from the cab, Terrill stood there expectantly, waiting for payment. Mixell had agreed to pay him cash, keeping the transaction under the table so no taxes would be due. However, Terrill knew far too much. He was connected to the container that Harrison and others were searching for, and he knew where Mixell's warehouse was.

Mixell pressed the garage door controller, and the door slid slowly closed.

"About the money," Mixell said. "There's been a change in the payment plan."

He reached for the pistol beneath his windbreaker.

After placing Terrill's body in the truck cab, Mixell made a call, informing the man awaiting his return from Baltimore that he was now available. While he waited, he cut the seal on the CONEX box and opened the doors, then examined its contents.

Futtaim was a true professional, delivering exactly what he had ordered.

Mixell waited outside for the next appointment, standing on the dilapidated wharf behind the warehouse, surveying the surroundings. To the south, the Woodrow Wilson Bridge spanned the Potomac, with Maryland's National Harbor in the distance. Across the water was Joint Base Anacostia-Bolling, occupying the majority of the opposite shore.

At the appointed time, a boat approached, angling toward the wharf. Behind Mixell, the garage door was closed, so nothing unusual would catch the man's attention during the transaction. Mixell was just a guy on a wharf, buying a boat.

The boat driver, Eric Dahlenburg, cut the engine, then tossed him a line as he drifted in. Mixell tied it to a rusted cleat, then climbed aboard the boat to check it out.

The boat he had selected from the classified ads was a Sea Ray SPX 190 with a MerCruiser 250 horsepower outboard. It was a used boat, but Mixell would need it one time only, so there was no point in buying something new. He required something reliable and fast, and the nineteen-footer with a 250 HP outboard would certainly haul ass.

After taking the boat for a test ride to confirm it was reliable, they returned to the wharf and Mixell made the transaction. Dahlenburg left the boat behind and took an Uber back to the marina where his new love was tied up—a twin-diesel forty-foot Mainship Sedan Bridge with one good engine.

Mixell returned to the warehouse and unpacked a few items he had picked up the previous day: a laptop, cellular internet hub, three additional displays, and three cameras, then began setting things up on a six-foot-long folding table he had also procured. The computer was soon up and running, with the displays ready to receive the desired video inputs.

The last step was the camera placement, which would take the rest of the day. Mixell had preplanned their positions during previous trips to the area, selecting locations where they could monitor the desired activity without being noticed. By tonight, everything would be ready.

60
GULF OF MEXICO

A deep red glow was receding from the horizon as a helicopter beat a steady path through the darkness, south across the Gulf of Mexico. Beneath the Sikorsky S-70B Seahawk, the ocean was mostly a vast, empty expanse with intermittent yellow dots on the dark water marking the location of oil and natural gas platforms far out to sea. Inside the helicopter, Captain Murray Wilson stared out the passenger side window, his eyes fixed on the fading horizon while his thoughts dwelt elsewhere.

Six hours earlier, he had boarded a flight from Norfolk to Naval Air Station Corpus Christi in Texas, where he'd transferred aboard the awaiting Seahawk helicopter for the second leg of his journey; USS *North Carolina* was already out to sea, heading south at maximum speed to reach the ASW barrier being established as soon as possible. The submarine had probably slowed and surfaced by now, since the Seahawk was approaching the rendezvous point.

A change to the beat of the helicopter's rotors and the feeling of his seat falling out from under him announced the aircraft's descent. A glance at the navigation display across from the pilot verified they had reached their destination. Wilson peered through the window, searching the ocean for the silhouette of a submarine against the dark water, eventually spotting the hazy outline on the surface.

The Seahawk slowed to a hover fifty feet above the submarine, the downdraft from its blades sending circular ripples across the calm ocean surface. Wilson moved aft into the cabin where two crewmen helped him into a harness, which they attached to a cable along with Wilson's duffle bag.

Wilson was lowered from the side of the helicopter, the metal cable paying out slowly, the duffle bag swaying in the downdraft as the helicopter crew aimed to land him in the submarine's Bridge cockpit. The submarine's Lookout grabbed the duffle bag as it swung by, then pulled hard on the lanyard, guiding Wilson into the Bridge.

"Welcome aboard *North Carolina,*" Commander Jerry Maske shouted over the roar of the helicopter rotor.

Wilson returned the greeting as a seaman helped him out of his harness and unhooked his duffle bag, then the helicopter pulled up and away, its cable swaying in the wind as it headed north toward the Texas coast.

Commander Maske descended to the Control Room and Wilson followed.

"Rig the Bridge for Dive," Maske ordered, then turned to Wilson for additional guidance.

"Let's talk in your stateroom," Wilson said.

Maske closed his stateroom door, then waited expectantly for Wilson to explain why *North Carolina* had been ordered south at maximum speed and he had been transferred aboard. Although Maske and his crew knew something was up—the entire Atlantic Fleet had been sortied to sea and several P-8A squadrons had been transferred from PAC to support the effort—the specifics had not been shared widely. That the Fleet was searching for a Russian submarine approaching the East Coast seemed obvious, but the Fleet's orders to sink *Kazan* had been transmitted only to the units participating in the effort.

Wilson pulled an orange folder containing the sensitive order from his duffle bag, along with the directive to replace Maske as the submarine's commanding officer, both of which were a surprise to Maske.

"Wow," Maske said as he sat down, although Wilson wasn't sure to which directive he was responding.

Wilson tried to assuage the younger man's presumably hurt feelings—COMSUBLANT had deemed him inadequate for the task.

"This is nothing against you," Wilson said. "It's just that given the unique circumstances surrounding *North Carolina* and her crew, Admiral Andrea wanted a more experienced officer in command."

Maske took it better than Wilson expected. "I understand, sir. This is my first trip to sea as a commanding officer, with an untested submarine and a green crew. To tell you the truth, given these orders, I'm glad you're aboard. I would've second-guessed every decision I made."

"All right, then," Wilson said. "Let's break the news to the crew."

Maske entered the Control Room, followed by Wilson, who picked up the 1-MC microphone.

"Attention, all hands," he began.

He revealed the submarine's new order, which was met with a mix of enthusiasm and consternation from the Control Room watchstanders. Personally, Wilson shared the latter. Detecting, tracking, and prosecuting an enemy submarine was far more complex than illuminating a target with radar for a few seconds and launching a fire-and-forget missile. It required experience, intuition, and teamwork that took months to develop and sometimes hours to execute. The cat-and-mouse game between two blind opponents, listening to decipher the other's location and movements, was often a painstaking ordeal.

Wilson paused a moment to let the crew absorb their new order before discussing the second, rather delicate issue. When he explained he was taking command of *North Carolina,* all eyes in the Control Room shifted to Maske. To his credit, Maske stood beside him stoically, displaying no hint of resentment.

Wilson replaced the 1-MC microphone, then prepared to relieve Maske as commanding officer. Although Wilson had been aboard plenty of Virginia class submarines while training new commanding and executive officers, he took a moment to refamiliarize himself with the Virginia class's unique characteristics, a departure from traditional submarine design and operations.

The most obvious difference was that Sonar was in the Control Room instead of a separate room, with sonar technicians manning the consoles on the port side while fire control technicians manned the starboard consoles. Although Sonar had been added to Control, the periscopes had been removed. Virginia class submarines employed two photonics masts, which didn't penetrate the pressure hull—there was no periscope to press your eye against or dance with in endless circles for countless hours. The Officer of the Deck instead sat at a tactical workstation, raising and lowering a photonics mast with a flick of a switch and rotating it with a joystick, while monitoring the image on one of two displays at his workstation.

The most unsettling aspect of the Virginia class design changes, as far as Wilson was concerned, was ship control. The four watchstanders on previous submarines—the Helm, Outboard, Chief of the Watch, and Diving Officer of the Watch—had been replaced by two watchstanders: the Pilot and Co-Pilot, who manned the Ship Control Station. The Pilot controlled the submarine's course, speed, and depth while the Co-Pilot adjusted the buoyancy and raised and lowered the masts and antennas. Wilson figured that someone in the design shop must have forgotten they were building submarines and not aircraft; it all amounted to a horrendous break in nautical tradition.

If that weren't enough, normal control of the submarine had been delegated to the submarine's computer. On Virginia class submarines, when the Officer of the Deck ordered a new course or depth, the Pilot entered it into the Ship Control Station and the computer automatically adjusted the submarine's rudder, or bow and stern planes, to the optimal angle. If desired, manual control could be taken by giving the Pilot a specific rudder order or ship angle, but it was normally a hands-off operation aside from tapping in the new course or depth. The computer did the rest.

Wilson spent the next few minutes receiving a turnover report from Commander Maske, discussing the ship's operational status and material condition. Once satisfied he knew enough—he would spend the next few hours reviewing the submarine's status and the crew's proficiency in more detail—he relieved Maske of his command.

"Attention in Control," Wilson announced. "This is Captain Murray Wilson. I have command of *North Carolina*."

The Quartermaster entered the event into the ship's log as Wilson ordered the Officer of the Deck, "Submerge to four hundred feet, then come to course one-seven-zero, ahead flank."

61

BALTIMORE, MARYLAND

Located primarily on the 400 block of East Baltimore Street, The Block is home to several bars, strip clubs, and sex shops. Originally several blocks long and famous for its burlesque houses in the early twentieth century, the strip had shrunk and become seedier by the 1950s, marked by a notable increase in crime, prostitution, and drug dealing. Many considered the criminal activity ironic, considering the location of Baltimore Police Department's Central District headquarters—at the east end of The Block.

Harrison had taken Kendall's advice and spent a few hours with Angie, then headed toward The Block to chase down the stripper lead. It was a long shot it would amount to anything, but if Mixell had been serious—that the stripper was his *soul mate*—now that he was back in the area, perhaps they had reconnected. Find *her,* and he might find Mixell.

This time of night, the traffic was heavy and the bars full as he drove east, searching for the Player's Club. He parked in a garage not far away and entered through a small door to find a surprisingly upscale establishment with a retro decor harking back to Baltimore's burlesque days, along with two dancers hanging upside down on a two-story stripper pole. Two other women were working walkways on either side of the main stage, with the edge crowded with men waving folded dollar bills at the dancers.

The bar was likewise crowded, but Harrison found an opening and waited his turn for service. The bar was tended by a woman who was as attractive as the dancers onstage, if not more so. She finished serving a customer, then approached Harrison.

"What can I get ya?" she asked.

"What do you have on tap?"

"How about a Topless Blonde?"

The woman smiled, giving Harrison a moment to realize she was talking about a beer and not one of the blond dancers onstage.

"It's pretty good," she added, "made by a local microbrewery, Chesapeake Brewing Company." She leaned closer and placed her elbows on the bar, providing Harrison a clear view of her cleavage. "It's got a nice body. You should give it a try."

Harrison nodded and a cold beverage was soon in his hand. He took a long pull and agreed with the bartender—the Topless Blonde was quite good. After a few more sips, Harrison caught the bartender's attention.

"Can I talk to the manager?"

She eyed him suspiciously. "What for?"

"Nothing to be worried about. I need some help."

"What kind of help?"

He pulled up a picture on his cell phone. "Recognize this guy?"

Harrison already knew the answer. The bartender looked to be in her mid-twenties, and Mixell had frequented this place fifteen years ago. She would've been around ten years old.

After she shook her head, Harrison said, "I'm hoping your manager remembers this guy."

"Why are you looking for him?"

Harrison debated whether to continue with the bartender's inquisition. She was doing an admirable job running interference for her boss.

He smiled. "Manager, please."

She cast another suspicious look at him as she pulled a cell phone from under the bar and dialed. She explained the situation, listened for a few seconds, then hung up.

"He'll be out in a minute."

A short while later, a tall, lanky man with long black hair and heavily tattooed arms and neck emerged from a back room. He eyed Harrison as he approached, then stopped beside him.

"Name's Steve Reed," he said. "And you are?"

"Jake," Harrison replied. Not wanting to spook the manager with the details of his current employment, he chose a different tack. "Former

Navy guy, working a new gig." Attempting to ward off additional inquiries, he said, "The gig's not important."

Reed evaluated Harrison's assertion, then replied, "How can I help?"

"I'm looking for a guy who dated a stripper who used to work here." Harrison showed him Mixell's picture. "Would've been a customer about fifteen years ago. Recognize him?"

Reed studied the photo, then replied, "Yeah, I recognize him. Don't remember his name though. Big guy, well built, with a temper. Like you said, he dated a stripper. A platinum blonde who went by the stage name of Angel, but the guys called her Trish the Dish."

"Trish the Dish?"

"Yeah. She was pretty hot and she dished out what she had to the guys, if you know what I mean."

Harrison nodded. "What was her name?"

Reed shook his head. "I don't recall."

"Do you have any employment records, something with her name and address?"

"Nothing that far back. Just seven years, for tax purposes. In this line of work, the fewer records the better."

"Do you know what happened to her?"

"She quit one weekend. Got engaged to some guy and was going to start her life over, or so the story went. Haven't seen her since."

Harrison pointed to Mixell's photo. "To this guy?"

"Don't know for sure, but I reckon so. She was pretty tight-lipped about personal stuff."

"Can you describe her?"

Reed shrugged his shoulders. "White girl, average height and build. Beautiful face, nice tits and ass, lean legs. Platinum blonde most of the time, but sometimes dyed her hair pink or purple."

"Did she have any friends or family?"

"No family I know of, and the girls around the club were the only friends I saw her hang out with. But I can't help you there either—those girls are scattered to the winds. I'm lucky to hang on to someone for two or three years."

"Is there anything else you remember that might be helpful? Where she went to next? What she might be doing now?"

"She said she was paying her way through college, going to have a respectable life. But I'd take that with a grain of salt. Her story was the same as every stripper. Deep down, they're all good girls working nights to pay for college or to put food on the table until they get that *big break* in their acting or dancing career. At least that's what they tell the guys."

"Got it," Harrison replied.

As he searched for another line of questioning that might produce a lead, the manager asked, "So why all the sudden interest in this stripper?"

Harrison was surprised by the manager's question. "What do you mean, *all* the sudden interest?"

"A woman was in here earlier today, asking the same questions."

"Did you get her name?"

Reed shook his head. "But she's hard to miss—a tall Arab chick. A real looker. I offered her a job and she gave me a look to kill. Daggers for eyes, that girl. Know her?"

"Maybe," Harrison replied, although he was sure it was Khalila. Why was she running down this lead, and why without him? Was she trying to help, or was she trying to get to the stripper before he did? If the latter, what were Khalila's plans if she caught up to her?

As usual with Khalila, there were more questions than answers.

Harrison pulled a Bluestone Security business card from his wallet and handed it to the manager. "If you remember anything that might be helpful, give me a call."

62
ALEXANDRIA, VIRGINIA

Lonnie Mixell sat at the table in the warehouse, working into the evening as he set up the last element of his plan. The three displays were energized and connected to video feeds from the cameras he had placed the previous day, and he tweaked the angles and played with the zooms, adjusting each camera to the optimum settings.

Everything was proceeding smoothly. His biggest concern had amounted to nothing. Earlier today, he had climbed inside the CONEX box and checked out the equipment. It energized without any issues, and instructions had been provided as requested. He had spent the better part of the day reviewing the procedures. As Futtaim said, the instructions were easy to follow.

The warehouse's heavy metal entrance door began to grind open, and Mixell turned to find the realtor, Sandy Perry, stepping inside. As he wondered how she unlocked the door, he remembered he had rented and not purchased the warehouse, and Sandy still had a key.

She pushed the door closed, then greeted Mixell. "I hope I'm not intruding. I was in the area and thought I'd stop by. No one answered my knock, but the lights were on, so I thought I'd check to be sure."

Mixell realized he must have missed her knock as he concentrated on the camera adjustments.

"I was hoping you were available," she said, "because . . . Well, you know. I thought we had a great time the other day." As Mixell rose to greet her, she asked, "Are you busy?"

He was indeed busy, and was also quite irritated at her unrequested return, but his annoyance quickly faded as his eyes swept over her body.

She had come to please. She wore tight jeans, and despite the cold weather, a stomach-baring halter top clinging to her breasts. Her hair was neatly arranged and her lips glinted with freshly applied strawberry-colored lipstick.

"I *am* busy," he answered, "but could use a break." He flashed a smile.

She returned the smile and moved toward him. As she approached, she glanced over his shoulder, then gave Mixell a curious look. Her eyes shifted to the left and she stopped, standing there with an air of uncertainty.

Mixell suddenly realized the displays were still energized, and she had noticed what his cameras were monitoring. There was also a pistol lying on the table.

Sandy Perry had seen too much.

She realized it as well.

"If this is a bad time," she said, her voice quavering, "I—I can come back later."

Mixell started toward her.

"Actually, now—now that I think about it, I need—I've got an appointment in a half-hour."

She began backing toward the door.

"I really shouldn't have used my key. I—I'm so sorry. I—I'll be going now."

Sandy turned to leave, but the door was heavy and opened slowly. Mixell closed the remaining distance and placed a firm hand on the door before it opened wide enough for Sandy to slip outside. He pushed it shut as he wrapped his other arm around the woman's waist and pulled her close. He kissed her on the lips as he let his hand move slowly down her ass. When she didn't respond to his touch, he realized, with some amusement, that she was too afraid to move.

Sandy's fate was sealed, but he couldn't waste the opportunity to toy with her.

"Actually, this *is* a bad time, and I regret what happened between us the other day. You see, I'm in a committed relationship and it would be unfortunate if word got out that I've been messing around. My soul mate is the jealous type, and I'd hate for anything to happen to you."

"I—I won't say a word. I promise. No one will find out."

"You're right," Mixell replied. "No one will find out."

He had no weapon on him—his pistol was on the table—but considering the victim, he didn't need one.

He spun Sandy around and pressed his body against hers, pinning her against the wall.

"PLEASE! I WON'T TELL ANYONE!"

Mixell grabbed her head with both hands and twisted it forcefully, turning her face around toward his. Her body squirmed as she tried to break free, her neck muscles straining as she fought the rotation. She tried to speak, but the force on her jaw from Mixell's hands prevented her from talking. He could tell she was pleading for her life, but the only thing he heard was a desperate whimper.

As her head twisted slowly toward him, he saw the pain on her face and the panic in her eyes. He leaned in for a lingering kiss, then pulled back and twisted her head with all his strength until her neck gave way with a sickening sound of shredding tendons and cartilage.

She dropped to the floor when he released her, and he knelt beside her as she stared at him. She was paralyzed but still conscious, and she opened her mouth to scream. Mixell placed a hand over her mouth and nose, suffocating her, watching the illumination fade from her beautiful hazel eyes.

63

MAD FOX ZERO-FOUR • K-561 *KAZAN*

MAD FOX ZERO-FOUR

The P-8A Poseidon, call sign *Mad Fox zero-four,* cruised at thirty thousand feet, circling above its station in the Gulf of Mexico. The P-8A, a modified Boeing 737-800ERX, was the replacement for the venerable P-3C Orion submarine hunter aircraft, sporting an array of technological improvements coupled with next-generation GPS-capable sonobuoys and a significant enhancement in weapon payload. The P-8As carried five HAAWCs (High Altitude ASW Weapon Capability)—MK 54 torpedoes with wing kits. Once the torpedo was ejected, the HAAWC's wings popped out and guided the torpedo, changing its descent angle and course as required, aiming for a GPS coordinate in the ocean.

Despite the improvements incorporated into the P-8A, there had been two steps backward in the new aircraft's design. The first was that the P-8As lacked the magnetic anomaly detection equipment carried aboard its predecessor, since it patrolled at a much higher altitude, and the second was a minor but somewhat annoying deficiency: Lieutenant Commander George Stringer, the crew's Tactical Coordinator or TACCO, in charge of the personnel in the aircraft's cabin, had no window to look through.

The P-8A had only two observer windows in the forward portion of the cabin. If he'd had a window, Stringer might have been able to spot another of the P-8As forming a line stretching six hundred miles across the Gulf, from Mexico to the Florida Keys.

Stringer took a break from his duties and leaned back in his chair, glancing at the other four watchstanders in the cabin: Sensor One and

Sensor Two monitored the data relayed from the sonobuoy field floating below, and Sensor Three manned the surface search radar and infrared sensor, capable of detecting submarine periscopes or the hot exhaust from a snorkel mast in case a submarine was running its diesel generator. Lieutenant Jeff Hanover, the crew's Communicator and only other officer in the cabin, sat at the NavCom station.

Stringer pressed his hands to his headphones, listening closely to the report being transmitted over the aircraft's Internal Communication System.

"TACCO, Sensor Two. Have a contact, buoy two-one, bearing two-four-eight, up doppler. Contact is approaching distro field from the south, classified POS SUB Medium. Request box sonobuoy pattern built off buoy two-one."

Sensor Two had detected a contact with a medium probability it was a submarine, approaching buoy 21 on a bearing of 248. But the sonobuoys in the distributed field were spaced so far apart that they held the contact on only one buoy, so they needed to drop a more closely spaced sonobuoy field to determine the contact's position, course, and speed.

Stringer turned his attention to his display, noting the location of sonobuoy 21, which transmitted its position to the P-8A sensor suite, waiting while Lieutenant Hanover calculated the placement of the new buoys in the box pattern built off buoy 21.

"TACCO, NavCom. All expendable drop points calculated."

After reviewing the coordinates for the new buoy field, Stringer sent them to the cockpit. "Flight, TACCO. Here's your expendable points."

The Patrol Plane Commander replied, "TACCO, Flight. Coming left to Expendable One."

Mad Fox zero-four turned west as the crew prepared to drop their closely spaced field of sonobuoys. A moment later, the buoys left the P-8A one by one, splashing into the ocean.

K-561 *KAZAN*

"Command Post, Hydroacoustic! Close aboard splashes, port and starboard sides!"

Captain Lieutenant Urnovitz acknowledged Hydroacoustic's report, then selected the Captain's stateroom on his communication panel, requesting his presence in the Command Post.

Plecas arrived a moment later. "What have you got?"

"Close aboard splashes. Looks like a sonobuoy field is being laid around us. First pass on an east–west axis."

Another announcement over the Command Post speakers interrupted Urnovitz's report. "Command Post, Hydroacoustic. Another series of splashes ahead."

"Man Combat Stations," Plecas ordered. "This is the Captain. I have the Conn."

Urnovitz passed the order to man Combat Stations, followed by an order to Hydroacoustic. "Send triangulation ranges from the spherical and towed arrays to fire control."

Although *Kazan*'s passive sonar systems could normally determine only a target's bearing, if the contacts were extremely close, such as the buoys being dropped around them, their range could be estimated by triangulating the bearings from the spherical and towed array sonars. As Plecas peered over the nearest fire controlman's shoulder, the buoys appeared on the geographic display. Two rows formed, each with four sonobuoys, both rows almost perpendicular to *Kazan*'s course. They were passing through the first row now, two buoys to starboard and two buoys to port, with the second row two thousand yards ahead.

"Command Post, Hydroacoustic. Third row of buoys being dropped."

A third row of contacts appeared on the screen, beyond the first two rows. *Kazan* was passing through the sonobuoy field, and the only thing they could do until they exited was maximize their distance from each buoy, splitting the distance equally between them.

"Steersman, come right to course three-five-zero," Plecas ordered. "Ahead one-third."

Kazan turned slightly right, threading its way between the second row of sonobuoys, slowing to reduce the signature from its main engines and screw.

In the Command Post, the submarine's First Officer and another twenty men hurriedly donned their sound-powered phone headsets, energizing the dormant consoles and plot displays. Combat Stations brought the ship to a combat footing as the crew prepared to fight and defend itself. But against an aircraft dropping sonobuoys, there was nothing to attack. Their sole aim was to protect themselves if the aircraft dropped a torpedo, speeding away from the Splash Point as soon as possible while they tried to fool the torpedo with decoys.

MAD FOX ZERO-FOUR

George Stringer adjusted the GEN track on his screen so it agreed with the data from the two buoys holding the contact. A submarine in the middle of a buoy field this tightly packed would normally have been held on at least four buoys, but if this was a submarine, it was a quiet one indeed, held on only two. But now that they held the contact, he needed to determine the target's solution.

The contact parameters on Stringer's display turned from amber to green, indicating the automated algorithms agreed with his solution for the target's position, course, and speed. The next step was to decide whether the contact was a submarine. After assessing the indications, he made the call.

"All stations, TACCO. Set Battle Condition One."

Each member of the crew, from the pilots to the Sensor Operators, pulled out their weapon release checklists, methodically accomplishing each step.

Stringer continued his calculations, determining the Splash Point for their torpedo, placing it in an optimum position to detect the submarine once the torpedo entered the water and began its search. As a P-3C TACCO, Stringer would have then calculated the Release Point—the location where the aircraft would drop its free-falling torpedo, so that it landed at the Splash Point. However, that was no longer necessary, since HAAWCs could fly to their destination, as long as they had enough glide path.

After verifying that was the case, Stringer reported, "Flight TACCO, weapon is in the launch basket. We are Weapons Red and Free. Give me bomb bay open, Master Arm On."

The aircraft shuddered as the bomb bay doors swung open, clearing the way for one of its lightweight torpedoes. Stringer selected Bay One, holding his hand over the Storage Release button.

On Stringer's console, an amber light illuminated.

"Flight, TACCO. I have a Kill Ready light. Standing by for weapon release."

"TACCO, Flight. You are authorized to release."

Stringer pressed the Storage Release button for Bay One, sending the HAAWC toward its destination.

64

K-561 *KAZAN*

"Command Post, Hydroacoustic. Additional splash, bearing three-three-zero." But before Plecas could acknowledge, Hydroacoustic announced, "Torpedo in the water! Bearing three-three-zero!"

Plecas overrode his instinct to order torpedo evasion. In this scenario, it would do more harm than good. Torpedoes didn't hold their target at first: submarine-launched torpedoes were usually launched well beyond detection range and were given a course to travel that would bring them close enough to the target submarine to detect it. Air-launched torpedoes also didn't hold the target when they entered the water—they executed various search patterns to detect the nearby submarine.

Torpedo evasion tactics were designed for the submarine to depart the area before the torpedo got close enough to detect the submarine, often deploying decoys and jammers to distract or inhibit the torpedo's sonar.

In this case, Plecas figured the air-dropped torpedo was doing a circle search, using both active and passive sonar to detect *Kazan*. If Plecas ordered ahead flank, *Kazan*'s main engines and screw would put an enormous amount of noise into the water, which was of little concern against submarine-launched torpedoes, which typically began their transit miles away. This wasn't the case with the air-dropped torpedo. It was likely very close, and increasing *Kazan*'s speed to ahead flank would light up the torpedo's passive sonar. Against a lightweight torpedo dropped nearby, playing possum worked better.

However, modern torpedoes also employed active sonar, and an object as large as *Kazan* would easily register as a valid sonar return, prompting the torpedo to travel toward it to investigate. Plecas needed a way to interfere with the torpedo's active sonar without giving away the submarine was nearby to its passive sonar or the aircraft crew above, which meant ejecting a broadband sonar jammer wasn't an option.

As Plecas searched for a solution, he recalled that during *Kazan*'s trip to the surface to cut away the tangled net, they had passed through a strong thermocline, with its lower boundary at sixty meters.

The thermocline was a thin layer of water where the temperature transitioned rapidly between the warm surface heated by the sun and the cold water beneath. Submarines used thermoclines to their advantage because the rapid temperature change bent sound waves as they traveled through the layer, reflecting the sound back toward its source like light reflecting off a window. Depending on the frequency and angle of the sound wave, some tonals wouldn't make it through. If Plecas could place *Kazan* on the other side of the layer before the torpedo detected it, they'd have a chance.

"Hydroacoustic, Command Post. Report torpedo detection angle."

"Command Post, Hydroacoustic. Spherical array detection angle is down ten degrees."

The torpedo was below *Kazan,* which meant it was also below the layer.

"Steersman, all stop. Compensation Officer, hover to forty meters."

Kazan's main engines went silent as the Compensation Officer pumped water from the variable ballast tanks. As *Kazan* rose toward the surface, the questions in Plecas's mind were—would they rise above the layer before the torpedo's circle search lined up toward *Kazan,* and was the layer strong enough to deflect the torpedo's sonar pings?

Plecas turned up the audio from the spherical array hydrophones. Unlike the powerful surface ship sonars that transmitted reverberating pings, the torpedo sonar had far less power and pinged at a higher frequency, which sounded more like a bird chirp. The strength of the chirps was steadily increasing—the torpedo was turning toward them.

"One hundred meters," the Compensation Officer reported.

Kazan rose steadily, the torpedo chirps increasing in volume as well. When *Kazan* passed through the layer, the chirps faded. Plecas breathed a sigh of relief; if they couldn't hear the torpedo, it couldn't hear its return pings either.

The Compensation Officer flooded water back into the tanks, halting *Kazan*'s ascent.

"On ordered depth," he reported. "Steady at forty meters."

Now that *Kazan* was shallow and the torpedo on the opposite side of the layer, Plecas worried about detection from above. At forty meters, the top of *Kazan*'s sail was only twenty meters from the surface. However, the torpedo had likely been dropped by a P-8A maritime patrol aircraft, which lacked the magnetic anomaly detection equipment carried by its predecessor. With twenty meters of water between *Kazan* and the surface, it was most likely safe from visual detection as well.

It was quiet in the Command Post as Plecas and his crew waited—until the silence was broken by a report.

"Command Post, Hydroacoustic. Have regained the torpedo's sonar."

On the spherical array speaker, Plecas detected the faint chirp.

The torpedo was rising above the layer to take a look.

"Compensation Officer, flood all tanks at maximum rate. Hover to one hundred meters."

Plecas ordered *Kazan* to just below the layer, the best place to hide from someone, or something, searching above it.

As *Kazan* dropped below the layer, the torpedo pings faded again. Thus far, they'd been lucky, vacating the water column the torpedo was searching in before they were detected.

Silence returned to the Command Post as Plecas and his crew waited tensely for indication the torpedo had locked on to their submarine. After a while, Plecas checked the Command Post clock. The torpedo had been dropped thirty minutes ago and had likely run to fuel exhaustion by now.

Erik Fedorov, *Kazan*'s First Officer, approached. "What now?" he asked.

"We wait. We convince the air crew that it was a false detection."

65

USS *NORTH CAROLINA*

"Conn, Radio. Download in progress."

Murray Wilson sat in the Captain's chair in the Control Room, listening to the report. *North Carolina* had just arrived in its assigned operating area and had gone to periscope depth to download the latest round of naval messages, which Wilson hoped included information on *Kazan*'s location.

Submarines were the most effective platform against other submarines, but the detection range was still limited. Had Wilson been forced to build an effective ASW barrier across the Gulf with just submarines, it would have taken at least thirty. Thankfully, the P-8As had been quickly repositioned, establishing the desired barrier, and *North Carolina* had been assigned a station in the center of the second layer. However, the probability *Kazan* would travel through *North Carolina*'s operating area was low, and Wilson and his crew awaited queuing information.

That information finally arrived. A radioman handed Wilson the message board with the pertinent message on top. A P-8A had detected a contact classified as POS SUB Medium and dropped two torpedoes, neither of which homed to detonation. The P-8A in question was monitoring their sonobuoy field and hadn't regained the contact, and had reclassified their initial detection as a false target.

This wasn't a surprise to Wilson. Most people untrained in antisubmarine warfare had no appreciation for how difficult it was for surface and air crews to detect a submerged contact, much less verify it was a submarine. In the Falklands War between the United Kingdom and Argentina, for example, the British Navy expended more than one thousand torpedoes without sinking a single submarine. After the war, following an analysis of the Argentinian submarine movements, the British Navy reluctantly concluded that all one thousand attacks had been against false targets. A common joke after the war was that the British Navy had launched a torpedo against every whale fart in the ocean.

Submarines, however, had an advantage over their surface and air brethren. They operated in the same environment as their opponent, with better sensors and better trained crews when it came to acoustic processing. Below the surface, submarines operated blind and sonar was their lifeblood. While surface and air crews often couldn't identify a submarine as friend or foe—they attacked anything submerged in their waterspace if they were weapons free—submarine crews could analyze down to the individual submarine class and sometimes even to the specific submarine if it had a unique tonal.

Wilson finished reading the message, contemplating the P-8A encounter. *Kazan* was the newest and quietest Russian submarine; it was possible the false target was indeed *Kazan*.

After debating the matter, Wilson decided it was better to run down a lead rather than sit around doing nothing. He buzzed the submarine's Communicator on the ICSAP panel.

"Draft a message requesting the waterspace behind *Mad Fox zero-four,*" Wilson ordered.

While the submarine's Communicator worked on the message, Commander Jerry Maske approached, informing Wilson the Battle Stations watchbill had been updated. After relieving Maske of his command, Wilson had pondered what to do with Maske, the most experienced officer aboard aside from him. After considering the issue, he decided to assign Maske as the submarine's Fire Control Coordinator during Battle Stations.

As Executive Officer on his last submarine, Maske had spent two years as Fire Control Coordinator, all of it on an operational submarine, while *North Carolina*'s current Executive Officer had never prosecuted a real submarine as FCC—only simulated trainer contacts thus far. With the Executive Officer freed up, Wilson reassigned him as Battle Stations Officer of the Deck, tapping into his experience as well.

The Communicator approached with the draft message, which Wilson approved for release, and it was quickly transmitted.

While they waited for a response, Wilson decided to move *North Carolina* toward the edge of their current operating area, where they would go back to periscope depth. Hopefully, by then they would be assigned the desired waterspace behind *Mad Fox zero-four.*

"Officer of the Deck, come down to four hundred feet and course two-six-zero. Increase speed to ahead flank."

66

MCLEAN, VIRGINIA

"This could take forever," Harrison said.

"Not forever," Kendall replied, "but close."

It was like looking for a needle in a haystack.

The thought crossed Harrison's mind, not for the first time, as he sat beside Kendall in the NCTC, shifting through real estate leads on his computer, searching for places Mixell could store a CONEX box. They were making slow progress due to the sheer volume of possibilities; there were more than fifty thousand properties on the market in the Washington, D.C., area. Even after they were winnowed down to those that could hide a CONEX box—warehouses and rural listings with a barn or forested land—a painstaking satellite review of each property was required, and in many cases, eyes on target from agents or officers visiting the property.

Harrison leaned back and took a swig of lukewarm coffee from his fifth cup of the day, taking a break as he gazed across the main floor of the NCTC, packed with analysts scouring data. They had been at it nonstop for the last two days, with Kendall getting things started shortly after their visit to the Port of Baltimore, and Harrison joining her the next morning. Thus far, however, their efforts had yielded nothing.

To help track Mixell down, the NCTC had released his image, captured as he debarked the flight at Dulles International Airport, but the effort was suffering because the issue hadn't been designated a National Special Security Event by the Department of Homeland Security. They hadn't yet determined what Mixell's target was—person, place, or event—nor even what type of weapon had been shipped to Baltimore.

As a result, the NCTC wasn't entirely focused on Mixell, spreading its resources across several potential terrorist actions.

Nonetheless, potential leads had been flowing into the NCTC via phone calls and emails from various law enforcement agencies in the area. Kendall was flicking her way down a plethora of email reports from the Maryland State Police, and he could tell she was reconsidering her decision to involve the state troopers. Still, scouring through police reports seemed infinitely more interesting than reviewing properties for rent or sale, and Harrison had been helping Kendall, while the real estate review had been delegated to a dozen other analysts allocated to them by Jessica Del Rio, the NCTC supervisor.

Harrison returned to his computer, scrolling down the emails, reviewing the subject of each before moving on, when his eyes stopped on a missing person report. Wondering what a missing person report had to do with Lonnie Mixell or places he might hide a CONEX box, he read further. When he got down to *Missing Person's Occupation,* his eyes halted.

He nudged Kendall on the shoulder. "What do you think?" he said, pointing to the screen.

She leaned over and read the report. "A missing realtor?"

Her eyes moved down to the woman's home address.

"Alexandria. Close to D.C. and minutes from I-395 and I-495. Sounds like a decent location for Mixell, assuming he's found a warehouse. What type of property does she specialize in?"

Harrison scanned the report. "Doesn't say."

He picked up the phone and dialed the Alexandria City Police Department, and after two transfers, was connected to the officer who filed the report.

"Sandy Perry?" he repeated back to Harrison. "Yeah, she's a realtor. Actually, she has her own company. Her secretary reported her missing this morning; she missed several appointments and she's not answering her phone. Her secretary stopped by her townhouse, but she wasn't home either."

"What type of properties does she specialize in?"

"Mostly commercial. Offices, retail space, warehouses, that type of thing."

"Do you know if she's rented any warehouses in the last few weeks?"

"Don't have a clue," the officer said. "I only took down the missing person details. You'd have to talk to her secretary."

"Got her name and number?"

"The name's Ashley Gonzalez," the officer replied, then provided her home, office, and cell phone numbers.

After thanking the officer and hanging up, Harrison dialed Ashley's cell phone. The woman answered and Harrison identified himself, then asked if her boss had rented any warehouses recently.

"A couple," was the response. "Why do you ask?"

Harrison explained they were searching for a man who might have something to do with Sandy Perry's disappearance—a man who was likely looking for a warehouse to rent—then asked for the addresses.

"I don't have them with me. I'd have to check the computer at work."

"Hold on for a second." He turned to Kendall, placing the phone on mute. "What do you think? Worth checking out tonight? The fresh air would do us good."

Kendall leaned back in her chair and stretched, extending her arms behind her head.

"Good idea," she said. "I could use the break, plus we can stop for a decent dinner while we're out, instead of the crappy cafeteria food."

Harrison unmuted the phone. "Where's your office?" He wrote down the address, then asked, "Can you meet us there tonight?"

"Sure. What time?"

"We can be there in . . ." He turned to Kendall, who said, "A half-hour."

Harrison made the appointment, then he and Kendall retrieved their weapons from their lockers and left for the garage. Kendall offered to drive since she knew the area, and a few minutes later, they were on their way.

As Kendall's car pulled from the parking garage onto Lewinsville Road, a dark blue Hyundai Tucson followed, trailing far enough behind to escape notice. In the driver's seat, Khalila Dufour slipped sunglasses on as her SUV turned toward the setting sun.

67

K-561 *KAZAN*

Aleksandr Plecas leaned over the fire controlman's shoulder, studying the geographic display on his console. *Kazan* was proceeding at three knots on its electric drive, the minimum speed possible for bare steerageway, at a depth of one hundred meters, just below the thermocline. Stealth was paramount, and *Kazan* was rigged for ultra-quiet. Only the essential personnel were on watch, with all others confined to their beds, minimizing the possibility of a watertight door being closed too forcefully, someone dropping a tool on the deck, or even a toilet seat slamming down too hard, with the sound transmitted through the submarine's steel hull into the ocean.

Plecas had no choice but to take the risk of being detected again—he had to extract *Kazan* from the sonobuoy field; they couldn't sit there forever. He had a schedule to meet, and they had burned through most of the reserve time he had incorporated into their transit.

Thus far, the extraction appeared to have worked. *Kazan* had slowly slipped past the sonobuoys and the twelve-buoy field was drawing farther behind them with no indication the maritime patrol aircraft above them had reacted.

Plecas maintained *Kazan* at three knots until they were ten thousand meters away from the sonobuoy field, then increased speed to ten knots. He stopped beside the navigation table and queried Michman Korzhev, the Navigation Party Technician.

"What is the required speed to reach the launch point on time?"

Korzhev measured the distance and replied, "Eighteen knots, Captain."

Plecas turned to his Watch Officer. "Shift propulsion to the main engines and proceed at ahead full, shaft turns for eighteen knots."

After the Watch Officer acknowledged and issued the orders, Plecas turned back to Korzhev.

"Time to launch point?"

"One hour and ten minutes, sir."

68

ALEXANDRIA, VIRGINIA

Dusk was falling, shadows creeping across the city as Kendall pulled into a parking spot in front of the Perry Realty Company on Duke Street, not far from city hall. Ashley Gonzalez met Harrison and Kendall at the front door and ushered them into a small, but well-appointed reception area containing several plush chairs and a single desk. After introducing herself, she slid into the desk chair as the two CIA officers moved behind her.

She had already pulled up the recent sales and rental agreements Sandy Perry had arranged over the last month, and had them sorted by type of property. She scrolled down to the warehouse section, where three buildings were listed. All were in Alexandria, and one was purchased while two were rented.

"Do you know who the buyer or renter is for each one?" Harrison asked.

"Certainly," Ashley replied. She clicked on each entry, which expanded them to show the details.

One was purchased by a woman, which temporarily ruled that one out, while the other two buildings were rented by men, neither of whose names Harrison recognized: Jim Patton and David Morrell.

"Do you know when she signed those two rental agreements?"

Mixell hadn't been in the country for long, and assuming he evaluated the property in person before signing the rental agreement, there was a narrow window to work with.

"Let me check the paperwork," Ashley replied.

She navigated through the computer's file directory, opening the rental agreements for the two properties in question. The first had been signed two weeks ago, well before Mixell had returned to America. The second date, however, fit perfectly. It was signed the same day Mixell had flown into Dulles.

"That's it," Kendall said, who pulled up the map app on her phone and typed in the address. "Just a few blocks away."

69

K-561 *KAZAN*

"Entering launch basket."

Captain Lieutenant Mikhail Alekhin, *Kazan*'s Weapons Officer, made the report.

"Verify each target is within range," Plecas ordered.

Plecas waited as Alekhin ran the target package through fire control, checking the distance to each target. Once the fire control system completed its calculations, Alekhin announced, "All twenty targets are within range."

To his Watch Officer, Plecas ordered, "Slow to ten knots."

Captain Lieutenant Ludvig Yelchin, this section's Watch Officer, relayed the order to the Steersman, and after *Kazan* coasted down to the ordered speed, Plecas picked up the tactical communication microphone.

"Hydroacoustic, Captain. Perform detailed acoustic search, all sectors. Report all contacts."

A few minutes later, after analyzing the broadband and narrowband sensor data, Hydroacoustic reported, "Captain, Hydroacoustic. Hold no contacts."

That was good news, but the Kalibr missiles would leave behind a white smoke trail, pinpointing *Kazan*'s position for any nearby warships or military aircraft.

Caution was prudent. Plecas had been surprised by the maritime patrol aircraft they had encountered a few hours earlier. The Americans had apparently established an ASW barrier across the Gulf of Mexico, in addition to the one he expected to be arrayed along the United States' East Coast. Whoever was in charge of the American ASW forces was astute indeed, recognizing that launching from the Gulf of Mexico would produce even more devastating results.

It was clear that the Americans had placed P-8A assets in the Gulf, but what else? As for submarines, he doubted there were any in the Gulf. All of the Atlantic Fleet submarine home ports were on the East Coast, with the nearest fast attack port being in Norfolk, Virginia. It seemed unreasonable to route a submarine to the Gulf when it was far easier to position maritime patrol aircraft there.

The only remaining task was to verify there were no warships on the horizon or military aircraft circling above, waiting to attack.

Plecas turned to his Watch Officer.

"Man Combat Stations and proceed to periscope depth."

70

ALEXANDRIA, VIRGINIA

The warehouse was at the end of Oronoco Street, built on the bank of the Potomac River and nestled between Oronoco Bay and Founders Park. Kendall eased off the gas as they approached the last intersection before the river. The warehouse was on the far left corner and mostly shrouded in darkness, with only a few sporadic streetlights illuminating the area.

Kendall turned right and went a block before doing a U-turn, then parked in the darkness alongside Founders Park. She pulled her pistol from its holster as she stepped from the car, holding it down by her side away from the street, so any passing cars or pedestrians wouldn't notice. Harrison did the same, accompanying her to the corner of North Union and Oronoco, where they stopped in the shadows to survey the warehouse.

There were no windows or doors on the short side of the building, and a single door and several multipaned windows spanned the long side. Harrison checked the warehouse for evidence of a security system—cameras or motion detectors—but didn't spot any telltale signs.

As they prepared to cross the street, they had a short discussion concerning who would lead. Kendall seemed well trained and proficient with a firearm—her movements were fluid and thus far she'd been composed under pressure—but she quickly conceded that Harrison was likely far better trained and more experienced in combat, and agreed to let him lead.

She followed Harrison across the street, where they stayed close to the building, working their way toward the door, a heavy metal contraption with a lever-type handle. Harrison tried to lift it slowly and hopefully silently, but it didn't budge. The door was locked.

Harrison moved toward the nearest window, which was a multi-pane design that couldn't be opened, and peered inside. The window was too filthy to see through, so he wiped most of the grime away with his sleeve; enough to get a decent look.

Inside the building was an eighteen-wheeler truck cab attached to a flatbed trailer, atop which sat a CONEX box. In the truck cab, a man sat slumped in the driver's seat, either asleep or dead. Nearby was a table with a laptop connected to several video monitors. A small desk lamp illuminated a man seated at the table with his back to the window. Also inside the warehouse was a green Ford Fusion, matching the description of the missing realtor's car.

Jackpot. They had found Mixell and whatever he had purchased from Futtaim.

There was no one else in sight, although Harrison didn't have a clear view of the entire interior. He searched for another entrance, scanning the other two walls. Unfortunately, the only feature was a large garage door on the opposite wall, which was shut.

There didn't seem to be a way to enter the building without alerting Mixell. The metal door looked too heavy to break through, and the last thing they needed was to give away their presence in a failed attempt. The window panes were large enough to squeeze through, but that was a bad idea. Mixell would be alerted the moment they broke the glass, and they'd be easy targets as they pulled themselves into the building.

He let Kendall take a look. Her eyes canvassed the interior, then she dropped below the window. "The garage door in the back. It's a long shot, but maybe there's an external controller."

Harrison led the way around the building, stopping beside the industrial-sized garage door. But there was no external controller.

They'd have to call for backup, requesting a unit with forced entry capabilities. It was times like this when Harrison missed being a Navy SEAL. A single four-man fire team would have been sufficient. Fire teams typically included a breaker—a SEAL trained in explosives—who was an expert at blasting entrances open.

Kendall retrieved her cell phone and pulled up her contacts, selecting an FBI card. She scrolled through the numbers, then selected one and placed the phone to her ear.

"Tony, this is Pat Kendall. We've found Mixell. He's in a warehouse in Alexandria on the corner of Oronoco and North Union." There was a short pause, then Kendall said, "Just my partner, and Mixell is alone as far as we can tell. But his CONEX box is inside, and there's no telling what kind of weapons he's got." There was another pause. "No, no, no," she said. "I need more than just firepower. I need a unit that can bust in. How about the HRT?"

She looked at Harrison for corroboration. The HRT was the FBI's Hostage Rescue Team, manned by over one hundred specially trained FBI agents. Renowned for its low subject fatality rate and frequently idle without any hostages to rescue, it often served as an elite FBI SWAT unit. There were three tactical units, one based in Washington, D.C.

Harrison nodded his agreement while Kendall waited for an answer.

"Thanks, Tony. I owe you one."

After she hung up, she said, "They're sending an HRT unit."

"How long?"

"About an hour."

Harrison didn't like the prospect of sitting around for an hour, but Mixell didn't seem to be up to anything nefarious at the moment.

"Let's move back to the other side, where we can monitor what he's up to."

Kendall nodded her agreement.

71

K-561 *KAZAN* • USS *NORTH CAROLINA*

K-561 *KAZAN*

Kazan tilted upward, rising toward periscope depth as the Watch Officer kept his face pressed to the attack periscope, the aft of the submarine's two scopes. Despite the crowded Central Command Post, now at full Combat Stations manning, it was quiet while *Kazan* rose from the deep.

Captain Lieutenant Yelchin announced, "Periscope clear," and began turning the scope swiftly, completing several sweeps in search of nearby contacts.

Kazan settled out at periscope depth as Yelchin declared, "No close contacts!"

Conversation resumed now that there was no threat of collision, and Yelchin completed a more detailed scan of the ocean and sky, searching for distant ships or aircraft.

While Plecas waited for Yelchin to complete his search, he focused on the pending launch. From *Kazan*'s launch point, its missiles could destroy all designated targets, which had been loaded into *Kazan*'s Missile Control System: the twenty largest military command centers in the United States aside from the Pentagon itself. There would be casualties, but the targets were military, which had been a key reason Plecas had agreed to the plan.

The American paying for his daughter's medical treatment was being funded by a Middle Eastern organization, and he had convinced its leadership that the proper targets were military and not civilian. By attacking military command centers, they could defeat the American claim that they were terrorists, and instead demonstrate that they were soldiers in a war against Western aggression. The only arguably civilian target was the White House. However, the president of the United States was the head of its military, and thus met the criteria in Plecas's mind.

The missile strikes would still claim many lives, but not more than those suffered by the Russian Navy at the hands of the Americans a few months ago. It was a fair quid pro quo as far as Plecas was concerned, an acceptable request in return for his daughter's treatment.

"Hold no contacts."

Yelchin had completed his search; there were no surface or air contacts within visual range.

Kazan had spent fifteen days traveling from Gadzhiyevo Naval Base through the Barents Sea, the Atlantic Ocean, and had finally reached the designated launch point in the Gulf of Mexico.

After Yelchin's report, the men turned toward Plecas, one by one, awaiting the next order.

It was time.

Plecas announced, "Prepare to Fire, full Kalibr salvo, vertical launch tubes One through Four."

The Weapons Officer acknowledged and prepared to launch all twenty missiles.

"All missiles are energized," he reported. A moment later, he said, "All missiles have accepted target coordinates."

Yelchin initiated the next step. "Open missile hatches, tubes One through Four."

The hatches atop the submarine's port and starboard sides began retracting.

USS *NORTH CAROLINA*

"Conn, Sonar. Detect mechanical transients, bearing two-four-one, designated Sierra four-five."

As the Officer of the Deck acknowledged the report, Wilson stood and evaluated the bearing on the navigation table. His request to move *North Carolina* to the waterspace behind *Mad Fox zero-four* had been approved, and *North Carolina* had entered its new operating area ten minutes ago, slowing for an initial sonar search. The search had turned up nothing, and Wilson had decided to return to ahead full and proceed to the middle of their new operating area.

Given Sonar's report, he now reconsidered. At high speed, the turbulent flow of water across the submarine's sensors reduced their effective range. They needed to slow and evaluate the mechanical transient.

Wilson ordered the Officer of the Deck, "Slow to ten knots."

Shortly after *North Carolina* slowed, Sonar reported, "Hold a new contact on the towed array, designated Sierra four-six, ambiguous bearings two-four-two and two-nine-eight."

The bearing to the southwest correlated to the mechanical transient, and Wilson waited as Sonar evaluated the frequencies and broadband noise received.

"Conn, Sonar. Sierra four-six is classified submerged."

They had found Kazan.

Wilson focused on the mechanical transient.

Kazan was preparing to launch.

He turned to his Officer of the Deck.

"Open outer doors, all torpedo tubes."

During the transit, Wilson had loaded all four torpedo tubes and powered up the weapons, completing their diagnostic checks. The torpedoes were ready for combat, but his crew wasn't.

"Man Battle Stations."

K-561 *KAZAN*

"Missile hatches, tubes One through Four, are open."

Plecas glanced at the missile tube panel, verifying the indicating lights for hatches One through Four were green, while *Kazan*'s Weapons Officer verified all launch criteria were met.

"Ready to fire, full Kalibr missile salvo."

Plecas evaluated the tactical situation, plus the readiness of his submarine and crew, one final time, then gave the order.

"Launch all missiles, tubes One through Four."

USS *NORTH CAROLINA*

"Loud transient on the bearing of Sierra four-five!"

The Sonar Supervisor almost shouted the report, even though he was standing only a few feet from Wilson and the Officer of the Deck, supervising the Sonar consoles on the port side of the Control Room.

The supervisor followed up, "Missile launch transient!"

A sick feeling settled low and cold in Wilson's gut.

They were too late.

Despite the trepidation, he responded instantly.

"Quick Reaction Firing, Sierra four-six, tube Two!"

This wasn't the situation Wilson had hoped for. Battle Stations weren't yet fully manned, plus they didn't have a firing solution for *Kazan;* they had just begun the process of determining the submarine's course, speed, and range. However, they didn't have time for an accurate shot. Wilson needed to stop *Kazan* from launching as soon as possible, which meant getting a torpedo into the water fast, regardless of its probability of hitting the Russian submarine.

If there had ever been a true test of the Submarine Force's land-based training program, its crew toiling for endless hours in tactical training labs, this was it. *North Carolina* hadn't been to sea in over two years, and this crew had never operated at sea together before today. Wilson was pleasantly surprised, however.

The nearest fire control technician promoted his solution to master, sending his best guess at the contact's course, speed, and range to Weapon Control, while the fire control technician beside him configured his workstation into the Weapons Control Console, then sent the target solution and search parameters to the torpedo in tube Two.

After verifying the torpedo accepted the presets, he announced, "Weapon Ready!"

Wilson gave the order. "Shoot tube Two."

The torpedo was ejected from its tube and turned onto its ordered course. Wilson had no idea if the shot was good enough to get a hit, but the torpedo's primary purpose was to distract *Kazan*'s crew. He had deliberately fired from a torpedo tube facing *Kazan,* increasing the chance their sonarmen would detect the unique sound of a torpedo launch, which would force them to commence evasion procedures, terminating their missile launch.

Stopping the launch was the immediate goal. Sinking *Kazan* would come next.

72
K-561 *KAZAN*

"Torpedo launch transient, bearing zero-six-two!"

Plecas spun toward the nearest sonar display, spotting a bright white blip on the reported bearing. As he wondered whether Hydroacoustic had identified the transient correctly, another report followed.

"Torpedo in the water, bearing zero-six-two!"

A red bearing line appeared on the torpedo fire control consoles, radiating outward, accompanied by a bright white trace burning into the sonar display.

"Terminate the launch!" Plecas ordered.

While the Weapons Officer shut the missile tube hatches, Plecas commenced torpedo evasion.

"Steersman, ahead flank!"

The Steersman rang up maximum propulsion as Plecas determined the best evasion course. He decided to place the torpedo twenty degrees aft of the beam, so *Kazan* could open range while evading.

"Steersman, left full rudder, steady course three-one-zero."

To his Watch Officer, Plecas ordered, "Launch torpedo decoy!"

Kazan swung around as it increased speed, and a decoy was launched in its wake, which would hopefully distract the torpedo long enough for *Kazan* to slip away.

Once they had put enough distance between the submarine and the decoy, Plecas ordered, "Launch jammer!"

A broadband sonar jammer was ejected from the submarine, which would mask *Kazan* as it sped away, leaving only the decoy as a tantalizing target for the incoming torpedo.

Hydroacoustic's next report confirmed what Plecas already knew. "Incoming torpedo is an American Mark forty-eight."

Now that *Kazan* was on a good evasion course and countermeasures had been launched, Plecas returned his attention to the incoming torpedo. It hadn't been a very good shot. The bearings were drawing steadily aft, indicating it had either been fired down a specific bearing or the American crew had been forced to shoot with an immature solution. Either way, it didn't matter; the torpedo would miss unless the American crew steered it onto *Kazan*'s new track. Plecas planned to ensure that didn't happen.

It was time to put a torpedo—or two—into the water.

Hydroacoustic didn't hold the American submarine. All they had was the launch bearing, which meant the American submarine could be headed in any direction. To increase the odds of getting a hit, Plecas decided to launch a horizontal salvo: two torpedoes running side by side.

"Prepare to fire horizontal salvo from tubes One and Two, bearing zero-six-two."

The bearing and salvo search parameters were sent to the torpedoes, then the Weapons Officer announced, "Ready to Fire, tubes One and Two."

Plecas examined the torpedo settings, and satisfied they were adequate, gave the order.

"Fire tubes One and Two."

Both torpedoes were ejected simultaneously from *Kazan,* one from each torpedo bank, and turned onto the ordered bearing.

Now that the MK 48 torpedo had passed astern and two torpedoes were on their way to keep the American crew busy, Plecas decided to slow and search for the enemy submarine.

"Steersman, ahead two-thirds. Right ten degrees rudder, course three-three-zero."

Plecas turned *Kazan* slightly to starboard as it slowed, presenting a beam aspect to the likely position of the American submarine, bringing both of *Kazan*'s primary sensors into play: the spherical and towed arrays.

He had agreed to launch all twenty missiles in return for his daughter's medical treatment, but thus far had launched only one. Nineteen more to go.

But first, he had to find the American submarine and sink it.

73

WASHINGTON, D.C.

In the Oval Office, with an emerald-shaded lamp illuminating the papers on his desk, the president worked late into the night, not because he had a backlog of documents to review, but because he couldn't sleep. The last few days had passed slowly, and he had stayed up late each night as the predicted time for *Kazan*'s missile launch came, then went.

One of their assumptions had proven wrong, and as hope grew that their conclusion *Kazan* intended to strike the United States was incorrect, he'd been briefed yesterday that a new ASW barrier was being established in the Gulf of Mexico. The Navy believed the Russian submarine captain planned to launch from the Gulf, where his missiles would threaten over eighty percent of the country, and would most likely launch within two days.

He had again briefly considered issuing evacuation orders, but his secretary of homeland security, Nova Conover, had pointed out the obvious again—the roads couldn't handle the simultaneous evacuation of almost three hundred million people. Even if they could, where would they go? They couldn't just park themselves in the middle of nowhere; food and water would be an immediate issue, followed by shelter and sanitation.

If *Kazan* didn't launch soon and an extended evacuation was required, they needed infrastructure—some way to feed and house the population long-term—and the country's emergency plans and supplies could handle only a fraction of the requirement. Hurricane Katrina had highlighted the difficulty in evacuating New Orleans—a single metropolitan city—while an effective response to *Kazan*'s potential launch could produce hundreds of Katrina-level nightmares. A mass evacuation was far more complex than he had realized, and after concluding it would be ineffective within the time frame expected, he relented.

The phone at the president's desk rang and he picked it up. Secretary of Defense Tom Drapac was on the other end. Satellites surveilling the Gulf of Mexico had detected a cruise missile launch a few minutes ago.

Kazan had commenced launching.

The president's blood chilled as images of incinerated cities flashed in his mind.

"How many missiles?"

"Just one, so far."

"Where is it headed?"

"Toward the Northeast. Most likely Washington, D.C."

"How much time do we have?"

"The missile is traveling at 0.8 Mach speed. If D.C. is the target, you've got ninety minutes left, depending on which route it takes. Now that the missile is overland and hugging the terrain, we've lost track of it, but we should pick it up again once it approaches any of our anti-air missile batteries, which are positioned in every major city."

Special Agent Ashley Tobin, tonight's shift leader for the President's Protection Detail, entered the Oval Office, having apparently been apprised of the issue.

"We need to leave, sir."

To Drapac, the president said, "Keep me informed," then hung up.

Tobin added, "We're helping the First Lady and rounding up all personnel in the White House. Marine One is on its way to take you to Joint Base Andrews, where you'll board Air Force One."

74

USS *NORTH CAROLINA*

As *North Carolina* raced toward *Kazan*'s last known position, Wilson studied the sonar displays. The Russian submarine had faded from *North Carolina*'s sensors, and Wilson had chosen to close the distance aggressively, increasing speed to ahead full, but turning thirty degrees to starboard in case *Kazan* counterfired, which was likely.

"Torpedo in the water! Bearing two-five-two!"

Sonar's report confirmed Wilson's assessment, and a red bearing line appeared on the geographic display. As Wilson evaluated the best evasion course, Sonar made another report.

"Second torpedo in the water, bearing two-five-four!"

The Russians had fired two torpedoes; a horizontal salvo by the look of it. Torpedo evasion just got harder. However, assuming both torpedoes were heading in the same direction and running side by side, which was typical for Russian salvo tactics, the pair could be treated as a single torpedo with a wider target acquisition range. An evasion plan that worked for one torpedo should work for both.

"Pilot, ahead flank! Hard right rudder, steady course three-five-zero."

To his Officer of the Deck, Wilson ordered, "Launch countermeasures!"

A decoy was launched into the water as *North Carolina* changed course and increased speed, followed by an acoustic jammer that would interfere with the torpedoes' ability to detect the submarine.

As *North Carolina* reached ahead flank, Wilson evaluated the incoming torpedo bearings. Both were drawing aft, indicating the torpedoes remained on their original course; they hadn't detected *North Carolina*, nor had steers been inserted.

That indicated the Russian crew didn't hold *North Carolina* on its sensors either, which meant the first submarine to regain the other would have the advantage. Even though *North Carolina* was the older vessel, Wilson was confident he had the acoustic advantage. The hydrophones in the Virginia class submarines were likely better, plus *North Carolina*'s sonar processors and detection algorithms had just been upgraded to the latest versions.

Wilson waited until both Russian torpedoes drew aft, verifying they remained steady on a course away from the submarine, then slowed to increase the range of *North Carolina*'s acoustic sensors.

"Pilot, ahead two-thirds."

Once *North Carolina* slowed to ten knots, Wilson ordered, "Sonar, Conn. Report all contacts."

Sonar performed a detailed search in all sectors, then reported no contacts.

Wilson examined the geographic plot again. The launch transient had come from a bearing of two-four-two and the first Russian torpedoes had been picked up on a bearing of two-five-two, which told Wilson *Kazan* had turned north after terminating its missile launch.

However, *Kazan* could have turned again after launching the torpedo salvo and could be headed in any direction now. After considering their failure to regain *Kazan* on sonar, Wilson concluded the Russian captain was running away, hoping to elude American forces and reposition his submarine where it could complete its launch.

The only way to catch *Kazan* was to increase speed and correctly guess which direction *Kazan* was going, or perhaps go active. As he evaluated which direction to head, Sonar made another report.

"Conn, Sonar. Hold a new contact, designated Sierra four-seven, bearing two-six-five. Simultaneous gain on spherical and towed array sensors. High signal strength. Analyzing."

Sonar's report caught Wilson by surprise. Contacts were normally picked up first on the towed array, then on the spherical array at a closer range. A simultaneous gain on both sensors, especially a high signal strength, made no sense.

Unless . . .

The realization coalesced in Wilson's mind a moment too late.

"Torpedo launch transients, bearing two-six-five!"

The Russian captain hadn't run away. He had turned toward *North Carolina,* hiding above the thermocline while its towed array drooped beneath it, giving him a clear look at the water below, detecting *North Carolina*. The two submarines had been closing on each other quickly, and *Kazan* had dropped below the layer at the last moment to gain *North Carolina* on its spherical array sonar, so its crew could refine its solution before firing. The Russian captain was savvy, indeed.

Wilson filed that information away as he focused on evading the incoming torpedo.

"Pilot, ahead flank! Hard left rudder, steady course one-six-zero!

"Launch countermeasures!"

As *North Carolina* changed course, Wilson decided to return fire.

"Quick Reaction Firing, tube One, bearing two-six-five!"

The fire control technician manning the Weapon Control Console entered the ordered bearing and sent it to the torpedo, along with normal submerged search presets. The torpedo communicated back, acknowledging receipt.

"Weapon ready!"

"Shoot tube One!" Wilson ordered.

As Wilson shifted his focus back to the incoming torpedo, he realized something was amiss. Following his order to launch their torpedo, there had been no characteristic whirr of the torpedo ejection pump, impulsing the torpedo from the tube.

"Cold shot!" was called out by Lieutenant Jeff Johnston, the submarine's Weapons Officer.

The torpedo hadn't been ejected.

There had been a failure either in the starboard torpedo bank or in the torpedo itself. It was counterintuitive, but the combat control system didn't fire the tube; the torpedo did. The firing signal was sent to the weapon, which did a final check of its systems, target solution, and search parameters, and if everything was satisfactory, it sent the firing signal to the torpedo tube. The fault could be in the torpedo, the tube, or something affecting both tubes in the starboard bank.

By design, the port and starboard tubes were independent, so that a fault on one side wouldn't affect the other. Earlier, they had fired a torpedo from tube Two, which indicated the port bank was operational.

"Shift to tube Four!" Wilson ordered.

Lieutenant Johnston sent the target bearing to the torpedo in tube Four, then reported, "Weapon ready!"

"Shoot tube Four!"

This time, Wilson heard the whirr of the torpedo ejection pump as the torpedo was launched from the tube, accelerating from rest to thirty knots in less than a second. On the port side of the Control Room, sonar technicians monitored the status of their outgoing torpedo, referring to the tube it was fired from so there would be no confusion if multiple torpedoes were in the water at the same time.

"Tube Four is in the water, running normally."

"Fuel crossover achieved."

"Turning to preset gyro course."

"Shifting to medium speed."

North Carolina's torpedo was headed toward its target.

Wilson focused again on the incoming torpedo, which was drawing aft now that *North Carolina* had changed course and increased speed. However, Sonar's next report was troubling.

"Up doppler, incoming torpedo! Torpedo is turning toward!"

Kazan's crew had inserted a steer, turning their torpedo back toward *North Carolina*.

Wilson needed to maneuver again.

"Helm, left full rudder, steady course zero-seven-zero. Launch countermeasures."

North Carolina turned east as the Officer of the Deck launched a second torpedo decoy, followed by another acoustic jammer.

Wilson examined the geographic plot on the navigation table, noting the appearance of white scalloped circles marking the location of *North Carolina*'s countermeasures. Wilson watched intently as *Kazan*'s torpedo approached the first one, hoping the countermeasures confused the torpedo long enough for *North Carolina* to slip away.

The torpedo sped past the decoy, ignoring it. It had either figured out the five-inch-diameter decoy wasn't a submarine, which wasn't hard to do if the torpedo was loaded with the proper algorithms, or it had detected the much larger *North Carolina* speeding away. The torpedo blazed past the acoustic jammer, then adjusted its course toward *North Carolina* and increased speed.

The telltale signs were reported by Sonar. “Torpedo is homing!”

75

ALEXANDRIA, VIRGINIA

Harrison and Kendall leaned against the warehouse, doing their best not to appear suspicious and draw attention, occasionally peering through the window to ensure Mixell was still seated at the table, working on the computer. Thankfully, there was little traffic at this time of night, either vehicular or pedestrian, and no one took interest in the man and woman standing beside the old building.

Harrison was checking his watch again, counting down the time until the HRT unit arrived, when he suddenly realized Mixell was doing the same. He peered through the window just in time to catch Mixell glance at his watch, then return to his computer. He studied Mixell more closely, then realized he wasn't working on the computer at all. He was just sitting there. Waiting.

Waiting for what?

A phone call? An event?

Harrison searched his memory for clues, then recalled the Swiss account dendrite shown at the NCTC, connecting Mixell to Futtaim and the three men tied to *Kazan*. Then the obvious answer dawned on him. He was waiting for Plecas to launch.

But then what?

A red border flashed around one of the displays, and Mixell leaned toward it. Harrison wiped the window pane a bit more. On the monitor was a video of the White House South Lawn, with the president and an entourage hurrying toward a green and white helicopter as it settled onto the grass, flanked by three identical helicopters landing nearby. Harrison recognized the Sikorsky Sea Kings, painted in the characteristic two-tone white over green presidential livery. The president was boarding Marine One.

The four helicopters lifted off simultaneously, immediately shifting their positions in an endless shell game, obscuring the location of the president from would-be assassins on the ground.

A second display on the table flashed with a red border, and Mixell turned to observe. On the monitor was a large aircraft hangar, whose doors pulled slowly apart, revealing a Boeing 747 jetliner.

Harrison put the clues together: the president was evacuating Washington on Marine One, heading to Joint Base Andrews where he would board Air Force One, which was being pulled from the hangar. Harrison reached one more conclusion, and a cold shiver ran down his spine.

Kazan had launched.

As Harrison wondered why Mixell was so interested in the president's evacuation, his eyes went to the CONEX box, and he suddenly realized what was likely inside: a surface-to-air missile launcher.

Mixell was planning to shoot down Air Force One.

He pulled Kendall to the window and explained.

When he finished, he said, "We can't wait for the HRT. We have to stop him. There must be a way inside."

His eyes went to the metal front door, then to the window. The window was their only option. Perhaps if they broke through separate windows, one of them might make it through while the other provided cover.

"You want a way in?" Kendall asked. She pointed to the window pane. "Wish granted."

Harrison took a look. The large garage door on the other side of the warehouse was rising upward.

He led Kendall around the building, stopping when they reached the garage door opening. Peering inside, he spotted Mixell at the back of the CONEX box. He had opened the doors and was extracting two heavy metal ramps from inside, muscling them into place. He was armed with a pistol in a shoulder harness, but as he set the second ramp in place, he was oblivious to Harrison poking his head around the edge of the garage door opening.

Harrison scanned the rest of the warehouse, spotting a woman's body sprawled on the floor by the front door, her head twisted into an unnatural position. The realtor must have stopped by and seen too much. Aside from the dead woman and the man in the truck cab, there was only Mixell inside.

Outside the warehouse, Kendall stood beside Harrison, her back pressed against the wall, her pistol held ready. His eyes locked on to hers and she nodded. He held his hand up, all five fingers and thumb extended, retracting one digit into a fist at one-second intervals. When his hand clenched, they surged into the building, leveling their pistols at Mixell, who had his back to them.

Harrison addressed his former best friend. "Put your hands in the air!"

Mixell raised his hands as he slowly turned around. His gaze settled on Harrison, then shifted to Kendall and back.

"My, my," Mixell said. "What a surprise." Then he smiled and said, "For you."

As Harrison tried to decipher his comment, Kendall swung her pistol toward Harrison's head. "Drop your weapon."

He turned toward her. "What the hell?"

"You've got three seconds to drop your firearm."

Harrison quickly concluded he had no viable options. Kendall was standing too far away to disarm her. Plus, even if he could, he'd then have to deal with Mixell, who had a pistol in his shoulder holster and would quickly react.

"One," Kendall announced.

The odds of defeating both of them were slim to none.

"Two."

Harrison let his pistol fall to the ground.

76

USS *NORTH CAROLINA* • K-561 *KAZAN*

USS *NORTH CAROLINA*

Murray Wilson's options were limited. The incoming Russian torpedo was less than two thousand yards away and closing rapidly on *North Carolina*. Minutes earlier, he had launched a set of countermeasures, which the Russian torpedo had ignored. Clearly, *Kazan* was carrying an improved version of Russia's Type 53 torpedo.

The most promising option was to employ the same tactic the Russian captain had—use the thermocline. *Kazan* had caught *North Carolina* by surprise by approaching above the steep thermocline, which created acoustic shadow zones on each side of the layer.

"Pilot, make your depth one-five-zero feet. Use thirty up."

The Pilot complied and *North Carolina* tilted to a thirty-degree up angle, shooting toward the surface at ahead flank speed.

Ordering such a shallow depth, combined with a large angle at ahead flank speed, was a recipe for disaster. Only an experienced Diving Officer or Pilot would know when to start reducing the angle and how rapidly, so the submarine didn't shoot all the way to the surface; Wilson had seen it happen many times aboard submarines with crews preparing for their upcoming deployment.

Wilson had faith in *North Carolina*'s Pilot, however. Reggie Thurlow was the Chief of the Boat, the senior enlisted man aboard and a master chief. He had never been to sea aboard *North Carolina* before this week, but he'd been the senior Pilot aboard his previous submarine, also a Virginia class. As the saying went, this wasn't his first rodeo.

As *North Carolina* shot upward, Thurlow expertly flooded water in as the submarine approached the thermocline, using the extra weight to more quickly halt the submarine's upward momentum. After *North Carolina* passed though the thermocline, Wilson executed his plan.

"Pilot, hard left rudder, steady course two-five-zero!"

The Virginia class submarines were quite nimble, especially compared with Wilson's *Michigan,* an Ohio class submarine almost two football fields long. At ahead flank speed and a hard rudder, *North Carolina* whipped around, sending anything unsecured sliding across consoles and the navigation table.

A significant portion of the submarine's speed bled off during the turn, and Wilson kept propulsion at ahead flank. They were now accelerating back toward the torpedo, but above the layer while the torpedo remained below.

North Carolina returned to ahead flank speed and seconds later, the torpedo punched through the layer behind *North Carolina,* still headed on the submarine's previous course of zero-seven-zero while *North Carolina* was now traveling in the opposite direction. With *North Carolina* and the torpedo moving in opposite directions at maximum speed, the torpedo was soon beyond reacquisition range, continuing to open.

After the torpedo faded from Sonar's sensors, Wilson decided to slow. They needed to find *Kazan*.

"Pilot, ahead two-thirds."

Wilson chose to remain above layer and let his towed array droop below, searching above layer with the spherical array and below layer with the towed array. He also needed to reload.

"Weapons, reload tubes Two and Four."

After Lieutenant Johnston relayed the order to the Torpedo Room, Wilson inquired about the starboard torpedo tubes.

"Any report on the starboard torpedo bank?"

"No, sir," Johnston reported. "All indications are normal in the Torpedo Room."

Wilson acknowledged the report. They'd have to troubleshoot later; now wasn't the time to tear into torpedo and combat control consoles.

A few minutes later, the Torpedo Reload Party completed their task.

Johnston reported, "Tubes Two and Four are reloaded."

"Very well," Wilson replied. "Flood down and open outer doors, tubes Two and Four."

Johnston complied and tubes Two and Four were made ready in all respects.

None too soon, because Sonar picked up a new contact.

"Conn, Sonar. Gained a new contact on the towed array, designated Sierra four-seven, bearing two-seven-seven. Analyzing."

Not long thereafter, the Sonar Supervisor reported, "Sierra four-seven is classified submerged. Tonals correlate to Sierra four-six."

Kazan.

Wilson announced, "Designate Sierra four-seven as Master one. Track Master one."

North Carolina's Fire Control Tracking Party went to work, determining the contact's course, speed, and range.

Reassigning Commander Maske as Fire Control Coordinator provided dividends; he instructed the three men determining *Kazan*'s solution to start with course zero-seven-zero, since *Kazan* had been following its torpedo toward *North Carolina,* and to assume a speed of at least ahead full for the Russian submarine, since it had to have been at high speed to keep up with *North Carolina*. The three operators quickly arrived at a consensus: course zero-seven-four, speed twenty-four knots, range five thousand yards.

"Conn, Sonar. Loss of Master one, all trackers."

Wilson focused on the unusual report. Contacts typically faded, their tonals or broadband noise growing weaker as range increased. A sudden loss of all frequencies, given the current acoustic environment, could only mean . . .

"Conn, Sonar. Regain of Master one on the spherical array."

Kazan was popping above the thermocline to take a look with its spherical array. If *North Carolina* could see *Kazan,* then *Kazan* could see *North Carolina*.

The scenario was clear in Wilson's mind. The two submarines were facing each other, and like an old-fashioned Western standoff, it was a race to shoot.

This time, however, *North Carolina*'s crew had the advantage; they had been tracking *Kazan* on the towed array and were likely much closer to a firing solution.

"Firing Point Procedures!" Wilson announced. "Master one, tube Two primary, tube Four backup."

K-561 *KAZAN*

"Command Post, Hydroacoustic. Regain of Hydroacoustic two-one on the spherical array, bearing two-five-one."

"Steersman, ahead two-thirds."

Plecas ordered his submarine to slow to ten knots while he assessed the situation. The American submarine had gone above layer to evade their last torpedo. It would take a few minutes to figure out which way his adversary was headed, and at what speed and range.

A few minutes they might not have.

The American crew had likely been trailing their towed array below the layer as he'd done earlier, which meant they probably had a decent firing solution on *Kazan*.

There was no time to waste. If he could shoot first, he might be able to keep the Americans on the defensive. Sooner or later, one of *Kazan*'s torpedoes would home to detonation.

Plecas decided to fire down a line of bearing at the American submarine, rather than wait for a target solution. Additionally, he needed to address the thermocline; it was strong here in the Gulf of Mexico, providing a shadow zone that was proving to be a challenge if his torpedoes were cross-layer from their target.

There was a way to fix that.

"Immediate Firing, Hydroacoustic two-one, vertical salvo, tubes Four and Five."

Plecas intended to place one torpedo above the layer and the other below. No matter which side of the layer the Americans evaded on, there would be a torpedo to deal with.

This time, the American submarine would not survive.

77

ALEXANDRIA, VIRGINIA

As Pat Kendall stood with her arm extended, her pistol aimed at Harrison's head, he pieced together the clues.

Pat.

Patricia.

Trish.

Trish the Dish.

Kendall was the stripper—Mixell's *soul mate.*

He had missed the clues, including her comment at the NCTC about ending up back on the street if she didn't keep her nose clean. He had assumed she was local law enforcement prior to joining the CIA, patrolling city streets, but *back on the street* meant an entirely different thing in Kendall's case.

Her background also explained the DDO's comment the day they met at Langley, when Kendall entered Christine's office and Harrison stood to greet her. *No need for chivalry,* the DDO had said, *especially in Pat's presence.* It also explained Kendall's odd interaction with Max, the Baltimore police officer, when Kendall had commented about his wife not being happy if she found out about his exploits when he was younger. Max must have frequented the strip clubs while she was a dancer, engaging in who-knew-what in the private rooms.

Kendall had indeed begun a new life, as the strip club manager mentioned, but hadn't broken completely clear of the old one. She and Mixell were still together.

It amounted to a critical lack of insight on his part, a failure that might cost him his life. He realized that during the confrontation between Khalila and Kendall the day he'd met them at Langley, both women's accusations were correct. Khalila had been responsible for some of her partners' deaths, and Kendall was corrupt, as Khalila suspected.

The realization must have been evident on his face, because Kendall said, "You finally figured it out. I have to hand it to you, Jake. You're pretty dense.

"Oh, one more thing. About that FBI backup. It's not coming. There was no one on the other end of the call. It helps if you press the phone icon before talking."

"Well, well, well," Mixell said as he approached Harrison, kicking away his pistol on the floor. "Long time, no see. This is an unexpected bonus. I can't tell you how much I'm going to enjoy killing you. After, of course, you realize how miserably you failed in your mission."

Mixell waited for a response, but Harrison declined to respond. He wasn't going to feed into whatever sadistic plan his former best friend had in mind.

An irritated look flashed across Mixell's face.

"*What's the plan?* you ask. Surely, you're curious. Or perhaps you've figured it all out. Let me show you. As they say, a picture is worth a thousand words."

He climbed into the CONEX box and Harrison heard an engine rumble to life, then a green mobile missile launcher, as Harrison had suspected, crept down the metal ramps to the warehouse floor, and Mixell parked it near the garage door opening.

Harrison didn't know what model the launcher was, but from the look of things, it was a Russian short-to-medium-range air defense system. It was armed with twelve canister-mounted missiles most likely capable of distinguishing chaff and infrared decoys from the real thing, and the launcher system could probably guide multiple missiles simultaneously to separate targets or to the same one.

With Air Force One taking off from Joint Base Andrews across the river, the president's aircraft was well within range, and unlikely to decoy multiple missiles closing the distance in only a few seconds.

"I must admit, I developed a brilliant plan," Mixell said as he stepped from the launcher.

He waited for a response again, which Harrison refused to provide.

"What?" He placed his hand to his ear. "You want to hear all about it? Of course, you do. Inquiring minds want to know, and you always were the curious type."

He turned toward Kendall and smiled.

"Trish was kind enough to provide me with the president's schedule, and I picked a day for the launch when the president would be at the White House. If *Kazan*'s launch and incoming missile went undetected—I call that plan A—the president and a good portion of Washington, D.C., would be incinerated. Easy-peasy."

He paused, then asked, "You *have* figured out the missiles *Kazan* is carrying are armed with nuclear warheads, haven't you?" His eyes went to Kendall, then back to Harrison. "That would be *yes*. Trish has been keeping me up to date.

"However, there was always the possibility the president would be forewarned—perhaps if *Kazan*'s launch was detected or the incoming missile was spotted by air defense radars. In that case, I couldn't let the president slip away. That would be plan B." He pointed at the missile launcher.

"Personally, I've been hoping for plan B. I've got a camera ready to record it." He gestured toward one of the computer displays on the table. "Air Force One on fire, trailing red flames as it plummets toward earth."

Mixell went on to explain that the video would be played endlessly around the world, demonstrating Ayman al-Zawahiri's reach and the capability of his rejuvenated al-Qaeda organization. Al-Qaeda would absorb many of the jihadist organizations, and funds would flow into its coffers. With the additional networks and loyal followers, plus adequate funds, there was almost nothing Zawahiri couldn't accomplish.

"You've betrayed your country," Harrison said.

"It betrayed *me*!" Mixell's face turned red, his neck veins bulging. "*You* betrayed me!"

His fury passed quickly, his skin color returning to normal.

"Haven't you forgotten something?" Harrison asked. "The president is being evacuated, which means one of *Kazan*'s missiles is on its way here. Congratulations on plan A, but we're all going to die."

Mixell smiled. "I appreciate your concern for our safety, but don't worry. The missiles fired by *Kazan* carry only a one-hundred-kiloton warhead. We're six miles from the detonation point, which should be beyond the lethal radius. Just in case, however, I've got a boat tied up along the wharf outside. Air Force One should be in flames about thirty minutes before the missile arrives, and Trish and I will be long gone by then."

One of the displays on the table began flashing again, and Harrison noted movement on the monitor. Marine One and its three escorts were approaching Joint Base Andrews, flying low, with their flight path occasionally blocked by nearby buildings, which explained why Mixell was waiting for the president to board Air Force One. Lumbering into the clear sky after takeoff, it would be an easy target.

Marine One touched down and the president and another dozen men and women debarked the helicopter, hurrying toward the boarding stairs pushed up against Air Force One.

"Pardon me for being rude," Mixell said as he moved toward the missile launcher, "but I've got a president to kill."

78

USS *NORTH CAROLINA* • K-561 *KAZAN*

USS *NORTH CAROLINA*

"Torpedo launch transient, bearing two-seven-eight!"

Damn. Despite his crew's head start tracking *Kazan* below the layer, the Russians had fired first. *North Carolina*'s crew was well trained, but they were methodical and slow. They weren't yet proficient enough to execute Firing Point Procedures as quickly as crews that had completed a six-month workup preparing for deployment.

"Torpedo in the water! Bearing two-seven-eight!"

"Ahead flank!" Wilson ordered. "Hard left rudder, steady course two-one-zero."

A red line appeared on the geographic display, joined by a purple line.

"Second torpedo in the water, also bearing two-seven-eight!"

To the Officer of the Deck, Wilson ordered, "Launch countermeasures!"

North Carolina ejected a torpedo decoy and broadband jammer, then completed its turn to the ordered evasion course, accelerating to maximum speed.

Both torpedoes had been fired while *North Carolina* was above the layer, so Wilson decided to drop below.

"Pilot, make your depth four hundred feet."

As *North Carolina* tilted downward, Wilson turned to his Fire Control Coordinator, who was waiting on the three operators refining their target solution.

"Check Fire," Wilson announced. "Quick Reaction Firing, Master one, tube Two primary, tube Four backup."

Wilson canceled their normal torpedo firing process, implementing the more urgent version, which forced his Fire Control Coordinator to send his best solution to the torpedo immediately. The Russian captain wouldn't know how well aimed the torpedo was, and it was better to give him something to worry about instead of letting him refine his solution and send updates to his torpedoes over their guidance wires.

Commander Maske shifted his gaze between the three combat control consoles, then tapped one of the fire control technicians on the shoulder. "Promote to master."

Maske announced, "Solution ready!"

The submarine's Weapons Officer followed. "Weapon ready!"

"Ship ready!" the Officer of the Deck announced.

"Match Sonar bearing and shoot!"

Wilson heard the whirr of the torpedo ejection pump, verifying the port torpedo bank responded as expected, then listened to the sonar technicians monitor their torpedo.

"Tube Two is in the water, running normally."

"Fuel crossover achieved."

"Turning to preset gyro course."

"Shifting to medium speed."

North Carolina's torpedo was headed toward its target.

K-561 *KAZAN*

"Torpedo in the water, bearing zero-eight-zero!"

The American submarine had counterfired as expected. But Plecas had planned ahead; *Kazan* was already turning to an optimal evasion course, increasing speed to ahead flank.

Plecas checked the torpedo bearings, verifying *Kazan*'s new course was adequate. The torpedo bearings were drawing aft as desired. For added insurance, Plecas ordered a set of countermeasures launched: a decoy first, followed by a jammer.

The countermeasures were ejected, and after verifying the incoming torpedo was still drawing aft, Plecas focused on his outgoing torpedo salvo. The American captain had undoubtedly maneuvered his submarine as well, which meant both of *Kazan*'s torpedoes would speed by without a detection.

Plecas moved behind the two fire control technicians, who were updating their target solution for the American submarine. It had increased speed to ahead flank and turned to port. After analyzing further, its new course became clear. Their adversary had maneuvered to the southwest.

Plecas ordered his Weapons Officer, "Calculate steers, both torpedoes."

Captain Lieutenant Alekhin evaluated several steers on his Weapon Control Console, then announced, "Recommend course one-eight-five."

"Insert steer, both torpedoes, course one-eight-five."

USS *NORTH CAROLINA*

"Up doppler from torpedo!"

Wilson evaluated Sonar's report with concern. The Russian crew apparently held *North Carolina* on its sensors and had just steered the torpedo back toward them. Wilson considered using the strong thermocline to his advantage again. But first, he needed to determine what type of salvo the Russian captain had employed.

Earlier, after dropping below the thermocline, they held only one torpedo on *North Carolina*'s sensors, which meant the other torpedo was running above the layer or had experienced a failure. The most likely scenario was that the Russian captain had fired a vertical salvo, but Wilson needed to be sure.

"Pilot, make your depth one-five-zero feet."

North Carolina tilted upward, and as it traveled through the layer, Sonar lost one torpedo, but gained another.

Kazan had indeed fired a vertical salvo. This time, Wilson couldn't use the thermocline, and if the Russian crew kept inserting steers, they would eventually lead their torpedoes to *North Carolina*.

The Russian captain had kept the advantage, keeping *North Carolina* on the run. Wilson needed to change that. Up to now, both submarines had been shooting quick-reaction fastballs at each other, forcing their opponent to focus on evasion, inhibiting their ability to prosecute their adversary. It was time for a curveball.

But first, he needed to respond to the torpedoes closing on *North Carolina*.

"Pilot, left ten degrees rudder, steady course zero-six-zero. Make your depth four hundred feet."

Wilson turned to the northeast, placing the torpedoes on *North Carolina*'s port quarter and going deeper, where the submarine's propulsor worked more efficiently and produced less noise.

"Launch countermeasures!"

After the torpedo decoy and jammer were launched, and as *North Carolina* steadied on its new course and depth, Wilson examined the geographic plot. *North Carolina*'s torpedo was traveling west, while *Kazan* was evading to the north.

"Firing Point Procedures, Master one, tube Four."

Finally confident about *Kazan*'s estimated course, speed, and range, Commander Maske directed one of the fire control technicians to promote his solution to master.

Wilson received the required reports, then ordered, "Shoot tube Four!"

The torpedo was launched without incident, and Sonar monitored the torpedo as it turned onto the ordered course.

"Insert steer, tube Four, right twenty," Wilson ordered, followed by, "Pre-enable tube Four."

Maske and Lieutenant Johnston shot curious glances toward Wilson. They had finally nailed down *Kazan*'s solution, yet Wilson had ordered them to send the torpedo on a tangent, twenty degrees to the right. Additionally, Wilson had ordered them to make the torpedo dumb and blind.

Wilson offered no explanation, so the Weapons Officer sent the commands to the torpedo, steering it to the right and turning off its sonar and search algorithms.

Now that Wilson's plan was in motion, he focused again on the incoming torpedoes. The timing was apropos, because the Sonar Supervisor reported, "Up doppler on torpedo!"

The Russian crew had steered the torpedo below the layer toward *North Carolina* again, and based on the signal strength of its pings, it was close. The torpedo above the layer was likely paralleling its deeper mate.

Wilson decided to use the thermocline again. But for the evasion to be successful, he needed to get both torpedoes onto the same side of the layer first. That being the case, Wilson maintained course.

As the torpedo chasing them gained on *North Carolina,* several watchstanders in Control cast furtive glances in Wilson's direction. Wilson did nothing, standing beside the navigation table until the report he'd been waiting for arrived.

"Sonar, Conn. Torpedo is homing!"

Wilson reacted immediately. "Pilot, make your depth one-five-zero feet. Use ten up."

He ordered a low angle to make sure the torpedo could follow them through the layer, which it did, joining the other torpedo on the same side of the thermocline.

"One thousand yards!" the Sonar Supervisor reported.

Both torpedoes were dangerously close, but Wilson still had a half-mile to work with.

"Officer of the Deck. Launch decoy."

Once the countermeasure was ejected, which would hopefully garner the torpedoes' interest for a while, Wilson gave the evasion orders.

"Pilot, make your depth four hundred feet. Use thirty down. Hard left rudder, steady course two-four-zero!"

It had worked the first time, and if *North Carolina* could reverse course before the torpedoes followed it through the layer, it should work again.

It was a gamble. If one of the torpedoes went below layer before *North Carolina* reversed course beneath it, dropping down in front of the submarine, they'd have only a few seconds to react; insufficient time to do anything besides pray.

As *North Carolina* steadied on its new course and depth, Wilson examined the geographic display, showing his submarine heading toward the torpedoes, separated by the thermocline.

"Coordinator, calculate intercept time."

Commander Maske had one of the fire control technicians calculate the time the two torpedoes would be directly above.

"Fifteen seconds!"

It was only a quarter of a minute, but time seemed to slow as the seconds counted down.

"Ten seconds!"

Wilson examined the sonar displays. There was still no indication of either torpedo.

"Five seconds!"

When the time reached zero, Wilson waited a bit longer, then let out a deep breath. Seconds later, both torpedoes descended through the layer, but they were too late.

With the torpedoes behind *North Carolina* and heading away at over fifty knots, plus *North Carolina* at ahead flank in the opposite direction, it wasn't long before both torpedoes were beyond detection range. *Kazan*'s crew could steer them again once they determined *North Carolina*'s new course and speed, but both torpedoes had been running fast for a while, and were likely low on fuel.

Plus, Wilson didn't intend to let *Kazan*'s crew steer the torpedoes anyway.

He studied the geographic plot, which presented a favorable picture. *Kazan* was still evading to the north while *North Carolina*'s first-fired torpedo was heading west. The second-fired torpedo, which Wilson had ordered pre-enabled, was approaching *Kazan* with an offset to starboard.

Exactly as planned.

"Weapons, steer tube Two right ninety degrees."

Lieutenant Johnston complied and the first torpedo turned sharply right.

Now came the critical part. Wilson's plan would work only if the Russian crew still held the first MK 48 torpedo on its sensors.

A moment later, the answer became apparent.

"Possible target zig, Master one," Commander Maske called out. "Target has turned to starboard."

Wilson's eyes went to his second torpedo, traveling to the right of *Kazan*'s original course. The Russian submarine had turned directly into the torpedo's path, only two thousand yards in front.

"Command enable tube Four!" Wilson ordered.

The command went out and the torpedo went active, its search algorithms turning on again.

"Detect!"

Lieutenant Johnston announced the data being sent back to *North*

Carolina over the torpedo's guidance wire. The torpedo had detected an object that warranted further investigation, and would ping several more times to verify the object's size and other required characteristics.

"Acquired!"

The torpedo had determined the object met attack criteria, and would now home to detonation.

K-561 *KAZAN*

"Torpedo in the water! Bearing one-five-zero!"

Plecas spun toward the hydroacoustic display. A bright white trace was burning in on their starboard beam. Based on the intensity of the trace, the torpedo was close.

"Steersman, left full rudder, steady course two-five-zero. Launch decoy!"

Kazan swung around quickly and a decoy was launched, which gave Plecas hope until Hydroacoustic's next report.

"Torpedo is increasing speed. Torpedo is homing!"

"Launch jammer!"

An acoustic jammer was ejected, but neither the decoy nor the jammer had an effect. The torpedo was locked on to *Kazan* and ignored the small device pretending to be a submarine. The jammer likewise proved ineffective; it had been ejected with the torpedo too close to *Kazan,* and the MK 48 sped past the noise field, locking back on to their submarine.

Plecas concluded that additional decoys and jammers would be ineffective. Their last chance was to try to lose the torpedo as *Kazan* passed through the thermocline.

"Compensation Officer, make your depth fifty meters. Use thirty degrees up!"

Kazan shot toward the surface, passing through the thermocline before steadying on ordered depth. But the torpedo chasing them had been too close; it followed *Kazan* in its wake, traversing the layer before Plecas could reverse course.

Only one option remained. "Emergency blow all Main Ballast Tanks! Compensation Officer, full rise on the stern and bow planes!"

Kazan's Compensation Officer pulled down on the emergency blow levers. High-pressure air spewed into the submarine's Main Ballast Tanks, pushing the water out through the flood grates in the bottom of the hull. Plecas grabbed the forward periscope as the submarine's angle reached thirty up, while other men held on to consoles near their watch stations. The air finished pushing the water out of the ballast tanks, then spilled out through the grates in the ship's keel, leaving massive air pockets in *Kazan*'s wake as the submarine sped toward the ocean surface, exactly as Plecas hoped.

But the American torpedo detected *Kazan*'s depth change before it was blinded by the turbulent bubbles, and calculated its target's upward trajectory. The torpedo's tail pitched downward, matching *Kazan*'s ascent toward the surface, and it burst through the turbulence into clear water just above the stream of bubbles exiting *Kazan*'s flood grates.

It pinged and received a valid return.

Another ping, and the contact was confirmed. Its target lay only a hundred yards away.

The torpedo armed its warhead, rolling its exploder assembly into position. All it had to do now was close the remaining distance.

Through the submarine's hull, Plecas heard the faint sonar pings from the incoming torpedo, growing louder. He tried one last-ditch effort—a sudden turn, which would leave a turbulent knuckle of swirling water from the submarine's rudder, potentially disrupting the torpedo's sonar returns.

"Steersman, hard left—"

The order was drowned out by a jolting explosion that knocked Plecas to the deck. A geyser of water surged into the Command Post from the level below, shooting up the access ladder and ricocheting off bulkheads and consoles. The wail of the Flooding Alarm filled his ears, followed by emergency reports detailing flooding in Compartments Two and Three.

Kazan tilted downward, increasing speed as it descended. Plecas struggled to his feet, fighting against the water rushing into the Command Post, already waist high. As he clung to the forward periscope barrel, he glanced at the digital depth detector. Its glowing red numbers increased as *Kazan* descended.

As Plecas watched the ocean pour into his submarine, he realized there was nothing more he could do; the flooding was beyond the capacity of their drain pumps, and their emergency blow with two flooded compartments would do no good.

Kazan was going to the bottom.

Plecas considered evacuating to Compartment One with the other men, but knew it was pointless. The ocean was more than two thousand meters deep here, well beyond *Kazan*'s crush depth. As *Kazan* descended, the intense water pressure would crumple all intact compartments as if they were made of paper.

His men stared at him with fear on their faces yet a glimmer of hope in their eyes. Somehow, he would save them.

They were wrong.

He had failed his crew and he had failed his family.

Two weeks earlier, as he hugged Tatiana tightly at the hospital, he had wondered whether he would be fortunate enough to see his wife and daughter again. He now had his answer.

USS *NORTH CAROLINA*

North Carolina shuddered and the sonar screens turned white as the shock wave from the explosion swept past the submarine. Lieutenant Johnston called out, reporting their torpedo had detonated.

"Loss of wire continuity. Final telemetry data correlates with Master one."

Cheers erupted in the Control Room, dying down as Sonar followed up.

"Conn, Sonar. Hull breakup noises, bearing three-three-five."

The cheers were replaced by a solemn quiet as Wilson, and no doubt the rest of the crew, thought about the men aboard *Kazan* who would never return from sea. Never return to the families waiting for them. It could just as easily have been them.

After a long moment, Wilson announced, "Secure from Battle Stations." He turned to the Executive Officer, who held up two fingers. "Section two relieve the watch."

Once the Communicator was relieved of his Battle Stations duty, Wilson ordered him to draft a message to COMSUBFOR reporting they had sunk *Kazan*.

To the Officer of the Deck, Wilson ordered, "Make preparations to proceed to periscope depth and transmit."

Hopefully, new waterspace assignments would arrive soon and *North Carolina* could begin its journey back to port.

The Officer of the Deck completed preparations to proceed to periscope depth, and as *North Carolina* tilted upward, Wilson reflected on what they had accomplished. They hadn't been completely successful. They had sunk *Kazan,* but the Russian crew had launched a missile armed with a nuclear warhead, which was on the way to its target.

79

ALEXANDRIA, VIRGINIA

Jake Harrison monitored the display on Mixell's table, watching the president and his entourage board Air Force One. Once the last person was aboard, the cabin door closed and the boarding stairs were pulled away.

Mixell climbed into the missile launcher control booth and energized its radar and fire control systems, watching intently as diagnostic start-up tests were run. When they completed satisfactorily, Mixell gave Harrison a thumbs-up.

As Harrison searched for a way to prevent Mixell from shooting down Air Force One, he realized the scenario in the warehouse had slightly improved. Kendall still had her gun pointed at him, but Mixell was no longer a factor; he was preoccupied with the missile launcher. The odds were still against him, since Kendall had him in her sights while he didn't even have a weapon; Mixell had kicked his pistol twenty feet away.

"Don't even think about it," Kendall said. She must have caught him eyeing his firearm on the floor.

Mixell entered a command into the missile control panel, and the twelve-canister launcher swiveled toward the garage door opening.

"Lonnie," Kendall called out, her eyes still on Harrison. "I don't see the point in keeping Harrison alive. We're not going to have much time after the missile launch."

Mixell glanced at the display monitoring Joint Base Andrews. Air Force One had begun taxiing for takeoff. He turned to Harrison.

"I was hoping to draw things out, Jake, cutting you into shreds and letting you bleed out. But as much as I like plan B, it has its drawbacks.

The missiles will be tracked back to their launch point, and Trish and I need to be on our way before then. That means I won't be able to hang around after the launch to provide you with a fitting farewell. Quick and easy will have to do."

He turned to Kendall. "He's all yours."

Kendall smiled. "It's been a pleasure knowing you, Jake."

As Kendall prepared to pull the trigger, the few options at Harrison's disposal flashed through his mind. He could try to dodge Kendall's aim and retrieve his firearm, but it was twenty feet away and she had a full magazine in her pistol; he wouldn't make it. His only option was to close on Kendall, somehow avoiding a bullet to his head—he could survive most body shots, at least temporarily—and wrest the firearm from her.

There was no more time to debate the matter.

Harrison lunged toward Kendall as a shot echoed through the warehouse.

He had expected his world to turn black with headshot, or at least feel the bullet tearing into his body.

Instead, Kendall lurched sideways, blood splattering from her right shoulder, her pistol falling to the floor as she struggled to stay on her feet.

Harrison missed Kendall with his lunge, rolling on the ground into a kneeling position not far away, and looked in the direction of the shot. Khalila was standing beside the garage door opening, shifting her aim toward Mixell, who was pulling his pistol from his shoulder harness.

Khalila squeezed off three rounds, forcing Mixell to duck below the launcher control panel, then kept firing at one-second intervals to prevent Mixell from shooting back at herself or Harrison.

Kendall had regained her balance and her eyes went to her pistol a few feet away, but Harrison dove for it first. Unfortunately, despite Khalila's efforts to keep Mixell occupied, he had a clear view of Harrison out the side of the missile launcher control booth, and took a shot. Harrison heard a crack and felt searing pain spider through his right shoulder; his shoulder blade had been shattered.

He fought through the pain, grabbing Kendall's pistol with his left hand as he rolled into a firing position. He could still move his right arm, but the effort sent shards of white-hot pain slicing through his body. He aimed at Mixell with his left hand, but Mixell fired first, putting a round into Harrison's chest.

As Harrison recoiled from the bullet, he had one succinct thought. *This wasn't going to end well.*

Mixell was fairly well protected in the missile launcher control booth, while Harrison was out in the open in the middle of the warehouse, with two bullets in him already. Additionally, Kendall was sprinting toward Harrison's gun, lying on the warehouse floor not far away.

Khalila must have come to the same conclusion. She shifted her aim and put a bullet into Kendall's back, dropping her to the floor, then swapped out magazines and rapid-fired at Mixell as she worked her way toward a clear shot at him through the side of the launcher control booth.

It was a bold but risky move. Khalila had left the partial cover she'd had by the edge of the garage door and moved into the open, firing to keep Mixell pinned down while she repositioned for a clear shot.

However, the former SEAL was ready, squeezing off a three-round burst when Khalila slid into view. Two of the bullets hit their mark, one in Khalila's chest and another in her abdomen, and she collapsed to the floor. She landed face-first, her pistol clattering onto the concrete floor.

Harrison had scant time to worry about Khalila's fate, but her aggressive attack had been fruitful. She had forced Mixell to focus on her for a few seconds, giving Harrison the time he needed. Kneeling with the gun in his left hand, he steadied his aim and squeezed the trigger, putting a bullet into Mixell's chest.

Mixell pulled back from view, into the missile launcher control booth, giving Harrison a chance to assess things. Khalila lay motionless on the floor while Kendall was pushing herself to her feet, not far from his pistol. Harrison got to it first, kicking it farther across the floor, taking aim at Kendall as she regained her feet.

Over Kendall's shoulder, Harrison spotted Mixell emerge from the missile launcher. Blood was spreading slowly across his left chest, but he had his pistol in hand and a laser-sharp focus in his eyes.

Harrison was in no condition for a shoot-out. He'd be firing with his left hand instead of right, while Mixell seemed unaffected, raising his pistol to the firing position.

Harrison moved behind Kendall, placing the pistol against her head, buying time to devise a plan. Kendall froze, as did Mixell, as all three evaluated the situation.

After a short silence, Mixell spoke first, "Isn't that chivalrous of you, Jake. Shielding yourself with a woman."

"Drop your weapon, Lonnie, or say good-bye to your soul mate."

"Not gonna happen, Jake. You're the one in the untenable position. Kill Trish and you're dead. Let her go and you're dead. The only question is whether you're taking Trish with you, and you're not that type of guy."

Mixell was right. There was no point in killing Kendall. Besides, keeping her alive offered the only hope of a favorable outcome.

Harrison debated whether to press the matter to a conclusion tonight—attempt to kill Mixell while firing with his left hand—or as the saying goes, *live to fight another day.*

"Here's the plan, Lonnie. We're going to call it a draw today. Kendall and I are going to walk toward the front door while you stay put, then I'll be on my way, leaving her with you. Deal?"

"I can't let you do that. You're not leaving this warehouse alive." He glanced at the computer display. Air Force One had reached the designated runway and was lining up for takeoff.

"I'm running out of time," Mixell said, "and patience!"

Harrison spoke to Kendall. "We're going to head slowly toward the front door. If you make a sudden move, you're dead."

"I can't walk," Kendall said, the pain evident in her voice. "I'm hurt too bad."

Harrison moved closer to her. "Then you're of no use to me. I'll have to take my chances with Lonnie, with you out of the way."

"On second thought," Kendall replied. "I can make it to the door."

Harrison raised his right hand slowly, fighting through the pain, until it rested on the back of Kendall's shoulder. He transferred the pistol to his right hand, aimed at the base of her skull, then wrapped his good arm tightly around her waist.

"One step at a time," Harrison said, "toward the door."

Kendall complied and they began their journey. Harrison kept her body between him and Mixell, with only half of his face visible behind Kendall's head.

Mixell moved toward them. "Jake! Don't make me do this!"

"You don't have to do anything, Lonnie. Just stay right there!"

Mixell gripped his pistol with both hands. "Let her go and settle this like a man!"

He kept approaching, and Harrison got the feeling his plan wasn't going to work. Mixell was an excellent marksman, and he was also cocky.

He was going to take the shot.

As Harrison continued toward the door with Kendall, he focused on Mixell's eyes, looking for the telltale signs he was about to pull the trigger. Mixell squinted as he adjusted his aim. As he exhaled slowly, which helped steady a shooter's aim before firing, Harrison jerked Kendall sideways a few inches, directly in front of him.

A shot rang out in the warehouse as Kendall's head snapped back, then her body went limp.

Harrison released Kendall and swapped the pistol back to his good hand, then aimed at Mixell, who stood frozen in shock as Kendall crumpled to the warehouse floor.

The glaze cleared from Mixell's eyes just before Harrison fired, Mixell lunging sideways to avoid the bullet. It hit him in his right arm and he lost the grip on his pistol. The force of the bullet, combined with Mixell's sudden move, sent the gun spinning across the floor, coming to rest beneath the missile launcher.

Harrison now had the advantage, a gun in his hand while Mixell had none, with the nearest firearm near Khalila.

The garage door was closer, and Mixell sprinted for the opening, changing direction along the way, hoping Harrison's aim with his left hand was poor. He was right. Harrison fired three bullets, missing Mixell each time, before Mixell sprinted through the opening, headed toward the shoreline, faintly illuminated by a nearby streetlight at the end of Oronoco Street.

Harrison followed him to the garage door, stopping as Mixell reached a speedboat tied up along the wharf. He leaned against the door opening and raised his left arm, taking aim as Mixell cast off the last line and gunned the throttle.

He squeezed the trigger and Mixell lurched sideways, collapsing onto the side of the boat, then his body slid into the river, disappearing under the water as the speedboat plowed on, captainless, vanishing into the darkness.

Harrison leaned against the warehouse wall and let the tension ease from his body. He had taken two bullets, but neither appeared to have hit a critical organ.

He heard a moan behind him, and turned to find Khalila on her back. He knelt beside her and assessed her condition. Her skin was pale and she had her hands pressed against her wounds, one in her abdomen and one in her chest, as blood oozed between her fingers.

He slipped his jacket off and gingerly removed his shirt—his right arm was almost useless—then ripped it in half with his good arm and a knee. He placed the linen over the wounds and applied pressure to one while Khalila placed both hands over the other.

"Did you kill him?" she asked. Her words were weak, but understandable.

"I think so. I put three rounds in him and he fell into the river. Hopefully, we'll recover his body to confirm."

In the background, Harrison heard the faint sound of approaching sirens.

"I called for backup before I entered," she said.

"How did you know I was here?"

"I've been following Kendall, hoping she'd eventually lead me to Mixell."

"Why?"

"I was working on the stripper lead, and I tracked down one of her friends from the club. She had an old picture of the two of them. The stripper was blond and younger, but it was Kendall."

Khalila turned her head slowly, glancing at Kendall's body on the floor, then returned her gaze to Harrison.

"I told you she was dirty."

Across the Potomac River, bright plumes of fire streaked upward. Harrison watched as a quartet of anti-air missiles rose skyward, curving southwest toward a small pinprick of red light speeding toward the District. The four missiles descended toward the target, with one of them scoring a hit, breaking the incoming missile into several pieces that spiraled to the ground.

One of *Kazan*'s missiles had been shot down.

Harrison waited tensely for more Kalibr missiles to arrive, but none appeared.

The steadily increasing sound of sirens, followed by lights flashing through the warehouse windows, indicated help had arrived.

As they waited for assistance to enter the warehouse, Khalila searched Harrison's eyes for a moment, then said, "It's Fatima."

"What's Fatima?"

"When we were in Damascus, you asked me what my real first name was."

"And your real last name?"

Khalila's body spasmed and she coughed, spraying Harrison's face with flecks of blood. After the pain subsided, she answered. "One day I might tell you." Then she smiled weakly and added, "If I don't kill you first."

80

WASHINGTON, D.C.

Christine O'Connor's black Lincoln Navigator traveled down West Executive Avenue, approaching the White House. During the short journey from Langley, she had paused from reviewing the file in her lap to stare at the District in the distance, imagining what the skyline might have looked like this morning if *Kazan*'s missile hadn't been destroyed.

The previous evening, she had returned to Langley after receiving the report that *Kazan* had launched, remaining through the night as additional reports filtered in: a single missile had been launched and shot down, *Kazan* had been sunk, and then there was the unexpected report that Mixell had been located and killed, with Harrison and Khalila seriously wounded. Both were at Inova Alexandria Hospital, with Harrison stable and doing well, while Khalila was in critical condition with the outcome uncertain.

A stunning revelation last night had been Pat Kendall's involvement with Mixell. PJ Rolow had been with Christine when they learned of Kendall's duplicity, and a dark mood had settled over the DDO, who seemed to be admonishing himself for his lack of insight. Harrison's injuries didn't seem to faze Rolow, but his mood had grown darker when he learned of Khalila's life-threatening wounds. It was clear there was a special relationship between her DDO and Khalila, and Christine filed that fact away.

The Lincoln Navigator passed through the White House gates, stopping outside the West Wing's north entrance. Christine stepped from her SUV and passed between the two Marines guarding the

White House entrance, then entered the Situation Room in the West Wing basement, joining several members of the president's cabinet and staff. The president and Chief of Staff Kevin Hardison entered a moment later.

Secretary of Defense Tom Drapac was the first to brief, covering *Kazan*'s missile launch and the Russian submarine's sinking. Concluding his report was a bit of good news: USS *Pittsburgh*'s crew had been rescued from the ocean bottom near Iceland; the Engine Room watchstanders had made it to a forward compartment after the torpedo explosion breached the hull, and the entire crew had survived. Secretary of Homeland Security Nova Conover went next, confirming what most already knew: *Kazan* had launched only a single missile, aimed at Washington, D.C., which had been shot down and the nuclear warhead recovered.

Christine followed, delivering information most were unaware of: Mixell had procured a Russian missile launcher from a Syrian arms dealer and had intended to shoot down Air Force One as the president evacuated Washington. There were stunned looks around the table after the revelation, although there was no visible reaction from the president.

Thankfully, Mixell had been located and killed before Air Force One took off, and the search for his body, which had slipped into the Potomac River, had commenced this morning. Christine decided not to delve into the details: Kendall's involvement and death, along with Harrison's and Khalila's injuries, although she intended to discuss the Kendall issue with the president once the investigation into her involvement had been completed.

Christine then provided new information uncovered by her DDA the previous day.

"We've tracked down the sixty-million-dollar payment made to Mixell, which he used to fund *Kazan*'s attack and the procurement of the missile launcher. It came from an account linked to al-Qaeda."

Christine went on to explain that Mixell had revealed the same to Jake Harrison, plus additional details: Zawahiri had survived the drone attack the previous year and had paid Mixell to orchestrate an attack even more devastating than 9/11, hoping to unite as many of the jihadist organizations under his leadership as possible.

"It's clear that al-Qaeda remains a significant threat and that more attacks are likely."

The president evaluated Christine's report, then replied, "Track Zawahiri down and work with SecDef on a plan to eliminate him. Brief me when you're ready."

81

LANGLEY, VIRGINIA

"What have you got?"

Christine O'Connor was joined at the table in her office by her DDO and Deputy Director for Analysis Tracey McFarland. The president's order had been clear—eliminate the man responsible for the havoc wrought by Mixell—and Christine and her deputy directors had been searching for a way to track down Zawahiri. They hadn't even realized he had survived the earlier drone attack, and if tracking down the top man at al-Qaeda was easy, they would have done so repeatedly, eliminating each new al-Qaeda leader. There seemed to have been a breakthrough, however, indicated by the DDO's request for a meeting this morning.

"We think we've found a way to track down Zawahiri," he began. "We learned from the bin Laden raid that no high-level al-Qaeda communications are transmitted electronically; no computers or phones—it's all done on paper or verbally, distributed to and from al-Qaeda leadership by couriers. Tracey's opinion is that Zawahiri wouldn't have transferred sixty million dollars to Mixell without meeting him first. That means one of Zawahiri's couriers would have brought Mixell to the meeting.

"Based on the date the funds were transferred into Mixell's account, that meeting happened while Mixell was in Pakistan. Analysis obtained additional camera footage around the time Mixell landed in Karachi, and he was picked up outside baggage claim by a man we've identified as Amir Zahed." Rolow turned to McFarland.

"After our drone strike on Zawahiri," she said, "all al-Qaeda couriers were considered compromised and we lost our leads to al-Qaeda leadership. However, based on Zahed meeting Mixell at the airport, we believe Zahed is now a primary courier for Zawahiri. Follow Zahed, and he'll eventually lead us to Zawahiri."

"Great work," Christine said. "So what's the plan?"

Tracey replied, "We have dedicated drone assets controlled primarily from Creech Air Force Base in Nevada. Let's put a twenty-four-seven surveillance on Zahed with an armed drone, ready to take out Zawahiri if he pops up."

Christine provided her concurrence.

82

INDIAN SPRINGS, NEVADA

Captain Mike Berger and First Lieutenant Dee Ardis were on duty again, seated inside the dimly lit, cramped, and chilly MQ-9 Reaper Ground Control Station trailer. Berger had his right hand on the joystick and his left on the throttle as his eyes studied one of fourteen displays built into the two-person control station, while Ardis, the Reaper's sensor operator, likewise studied her pertinent screens.

Another day, another mission.

A boring one at that.

For the last several weeks, Berger and Ardis, along with the other Reaper teams assigned to this control van, had been surveilling a guy in Karachi, Pakistan. It was clear the higher-ups were waiting for this guy to meet a designated target, because every time he met someone, the Reaper attack controller requested target verification. Thus far, it had been several weeks of negatives. It was also clear the designated target was high value; after circling their Reaper above the man's residence in Karachi for the last few weeks, Berger realized there were also agents on the ground surveilling the man's every move.

While it was challenging to maintain track of the guy while he traipsed about on foot in the city, tonight's task was as easy as it got. They were following the man's green sedan as it worked its way from the congested city into the sprawling suburbs, eventually entering an affluent development of gated residences where it stopped before a home's black metal gate.

The attack controller's voice came across Berger's headphones. "Prepare for visual target confirmation."

Berger acknowledged, then tilted his joystick, sending the Reaper down from its standard ten-thousand-foot surveillance altitude toward a better angle for facial recognition. As the drone descended, the gate pulled slowly aside and the sedan pulled to the end of the driveway.

The Reaper leveled off as the man stepped from the vehicle, where he was greeted by a man wearing a white dishdasha who emerged from the residence. Ardis zoomed in, taking a picture of the new man's face.

The photo appeared on one of Ardis's displays as they waited for the facial recognition program to finish its evaluation. Eventually, *Target Not Confirmed* appeared in red letters beneath his picture.

Another dead end.

After both men disappeared into the home, the attack controller agreed to let Berger return the Reaper to its standard surveillance altitude. A half-hour later, a black SUV arrived, stopping at the closed gate.

Berger and Ardis repeated the procedure, dropping the Reaper down for a better look as the SUV pulled forward and stopped behind the green sedan, then Ardis took pictures of four men who stepped from the vehicle. This time, a green *Target Confirmed* appeared beneath one of the photographs.

"We have confirmed jackpot," the attack controller declared. "Request weapon release."

The attack controller's request confused Berger. Why was he asking *him* for weapon release authority? It worked the other way around—attack controllers provided weapon release authority to Reaper control teams.

"What do you mean?" Berger asked. "You're supposed to provide that authority to me."

"I don't have the authority for this mission," the attack controller said. "Someone should be on-line momentarily."

As Berger pondered the unusual protocol, one of his displays reconfigured into a split screen, with a four-star Air Force general on one side and an attractive woman in her forties on the other. He had no idea who the woman was, but he recognized the four-star general as the man in charge of Air Combat Command, about as high up in the Air Force food chain as it got.

The woman seemed to be studying something off-screen, as her eyes were focused off to the side. Then she looked at the camera and said, "You are authorized for weapon release."

Berger hesitated. The last time he checked, the only civilian in his chain of command was the guy at the top, called the president. He shifted his gaze to the four-star general.

"Do as she says, Captain."

The woman added, "Two Paveways in the center of the house."

Wow, Berger thought. *Talk about overkill.*

It wasn't his call, however. He selected the first of the Reaper's two Paveway five-hundred-pound bombs, then waited as Ardis slewed the laser designator onto the center of the building.

Release solution valid appeared on the center console.

Berger armed the Paveway, its new status appearing on the display—*Master arm on.*

Finally, *Ready for release* appeared.

After verifying the laser designator was locked on to the center of the residence, Berger pressed the red button on his joystick, releasing the first Paveway.

As it fell toward its target, Berger repeated the process for the second five-hundred-pound bomb, and it soon followed.

Berger watched as the Paveways completed their journeys, first one, then the second, hitting the building dead center. An orange fireball erupted, followed by another, billowing upward above a trail of black smoke as debris rained down on nearby rooftops and yards.

Ardis waited for the dust to clear, then zoomed in on the area, searching for survivors. There was no movement. From his vantage point in the Reaper pilot seat, studying Ardis's display, he spotted a few charred bodies.

Post-mission analysis would be required to assess the results of today's mission, but Berger was confident the target's status on his display would be updated from *Target Confirmed* to *Kill Confirmed.*

The attack controller's voice came across Berger's headphones again. "You are released for further duties."

After Berger acknowledged, the woman on the video display spoke again.

"Well done."

83

LANGLEY, VIRGINIA

It was a small ceremony in the seventh-floor conference room. The table had been pushed to the side and covered with a white tablecloth, then laden with drinks, pastries, and fruit. The empty space in the middle of the room had instead been filled with two rows of chairs, with Harrison sitting in front between Khalila and DDO PJ Rolow, along with the DDA, Tracey McFarland. Seated behind them were the other CIA deputy directors, while Christine O'Connor and Deputy Director Monroe Bryant stood at the front of the conference room.

It had been two months since they tracked down Mixell in the warehouse in Alexandria, with Harrison and Khalila engaging Mixell and Kendall. Although Mixell's body hadn't been recovered, that wasn't surprising considering the Potomac was the fourth largest river on the East Coast, with thousands of small bays and coves along its banks as it emptied into the Chesapeake Bay.

Khalila's condition after the encounter had been tenuous, but she had pulled through. Today was the first time Harrison had seen her in those two months, and he noted that she had lost a good bit of weight during her recovery, but her personality hadn't changed. She ignored him upon entering the conference room, talking quietly with the DDO for a while before the ceremony began, not even acknowledging his presence when she sat beside him.

Bryant handed the two certificate folders to Christine, retaining the medals in his hands. Harrison and Khalila were being awarded the CIA Intelligence Star, one of a group of medals referred to within the CIA as *jock strap medals,* since they were often awarded secretly due to the classified nature of the respective operation, and subsequently couldn't be displayed or even acknowledged publicly.

Christine read the citations, which were identical aside from their names, then Harrison and Khalila were called forward to receive their medals. Christine opened the boxes for each to examine, then handed them their medals instead of pinning them onto their clothes as was customary in the Navy.

After Harrison and Khalila returned to their seats, Christine spoke briefly, amplifying the citations and commending both of them for their exceptional performance. The nation, as well as the president himself, owed them a debt of gratitude.

It was a short ceremony, and afterward, Christine invited the attendees to take a break from their busy day and socialize for a while. Harrison looked at Khalila, evaluating how best to break the ice between them, when she stood and approached the DDO without a word to Harrison. He shook his head slightly to himself. It was as if he had been the one who had almost killed his partner in Sochi; the one who had turned aggressive and threatening while interrogating the Russian they had captured.

Pushing Khalila from his mind, he enjoyed the refreshments while getting to know the other deputy directors, most of whom he hadn't met until today. After a while, some of the deputy directors departed, and Harrison's thoughts returned to Khalila.

To say their relationship was complicated would be an understatement. In Sochi, she had almost put a bullet in his head, and he'd left Russia convinced that Khalila had no conscience or regard for others. Yet in Alexandria, she had saved his life while risking her own. He was grateful for that, but still resentful about what she had almost done in Sochi.

Christine called the DDO over to join her in a conversation with another deputy director, which left Khalila standing by herself. Harrison decided to engage.

She eyed him as he approached, but said nothing as he stopped before her.

Harrison debated how to begin the conversation, and after considering his conflicting feelings toward her, chose to offer a compliment and a barb at the same time.

"So, how's my favorite sociopath doing?"

Khalila stared at him for a moment, then looked away, but not before he noticed the hurt expression on her face. Her reaction was unexpected, and Harrison regretted his words immediately.

"I'm sorry."

She turned back to him. "You're right. I know I'm a sociopath, but it hurts to hear someone say it."

"Isn't that a contradiction? A sociopath with feelings?"

"A *psychopath* has no conscience or feelings. A sociopath has . . . some. I suppose that's the easiest way to think about it."

"It sounds like you've had some counseling."

Khalila shrugged. "I know what I am, and I embrace it."

There was an awkward silence between them, and Harrison searched for a new topic. Lying on the floor of the Alexandria warehouse, Khalila had revealed her real first name, but not her last. He decided to try again.

"Okay, Fatima," he said, deliberately using her real first name. "What's your real *last* name?"

Khalila smiled. "You are *very* persistent. Unfortunately, I'm not authorized to divulge that information."

"Whose authorization is required?"

Khalila's eyes went briefly to the DDO, talking with Christine, before returning her gaze to Harrison. She moved closer to him.

"You already know too much."

Before Harrison could respond, she stepped back. "Take care, Jake."

Then she left the conference room.

Harrison watched Khalila leave, trying to figure her out. She was like a puzzle with pieces that didn't fit. It didn't matter at this point, however, since he wouldn't be working with her again.

The room was almost empty now, containing only Harrison, plus Christine chatting with Rolow near the exit. She glanced at Harrison, noting that he was no longer talking with Khalila, then wrapped up her conversation with the DDO, who also departed.

Christine waited expectantly as Harrison approached. Although his relationship with Khalila was complicated, it paled in comparison to his bond with Christine.

They had already discussed the pertinent issues in a meeting in Christine's office the week prior. Christine had suggested he stay on at the CIA, but Harrison declined. Angie had insisted he take a safer job, plus he'd spent more than twenty-five years in the Navy and been deployed for most of it, and a job on the East Coast with his family across the country wasn't an acceptable arrangement. He'd be heading home to Washington State to spend time with his wife and daughter.

"So," Christine said. "I take it you haven't changed your mind."

"I appreciate the offer, but I'm sure you understand my situation."

"Of course. If I were Angie, I'd want the same."

Christine extended her hand and they shook, but then she gave him a warm hug as well.

"Don't be a stranger," she said.

84

POTOMAC OVERLOOK REGIONAL PARK

Darkness had fallen by the time Christine O'Connor's SUV, with two Protective Agents in the front, sped south on the George Washington Parkway en route to her home in the Clarendon district of Arlington. In a scenic outlook on the northbound side of the parkway, several cars were parked, with most of their former occupants clustered near the edge of the outlook taking in the picturesque view: the Potomac Heritage Trail winding along the near bank of the Potomac River, the Washington, D.C. skyline in the distance, and the black water in between, reflecting the yellow lights illuminating the river's opposite bank.

Leaning against one of the parked cars was a man who noted the passing of a black Lincoln Navigator on the south side of the Parkway, which sent his thoughts into the past. Two months ago, he had crawled from the Potomac River onto the shore of Fort Foote Park in Fort Washington, Maryland, a heavily wooded area containing a neglected Civil War–era earthwork originally armed with twenty-five-ton cannons protecting the nation's capital from ironclad ships sailing up the Potomac.

As he lay on the shore in the darkness, evaluating his condition—Jake Harrison had shot him three times and he'd lost a significant amount of blood during his mostly underwater swim across the river—he couldn't get rid of the image seared into his mind: Trish Kendall's body on the floor near Harrison's feet, a bullet hole in her forehead and her eyes frozen open.

He knew the bullet came from his own pistol and that he had pulled the trigger, but neither of those details registered. The only thing that mattered was that Trish's death was Harrison's fault.

Several years ago, when Mixell had been released from prison,

Harrison had been on his list of people and institutions upon which to take his revenge. In light of recent events, Harrison had moved to the top and there was a new name on the list: Christine O'Connor, who had convinced Harrison to help track him down.

It left a sour taste in his mouth—that his two best childhood friends were working against him. However, the revenge would be sweet.

Mixell smiled at the thought.

AUTHOR'S NOTE

I hope you enjoyed reading *Deep Strike*!

For those of you who've read the first five books in the Trident Deception series, you probably noticed that *Deep Strike* was a different kind of book. I try hard to ensure each plot is quite different from the others, avoiding the cookie-cutter plot template approach, but the one constant in the first five books has been Christine O'Connor's involvement. You probably noticed she didn't have a large role in *Deep Strike* compared to the previous novels, especially in comparison to the last book, *Treason.*

As I mentioned in the author's note in *Treason,* the plot structure of each book in the Trident Deception series determines which characters play dominant roles, and Christine didn't have much to do in *Deep Strike.* Hopefully you enjoyed some of the new characters introduced, including Lonnie Mixell and Khalila Dufour. Unfortunately, thanks to Lonnie, not all of the Trident Deception characters make it to Book 8. (Books 6 to 8, which start with *Deep Strike,* form a trilogy for the secondary plot theme involving Mixell and his childhood friends, Christine and Harrison, and you'll note at the end of *Deep Strike* that there's a debt to be paid.)

There's also the Christine–Harrison storyline that's been running since Book 2 (*Empire Rising*), with many readers asking: *Are Christine and Harrison ever going to get together?* Books 7 and 8 will answer that question, secondary, of course, to the main plots in those books. Although in *Treason*'s author's note, I said that *Deep Strike* would make that clear, the necessary chapters ended up on the cutting-room floor; they didn't fit well with the main plot in *Deep Strike,* and it ended up being a case of *more is less:* the extra Christine–Harrison interactions detracted from the overall novel. However, those chapters will be included in the next book, where they fit better.

Finally, the usual disclaimer—some of the tactics described in *Deep Strike* are generic and not accurate. For example, torpedo employment and evasion tactics are classified and cannot be accurately represented in this novel. The dialogue also isn't 100 percent accurate. If it were, much of it would be unintelligible to the average reader. To help the story move along without getting bogged down in acronyms, technical details, and other military jargon, I simplified the dialogue and description of operations and weapon systems.

For all of the above, I apologize. I did my best to keep everything as close to real life as possible while developing a suspenseful (and unclassified), page-turning novel. Hopefully it all worked out and you enjoyed reading *Deep Strike.*

AMERICAN CHARACTERS

UNITED STATES ADMINISTRATION

Robert (Bob) Tompkins—vice president
Kevin Hardison—chief of staff
Tom Drapac—secretary of defense
Dawn Cabral—secretary of state
Nova Conover—secretary of homeland security
Thom Parham—national security advisor
Glen McGlothin (Captain)—senior military aide
Lars Sikes—press secretary

UNITED NATIONS

Marshall Hill—United States Ambassador to the United Nations
Mel Cross—Diplomatic Security Service agent
Jill Mercer—Diplomatic Security Service agent

CENTRAL INTELLIGENCE AGENCY

Christine O'Connor—director (DCIA)
Monroe (MK) Bryant—deputy director (DDCIA)
Patrick (PJ) Rolow—deputy director for operations (DDO)
Tracey McFarland—deputy director for analysis (DDA)
Jake Harrison—paramilitary operations officer (Special Operations Group)
Nizar Mussan—paramilitary operations officer (Bluestone Security)

Maxim Anosov—paramilitary operations officer (Sochi, Russia)

Pat Kendall—specialized skills officer (National Resources Division)

Khalila Dufour—specialized skills officer (National Clandestine Service)

John Kaufmann—specialized skills officer (National Clandestine Service)

Asad Durrani—collection management officer

OFFICE OF THE DIRECTOR OF NATIONAL INTELLIGENCE

John Rodgaard—Director of National Intelligence

Jessica Del Rio—National Counterterrorism Center (NCTC) supervisor

COMMANDER, SUBMARINE FORCES (COMSUBFOR)

Bill Andrea (Vice Admiral)—Commander, Submarine Forces

Rick Current (Captain)—chief of staff

Dwayne Thomas (Captain)—operations officer

Beverly King (Captain)—public affairs officer

Mark Graham (Captain)—training officer

USS *PITTSBURGH* (LOS ANGELES CLASS FAST ATTACK SUBMARINE)

John Buglione (Commander)—Commanding Officer

Rick Schwartz (Lieutenant Commander)—Executive Officer

Bob Cibelli (Lieutenant)—Navigator

Ed Reese (Lieutenant)—Weapons Officer

Bob Martin (Lieutenant)—Junior Officer

Bob Bush (Sonar Technician Chief)—Sonar Division Chief

Alex Rambikur (Sonar Technician Second Class)—spherical array operator

USS *NORTH CAROLINA* (VIRGINIA CLASS FAST ATTACK SUBMARINE)

Jerry Maske (Commander)—original Commanding Officer

Jeff Johnston (Lieutenant)—Weapons Officer

Reggie Thurlow (Sonar Technician Master Chief)—Chief of the Boat

MAD FOX ZERO-FOUR (P-8A AIR CREW)

George Stringer (Lieutenant Commander)—Tactical Coordinator (TACCO)

Jeff Hanover (Lieutenant)—Communicator

OTHER MILITARY CHARACTERS

Murray Wilson (Captain)—Commanding Officer, USS *Michigan* (BLUE) / USS *North Carolina*

Gil Bohannon (General)—Chairman, Joint Chiefs of Staff

Tom Blaszczyk (Admiral)—Chief of Naval Operations (CNO)

Pat Urello (Rear Admiral)—Director, Undersea Warfare Division (OPNAV N97)

Mike Berger (Captain, USAF)—Reaper pilot

Dee Ardis (First Lieutenant, USAF)—Reaper sensor operator

SERENDIPITY (TRAWLER)

Marc Manis—captain

Kirk Murphy—first mate

John Lojko—lead foreman

Dan Metzger—chief engineer

OTHER CIVILIAN CHARACTERS-MALE

Lonnie Mixell—former Navy SEAL

John Dehner—Director of the Federal Bureau of Investigation

Steve Reed—manager, Player's Club

Bill Sullivan—Puget Sound Naval Shipyard supervisor

Charlie Rooney—Port of Baltimore gate guard

Allen Terrill, sr.—independent trucker

Eric Dahlenburg—boat owner

OTHER CIVILIAN CHARACTERS-FEMALE

Ashley Tobin—Secret Service agent
Angie Harrison—Jake Harrison's wife
Madeline (Maddy) Harrison—Jake and Angie Harrison's daughter
Sandy Perry—realtor
Ashley Gonzalez—Sandy Perry's office assistant

RUSSIAN CHARACTERS

RUSSIAN FEDERATION ADMINISTRATION

Yuri Kalinin—president
Anton Nechayev—defense minister
Andrei Lavrov—foreign minister

FEDERAL SECURITY SERVICE (FSB)

Nikolai Barsukov—director
Nicholai Meknikov—agent
Pyotr Sobakin—agent

K-561 *KAZAN* (YASEN CLASS ATTACK SUBMARINE)

Aleksandr Plecas (Captain First Rank)—Commanding Officer
Erik Fedorov (Captain Third Rank)—First Officer
Mikhail Alekhin (Captain Lieutenant)—Weapons Officer
Ivan Urnovitz (Captain Lieutenant)—Central Command Post Watch Officer
Ludvig Yelchin (Captain Lieutenant)—Central Command Post Watch Officer
Eduard Topolski (Senior Michman)—Fire Control Technician
Erik Korzhev (Michman)—Electric Navigation Party Technician
Oleg Noskov (Starshina First Class)—Torpedo Division Petty Officer

OTHER MILITARY CHARACTERS

Georgiy Ozerov (Fleet Admiral)—Commander-in-Chief, Russian Navy

Eduard Simonov (Captain Second Rank)—intelligence center watch officer

GADZHIYEVO NAVAL BASE

Anatoly Bogdanov—ordnance supervisor

Vasily Morozov—ordnance supervisor

Andrei Voronin—senior ordnance supervisor

NORTHERN FLEET JOINT STRATEGIC COMMAND

Mikhail Korenev—command center watchstander

Arkady Timoshenko—command center watchstander

OTHER CIVILIAN CHARACTERS

Tatiana Plecas—Aleksandr Plecas's wife

Natasha Plecas—Aleksandr and Tatiana Plecas's daughter

Dr. Maxim Vasiliev—Blokhin National Medical Research Center lead oncologist

OTHER CHARACTERS

AL-QAEDA

Ayman al-Zawahiri—leader of al-Qaeda and ISIL factions in Afghanistan and Pakistan

Amir Zahed—courier

OTHERS

HASAN NASSIR—Syrian weapons dealer
ISSAD FUTTAIM—Syrian weapons dealer
AKRAM ABOUD—Futtaim's executive assistant